VIRIDIAN

THE DEMON AND THE SAVIOR
BOOK 2

I0526554

ASHLEY R. O'DONOVAN

"THOSE EYES
COULD
START A WAR,
AND THAT
SMILE WOULD
FINISH IT."

SUNDERLANDS

Irina's Ranch

Hunting Cabin

NORTHWESTERN DISTRICT

WESTERN DISTRICT

Marco's Cliffside Compound

Garden / Park ♡

Shoreline / Borderline
District border
Scale 1:13,500,000
0   500 Miles

SYNDICATE

C.
Here are the coordinates
42,62132.N, 73,12040
FUCK ORIN

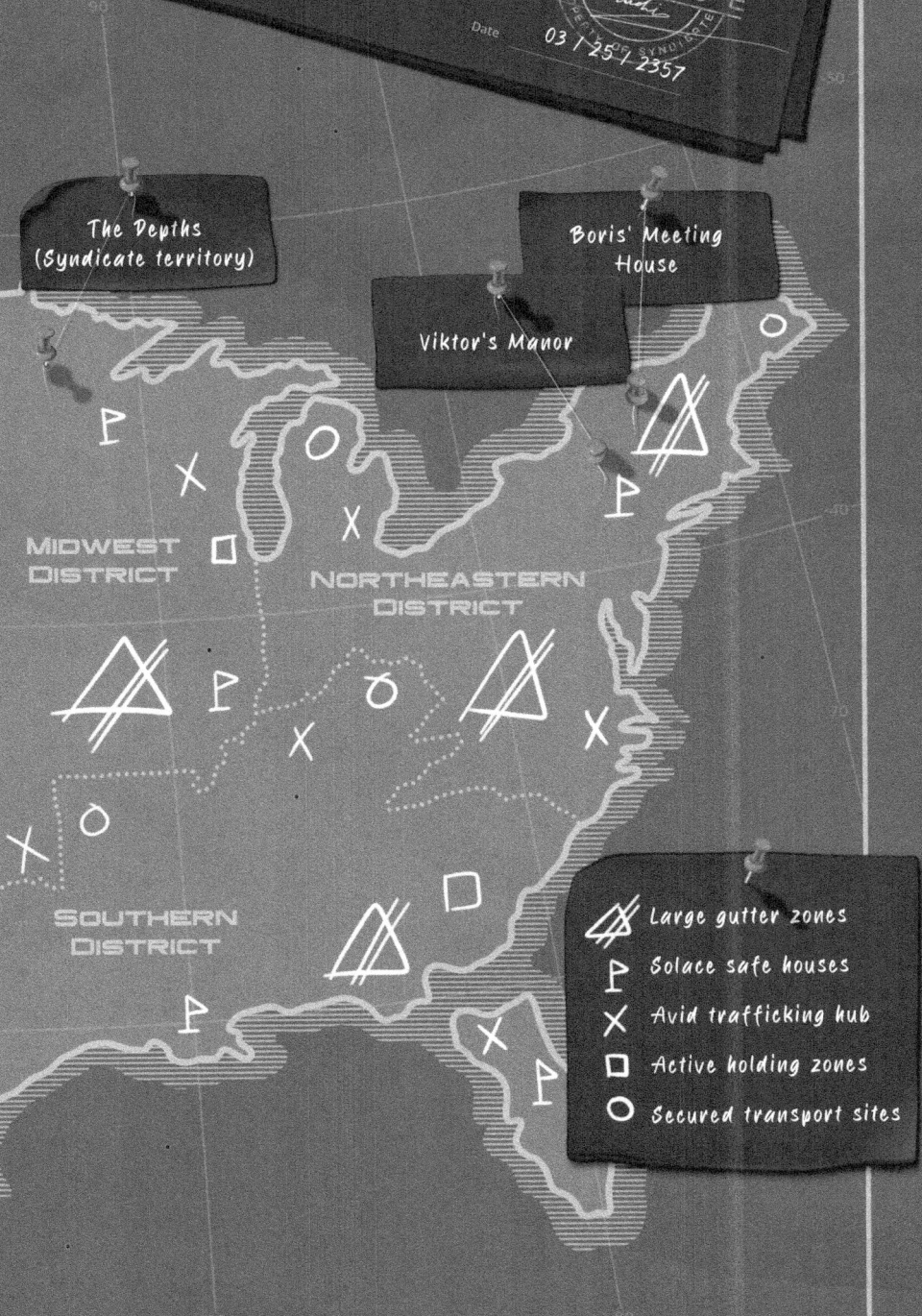

Viridian

By Ashley R. O'Donovan

Map by EKATHART Illustration

This is a work of fiction. All of the characters, organizations, and events portrayed in this novel are either products of the author's imagination or are used fictitiously.

FOR MCKENNA AND QUINN —
DREAM BIGGER THAN THE STARS.

CONTENT WARNING

Viridian is approximately 90,000 words, it contains sexually explicit scenes, mature language, and themes intended for adult readers. Please note that the story includes depictions of violence, the trafficking and exploitation of a gifted race, and other intense situations that may be triggering for some readers.

VIRIDIAN

The Demon and the Savior: Book Two

ASHLEY R. O'DONOVAN

Chapter One

LOG ONE - OBSERVATION BEGINS: WE SET OUT TO
BUILD A CURE, BUT WHEN SHE OPENED HER EYES, I
FEARED WE'D CREATED SOMETHING ELSE ENTIRELY.

THEY SAY DEATH IS FINAL, but I've seen enough ghosts to know the universe isn't that simple. Death. The afterlife. The thin, haunting line that separates the living from the dead ... I've walked it.

Nothing could've prepared me for Cade Calloway standing here, breathing, bleeding, and lying through his teeth.

Cade reaches for me, and I sidestep him.

What did he say? I was always meant to be his, and he's here to take me home?

I shake my head and find my voice.

"Are you working with Marco? Did you help him escape? Where did he even go, and what the fuck is this?" I hold up the tiny vial. A single drop of viscous dark-green substance remains.

"I'll explain everything, but please come with me first," Cade says, his bright-green eyes widening.

I study his face for a beat, his disheveled black hair, his tan skin and full lips. It's my Cade, only aged a bit. A huge part of me wants him to take me away from here, to escape, to forget the last several years of my life.

But that's not going to happen.

Maybe if he had found me sooner. Maybe if he had made this offer before this case with Viktor. But now, everything has changed.

I've changed.

"I can't go with you, Cade. We should be searching for Marco or warning the others. Malachi and his team are outside—"

He steps closer, shaking his head. There's urgency in the way he presses his lips together, like he's biting something back.

The rumbling sound hits first, sharp and violent. A split second later, the floor jolts beneath my feet like the world's coming apart. I'd think it was an earthquake if it weren't for the sound of the blast.

Cade's hand wraps around mine.

"Run," he says.

He pulls me toward the door, but we don't make it.

The door bursts open with a crack, and Malachi storms in, still wearing full tactical gear. His eyes find mine and then drop to Cade's fingers locked around my hand. His jaw tightens. I can practically hear the silent fury radiating off him.

"Where's my father?"

I yank my hand out of Cade's grip.

"He escaped," I say, stepping forward. "I don't know how, but he left this."

I hold up the vial.

Malachi's gaze never leaves mine as he takes it.

"Calloway," he says, his eyes narrowing as he brings the vial up to his face, turning it over and examining it closely, "get to the jeep. You're riding with Dante. We'll debrief later."

It's the tone that brooks no argument. He's done being nice ... if he ever was.

And if my mind hadn't fully processed it before, it does now—there's history here. A strong one. I can feel it in the tension between them, in the way Malachi calls him *Calloway* with disdain.

What surprises me even more? Cade listens.

He brushes past Malachi and heads for the doorway. No argument, no defiance, only quiet obedience that makes my spine prickle.

He pauses at the threshold. I glance up, half expecting him to say something. Instead, he waggles his brow.

He fucking winked at me.

I have no idea what the hell is going on, but I decide to hold my cards close for now. This isn't the place or the time for a meltdown. I need time to process, to figure out the right questions to ask. One thing's clear though. Both men are keeping secrets. Big ones. And I don't know if they're working together or plotting against each other.

Once Cade's footsteps fade down the hall, I turn to Malachi.

"What happened?"

"A bomb or some kind of device went off in my father's storage room downstairs," he says, eyes still scanning. "He must've detonated it before disappearing."

He tucks the vial into his pocket like it's nothing.

"What the hell was he hiding in that room that someone would risk blowing it up to keep it secret?" I ask, shifting my weight, my nerves coiled too tight to ignore.

"I don't know," he says, "but I'm going to find out. I've got a team searching what's left of it right now. First, I need to get you out of here."

He slides his arm over my shoulders, tucking me protectively into his side. I let him. For now.

Together, we move through the compound and out a side door, where a line of black vehicles with tinted windows are parked. And for some reason, I can't shake the uneasy feeling festering in my gut that I'm being freed from one prison and sent straight into another.

I try to dismiss it. It's insane, right? I know Malachi. I know what the Syndicate is doing. They're saving people. They're saving Avids.

They're saving me.

But if that were the whole truth, why does this sinking feeling in my gut keep feeling heavier by the second?

Malachi opens the passenger door of a black SUV, and I slide in. He jogs around to the driver's side, barking something to one of his men at the front of the property, then jumps in and starts the engine.

"Where are we going?" I ask, glancing out the window, hoping this is the last time I ever lay eyes on this place.

"We've got a safe house not far from here. I'm taking you there for the night. Tomorrow, we'll catch a flight off this damn island."

He doesn't look at me when he says it. The furrow in his brow, the tension in his jaw tell me he's deep in thought, probably ten moves ahead.

I should stay quiet.

I should let him think.

But the cacophony of questions firing through my brain is too much to keep bottled up.

"Malachi." I clear my throat. He glances at me, then focuses back on the road. "How do you know Cade? And why didn't you tell me he was still alive if you knew the connection between us? Why was he working under the alias Brian and—"

I stop myself. One question at a time. If I want real answers, I can't let him pick and choose what to tell me.

I breathe in slowly and turn to the window. The sky is stained with soft hues of orange and pink, serene and beautiful, a jarring contrast to the storm unraveling inside me.

"I've been working with Cade for a few years now," Malachi says. "Fuck, I didn't know for sure you were the girl he'd been searching for until the night we rescued Aurora and the other Avid. Cade was there. He's the one who took Aurora to our safe house nearby."

The memory flashes through my mind. One of the team members had stared at me a little too long. I couldn't see his face through all the gear, but I remember the way he tilted his head like he recognized me or I meant something. That was Cade. He was right there. And Malachi kept it from me.

I chew the inside of my cheek, fighting the urge to explode, to scream at him for every lie he let me believe.

"By the time I knew he was your Cade, it was too late. Call me an asshole, Kat, but I was already starting to feel something for you. And I had to keep Calloway busy. I needed to get to know you without him interfering. Without risking never getting the chance at all," he says, gripping the steering wheel tighter.

"That's no excuse. You're a real fucking asshole, Malachi," I say, all the rage and heartbreak I've swallowed surging. "I thought he was dead. He was my best friend. And all this time, he's been looking for me. He joined your twisted underground team to rescue Avids, all because he hoped he'd find me. And you deliberately kept us apart. All so you could get your dick wet." I say it before I can stop myself. It's bitter and ugly and exactly what I'm feeling. I won't take it back.

"It wasn't like that. You know me, Katja," he says. "My idea was—"

I cut him off before he can finish. "I barely know you, and yet I still chose to come with you over someone I've known my entire life."

I stretch my legs out and swipe a few strands of hair from my face, trying to keep my expression neutral. Why did I choose to go with Malachi? Why didn't I insist on talking to Cade?

I don't have a clear answer. Maybe it's instinct. Maybe it's confusion. Or maybe it's because Marco knew Cade too, knew him as Brian. And if Cade really is working both sides ... If he's been betraying Malachi and working with his father ...

I'm not comfortable making any assumptions. Not yet. And I sure as hell won't tell Malachi anything until I've talked to Cade under more rational circumstances.

Feels like I'm right back where I started.

Trust no one. Not even the dead.

"Katja, I care about you. I know I've really fucked this up," Malachi says, dragging a hand down his face. "But when we get to the safe house, we'll talk. I'll tell Dante and Cade to meet us there instead of boarding the plane with the others."

He glances at me, setting his jaw. "They can stay the night with us, and we'll all travel back together tomorrow. Should give you plenty of time to hear what Cade has to say."

I swallow hard. Am I being too hard on him? I don't know.

All I know is, I hate being lied to. And this entire situation has me on edge.

"Yes, I'd like that," I say quietly, turning back to the window.

"Now," he says, voice shifting, "as pissed as you are, we should probably still talk about Marco's escape. Care to explain how that happened?"

I huff a sharp breath. I don't care to talk to him at all right now, but I force myself to answer. "Cade showed up. At first, I thought I was seeing a ghost—until I realized Marco could see him too. We got distracted talking, and then ... Marco was just gone. I don't know what was in the vial, but I'm guessing it played a role."

Malachi nods, eyes narrowing. "Yeah. I need to go back to that cabin in the woods and search underground. I have a feeling we're about to learn my father's obsession with Avids goes way deeper than using their abilities."

I nod slowly. Marco did seem to know something about the Depths, and that alone makes me uncomfortable.

"He said we weren't looking hard enough. And that he got the idea from the Depths," I say, trying to recall what exactly he said. I should've paid closer attention, but I was too focused on the prospect of slitting his throat.

"I need to talk to Aunt Irina. This entire plan has gone to shit, and clearly my father has someone on the inside feeding him information about the Syndicate."

Malachi's grip tightens around the steering wheel. His knuckles are so white they look bloodless. I silently hope Cade isn't the one feeding Marco intel.

Outside, the fading sunset melts into murky shadows that stretch long across the road. The warmth of golden light is gone now, swallowed by gray and creeping black. I glance out the side window, watching the last trace of pink dissolve into ash-colored clouds.

A strange pressure builds in my chest. It feels like something is coiling tighter around us, like we're being watched.

Hunted.

"Malachi," I whisper, slowly turning to face forward as goosebumps spread across my flesh. My eyes widen.

A wall of black crashes against the windshield, thick and violent like a tidal wave made of smoke. The air around the car distorts, bending unnaturally. Shadows twist and spiral, not like mist but like living things with intent.

"What is that?" I gasp.

Malachi doesn't take his eyes off the road. His voice is low, tense, like he's afraid saying it too loud will make it worse.

"Not what," he says. "Who."

Chapter Two

THE CAR ENGINE cuts out suddenly, leaving the car drifting to an abrupt halt.

Everything goes still.

A chill creeps through the air, frosting my skin. It's like the warmth has been sucked out of the world. Fog smears the windows from the inside. I reach up to wipe the glass with my sleeve, but my hand stops.

The shadows outside are shifting.

They roll like smoke in water—thick, liquid, alive. And then they start to part.

A figure steps forward, emerging from the darkness. Her feet don't make a sound. She doesn't blink. She walks like the ground is bowing beneath her.

I stop breathing.

"Meadow," I whisper, my voice breaking.

Malachi moves fast. A blade flashes in his hand as he releases his seatbelt, ready to make the next move. "You know her?"

"She was one of Marco's Avids," I murmur, "but she never

lived in the compound. I only saw her once in passing. She looked human then."

Now she looks like something else entirely.

Her eyes are pits of black, glossy and endless. Her lips are sewn shut with thick black thread, the skin around them cracked and red. She tilts her head to the side like she's studying us.

Then her voice pierces my mind. "You're next, Katja."

It's not a whisper. It's a screech of rusted metal inside my skull. My entire body recoils. Her mouth hasn't moved. I know Malachi didn't hear it.

I clutch his arm. "Whatever happens, don't let her touch you."

He doesn't look away from her as he turns the hilt of his blade over in his hand. "Why? What happens if she does? And what the fuck is this smoke?"

I glance behind us. There's nothing but black, like the car's parked in the center of a void. No road. No sky. No headlights. The world has folded inward, and all that exists now is *her*.

"I don't know what the smoke is," I breathe. "But I've heard stories. If she touches you, she infects you. Leaves something behind."

Malachi finally glances at me. "Infects you with what?"

I shake my head. "With herself."

He swears under his breath.

"She'll be inside you. Always. No matter where you go, no matter what you're doing. She'll know. She'll feel you."

I can feel her even now, tugging at the edges of my presence. Not my body. My existence. Like she's reaching for me, not with fingers but with something far worse.

"She doesn't track you," I say. "She marks you." I don't even know how I know this information, but it floods my memory from somewhere forgotten.

Meadow stops a few feet from the hood of the car. Her head lifts, her black eyes fixed on mine.

Her shadow begins to move.

It rises from the pavement like smoke given shape, long, spidery arms stretching toward us. One slides across the ground, reaching for the driver's side. The other snakes in my direction.

Malachi tightens his grip on the blade. "What happens if it reaches us?"

I meet his eyes, my voice strained. "I have no idea. I'm not an Avid expert. I've spent most of my life locked in a pretty prison. Or did you forget that part?"

"Some Avidian backup would be nice right about now," Malachi mutters, seeming to realize the blade in his hand is useless. His eyes flick to the suffocating darkness outside, and I can see it on his face. He knows he's not equipped for whatever she is.

"I have an idea," he whispers.

He leans forward enough to keep his mouth hidden from Meadow's view.

"What is it?" I ask, lowering my head to mirror his movement, though I keep my eyes locked on the terrifying girl.

"Use your gift," he says. "Summon someone. See if they can stop her ... or slow her down."

I resist the urge to roll my eyes, not because it's a terrible idea but because he says it like it's as easy as flipping a switch. Like I haven't already been holding back everything inside me, trying not to lose control or go too far and fall into sleep for days again.

"She's not some phantom threat I can ghost away, Malachi," I whisper.

It isn't a terrible idea. Maybe I could open the Veil and drag her into it somehow. Trap her there. But I'd have to touch her, and the Veil is so unpredictable, especially with someone like Meadow. I don't know what would happen. I don't know if I'd come back. I'd like to ask her to come with us, but it looks likes she's beyond saving. Something about that look in her eye screams evil.

What did Marco do to you?

The door handle next to me jiggles.

I jolt, heart slamming into my throat. My eyes snap to the side door, then dart back to where Meadow still stands. She hasn't moved, but her head is tilted at a sickening angle, like her neck has unhinged. I swear she almost smiles.

BAM.

A blur of motion. A jeep slams into her with brutal force, sending her body flying into the air like a rag doll. The second she makes contact, the darkness surrounding us doesn't melt away—it vanishes. One instant, we're trapped in black. The next, it's a normal, open road again. Clear sky. Cold air. Light from the dimming sunset.

"It's Cade and Dante," Malachi says. "Stay here."

Yeah, right.

I'm already throwing the door open before he's finished. My shoes hit the pavement as I leap out after him, adrenaline lighting my veins on fire. He jogs toward the jeep, and I follow because there's no way I'm sitting back while everything falls apart.

Malachi reaches the jeep as Cade throws open the passenger door. I run straight past them, eyes scanning the rocky terrain, heart pounding in my throat.

I skid to a halt.

She's gone.

I turn in a slow circle, searching the brush, the shadows, the empty stretch of road, but there's no sign of her. Not even a footprint in the dust.

"She's gone," I mutter mostly to myself.

"Good," Cade says. "Let's get the hell out of here before Marco sends more of his experiments after us."

I glare at him. "She's not just an experiment."

"He's right," Malachi says, stepping beside me. "We need to move. We're losing daylight."

He places a steadying hand on my back. I fold my arms tightly around myself as the wind kicks up, stirring my hair and bringing with it the sharp scent of salt and stone. The silence feels heavier now. Too full of things we can't see.

Malachi exchanges a few quick words with Dante through the driver's window, then turns back to me.

We climb into the car. The engine roars to life on the first try, like nothing ever happened. Like the darkness hadn't swallowed us whole.

We drive the rest of the way in silence.

I PULL on a black shirt and pants. Thankfully, this place is fully stocked. They have every size imaginable, probably for situations like this, when they bring rescued Avids in and need to outfit them quickly.

The shower felt incredible. Hot water, clean skin, a few minutes alone to scrub away the day. I didn't realize how much I needed it until I stepped out feeling like a slightly more–functional version of myself.

I'm not sure what I expected when Malachi said safe house, but it wasn't this. I pictured something underground, hidden, mysterious. Instead, it's ... a house. Not too nice, not too rundown. Slightly isolated, tucked far enough back from the road that no one's spying on you, but not so far that it screams secrecy or wealth. It's the kind of place that avoids notice by being aggressively normal.

The decor is minimal, enough to get by. A few mismatched throw pillows and faded rugs. One wall-mounted screen. The only things that stand out are the closet full of weapons and racks of clothes with the tags still on. It feels like we're hiding in plain sight, which I guess is the point.

Both jeeps are parked in the garage, covered up. A white van sits out in the driveway, probably for appearances. Every inch of this place has been designed to blend in.

I glance around my room. The walls are painted sage green, the kind of color meant to be calming. There's a small window across from the bed, but all I can see beyond it is a stretch of dirt and rock. It's full night now, and the darkness outside feels still but heavy. Watching.

From what I gathered, the house has five bedrooms. The guys all took rooms upstairs. Mine's the only one down here past the kitchen. It's quiet. The place must be well insulated, because I can't hear a single footstep or voice above me. Maybe everyone's as exhausted as I am. Maybe they're putting off the debrief until tomorrow.

I pull back the thick tan comforter and climb into bed. My body aches, my brain won't settle, and even though I feel completely on edge ... I'm too drained to dwell on any of it.

Sleep is the only escape left tonight. And even that feels uncertain.

I roll onto my side and stare at the window, watching the faint outline of the field beyond shift with the breeze.

Mischka appears.

She curls into my chest, her little ghost body giving off a faint shimmer, like moonlight captured in motion. She wiggles with excitement, nose nudging under my chin, and I smile despite everything. I press a kiss to the top of her silvery-blue head and exhale, waiting for sleep to pull me under.

For the first time today, I almost feel safe.

Then she yips.

My eyes snap open. I don't know how long I was asleep.

A second later, I hear it ... the creak of my doorknob turning.

Chapter Three

LOG THREE - EMOTIONAL RESPONSE TRIGGERED:
SHE SMILED. IT DIDN'T FEEL HUMAN.

"YOU AWAKE?"

I know it's Cade, not from his voice but from the way Mischka lights up the second she sees him. She remembers him too, and my heart does a little squeeze at the sight of it.

She launches over my shoulder in a flurry of excitement, doing ghostly zoomies across the bed before circling his feet in frantic, happy loops. A fat smile spreads across my face.

"I didn't expect you to be this excited to see me," Cade says, his lips curling into a smile. "But honestly, it's a relief."

I shake my head, forcing my gaze off Mischka and up to his face. "What are you doing here?"

He takes it as an invitation, stepping inside and nudging the door shut with his foot before kicking off his shoes.

"Can I sit?" he asks, nodding toward the foot of the bed.

I shift upright and wave him over. "Be my guest."

He drops onto the edge of the mattress across from me, and an awkward moment passes. Not uncomfortable exactly but full of everything unsaid.

Mish curls into a ball right in Cade's lap.

Little traitor.

I open my mouth to hide the smile tugging at the corners of my lips.

"Before you say anything," Cade starts, running a hand over his dark hair, "let me explain."

I meet his emerald eyes and lean back against the headboard, bracing for whatever's coming.

It's strange, seeing him now. He still looks like the Cade I remember, but time has carved its way into him. His jaw is sharper, more defined. His black hair is a little longer, messier. And there are faint creases in his forehead that didn't used to be there. He's older, rougher around the edges, but underneath it all ... he's still him. I think.

"After the car accident, I was messed up," he says, taking a long breath. "But ... I went to your room. You were in a coma. The doctors wouldn't let me see you after that. They told me you died."

His eyes drop to the floor like the weight of the memory is too much to carry. Like if he looks at me while saying it, it might break something inside him.

"Why would the doctors tell both of us that the other was dead?" I ask.

"My question exactly." He leans forward slightly, elbows on his knees. "The corruption in this godforsaken country runs deeper than you can imagine."

His gaze meets mine and holds.

"I believed them, until I saw you one day in the back of a car. You were staring out the window." He pauses. "I did a double take, thought I was losing my mind. But it was you."

I think back to the endless errands, the suffocating car rides with Gladys, the sorry excuse for a foster mother who treated us more like chores than children. All those rides where I sat in silence, watching the world pass by, pretending I was some-where else.

"I don't understand." My voice cracks before I can stop it. "Why didn't you follow me, then? Why did it take so long for you to find me?"

Guilt flashes across his face, and I hate that I'm the one who put it there.

"I tried," he says, "but I was living on the streets, Kat. No car, no resources. I was moving in and out of gutter zones, doing whatever I could to survive. But seeing you that day ... It changed everything. It gave me something to live for again."

He reaches out and places his hand over mine. His calluses brush against my knuckles, rough, worn-in, familiar.

"After that, I was determined to find you. It seemed like I was always a few steps too late. Your foster mom—"

"Gladys?" I cut in, meeting his eyes.

He nods slowly. "Yeah, I found her."

There's something dark behind his expression now. "I had to torture the information out of her, but that's when I found out the truth about you being an Avid. About how she sold you like you were a piece of property."

My stomach twists, but not with sorrow. With satisfaction.

"She got what was coming to her," he says, reading my face. "And I made sure every single kid under her care was placed in a proper home."

I smile. A real one. The kind that blooms from somewhere bitter and vindicated.

"Good," I say, wanting to know exactly how he tortured her but refraining from asking. I'm glad she wasn't able to ruin any more kids' lives.

"Once I found out you were an Avid, I had to do some digging," Cade says, stretching one leg out over the side of the bed. "At first, I didn't believe it. I thought Avids were another overblown media invention—more corruption, more fearmongering. But the deeper I looked, the more the pieces started to fit."

"What pieces?" I ask. My pulse quickens, like my body already knows the answer won't be simple.

"Why the doctors lied to me at the hospital," he says. "They knew what you were, Kat. Somehow. Some kind of blood marker or something flagged you. I don't know the science, but someone up the chain gave orders. You weren't supposed to go home. You were supposed to disappear."

I blink. "Disappear ... into the foster system."

He nods. "That home wasn't random. It was controlled with enough freedom to keep you quiet, enough oversight to make sure you never learned the truth."

My thoughts catch on every unspoken memory of Gladys, her cold eyes, her locked office, the way she always knew when I was lying. Maybe one of the other foster kids didn't turn me and Aurora in, maybe Gladys knew what we were the entire time.

And then something clicks.

"If you're alive," I whisper, "then what about my parents?"

The silence that follows is too loud.

Cade presses his lips together, and that's all the answer I need. But he gives it anyway.

"They passed," he says gently. "I'm sorry."

I nod once. "It's okay. It wasn't your fault."

And it wasn't. *It was mine.*

I was the one driving that day. I'm the one who lived.

Cade's gaze sharpens. "It wasn't yours either, so wipe that look off your face."

I sit up straighter, forcing my shoulders back. The past claws at me, but I won't let it drag me under. Not tonight.

"So," I say, offering the barest hint of a smirk, "what

happened after you tortured my foster mom? Did you track down my doctor and torture him next?"

It's meant as a joke. Mostly.

Cade doesn't smile.

"Of course I did," he says without hesitation. "When you don't have money or power behind your name, the only way to get information is brute force. Trust me, I had to get into the best shape of my life to survive."

He chuckles lightly, and I let out a quiet exhale, dry amusement slipping through the chaos in my mind.

God, what has my life become? Joking about torture like it's a coping mechanism.

Maybe it is.

"So what did you find?" I ask, needing the shift, needing answers more than breath.

"That's when I first learned about Marco Volkov," he says somberly. "You know he owns that hospital, right? Actually owns it. The building, the board, the doctors, anyone worth their weight in that place is on his leash."

My stomach tightens.

"But ... Marco bought me at an auction," I say, trying to make sense of the twisted timeline. "He didn't even know I existed before that, did he?"

"Maybe he did," Cade says quietly. "And it wasn't a coincidence he happened to be at that auction."

I shake my head, the thoughts swirling too fast to hold onto. "Why even bid on me if he was basically controlling my life already? If he wanted me, he could've taken me at any time."

"Maybe Gladys wasn't supposed to sell you," he suggests. "Maybe she got greedy and stepped out of line."

He pauses, eyes flicking to mine.

"She did mysteriously disappear not long after my ... encounter with her."

The way he says it is casual, but the look in his eyes says otherwise.

I lean back against the bed, pulse ticking in my throat. Every piece of this is tangled, and Marco's at the center of it. Always.

I wish he were here now, tied up and at my mercy.

I wouldn't waste the opportunity this time.

"A lot happened after that," Cade says quietly, his gaze distant. "And not all of it I'm proud of. But somewhere along the way, I met Malachi. We realized we had a common goal, saving Avids from people like his father."

His thumb brushes along the edge of his knee. "I worked with him for years, taking down traffickers, waiting for the right time to get to Marco."

"You knew I was with him?" I ask, voice sharper than I intend.

"I didn't know for sure," he says. "I could never get close enough. Marco's compound was a fortress. His men, untouchable. I didn't know if he had you or if someone else did, but every mission I went on with Solace, I looked for you."

Something in me cracks, soft and painful.

"I thought you were dead, Cade," I say, heart aching. "If I'd known ... I would've tried to find you too."

I reach for him.

His hand is warm beneath mine.

But the doubt creeps in, slow and stubborn. I still don't know if Cade is the rat, if he's been working both sides. Marco knew him as Brian, and I can't forget what I saw in that vision. Cade killing Carmen.

I don't doubt he's killed before. Probably many times. Maybe even to save others. But doesn't that still say something about him?

A soft knock breaks the moment.

Mischka doesn't stir from her spot on the bed, which means it's probably Malachi.

"We'll talk more soon," Cade says. He gives my hand a gentle squeeze before rising and walking to the door.

When he opens it, Malachi is standing on the other side.

"I didn't realize you two were still talking," he says, and there's a careful neutrality to his tone that makes me look twice. He knew Cade was here. He let it happen.

Were they friends once? Allies? Did I come between something I don't understand yet? Or maybe Cade doesn't have friends. Maybe survival doesn't leave room for that.

"We're done," Cade says, stepping past him. "I'll see you in the morning."

Malachi watches him go, then looks back at me. "Do you want to be alone?"

I let a crooked smile pull at the corner of my mouth and shake my head.

"Of course not."

He runs a hand through his reddish-brown hair and exhales, the tension in his shoulders easing. His chocolate-brown eyes soften, like he was holding his breath, waiting for a different answer.

Chapter Four

LOG FOUR - SUBJECT UNSETTLED: SHE STARED AT THE WALL FOR HOURS. I THINK SHE'S LISTENING TO SOMETHING I CAN'T HEAR.

"DANTE and I were going through a couple of boxes he had stashed in the back of the jeep," Malachi says as he steps inside, a thick, weathered book in his hand. His boots are dusty, laces loosened. He nudges the door shut with his heel, crosses the room, and kicks off his shoes before lowering himself onto the edge of the bed.

"There's more," he adds, flipping the book open and glancing at a page before setting it aside on the nightstand. "A lot more. But my team loaded the rest onto the plane and left a few hours ago. We couldn't all fit here, and ... honestly, I didn't want them digging through this stuff yet."

He rolls his shoulders back, tension radiating from him. "From what I went through tonight, it's worse than I imagined."

I shift, my attention locked on him now.

"My father's been running experiments," he says, and I don't like where this is going. "Not only on Avids. Animals. Civilians. Anyone he could get his hands on. But it's not just him."

He leans forward, grabbing the book again and flipping to a page he's marked.

"This dates back to the year 2263."

My brain kicks into gear, doing the math automatically. If it's 2357 ...

"That's almost a hundred years old," I murmur. "How is that even still here? How did it survive everything?"

He shakes his head slowly. "I don't know, but someone's been protecting it. Preserving it. This goes deeper than bloodlines or political power."

"I only skimmed a few pages," Malachi says, holding the book out to me, the worn leather cover creaking slightly in his grip. "But I thought you should have it."

I take it from him carefully. The cover is soft with age, edges frayed, the binding barely holding together. Whatever's inside feels old. Important. Dangerous.

When I open it, the scent of dust and something abrasive, like a chemical, rises to meet me.

The pages are handwritten.

My eyes land on the top of one of them.

"Log Sixty-Three – Unverified Access: The numbers don't make sense. Neither does the way she knew them before I did."

I cringe.

"What is this?" I ask, though I already know. Somewhere deep inside, I think I've always known.

"A scientist's journal," Malachi says quietly. "It looks like it documents the first Avid."

I swallow hard. "I didn't know we've been around that long. I thought we were ... something caused by the environment, the food, or maybe a mutation passed down."

The truth never had a name before. Now it's inked in someone else's handwriting.

He watches me carefully. "I only got through a few entries,

but I think she was a normal person. Someone got too close to, and something about her changed."

I run my fingers along the edge of the thick paper.

"Thank you for giving it to me," I murmur. "I'll let you know if I find anything useful."

He nods, and I place the book on the nightstand beside me, careful not to look at it again.

I already know the truth hiding in those pages might not merely explain what I am.

It might ruin me.

"This day feels more like a week. I can't believe I almost lost you," he says, pulling back the covers and sliding into bed beside me. "We were so close to ending things with my father."

I shift to face him. "Is it even safe to go back to Irina's? Marco knows about the Depths now. He knows you want him dead. Lines have been drawn, Malachi ... and we still don't know who's playing both sides."

I hate adding to the weight already pressing down on him, but pretending otherwise won't help us. If Cade isn't the rat, I have no idea who it could be. Maybe Marco said it to shake us, but he knew things he shouldn't.

Malachi exhales slowly, eyes fixed on the ceiling. "I'll protect you. If he makes a move, we'll be ready."

He settles against the pillows and pulls me closer to him. His body is firm and warm against mine, his muscles wound too tight. He smells of fresh soap and rain, the kind that falls after a storm and sinks into the earth. It's intoxicating. Familiar. His scent curls around me, making it hard to remember why I'm supposed to be angry with him.

Right now, all I want is to forget, to lose myself in something that feels steady. Real.

His hand slides up, fingers curling under my chin, guiding my face to his. The moonlight slips through the window, painting silver shadows across his features. His eyes rake over me, as if he's trying to piece together the war still raging behind mine.

His fingers stay at my chin, thumb brushing slow strokes on my jaw. "Those gorgeous blue eyes of yours, they've been looking at me like you want to strangle me ... or maybe straddle me," he says, lips quirking up on one side. "Which is it?"

Amused but not wanting to show it, I narrow my eyes. "Strangle. Obviously."

He grins fully now, cocky and far-too pleased. "You sure? Because your body's saying otherwise."

"You're insufferable."

"And yet here you are. In my bed."

I shove his chest. "You're the one who came into my bed."

"You really going to push me away, Katja?" His voice fills my ears. "After the day we've had?"

"I'm mad at you, or did you forget?" I whisper as my fingers curl in the fabric of his shirt.

"Then take it out on me," he says, dipping his head until our foreheads nearly touch. "Yell at me. Hit me. Kiss me. I don't care. But don't shut me out."

I grab a fistful of his shirt and pull him to me, my mouth crashing into his. His lips are soft, his tongue warm, and the desire burns fast and bright inside me. My other hand slides into his hair as I climb onto his lap, kissing him until I'm out of breath.

I break the kiss and tug on his shirt. He lifts enough for me to pull it off.

"I might want you mad at me more often if this is how you take it out on me," he says, tossing the shirt to the floor.

I shove him back and kiss him harder, catching his bottom lip between my teeth and biting down.

A low, guttural sound rises from his throat. His hands lock on my waist, dragging me tighter against him.

"I told you ... demons like to bite," I whisper, releasing his lip and yanking off my own shirt.

He chuckles, but his gaze darkens, heat flaring in those chocolate eyes as they drag down my bare skin. My breasts ache under the attention, nipples hardening as if reacting to his stare.

He reaches up, cupping one of my breasts, his thumb dragging across my peaked nipple. I can feel the hard bulge of him pressing through his sweats, and I grind my hips down, desperate for more friction.

"You trying to kill me, Kat? 'Cause this feels like slow, sweet murder," he groans.

I lean in, lips brushing his jaw to feel the shiver that rolls through him. "You're the one who said to take it out on you. Can't handle me?"

His hands slide up my thighs, rough and warm, gripping my hips like he's staking a claim. "Oh, I can handle you," he says as he breathes me in. He kisses up the side of my neck, slow and possessive, until his mouth finds my ear. "Question is ... can you handle me?"

I sit up slightly, one brow arched as I roll my hips against him hard. "Guess we'll find out."

He tips me onto my back, one arm tight around my waist. He kicks off his pants, then hooks his fingers in mine and drags them down my legs. His body covers me, heat radiating off him as he takes my mouth.

It's a kiss that steals the air from my lungs and replaces it with pure fire. His teeth scrape my bottom lip, and I gasp, which only makes him smirk against my mouth. "Still mad at me, my little demon?" he murmurs, lips dragging a slow, wet trail down my throat.

"Yes."

"Liar."

His mouth moves lower, closing around my nipple. He bites—not hard but enough to make me squirm and arch into him. His tongue soothes the sting, licking slow circles until I'm trembling beneath him.

"But keep pretending. I like it when you make me earn it."

I thread my fingers through his hair as he dips lower, nudging my thighs apart with the slow press of his body. His breath ghosts over my skin before his tongue finds my center. He licks a slow stripe through my core before his mouth closes over my clit and sucks hard enough to make my hips jerk.

A moan slips from my throat as he slides a finger inside me, curling deep enough. I'm already drenched for him. When he works a second finger in, my grip tightens on the blankets, knuckles white as I fight to hold on to the last threads of control.

His tongue doesn't stop, circling and flicking in rhythm with every stroke of his hand, unraveling me with expert precision.

He pulls his fingers out, sitting up to look me over. "Still mad at me?" he says, an infuriating grin spreading across his face.

"I'm furious. Now, fuck me," I tell him, and his eyebrows shoot up in surprise.

He grabs my wrists and pulls my hands up over my head, holding them there with one of his. His other hand trails down my body, palming my breast and then finding its home on my hip, where he squeezes gently, holding me in place as the head of his cock presses against my wet entrance.

"You don't have to tell me twice," he says, then thrusts into me fully.

He doesn't wait for my body to adjust to him and doesn't

give it to me slowly. He pushes inside me, deep and hard, and I feel every glorious inch of him as I take him.

"Oh god, Malachi," I cry out, and he captures my moans with his lips, releasing my wrists and brushing my hair from my cheek. He grips one of my legs, lifting it up between us and somehow finding a way to press deeper inside me.

"I'd burn the world to keep you like this," he says, slowing his rhythm and exploring my body with his hands. He looks down at me through hooded eyes full of desire.

He feels so good—too good—I want him to stay inside me like this forever. He releases my leg and reaches between us, pressing his thumb to my clit and circling. I suck in a breath as my orgasm rips through me, causing my body to tremble beneath his.

He doesn't stop moving his thumb until my body stills and my cries of pleasure calm down. Then he finds his own release.

He stays inside me, pulling me onto him, and I rest my cheek on his chest as his hand runs up and down my back.

I must've drifted off, but I stir when the bed shifts and he slips out. A moment later, he returns from the bathroom with a warm washcloth, the gentleness of his touch as he cleans me pulling me fully awake. He climbs back under the covers, and I roll to face the window as he curls around me, his arm draped over my waist, his body a steady heat against my back.

Moonlight spills through the glass, silver and soft, and I find myself hoping no one heard us ... especially Cade.

It's strange having him here. Surreal, almost. I don't even know how I'm supposed to feel. He still holds a piece of my heart, and I can't wrap my head around the fact that he spent years trying to find me, trying to save me. There's still so much I want to ask him. Things I need answers to.

And Malachi ... Gods, as angry as I am at him for all the lies —for the things he kept from me about Cade and everything else—I can't pretend he hasn't worked his way under my skin and into my heart.

But I have to stay sharp and remember my number one rule I've always lived by: trust no one.

Not until I know the full truth. Not until I uncover what's really going on with the Syndicate and Marco.

If I must resort to asking the dead, I will. They might lie, sure, but they usually have fewer reasons to.

Chapter Five

LOG FIVE - ABERRANT VITALS RECORDED: HER
HEARTBEAT DOESN'T MATCH HER BREATH. I
WONDER WHICH ONE BELONGS TO HER.

"SO, how'd you get Malachi to let you ride with me?" Cade asks, glancing over from the driver's seat.

I turn the knob to crank up the heat. In the short time we were away, I forgot how bitter the cold is here in the Midwest District. The plane ride was uneventful, everyone too exhausted from the previous day. The tension between Malachi and Cade didn't help. The awkward stares they exchanged across the aisle felt like silent standoffs.

"He's not the boss of me, you know," I say, shifting my gaze to the snow-covered flatlands outside the window.

"Then why do you do everything he says?" Cade lifts a brow, eyes still on the road. I see what he's doing—trying to bait me.

"I don't. It happens that most of what he says, we agree on. If it suits me, I go along with it." I cross my arms and sit up straighter.

Why am I acting like this with him? He knows me, or at least he used to know me better than anyone.

"Fine," he says. "So if you don't do everything he says, that means you're not afraid of upsetting him?"

"No," I reply a little too quickly. "I'm not."

I glance behind us. No sign of the other vehicle. When we left, Malachi and Dante were still loading up the SUV with boxes of documents pulled from Marco's compound. We're supposed to be meeting them at his aunt Irina's house.

"Then let me take you somewhere," he says, piquing my interest.

"Where?" I ask instead of blindly agreeing like I probably would have in the past.

"I want to show you where I live. It'll give us a little time to talk before we rejoin everyone and the constant scrutiny starts up again." He casts a quick, almost pleading glance at me.

The mention of scrutiny lingers in my mind.

"Okay, Cade. Take me to your home," I say.

A smile breaks across his face, and he makes a sharp left turn.

"Wow, you really waited until the last second to ask me that," I say, laughing as I grip the door.

"Yeah, what can I say? You make me nervous."

I wrinkle my nose. "I make you nervous?"

"Yeah," he says, keeping his eyes on the road. "You've always been beautiful, Kat. But now? Now you're something else. Breathtaking."

I'm not sure what to say, not sure how to feel. It sounds nice, but what is that really supposed to mean? How beautiful do I have to be before people start telling me the truth? Or is that the reason they're lying?

"WHERE ARE WE?" I ask as Cade shifts into four-wheel drive, the tires crunching over snow as we climb a narrow road that snakes through dense trees.

The landscape looks eerily familiar. It reminds me of the forest Malachi and I hiked through ... before Orin found me.

"This is one of the last forested areas in the Western District," Cade says, eyes on the road. "No one knows its real name, but locals call it the Whispering Mountains."

I glance out the window at the snow-covered branches swaying gently in the wind. The name fits. There's something unsettling about the way the forest seems to watch us pass.

"If this really is the last forest," I say slowly, "then it has to be the one Malachi and I were in when I was taken."

Cade nods. "It is. But these mountains stretch for miles. I don't live near the cabin you two stayed in."

In the daylight, this forest is hauntingly beautiful. Snow clings to every surface like nature's lace, softening the world in a way that feels both gentle and dangerous. I've always thought snow and the ocean were the two most beautiful things Earth has left.

"We're here," Cade says, pulling me from my thoughts.

I blink and shift forward in my seat, eyeing the house nestled between two towering pines. Secluded, unassuming. A quiet kind of safe.

"I thought you'd be staying on Irina's land or maybe in one of the houses near the Depths," I say as he parks and turns off the engine.

He glances over at me with a small smirk. "Too many eyes there. I prefer to keep my peace where no one's watching."

"Hey, just because you don't see anyone doesn't mean no one's watching," I say, and push the door open. My boots sink deep into a pile of untouched snow.

Cade laughs, the sound warm against the bite of the cold.

"Right. Leave it to the girl who can see the dead to say creepy shit like that."

He comes around, and I take his elbow as he helps me through the thick powder toward the front door.

"I didn't get to ask you last night, but what's the deal with you and Malachi anyway? You've been working together for years, but there's some weird tension there. I know Dante and I both felt it during the flight," I tease as we reach the door.

He fumbles in his pocket for the keys.

"Malachi is a bit of a prick, no offense," Cade says, raising his hands in mock surrender, drawing a giggle from me. "Sure, we get along when we have to, but I wouldn't exactly call us friends. Maybe in the beginning we were, but now things are complicated, especially after the shit he pulled with you." He shakes his head, sighing as he pushes the door open and waves me inside. "He intentionally kept us apart, Kat, all because he wanted you to himself. Selfish prick. And he knows it."

I think back to Malachi's admission yesterday, and while I want to fault him for it, I can't fully bring myself to. Maybe I'm blinded by my feelings for him.

The first thing I see is a large sitting room with plush chairs, overstuffed couches, and a fire roaring to life in the cobblestone fireplace that dominates the entire far wall. Wait, there's a fire.

"Who's—"

A flash of red hair rounds the corner and crashes into me.

"Oh my God! Aurora."

She throws her arms around my neck, and I squeeze her tight. I haven't seen her since the night we rescued her from Viktor's estate. That night, Cade was there too, though I hadn't known it was him. And he's been taking care of her all this time. Something about that warms my chest in an unexpected way. I breathe her in. She smells like fresh soap and something sweet, fruity.

"I've missed you so much. I've been driving Cade crazy, bugging him constantly about when I'd get to see you. I told him to ignore his boss and go get you, but what do I know?" She releases me with a dramatic roll of her eyes in Cade's direction.

I turn toward him, crossing my arms. "Why didn't you tell me she was here?"

He shrugs, a playful glint in his eyes. "I thought it'd be a good surprise."

I look back at Aurora, who looks healthier now—rosy cheeks, that wild orangish-red curly hair shining in the firelight, freckles dusting her nose, and those striking light-green eyes. The last time I saw her, she was fading, her spirit dulled, but now she looks vibrant. Alive. Beautiful.

"Come sit. We have so much to talk about." She tugs at my hand, and I let her pull me down onto the cream-colored sofa beside her.

"I must know everything. I heard you have a fling going with the boss. What's that about? And this place, the Depths, Bash—I mean, the things he's doing with the other Avids? Crazy, right?" she says, talking a mile a minute.

All I can do is smile like an idiot before I manage a response.

"First of all, I don't know if I'd call Malachi the boss," I say, tucking my legs under me on the couch. "He's the head of Solace, but he's not running the whole Syndicate."

Aurora rolls her eyes, bobbing her head like she's heard this argument before. "Yeah, yeah, semantics."

"And what Bash is doing ... I mean, I don't even fully understand it yet. It's incredible and slightly terrifying at the same time."

Cade settles into the armchair beside the fire. The flames throw a golden glow across his face.

"So you've been staying here the whole time with Cade?" I ask, glancing between the two of them.

"I was at a safe house for a while with Cade and a few others, not far from where you found me. Then I came here. Got to see the Depths. Met some of the other Avids. And Cade thought it'd be more comfortable for me to stay here than in one of those pop-up Syndicate houses. You know, the ones with walls that feel like they're watching you." She shivers dramatically, though the fire is blazing.

I nod slowly, trying to calculate the timeline. How long has she been so close without me knowing? Has it really only been several weeks at most? Malachi didn't mention any of this—not that I'm shocked. This all circles back to him not wanting to lose me to Cade. He kept me away from her, like he kept Cade away from me.

I sigh, barely catching what Aurora's saying.

"And once Cade figured out we were in the same foster home, he wanted a full download of our time together. I had to fill him in on all things Kat." She grins and throws a teasing look at Cade, who clears his throat like he's been caught snooping through my diary.

"You didn't let Bash run any tests on you, did you? Put you through his machine and try to extract Avid essence or whatever he does?" I ask, watching her closely.

Aurora shakes her head, curls bouncing. "No, but ... I think I'm going to. He said it doesn't usually hurt, and honestly, I'm curious. I want to see more of what he's doing in that lab of his."

I chew on the inside of my cheek. "I've thought about it too," I admit, "but I'm not sure yet. Don't do anything without me, okay? If you go in there, I want to be with you."

Her grin grows. "Of course. I just got you back. We're going to be besties again in no time."

I laugh, and it surprises me how easy it is to enjoy myself

around her. I haven't had a real friend in what feels like forever. Not one who knew me before all of … this. And now I'm sitting here with the only two people who ever truly did. It doesn't feel like real life, more like a memory I'm not ready to forget.

"Alright, you two can finish catching up later," Cade says, leaning forward in his chair. "We've got more serious things to talk about before your boyfriend shows up and kicks down my door."

I scowl. "Don't call him that."

"What?" Cade smirks. "Boyfriend too casual? Should I say your future husband? Your lover?"

I roll my eyes, but the heat crawling up my neck betrays me. "Labeling feels … unnecessary," I mutter.

Cade chuckles and leans back in his seat. "Sure, Kat. Whatever helps you sleep at night."

I turn toward him. "Alright then. The floor is yours."

His smile fades. His posture shifts slightly, enough for me to sense a change in the air. Whatever he's about to say, it's important, but he doesn't come right out with it.

"Fuck, what is it? I feel like you're about to tell me my dog died—oh, wait, that already happened," I say, hiding behind my sarcasm as something anxious starts to bubble up inside.

Cade pushes off the chair and disappears down the hallway. Aurora gives me a curious look but stays quiet, pulling her knees up to her chest like she's bracing herself for something.

A moment later, Cade returns with a thin weathered folder clutched in one hand. The edges are frayed, and the label across the front is so faded I can barely make out the lettering.

VIRIDIAN

He hesitates before handing it over, fingers clenching like he's still deciding whether to go through with it.

"I found this in one of Marco's old facilities almost a year ago now," he says, eyes fixed on mine. "One that hadn't been cleared out yet. Hidden in a false panel behind a rusted vent. Most of the tech had already been stripped, but this was buried deep. Someone didn't want it found."

I take the folder from him slowly, our fingers brushing for a second. The paper is cold.

"Were you working for Marco when you found this? Are you the one who's been playing both sides? Feeding Marco information about the Syndicate?" I ask.

He runs a hand through his hair, letting black strands fall back across his forehead.

"I'm not a rat, Kat, if that's what you're asking. And when it comes to sides, the only side I'm on is my own."

I narrow my eyes.

"And by my own, I mean ours—me and you," he adds quickly.

Aurora clears her throat.

"And Aurora." He smirks.

"Now open it. I didn't understand all of it, but the parts I did get ... messed with my head. You need to see for yourself."

I glance down at the folder, then back up at him, feeling unsure.

"Why are you showing me this now?"

"Honestly? I think you've already been through enough, and you deserve the truth."

That pit in my stomach returns in full force as I peel the folder open.

The first few pages are thin and brittle, the edges yellowed from time. Faded printouts. Data logs. Scanned handwritten notes that bleed into the page like shadows. A photograph slips loose and flutters onto my lap—blurry, grayscale, the date printed across the top corner: March 3, 2266.

I hold the folder up and squint at the image.

A girl in a hospital gown stares back at me through a glass

window. Her hair is long and tangled, her eyes pale and haunting, barely clinging to the life in them. But the face—

My blood goes cold.

Aurora leans over my shoulder, breath catching. "Wait, is that—"

"It's you," Cade finishes for her. "Or someone who looks exactly like you. The timestamps on the logs go back nearly a century."

Chapter Six

I CAN'T STOP STARING. My fingers tremble around the edges of the photo.

"She was Subject One," Cade continues, quieter now. "They called the project Viridian. There are notes in there about cellular regeneration, psychic transference, emotional dampening ... It sounds a lot like Avidian, only more volatile. Less refined. There's something in there about trying to create a cure or a weapon. I couldn't tell which. Maybe both."

I flip to the next page and find a scan of an old journal entry. The ink is faded and smudged in places, but the writing is still readable.

"Subject exhibits spontaneous cellular recovery at unprecedented speed. Blood reacts violently to direct stimulation, stabilizing only in proximity to another enhanced specimen. Emotional tethering may be the key to regulating destructive potential. Recommend cross-examination with Project M. Further testing required."

"Malachi gave me a journal last night," I murmur. "I didn't bring it, but it's in my bag on it's way back with him. The notes sounded almost identical to this and are dated three years before this photo. He thinks it's about the first Avid, one they made by accident."

Aurora leans back against the cushions, shaken. "This is the kind of shit that makes me miss the days when my biggest worry was finding my next meal, not unraveling the origin story of some lab-made demigod."

I exhale slowly, eyes drifting back to the photo. "It's not me. I mean, it can't be. But what if she's related to me somehow?"

Cade nods. "That's what I wondered. When I first saw it, I thought I'd found you. But the date … didn't make sense. Could be your grandmother. Or great-grandmother. Hell, a clone for all we know. If you look closely, there are subtle differences, but you have to be related."

"I didn't know any of my grandparents. I was told they died before I was born," I say, but I'm starting to question everything I was told.

Everything I thought I knew about who I am.

"Kat, I know you've never liked using your gift—at least not back then—but maybe it's time you start using it for your own answers," Aurora says gently. "Stop letting everyone else benefit from it. Use it for you."

"She's right," Cade adds. "I've heard what you can do. We need answers, and now you've got a photo. Why not try to reach out to whoever this is?"

A flush creeps up my neck, too hot all of a sudden. My chest tightens. I push off the couch and start pacing in front of the fire, needing to move, needing space to think.

"It doesn't work like that," I say quickly. "Sure, maybe I can try with her—whoever she is—because I have the photo, but I don't have a name. I don't know *anything* about her. That makes it harder."

But then something occurs to me. "What about Banks?"

Cade frowns. "Marco's security guy?"

"Yeah. He was locked in the basement with me. I think he tried to help me. I asked Malachi about him on the flight, and he said he didn't think he survived."

I can't stop pacing, the heat from the fireplace getting uncomfortably hot. My thoughts are spiraling. Too many things are happening too fast.

"Banks knew things. He was close to Marco, and if he's dead, he doesn't have a reason to stay loyal anymore. He should want revenge," I say, spinning on my heel to face them. "For fuck's sake, Marco had him beaten and tied up. He has to want revenge."

"Okay," Aurora says slowly, raising a brow, "can you sit down before you wear a hole in the floor?"

I sigh and drop onto the cobblestone ledge, facing them. The flames crackle behind me, and I feel them both watching me closely.

"Banks was ... He was decent to me. As decent as someone keeping you under lock and key can be. But he's seen things. He knows things. And if I can reach him, if he's on the other side ... he could be exactly what we need."

They both nod, like this is something I should've tried already. And maybe they're right, but it's only been a day.

"You should do it now," Aurora urges.

I push to my feet and glance at Cade.

"Yeah, she's right," he says, rising with a stretch. "We need to get you back to Irina's before they come looking. Better to do this now, then we'll head into town."

I nod once, my nerves flaring. "This will work better if you're both not staring at me."

Cade steps back and plops down next to Aurora on the couch, and I turn toward the fireplace and the crackling flames.

I exhale and close my eyes, centering myself as the familiar buzz of pressure begins to hum in my blood.

Banks didn't cross over that long ago. It should be easier to reach him because he knew me. Respected me in a strange, guarded sort of way. I conjure his face in my mind: the stern line of his jaw, the faint scar above his right brow, and those eyes, so dark they looked black under dim light. That's where I focus. The eyes. They always hold the strongest connection.

I feel it then—the whisper of cold brushing the back of my neck. The tiny hairs on my arms rise like a silent alarm.

I open my eyes.

He's there. Sitting exactly where I was moments ago by the fire.

"I'd say it's good to see you, Miss Sinclair, only I wish it were under different circumstances," Banks says, his voice the same deep, even tone I remember, only now it echoes faintly, like it's traveling through water.

I give him a half smile. "I don't remember everything that happened, but I know you tried to help me. Thank you for that."

He dips his head in acknowledgment, his form wisping faintly at the edges like smoke.

"Are you okay?" I ask before I can stop myself. It's a rare question for me to ask a spirit. I've seen enough of the afterlife to know it's not something I want details about.

His eyes narrow. "I'll be at peace when Marco and Orin pay for what they did to me."

Good. That frustration—that tether of unfinished vengeance—I can work with that.

He's already beginning to fade, his silhouette thinning. I grit my teeth and force my will into the room, anchoring him with my focus.

"Banks, listen to me. I need to know what Marco was doing.

The experiments. The hidden labs. Is there anything you can tell me, especially about a vial? It was filled with viscous dark fluid. What is it?"

His image steadies slightly, drawn back by my urgency.

One question at a time, Kat.

"I don't know anything about a vial or dark fluid, but I do know of three hidden facilities he was doing work in," Banks says, his voice low and crackling like static through the Veil.

That's something. Better than nothing.

"Do you have a map?" he asks.

I spin toward Cade, who's still sitting on the couch tense and watching me like I'm speaking in tongues. "Bring me a map."

He nods, disappearing down the hall. A few drawers slam, and then he's back, unfolding a large map of Sunderlands across the coffee table. It's nearly identical to the one I saw in Malachi's office, riddled with marks indicating safe houses and trafficking hot spots. A network of secrets etched in ink.

I take it from him and kneel by the fire, laying it flat on the floor. The paper crackles beneath my fingertips as I turn back toward Banks, who flickers with a faint pulse of energy. "Show me anything you can."

Cade hands me a marker, and I pop the cap off, waiting for Banks.

He moves slowly, reaching out with a translucent finger. It passes through the paper, and he pauses, looking at his finger like he's not used to that happening.

"It's here somewhere. Close to the cabin Orin took you from. Where the wolves prowl."

I quickly mark the spot he gestures to with a small star.

"It's underground, right? Like a silo?" I ask.

He shakes his head. The motion sends a cold ripple across the back of my neck, sharp despite the flames behind me. "No, it's built into the side of the mountain. I think it used to be a mining site."

I nod, my hand already hovering over the map, heart starting to pound. "Next."

He points to another spot south of the hunting cabin. Too close for comfort. The lines on the map blur for a second.

"Why two so close together? Are you sure?"

He nods again, slow and certain. I mark it and wait.

"This last location is the one I would go to first."

He points again, this time farther north. My stomach drops. The spot is directly in the center of the largest gutter zone in the country, not far from Viktor's compound.

"Why would you start there?" I ask.

But when I glance up, he's gone. Vanished.

"Damn it," I mutter, glancing up at Cade and Aurora who are hovering over me, their eyes fixed on the new marks. Cade's jaw clenches, and Aurora's brows knit together as she hugs her arms.

I take a breath and walk them through the conversation, which leaves a strange weight in my chest. I can't shake the feeling that whatever Marco's building, it's already in motion.

And we are closer to it than we should be.

"Why didn't you ask him more questions?" Aurora says, watching me.

I rise to my feet and start folding the map. "I wanted to but couldn't hold him any longer. Maybe I'm not strong enough yet. Or maybe the connection was weak. The spirit fades if I lose focus, and I was already pushing it."

"Then you need to let Bash run some tests on you. Make you stronger," she says, insistent. Right now, that doesn't sound like the worst idea.

I give her a weak smile instead of an answer.

Cade grabs his jacket from the back of a nearby chair.

"Come on. I better get you back before the search party shows up at my door."

I elbow him lightly in the chest. "Very funny."

"Are you coming with us?" I ask, turning to Aurora.

"Of course. We'll have the whole drive to catch up," she says, beaming as she slips on a pair of boots and shrugs into her coat by the door.

"Sounds lovely," Cade mutters.

I roll my eyes at his sarcasm, but a smile tugs at the corner of my mouth. For a brief second, things feel almost … normal.

"Wait." I reach for the Viridian folder still resting on the couch and pull out the small grainy photo of the girl behind the glass. "Can I keep this?"

Cade drops the folder onto the table with a soft thud. "Sure, I don't need it."

I slide the photo into the inside pocket of my jacket, pressing it flat against my chest like it might whisper answers if I keep it close enough.

"I might try to contact her later. The photo will help." My voice is quiet, thoughtful.

We step outside, the cold air biting against our skin as we pile into the SUV. The image of the girl still lingers in my mind —those light eyes, that hospital gown, her face caught in a moment that looks too much like mine.

Who are you?

And what the hell are you to me?

Chapter Seven

AURORA SPENDS the next thirty minutes of the drive spilling everything that's happened to her since we were torn apart. She bounced from house to house, passed through a couple of auctions, until her gift started to evolve. She didn't merely heat things anymore. She could ignite them. Melt steel. Reach temperatures no human should be able to withstand.

That's when someone finally took notice.

A buyer from the Southern District—rich, connected to the black market—snatched her up. Not political, not affiliated with any of the ruling families. A weaponsmith with deep pockets and a hunger for power. He treated her ... well enough, she says. Used her to melt and mold metal faster than any furnace. Her hands created blades that could cut through anything, shaping parts that no forge could match. She was his secret weapon. His edge.

But then he made the mistake of owing the wrong men money.

That's when everything changed. She was taken one night, ripped from his estate by men she's sure were working for

Viktor, and locked away in one of the holding cells beneath that cursed barn, waiting to be sold again or worse. She spent weeks there, half starved and terrified, until the night we found her. Her and a boy named Freddy.

I remember him now. The one with the wide eyes and the bruised ribs. She tells me he can breathe underwater, something that sounds almost laughable out here in the cold mountains. I don't know how useful a gift like that really is, but apparently, Bash does. She hasn't seen much of him since. He's been working directly with Bash in the lab since they arrived here.

"I hate to ruin what's been a surprisingly good day, but we're almost to Irina's, and while I've got you both trapped in here, I need to know how you really feel about pulling Malachi into the loop with us." I scrunch my nose, bracing myself.

They speak in unison. "Absolutely not."

Aurora follows it up immediately. "Are you crazy? We don't even know if we can trust him. He's too close to all of this."

I let out a long, slow sigh. "I know I haven't known him that long, but I trust him and care about him. And if I'm being honest, we need him. We can't raid these labs or uncover whatever the hell Marco is doing without his help."

Aurora leans back in her seat, her arms crossed. Cade takes it from there.

"I don't know if we can trust him either, Kat. I've known him longer than you have. Yeah, he usually tries to do the right thing, but he's deep in the Syndicate. Irina is his aunt. And Marco—"

"Marco is my fucking nightmare," I cut in. "And Malachi isn't him."

"I'm not saying he is, but Aurora's right. He's too close."

I cross my arms, staring out the windshield, frustration

building like a slow burn in my chest. "Too close? I'm at the center of all of this and want him involved. What's your plan otherwise? The three of us sneak off with a couple of knives and storm secret facilities on our own? You think we'll get far?"

Cade stares out the window, the snow-covered trees blurring past. When he finally looks back at the road, his voice is quieter.

"Alright, Kat. You're right. It would be easier if we had his help, but we have to be careful. We don't know who we can trust. I don't even trust everyone in Solace anymore. The Syndicate could have spies. My team could have spies."

I breathe out slowly, relieved.

"But don't rush it," Cade continues. "Give it a day. Feel him out. Ask hard questions. Be smart. After that, if you still believe he belongs in this, then tell him."

"Okay. You're right." I nod. "I promise I'll be careful and make sure it feels right before I say anything. And if I get a moment to myself tonight, I'll try to contact the girl in the photo."

For once, we're all in agreement.

"Are you coming in when we get there?" I ask as Irina's ranch starts to come into view.

Cade scoffs, "No. We'll meet you in Bash's lab tomorrow around noon."

Aurora pulls her hood up.

"Alright. It's a plan then."

I debate asking Cade to drop me at the edge of the property, closer to Malachi's side of the estate, but it's freezing out—and he's probably at Irina's anyway. So I find myself standing awkwardly at her front door. Do I knock? Walk in? I'm not sure of the protocol here, and the cold wind biting at my face isn't helping me think straight.

I knock once, then glance back to wave off Cade and

Aurora. They don't need to wait. They're already halfway down the icy driveway by the time the door creaks open.

"Katja," Irina says, her smile warm. "I'm glad to see you're all right. You gave everyone a bit of a scare. Come in, it's freezing."

I step inside, pulling off my gloves and stuffing them in my coat pocket, rubbing my hands together to bring back some feeling. Her house smells like cinnamon and cloves, something warm and old-world comforting.

"Is Malachi here?" I ask, my eyes scanning the quiet foyer.

"He's downstairs. Took the boys over an hour to haul in all the boxes from my brother's compound." Her mouth tightens slightly. "Will be interesting to see what we can uncover."

She waves me toward the kitchen, where a pot of cider simmers on the stove. She ladles some into a thick ceramic mug and passes it to me. The warmth seeps into my hands immediately, and I inhale the steam like it might steady the nerves dancing beneath my skin.

"You were so close to finally putting an end to my miserable brother's life," Irina says, lifting a mug and settling onto one of the bar stools by the kitchen island. "I heard he had some sort of vial on him when he disappeared. Any idea what it could be?"

I pause, the rim of my cup hovering near my lips. That's not idle curiosity. Malachi must have already debriefed her—told her I didn't know what the vial was. So why is she asking me now? Is this small talk? She doesn't strike me as someone who wastes breath without a reason.

"No," I say simply, keeping my expression neutral, "I'm not sure."

I have theories, ideas that make my skin itch when I think about them. But I've learned the hard way it's smarter to keep my cards close. Maybe Cade's paranoia is rubbing off on me.

She takes a slow sip, eyes never leaving me. "Well, you and

Malachi are going to be running a bit of a skeleton crew here and over at the Depths for the next few weeks."

That gets my attention.

"A skeleton crew?" I echo, watching her for a deeper explanation.

Irina nods, idly fiddling with a stack of napkins on the counter. "Yes. I'm sending Rain and her team to occupy Marco's compound. I want it fully secured, and I want them to dig—see what he left behind before he has a chance to reclaim anything."

I exhale, relieved it's not Malachi's team being assigned. The last place I want to step foot in is that house again. "I don't think he'll try to take it back."

"Neither do I," Irina says, brushing a hand through her long blonde hair. She looks tired. The faint creases at the corners of her eyes seem deeper than before. "But that's what worries me. He has other places to go, too many. And I'm sure by now Viktor knows everything he does."

She lifts her mug and takes a sip, pausing like the weight of everything is catching up to her. I tilt my head. "If Rain's team is going there ... where are you going?"

"A summit in the Southern District." She meets my eyes. "There's unrest among Syndicate leadership. Whispers of defectors. I'm hoping this meeting brings clarity ... before someone does something that can't be undone."

A summit? My pulse quickens. "You'll be gone for weeks?"

"There are other facilities I need to visit as well," she replies vaguely. She stands, taking our empty mugs to the sink. "Ties that need tightening. Concerns that need addressing. You understand."

Not really. But I nod anyway.

"Go find Malachi. He's downstairs, and I'm sure he'll be

glad to see you." Her expression softens slightly. "I need to finish packing."

Before I can say anything, she disappears down the hallway.

"MIND IF I JOIN YOU?" I call out to Malachi as I descend the last step into the basement and kick off my boots.

The space surprises me. It's not cold or cement walled like I'd expected. Instead, it feels lived in, curated in that effortless, masculine way—dimly lit, warm, and quiet with plush beige carpet beneath my socks and the lingering scent of cedar and smoke in the air. An old leather couch sprawls across one wall, well-worn but inviting. A relic of a television sits across from it, the kind you'd only find in black market shops now, probably useless unless paired with an antique Blu-ray player. The idea that he'd even have one makes me smile.

The rest of the basement is a strange blend of chaos and order. Tall stacks of boxes line one entire wall, some sealed tight with crisp new tape, others frayed and faded, their edges curling like old photographs. The desk in the corner—sleek and angular—is buried beneath files and papers, a single overhead lamp casting a soft pool of light around him like a spotlight.

Malachi is perched there in the center of it, leaning forward as he flips through documents with a crease between his brows. His dark hair is tousled, and his sleeves are pushed to his elbows, exposing strong forearms veined and dusted with ink smudges. He looks up when he hears me, and the second our eyes meet, the serious expression vanishes. Something else replaces it—warmth, hunger, relief.

"Look who survived the mountain," he says, pushing back slightly in the chair, amused. "Thought you might have decided to stay up there in a cabin with your ex and your best friend forever."

I peel off my jacket, draping it neatly over the edge of the couch. My body still feels chilled, but the room radiates heat from somewhere—maybe him. I cross the floor, dragging my fingers along the wall of boxes as I approach. The silence is comfortable now, familiar.

"I figured you'd miss me too much," I murmur, stopping right beside him.

One of his hands slides around the back of my thigh, the other curling around my waist as he pulls me forward into his lap. My breath catches as I settle there, knees straddling his thighs, hands bracing against his chest.

"Oh, my little demon, I'd miss you like a sinner misses sin, like the dark misses the stars," he murmurs, voice low and sultry against my ear. "But don't get too cocky about it."

His hands tighten slightly, possessive. Confident. Like I'm already his and he knows it.

"I was starting to think you might be avoiding me." His lips curl into a smirk, but his eyes search mine—still sharp, still reading every inch of me.

"Not avoiding," I say, letting my fingertips drift across the top button of his shirt. "I needed time to process a few things. You know, top secret mountain business."

"Right," he says, drawing it out. "Secret rendezvous with Calloway. Cozy fireplace. Dangerous revelations." He leans forward enough for his nose to brush mine. "I'd be jealous if I wasn't so damn confident in how much you want me."

My pulse answers before I can. Still, I arch an eyebrow. "You sure about that?"

Instead of answering, his hands slip beneath the hem of my shirt and rest at my waist, thumbs brushing bare skin. His gaze drops to my mouth.

"Dead certain. But if you need a reminder, I'm happy to provide one."

I swallow, my skin buzzing from his touch. He tilts his head like he's waiting, teasing, letting the air between us stretch taut.

Then he adds, "I'm glad you're back, Katja. I could use your help going through all of this." He looks over at the stretch of boxes, and the moment's gone.

I clear my throat and rise to my feet, brushing my hands down the front of my pants. "Where should I start?"

Malachi lifts his head slightly from the desk, his eyes dragging over the wall of towering boxes behind me. "Anywhere you'd like."

I choose one that looks like it hasn't been touched yet and slide it toward me. I grab a couple of pillows from the couch, toss them to the floor, and sink into the soft carpet, tucking one behind my back as I cross my legs beneath me.

The files inside are layered in careful rows. I start pulling them out one by one, spreading them into loose categories around me. Names. Locations. Lab reports. The smell of old paper mixes with the faint scent of cedar from the box itself.

Malachi speaks again, quieter this time. "How was seeing Aurora?"

I glance up, surprised he asked. His eyes remain on the file in front of him, but I can tell he's listening, waiting.

"It was really great actually," I say, flipping over a page with a rusted paperclip attached. "She seems like she's settling in at Cade's place."

He hums in response, and the room goes quiet again except for the occasional rustle of papers between us.

"Why aren't any of these files digital?" I ask, flipping through a folder thick with faded auction records. "I know I've seen Marco on a computer before, so what's with the archives?"

Malachi finishes reading the page in front of him, sets it aside, then leans back in his chair.

"My father doesn't trust digital systems," he says. "Anything connected to a network can be hacked, leaked, or traced. Paper has no remote access. No spyware. No digital fingerprint."

I glance around at the towers of boxes stacked against the wall. "I guess that's fair, but it didn't stop us from getting our hands on all of this."

"Well," he says, letting out a breath, "not all of it. A good portion of his files caught fire in the explosion. What we have here is only what survived."

He grabs another fresh stack of folders out of the box next to him, then adds, "Gary and Orin had both been pressuring him to digitize more of it. I think he started to, but most of these records predate my father's leadership. A lot of it was inherited. Passed down from the men who came before him I guess."

So paranoia runs in the family, great.

I don't know how long we've been reading through these files, but it's long enough that my eyes feel like sandpaper, and the words on the page blur together like melting ink. At some point, Irina came down to tell us she was leaving, but that feels like hours ago.

Most of what I've sifted through is useless: scraps of old auction records, faded lists of names and numbers, handwritten tallies of prices paid and buyers labeled only by initials. There are black market receipts for shady deals that lead nowhere and pages of coded memos that reference conversations, with no clear sender or recipient. It all feels ... sanitized. Too clean. Like someone packed it intentionally to look damning without actually giving away anything important.

Maybe this whole stash was curated to throw us off. Maybe

everything that mattered went up in flames the night he escaped.

I'm about ready to toss in the towel and find something to eat, but Malachi's been silent for so long I glance over to make sure he's still breathing. He hasn't looked up once. Whatever he's reading has his full attention, so I figure I'll give it one last try before I disturb him.

The next box catches my eye because it looks nothing like the others. It's not weathered or falling apart at the corners. No yellowing tape, no brittle edges. This one is new. Pristine. Like someone packed it last week.

Something about that makes the hairs on my arms stand up.

I drag it toward me and peel back the crisp edge of the tape. It opens with a clean rip, the kind you only get from a fresh seal. Inside, the first thing I notice is the lack of dust. The second thing is that everything inside is perfectly organized. Not a single page out of place.

This wasn't abandoned. It was preserved.

With a flutter of unease starting to fester inside me, I lift out the top folder. It's unmarked on the front, but the tab has two words in bold block letters.

PROJECT GRAFT.

Chapter Eight

LOG EIGHT - REFLEXES BEYOND CONTROL: SHE MOVED BEFORE THE NEEDLE TOUCHED HER. EYES CLOSED. STILL SMILING.

PROJECT GRAFT.

I crack open the folder and immediately slam it shut, heart lurching into my throat. My pulse stutters. There is a photo of a monstrosity. At first glance, it looks like a fox, or maybe it used to be, but it is now something else. Limbs stitched where they shouldn't be. Eyes too large, too human. The fur patchy, wiry, and singed.

I take a breath, then another, forcing the bile back down my throat.

You have to look. You have to know.

I open it again, slower this time, blinking fast as my eyes skim over the grotesque image and drop to the page beneath it. Black ink. Sharp, clinical. Unfeeling.

I flip through the documents, each page worse than the last. Organ grafts. Genetic manipulation. Neurological rewiring. They're not simply testing on animals; they're trying to remake them. Rebuild them. Strip them down to muscle and bone and insert something else in their place. Something Avid.

I read, *Cognitive Enhancement Trial #6. Increased aggres-*

sion noted. Subject terminated after breaching enclosure. Another line is scrawled in the margins. *No tranquilizer necessary. Subject responded to heat signature, nearly intelligent.*

My hands tremble as I keep reading.

Project Graft isn't some theoretical idea; they've already done it. They're giving animals powers. Trying to gift them strength, speed, even perception. As if the world isn't already a nightmare.

And then it hits me like ice water down my spine.

The wolves that tore through the forest in the snow. We knew something was off. They were too fast. Too organized.

I squeeze the folder tighter until the paper crumples at the edges.

Marco. This has his corruption all over it.

I don't know how anyone could justify this. Why would anyone need this kind of weapon, this kind of creature?

But someone does. Someone wants this army and thinks the only way to win is to play God. And they've already started.

If they're trying to give animals powers like Avids, then I don't even want to think about what kind of experiments they've done on actual Avids to make that happen. The folder in front of me is bad enough. But there's more out there. Worse. I know it.

Meadow.

She wasn't herself. Stronger, yes, but something had been twisted inside her and stitched back together incorrectly. They did something to her. Changed her. Used her.

I know she wasn't the first.

And she won't be the last.

Every single person behind this deserves to burn for it.

Torture would be a kindness compared to what they've done. And I don't care if that makes me sick or depraved. I would deliver the pain myself, smiling, if it meant they paid for what they did.

I have to go to this facility. I will find a way in. I will tear down everything the Volkovs have built. And anyone helping them—anyone complicit in this horror—will fall with them. This world is already hanging on by a thread. We've poisoned the planet, ripped each other apart, turned survival into a currency only the powerful can afford. Society is fractured beyond recognition. Still, we don't stop.

Natural disasters used to humble us; earthquakes, floods, the kind of events we couldn't control. They reminded us how fragile this earth is. How small we really are. But even after the planet fought back, even after half the population died ... we didn't unite. We didn't learn.

We found new ways to destroy each other.

I think about what I read in the scientist's journal that Malachi gave me. The first Avid wasn't born. She was made. A terrified girl experimented on in some desperate attempt to cure a plague we brought on ourselves. Millions died. And we turned on our own. We created monsters and then blamed them for existing.

We are the problem. And we're not only killing each other. We're killing everything—every innocent soul still trying to live on this scorched Earth.

"Are you all right?"

Malachi's voice breaks through the spiral, and I turn away quickly, blinking back tears before he can see. I hate feeling this way, hate letting the darkness inside me swell to the surface. I want to believe in people. There's still good left in this world, but every time I think I've found it, something like this rips it away.

This godforsaken lab full of cages and needles and screams will fall. I will tear it down myself if I have to. I'm going to put myself through Bash's machine. Whatever it takes. I have to get stronger. I need to be ready. Because there *will* be a mission. I'll lead it if I have to.

Marco thinks I hated him before? That was before I knew how deep his sickness runs. Before I understood what kind of monster he really is. I let myself be blind. Let myself believe ignorance was protection.

That ends now.

Every hand that touched this, every mind that approved it —they all have blood on their hands, and I won't let them walk away from it.

"Kat?" Malachi's hand finds my shoulder, grounding me for a beat. I pass him the folder, swiping at the tear that escapes before he can notice.

"Project Graft," he mutters.

He flips through the pages, his expression tightening with every turn. His brows knit together, then his jaw locks. I watch his hand clench around the paper, the tendons straining with a soundless fury as he exhales through gritted teeth.

I don't need to look again. The images are already burned into my mind.

And this is only the first folder.

My gaze drops to the box still full beside me. Whatever else waits inside, I'm not sure I'm strong enough to face it tonight.

Malachi closes the file and sets it down. His arm slips around my shoulders, pulling me into him.

"That's enough for tonight," he says gently. "Come on. Let's get you something to eat."

I lean into his warmth, into the steady thrum of his heartbeat, and let myself sink there for a moment. For all the cruelty and chaos clawing at the edges of this world, somehow, I still found him—this calm, this good.

We barely make it halfway to the kitchen when I hear something.

A sharp beep.

Then another.

Malachi stops in his tracks. I freeze, the sound cutting through the quiet.

"What is that?" I whisper.

He pivots on his heel and strides back toward the basement. I follow, heart thudding.

The beeping grows louder as we descend the steps.

Malachi drops to his knees in front of the box, yanking away folders until his hand closes around a small black device nestled deep in the center. The LED on its face pulses red.

"Shit," he mutters, holding it up. "It's a tracker. This box—it's not records. It's bait."

A cold rush spreads through my chest.

"We need to go." He's already on his feet, rushing past me toward the stairs. "Now."

I snatch my jacket off the couch, fingers trembling as I shove my arms through the sleeves.

"They know we have it," I say, frantic.

"And they're coming to take it back," he says, voice sharp. "That sound—the tracker beeping means they're close."

I whip my head toward him. "Who's close?"

My mind's already scanning for allies. Irina is halfway across the country or still on a plane—either way, unreachable. Rain and most of Solace are headed west, gone with the last convoy. Cade and Aurora are tucked away in the goddamn mountains.

We're alone.

I glance out the nearest window, the snow outside drifting peacefully.

"Malachi," I say, stepping closer, "who the hell did your father send?"

He spins toward the hall closet, yanking it open and grabbing a black tactical pack. He tosses in whatever supplies he can grab. I can barely see with all the lights off and don't know how he can tell what all this stuff is.

I stand there like an idiot, empty-handed. Shit. I haven't even changed clothes. Still in these all-black safe house sweats, no boots, no weapon. My eyes flick to the kitchen. A knife block sits on the counter, maybe eight feet away.

I take one step, but a soft sound stops me cold. Malachi freezes too and turns to me, lifts one finger to his lips.

The next sound is a faint click.

The handle of the front door turning, slow and careful. Someone's picking the lock.

No—*not someone trying to get in.*

Someone trying not to be heard. If it were Orin, he'd kick the damn door in. No subtlety. No games.

And that makes it so much worse.

Malachi slips the backpack over his shoulder and reaches for my hand. His grip is tight, steady. He doesn't speak as he guides me through the house, bare feet silent against the hardwood.

I try not to breathe.

Every creak, every distant shift of weight sounds like thunder in my ears.

We reach the back door as the front door creaks open behind us.

They're inside.

Whoever or whatever is here, and they're in the house.

Malachi opens the door slowly, holding it just enough for us to slip through. The icy night air hits my face like a slap. He pulls me with him into the snow, the door closing behind us with a muted click.

There's only one thing left to do.

We run.

Chapter Nine

LOG NINE - VOCAL SHIFT RECORDED: SHE SPOKE TODAY, BUT NOT IN ANY LANGUAGE I KNOW. THE MACHINES TRANSLATED IT AS GRIEF.

WE RUN IN SILENCE, our footsteps muffled by a fresh dusting of powder, breath clouding in the air as we cut through the darkness toward the far end of the property. Malachi's cabin looms ahead, and we don't slow until we're inside.

He locks the door behind us, eyes scanning the space as he moves room to room. I stand in the center, heart hammering, ears straining for any sound behind us. The place looks untouched.

"No one's been here." His voice is hushed. "Don't turn the lights on. Grab anything you need and wait for me here. If I'm not back in five minutes, get in the jeep and drive straight to Cade's. Don't stop for anyone. You understand?"

I blink at him, stunned. "You're not leaving me. Wherever you go, I go. Try and stop me, Malachi."

He lets out a sharp breath and crosses to me in three long strides. "Goddamn it, Kat." Without warning, he lifts me off the ground and drops me gently onto the couch. "I didn't realize you left your shoes."

My feet are burning from the cold now that I've stopped moving. He crouches, pulls off my soaked socks, and starts rubbing warmth back into my feet. Then he lifts them to his mouth, blowing hot air across my numb toes over and over.

I want to tell him to stop treating me like something breakable because we don't have time for this, but I can see it in his face that this is important to him.

He disappears into the bedroom and comes back with thick wool socks and a pair of my old loafers. "They're not boots, but they'll have to do."

I shove them on as fast as I can. By the time I'm on my feet, he's slinging a duffle bag over one shoulder, stuffed with clothes —his and mine.

"Follow me. Stay low. Stay quiet."

I fall in step behind him.

A lone jeep waits behind the cabin, dusted in snow. Malachi drops the duffle and the backpack beside the back tire, his breath misting in the frigid air. Then he takes my hand again, fingers tight around mine, and leads us away from the cabin—not back toward the road but through a narrow path behind the barn.

The trees here are sparse, thin skeletons veiled in white. We keep low, weaving through shadows and using every bit of cover we can find until Irina's house comes into view again from a new angle.

The front door is shut. It's quiet.

Malachi halts behind an old feed trough, snow crunching softly beneath his boots. He pulls a small pair of binoculars from his coat pocket, one of the things he must've grabbed before we fled, and presses them to his eyes.

I stay close, the cold cutting through every layer I have on. A fresh flurry begins to fall, the flakes burn against my cheeks, collecting on my eyelashes, clinging to my hair and nose. I squint toward the house, trying to see what he sees.

Two men step out the front door, both dressed in dark clothes. I don't recognize the first one. He's lean with shoulder-length blond hair and a strange stillness in the way he walks, like he's listening to something only he can hear. But the second man ...

I freeze.

Tall. Slicked-back hair. That smug, polished arrogance in the way he holds himself.

Gary Volkov.

Malachi's brother.

The one I used to think was the reasonable one between him and Orin. The quiet one. Now, watching him from the shadows, I realize I was wrong. He's cold, empty, and right now he has a leash in one hand ... and a fucking wolf on the other end of it.

It's massive with mangy black fur that hangs off its thick frame in patches. Its eyes glow with an unnatural yellow light that seems to cut through the night and land directly on us.

Gary lifts his chin like he's sniffing the wind, and the wolf mirrors the motion.

I swallow hard, trying to stay calm, but the sight of the creature makes my heart thud rapidly in my ears. Whatever part of me used to believe Gary would take me back to that pretty prison is long gone. I don't think he'd hesitate to let that monster rip me apart.

The front door creaks again.

A third man walks out, heavier build, face obscured by the collar of his coat. He's holding something—metal in one hand, red in the other.

Malachi grips my hand tight.

"Fuck," he breathes.

The red thing isn't a weapon. It's a gas can.

We crouch lower, and Malachi tugs me gently but urgently back toward the tree line, moving fast, barely making a sound as the snow flurries pick up all around us.

We reach the jeep without speaking, without looking back. But I know what I saw and what's about to happen to Irina's house.

We slip inside the jeep, both of us easing the door shut so slowly it barely clicks. Still, I wince. My eyes squeeze shut on instinct, bracing for a sound I already know the wolf will hear. Every noise feels loud.

Malachi sits frozen, one hand on the ignition, the other gripping the wheel. We're both listening.

Waiting.

Boom.

Irina's house erupts into flames behind us. The blast punches through the night like thunder, followed by a shockwave that makes the jeep tremble beneath us. A flash of orange light swallows the darkness for a split second, fire blooming out of the windows and licking the sky.

Malachi doesn't flinch. That was the sound he was waiting for.

He starts the engine, throws the gear into drive, and we tear off the property, no headlights, no warning, only snow and speed as we veer off road into the trees behind the cabin.

I twist in my seat, eyes wide, scanning the fields through the rear window. My breath fogs the glass. I'm searching for movement. A car. A silhouette. Glowing yellow eyes. Anything.

But there's nothing but darkness.

And behind it, the distant, rising glow of Irina's property burning to the ground.

"Fuck, did you see Gary? Did you see the wolf he had with

him?" I say once I realize no one's following us. My heart is still hammering against my ribs from whatever the hell happened back there.

"Gary's doing whatever he's told, like a good boy, always acting like a fucking puppet." Malachi doesn't look in my direction, doesn't slow down. The speedometer needle keeps climbing. "It's not Gary I'm worried about. Did you see the guy with long hair?"

He gives me a quick sideways glance, and I catch something dark flickering in his eyes.

"Yeah, I did. And the third man who came out with the gas can, but I didn't recognize either of them." I buckle my seatbelt with shaking fingers and turn to face him fully, studying his profile. There's something he's not telling me. "Who were they?"

Malachi's silent for a long moment, like he's debating how much to reveal. Finally, he exhales. "I don't know who the third guy was, but the one with long hair is named Rupert. And he's not only friends with Irina. He's a Syndicate member."

My mouth falls open, and I stare at him, trying to process what this means. "You're telling me one of her allies torched her house?"

"I don't think she's the target," he says. "We are."

"Where are you taking us now?" I ask, in disbelief about the turn of events tonight. My mind is reeling, trying to piece together what happened.

"Now we'll go to your boyfriend's house." His mouth curls up on one side, that infuriating smirk I know too well.

"Don't call him that," I snap, and slap his shoulder hard enough to make him wince. "I don't know how you can smile right now after what's going on." I scowl at him, but he chuckles, the sound dark and a little unhinged.

"Kat, I'm not going to lie. This is all sorts of fucked up, and all I can do right now is laugh about it." He chuckles again, shaking his head. "Otherwise, I might lose my damn mind."

"Are you insane?" I stare at him like he's completely lost it. "Why Cade's house of all places?"

Mish appears in my lap, her ghostly form materializing like smoke. She stretches her ethereal limbs before curling into a ball, and I feel that familiar coolness against my thighs. She always knows when I'm stressed.

I stroke her translucent fur, the sensation like touching mist, and wait for Malachi to elaborate.

"Calloway has a knack for staying below the radar. There are very few people who know where his property is." His tone shifts, becoming more serious. "It should be safe for us to stay there and regroup."

The thought of all four of us staying under the same roof makes my stomach flutter with a mixture of excitement and dread. Cade and Malachi in the same space for more than five minutes?

They're going to kill each other.

"WHAT'S HAPPENED?" Cade asks as he opens the door for us. It's late, and by the looks of it he just tumbled out of bed. His dark hair is sticking up in every direction, and he's only wearing gray sweats that hang low on his hips. The sight of his bare chest makes my pulse quicken despite everything that's happened tonight.

"Put on a fucking shirt, Calloway, and tell me you have a phone line that reaches this place." Malachi brushes past him without ceremony, hanging his jacket on the rack and heading straight for the kitchen where an old rotary phone hangs on the wall.

Cade smirks at me as I walk by, his eyes lingering on my face like he's reading every detail of what I've been through. I settle in front of the fireplace where embers are still glowing with stubborn life, and Mish immediately curls up beside me at the hearth.

"Here, let me help." Cade grabs the poker and starts coaxing the flames back to life, adding fresh logs until the fire roars and crackles. The warmth hits my skin, and I practically melt with relief, pulling off my jacket and shoes to soak up more heat.

"What's going on?" Aurora appears from down the hall in cute pink button-up pajamas, her wild curly hair creating a halo around her sleepy face. She looks like she stepped out of a fairy tale, all soft edges and innocence.

Malachi hangs up the phone with a sharp click and comes to sit beside me on the floor. "I talked to Bash. He's working late in the lab and says everything's fine there, but he's put the Depths on lockdown. We'll go there first thing in the morning."

"Hi, nice to see you again. I'm Aurora." She gives Malachi a pointed look, her voice dripping with sarcasm. "Now, can you tell me what the hell is happening?"

I bite back a giggle. Aurora's sweet exterior hides a backbone of steel.

Cade returns from down the hall, pulling a gray T-shirt over his head. The fabric clings to his chest as he settles on the couch across from Aurora, and I force myself to focus on Malachi.

"Everything's gone. Gary, Rupert, and someone else I didn't recognize showed up and burned the entire property to the ground."

Cade sits up straighter, tension coiling through his shoulders. "Irina?"

His face pales.

"She wasn't there. She packed up earlier and left for the Southern District. It was only me and Katja." Malachi's voice is carefully neutral, but I catch the undercurrent of something I can't place.

"There was a tracker in one of the boxes from Marcos," I add. "We heard it go off before they arrived."

"Shit." Aurora tucks some wild strands of hair out of her face.

"You think they wanted to kill you and Kat?" Cade leans forward, deadly serious. The playful smirk is completely gone now.

"I'm not sure. They searched the house before they blew it up, but we'd already snuck out." Malachi's jaw tics. "Maybe they would have captured us. One thing's certain—they didn't want us going through those boxes, and my father's clearly pissed. He's not afraid to take it out on his sister anymore."

"Yeah, I never thought he'd do something like this to Irina." Cade shakes his head. "What does this mean for the Syndicate? How is Rupert involved?"

Malachi runs a hand down his face, and I notice how exhausted he looks—more than I've seen him in weeks. The events of the last few days are catching up to him. "I don't know. I need to get hold of my aunt. I'll try her again before I go to bed, but you guys should get some sleep."

He looks over at me and reaches out to rub slow circles up and down my back. The touch is possessive and comforting all at once.

"About that, there are only two bedrooms," Aurora starts, but Cade jumps in before she can finish.

"You two can take my bed. I'll sleep on the couch."

Malachi makes a face like he tasted something rotten, clearly disgusted by the thought of either of us anywhere near Cade's bed.

"Kat can sleep with me, and you boys can figure out your shit." Aurora gets to her feet and reaches for my hand, tugging me up with surprising strength for someone so small.

But Malachi stands too, intercepting me before Aurora can drag me away. He pulls me close to his chest, looking down at me with those dark eyes that seem to see straight through my soul. His fingers brush the loose strands of hair from my face with infinite tenderness.

"Are you sure you're all right?" he asks.

I nod, acutely aware of Cade and Aurora watching us, but Malachi continues like we're the only two people in the world.

He leans down and gives me a long, devastating kiss. He takes his time, tasting me, exploring my mouth like he's trying to memorize the shape of my lips. When he finally pulls away, I'm breathless and dizzy.

I clear my throat, feeling heat bloom across my cheeks. I'm sure they're bright pink after that display.

"Careful, Kat. Keep looking at me like that, and I might forget we have an audience."

I shove his chest and laugh it off, trying to ignore the way my pulse races at the thought.

"Goodnight."

I follow Aurora down the hall, but before I close the door, I hear Malachi's voice carrying through the house. "I'll take the couch, but we need to talk."

My stomach clenches. What are they going to discuss? Me? The situation? The obvious tension between all of us?

"I know the room is nothing special—Cade is no decorator —but at least we have our own bathroom and heated blankets." Aurora beams at me, her energy infectious despite the late hour. She goes over to the dresser and starts pulling drawers open.

I remember then that my duffel bag with some of my clothes is still sitting in the jeep. Great.

"Here, you can wear some of my pajamas." She hands me a neat stack of soft cotton clothes that smell like lavender, and I stack them on top of the jacket I'm already carrying.

"I think I'll take a shower too," I tell her, suddenly desperate to wash away the day.

Aurora yawns, already climbing into bed and pulling the covers up to her chin. "Mmm, good idea. The water pressure's amazing here." She nods sleepily, her curls splaying across the pillow.

I set the stack of clothes down on the wooden countertop, my fingers lingering on the soft fabric. The bathroom is amazing—nothing too fancy, but spacious and calming. There's a large walk-in shower covered in midnight-blue tiles with little swirls that remind me of the ocean at night, deep and mysterious.

I turn on the water, and both showerheads spring to life—a large rainfall one mounted on the ceiling and another on the wall. To my surprise, they heat instantly, sending clouds of steam billowing against the glass walls like morning fog.

I strip off my clothes, each piece a reminder of how quickly everything can burn, and drop them into the wicker laundry basket in the corner. But before I step into the sanctuary of hot water, something makes me pause.

I move past the pajamas and grab my jacket, my fingers fumbling through the pocket until I feel the familiar edges of old paper. I pull out the photograph, my heart clenching as I stare at the girl in the picture. Her face is etched into my soul, but I force myself to memorize every detail again—the curve of her mouth, the light in her eyes, the way her hair falls across her shoulder.

I tuck the photograph back into my jacket pocket, then step into the shower. The hot water hits my skin, and I breathe in the thick, warm steam, closing my eyes as it washes away the remnants of the day.

Let's see if the dead are awake tonight.

Chapter Ten

LOG TEN - MIRROR RECOGNITION FAILURE: SUBJECT STUDIED HER REFLECTION, TOUCHING THE GLASS REPEATEDLY. WHEN ASKED WHAT SHE SAW, SHE WHISPERED "SOMEONE ELSE."

THE HOT WATER feels great against my skin, and the way the shower is designed—with that massive glass wall—all the steam collects and swirls around me like a personal sanctuary. The heat seeps into my muscles, dissolving the knots of tension that have been building all night.

I keep my eyes closed and clear my mind of everything except this moment—me and the warm cascade at my back. I think about the girl in the photograph, her face floating behind my eyelids. I don't know her name or who she is, but I will her to come to me. I implore her to communicate with me, reaching across whatever divide separates us.

I try to imagine the Veil thinning, search for that perfect frequency where the living and the dead can touch.

Suddenly, I feel it. Something spreads across my skin like a thousand tiny pinpricks, electric and foreign. An overwhelming wave of worry crashes over me—but it's not mine. These aren't my feelings, this crushing anxiety that tastes like copper and fear. They're hers.

A soft buzzing fills my head, growing louder, and I open my eyes to shake it away.

The shower is gone.

I didn't mean to go this deep. I was willing her to appear with me in the bathroom, but somehow, I've been pulled into her space instead. I'm standing in an all-white room that feels sterile and cold—hospital-like, maybe medical. The air smells of antiseptic and something else I can't name.

The girl, the woman, really, is sitting on a metal gurney in the center of the room. She tilts her head to one side, studying me with the same intensity I'm using to study her. Her eyes are wide, startled but not afraid.

"I'm Kat," I say, not daring to move, barely daring to breathe. Also realizing I'm completely nude, but there's nothing I can do about that now. "Can you tell me your name?"

"YOU'RE ASKING the wrong questions, Kat. The question isn't who I am. It's who you are."

I blink at her, confused. I told her who I am. What else does she want to know?

"What happened to you? How did you die? Are you the first Avid?" The questions tumble out before I can stop them, and I mentally remind myself to keep it to one at a time. Spirits get overwhelmed easily.

The room distorts around us, the white walls rippling like water before snapping back into focus. I venture a step closer to her, my bare feet silent on the cold floor.

"Avid is not a word of my time." Her voice carries a strange sadness, like she's speaking from somewhere very far away. "You'll see. Your gifts are only beginning to surface."

I don't know what she means. What did her folder say again? Oh yes, Project Viridian.

"Is your name Viridian? Does that mean anything to you?"

The change is instant and devastating. Her anxiety tears through my chest like a physical blow, followed by grief so crushing and raw that I have to consciously remind myself to breathe. My lungs seize up, my chest threatening to cave in on itself under the weight of emotions that aren't mine.

"What's wrong?" I stutter, gasping for air. "I can feel you so strongly."

The room wobbles violently, reality fracturing at the edges. Through the distorting white walls, I catch glimpses of midnight-blue shower tiles bleeding through like watercolors in rain.

"The cage is beautiful—"

She keeps speaking, but all I see are her lips moving in silent desperation. The sound of water rushes back, the shower drowning out her voice like a roaring tide.

No. Not now.

I stare at her, stepping closer, my heart hammering as I focus on her mouth, willing her to stay with me—or me to stay with her. I don't know who's anchoring who in this dissolving space between the Veil.

"The eyes never lie, even when everything else does."

The room starts to shake violently, the white walls cracking and splintering like broken glass.

Her eyes widen with something that looks like panic, like she has so much more to tell me, but time is running out. As she begins to fade, becoming translucent against the fracturing room, I hear her again.

"Find the door."

Then she's gone. The white room collapses like a house of cards, and I'm left gasping and disoriented, staring at nothing but midnight-blue shower tiles and my own reflection in the steamed glass wall.

I turn off the water and towel myself dry, but I still feel unsettled and chilled despite the scalding heat. Find the door, my gifts are beginning to surface, and a bunch of other cryptic nonsense. I'm more confused now than I was before I contacted her.

Maybe my connection was poor because I'm so exhausted. I'll have to try again soon, when my mind is clearer.

I slip into the shorts and matching button-up pajama top Aurora gave me—soft black cotton scattered with tiny blue and white flowers that remind me of my garden, the one I first met Malachi in. I miss that garden. It's probably the only thing I'll ever miss about that life. I turn off the light and tiptoe to the bed, sliding carefully under the covers. She was right about the heated blankets, which feel like pure luxury as I ease into the warm embrace of the comforter.

"That was a long shower," Aurora says, rolling onto her back in the dark.

"Sorry, I didn't mean to wake you."

"I'm a light sleeper." I can sense her smiling. "So, that Malachi is pretty hot up close. You think it's serious?" Her tone shifts, becoming conspiratorial. "Did you see the way Cade was eye-fucking you during that kiss?"

I have to clap my hand over my mouth to stifle my laugh. "Aurora!"

"What? I'm saying what we were all thinking." She sounds completely unrepentant.

"Cade is a friend now, nothing more. And Malachi ..." I pause, my chest tightening at the thought of him. "I fear I'm falling hard for him. I try to rein it in, to remind myself I haven't known him that long and need to be careful, but the way my stomach does flips when he's near ... The way my pulse quickens ..."

"Oh, Kat, you have it bad," she says, her laughter warm and knowing in the darkness.

"I know I do, and I feel bad because Cade went through so much to find me. All these years of searching, it's tragic and romantic, like the ultimate gesture of love."

"I'm sensing a 'but' coming on."

I sigh, my chest feeling heavy with guilt and confusion. "But I've been falling in love with Malachi since the moment I met him, if I'm being honest with myself. The feelings I once had for Cade don't even compare to what I feel for Malachi now."

I feel almost guilty for saying it out loud, like I'm betraying something sacred.

"Don't feel bad for not reciprocating Cade's feelings," Aurora says, like she can read my mind. "He's a big boy, and like you said, it's been years. You two are different people now." Her tone becomes more playful. "Besides, you have that hot boss man wrapped around your finger."

She dissolves into giggles, and I swat blindly at her, hitting her shoulder, I think.

"Aurora, my God!" I laugh despite myself, the sound bubbling up from somewhere deep in my chest. It feels incredible to laugh and have girl talk—something I haven't experienced in far too long. Something I didn't realize I was starving for.

"Tomorrow at breakfast, I'm going to tell Malachi about everything. The four of us need to work together, especially after what happened tonight. I know we can trust him."

"You're assuming we'll even have breakfast. Have you looked inside Cade's fridge?" Aurora jokes but then clears her throat. "You're right, Katja. If you feel strongly about Malachi and think he can be trusted, then I'll support your decision. Cade will deal. Don't worry about him."

My stomach chooses that moment to growl loudly, and I'm suddenly starving thinking about breakfast. I try to remember the last time I ate anything substantial. We were about to make dinner when all hell broke loose earlier tonight.

"Were you serious about Cade's fridge?" I ask, completely fixated on food now.

"No. Well, kind of. He doesn't have a lot of options, but he still has better food than I ever had in the South. The other day, I had some protein wafers for breakfast, and I don't recommend them. Chalky and synthetic. Like vanilla-flavored dirt." She giggles at the memory.

"The apple flavor is marginally better, but I know what you mean," I say, grimacing.

"After lots of complaining, Cade finally got some good stuff. He has a jug of synthetic eggs, but they actually taste really good. We can make omelets with toast. He even has jam." Her voice brightens.

My mouth waters. "Sounds perfect."

I turn onto my side as Mish hops up onto the bed, doing a quick zoomie session over both of us before curling up right against my chest. Her ghostly warmth settles into that familiar spot she's claimed as hers for years.

As if reading my mind, Aurora says quietly, "Do you still see your dead dog?"

I look down at Mish's translucent form and close my eyes, feeling that bittersweet ache that always comes when I talk about her. "Yeah, I still see Mischka. She's here now, cuddling me, still faithful after all these years."

"That makes my heart happy. After everything you've been through, at least you've always had your girl watching over you."

"HE MIGHT BE EVEN CUTER when he's asleep," Aurora whispers as we tiptoe past Malachi passed out on the couch. We decided to make breakfast for everyone before they wake up, a small peace offering after the shitstorm of a night.

"Shhh." I peek at him anyway, my heart doing that familiar flutter. He looks peaceful when he sleeps, the normally hard lines of his face softened into something almost innocent looking. His brown hair is tousled across his forehead, and one arm hangs loosely off the edge of the couch.

Aurora starts brewing coffee—lab-grown coffee substitute, but it tastes remarkably close to the real thing. I grab the big carton of Goldenscram from the fridge and pour the yellow mixture into a pan, moving it around with a spatula to make enough scrambled eggs for all of us.

As I slide the carton back into the fridge, I catch sight of the label and can't help but smirk. There's a cartoon picture of a ridiculously happy chicken giving an enthusiastic thumbs-up. The slogan in cheerful yellow letters reads, *Luxury you don't have to hatch!*

The absurdity of it makes me shake my head as I push it back onto the shelf.

Cade emerges from down the hall, scratching the top of his messy hair and yawning, but thankfully fully clothed this time. He's wearing a simple gray T-shirt and dark jeans, looking slightly more put together than he did last night despite clearly having rolled out of bed.

"Make yourself useful and set the table," Aurora says, swatting Cade away as he tries to grab a handful of fluffy eggs straight from the pan.

His lips pull back in that guilty, caught-red-handed grin that makes me laugh despite myself. "I don't remember her being this bossy," I tease.

Aurora winks at me, handing Cade a stack of plates and forks with mock authority.

"These are ready. You got the toast?" I ask her.

"Yeah, we'll set everything on the table. Go wake up your man."

Something about the way she says it makes me cringe. It feels awkward with Cade right here, though I can't pinpoint exactly why.

I sneak over to the couch and stare down at Malachi. He's normally not such a deep sleeper, and I wonder how late he stayed up last night talking with Cade. Poor guy probably got no rest at all.

I lean down and press a gentle kiss to his forehead, brushing the dark strands of hair away from his face. Before I can pull back, his hand shoots out and grabs my wrist, tugging me down on top of him.

"Good morning, beautiful," he whispers as he breathes in my hair and presses a soft kiss to the top of my head.

My pulse quickens at the intimacy of it, the way he holds me like I belong there. "Come on, we're all awake. It's time for breakfast and coffee," I say, grabbing his hand and pulling him up off the couch with me.

I settle at the small rectangular table across from Cade and next to Malachi, the seating arrangement feeling both natural and charged with unspoken tension. Aurora places a steaming mug of coffee in front of each of us, the rich aroma filling the kitchen.

She takes her seat next to Cade, completing our little circle, and we all start loading our plates with the fluffy Goldenscram. The synthetic eggs are surprisingly good—light and buttery with none of the chalky texture I was expecting after Aurora's protein wafer horror stories.

I grab a piece of toast and spread some dark-purple jam

across it. I don't know what fruit it's made from and honestly don't care because I'm absolutely starving. The jam has a sweet, berrylike flavor that makes my taste buds sing after days of barely eating.

I devour the entire piece and all of my eggs before I even take a sip of my coffee, eating with the kind of desperate hunger that comes from surviving chaos. Only once my stomach starts to feel satisfied and the gnawing emptiness begins to fade do I venture to speak.

"Now that we're all refreshed and together, I'd like to discuss something important."

The atmosphere at the table shifts instantly. Malachi turns his head toward me, his brown eyes alert and curious. Aurora gives me an encouraging nod before strategically burying her face in her coffee mug, trying to look invisible. Cade's eyes narrow with suspicion, his fork pausing halfway to his mouth.

This is going to be great.

Chapter Eleven

LOG ELEVEN - REFUSED SEDATION: THE SERUM
DIDN'T TAKE. SHE TOLD US IT WOULDN'T BEFORE
WE TRIED.

"MALACHI, there's something we need to share with you, and I've assured Aurora and Cade that we can trust you."

Malachi's expression hardens, his coffee mug freezing halfway to his lips. I can see the wheels turning in his head, analyzing what kind of secret could require this kind of formal announcement.

"Kitty Kat, are you sure you know what you're doing?" Cade says in a mocking singsong voice from across the table, challenging me.

"Don't call her that," Malachi barks, his entire body going rigid. "It may have been cute when you were kids, but she's a grown woman now—my woman—and I don't want you calling her pet names, for fuck's sake."

I swallow hard, my stomach dropping as I realize this is already spiraling down a dangerous path. The testosterone in the room is making it hard to breathe, and we haven't even gotten to the actual revelation yet.

"Hey, hey," Aurora jumps in quickly. "We're still at the breakfast table. Let's all play nice, boys."

I silently thank her for the intervention, shooting her a grateful look across the table.

"You guys rekindled this friendship what, a day ago, and already you have inside secrets?" Malachi's says, his gaze flashing between Cade and me.

Cade's lips start to tip up on one side like he's enjoying the drama way too much. "Careful, Mal, you're starting to sound jealous. One might think you don't feel secure in your relationship," Cade purrs, deliberately baiting.

I slam my hands down on the table hard enough to make all the coffee mugs jump and rattle against their plates. "That is ENOUGH from both of you," I say, getting to my feet.

Aurora's eyes are wide as saucers, but she's smiling, and both men look like I slapped them.

"You are my friend, truly, Cade. I will always care about you, and I am so beyond happy you're alive and okay. I'm humbled you were searching for me all these years. I cannot tell you what it means to have you back in my life again. Suffice it to say, it means everything."

There's a look of complete bewilderment on his face. It's probably because I'm yelling, but I need them to stop tearing each other apart so we can actually trust each other and work together.

"And YOU." I whirl to face Malachi. "There's no need to be jealous of Cade because I'm clearly madly in love with you. So get your head in the game and start working with us, not against us, because there *is* an us here. Cade and Aurora will always be on my team, so if you're going to be in my life, then you need to get over it and step up."

Heat rushes to my face. Did I really declare my love for him for the first time while standing and yelling across a breakfast table, scolding everyone worse than my elementary school teacher used to do?

Yes, Kat, you did.

I slowly lower myself back into my chair, feeling the weight of everyone's stares. Aurora's smile widens across the table, and she mouths *Nice.* I close my eyes briefly, feeling equal parts empowered and ridiculous.

"I'm on your team, Kat, and I trust you," Malachi says, his voice much softer now—or maybe it's the harsh contrast after my yelling. "If you trust them, then I trust them. Now tell me what's on your mind. I'm listening."

I glance over at Cade, and he nods, releasing that antagonistic edge he's been carrying.

I fill Malachi in on everything—Viridian and the photograph of the woman who looks like she could be my ancestor. I explain how we don't know if we can trust the Syndicate anymore, and we definitely can't trust Marco. How everyone might be doing something horrific and calling it something noble.

He doesn't seem to like that part much, and I can see the conflict in his eyes. I know he genuinely tries to do good work, believes the Syndicate does good work, but he's not the Syndicate. After a long moment, he agrees that he doesn't know the full extent of any corruption—especially after last night's betrayal.

I tell Cade and Aurora about Project Graft and the sickening experiments I read about before the tracker went off. They both look equally disgusted but not entirely surprised, which tells me they've suspected darker truths for a while.

"Oh, and I contacted Banks's spirit yesterday," I add casually.

Malachi's head snaps back in my direction. "What? When?"

"When I was here before they drove me back to the ranch. I

needed to do it, and I may need to do it again because I got some useful information out of him."

Malachi starts shaking his head. "How do you know you can trust anything he says?"

"It's a feeling I have," I insist. "Besides, he's pissed at Marco and wants vengeance. That kind of anger doesn't lie."

The explanation seems to satisfy him, though he still looks uncomfortable.

"Tell him about the map," Aurora prompts.

Cade gets up and retrieves the folded paper from wherever he stashed it, bringing it back and spreading it out on the table between our plates and coffee mugs.

"These are the three locations he gave us, secret labs the Volkovs are using for their experiments, trafficking, or both. This is the one he said we should start with." My finger traces to the star positioned in the largest gutter zone north of Viktor's estate.

"I think we need to get ready to attack it soon," I say, and Malachi's eyes go wide.

"Whoa, Kat—attack?" He repeats it like I suggested we blow up a daycare center.

"Yes, attack, spy, infiltrate, whatever you want to call it. But we need to go see what's happening and put a stop to it." I cross my arms, meeting his stare head-on.

Malachi exchanges an unreadable look with Cade across the table, some kind of silent male communication passing between them.

"What was that? Why are you looking at him?" I demand, hating being left out of their nonverbal conversation.

"You're right. We need to investigate this, see what's going on, see who we can help. My father and uncle need to be stopped." He looks me over. "But I'm not letting you anywhere near this after everything that's happened."

My eyebrows shoot up so fast they practically hit my hairline. "You're not the boss of me, and I've already said you're not my fucking savior, Malachi. I need to do this. I'm meant to. I can feel it." The conviction in my voice surprises me. "So train me, study me, put me through Bash's equipment, whatever you need to do to be okay with this, because it's happening. I'm going with or without you."

Instead of getting upset or angry like I expected, he smiles, and it makes me want to reach over and shove him.

"So this was your plan? The three of you were going to attack an underground lab in the largest most-violent gutter zone in the country?" He snickers. "It would be near impossible for the three of you alone to even reach the lab, let alone infiltrate it."

I bristle at his condescending tone. I think he may be seriously underestimating us.

"Hey, we deserve more credit than that," Aurora says, starting to stack plates and clear the table.

I don't want this to escalate into another shouting match, and I'm trying my best not to be irrational or stubborn, so I take a deep breath and force myself to speak calmly.

"I'm going, Malachi, and I want you to come with me. Let's put together a small team of people we can trust."

Cade finally chimes in. "I know we can trust Dante. He would be down for something like this."

Malachi nods thoughtfully. "I trust Bash, but beyond that, I need to think about it. There's only a small crew left working in the Depths right now, and that's probably a good thing for us." He stands, already shifting into planning mode. "Let's get ready and head down there. We can talk more about a concrete plan when we get there."

"Great," I say. Progress feels good, even if it's baby steps.

Malachi leans down and kisses the top of my head, then

stands and heads outside. The simple gesture makes my heart do a little flip-flop.

Cade stretches his arms above his head, yawning as he gets to his feet. "I need a shower and more coffee." He refills his mug and disappears down the hall.

"Hey, all things considered, I'd say that went pretty well," Aurora says, plopping down in the chair next to me with a satisfied grin.

"I need a shower," Malachi announces as he comes back in with our bag slung over his shoulder.

"Down the hall to your left. You can use my room," Aurora offers casually.

His brows pinch slightly, eyes locked on mine with something between warning and desire. Then he turns and walks down the hall, leaving my pulse thrumming in the quiet.

"Go on. You know you want to," Aurora says with an amused expression, tilting her head toward the hall.

"Thank you for cleaning up," I say, already standing and trying not to look too eager as I hurry down the hall and slip into her room.

I can hear the shower running, steam already beginning to seep out from under the bathroom door.

I didn't tell the others about contacting the girl in the photograph last night. I'm not sure why, but it feels like something I ought to keep to myself until I find out more. There's something about that connection I have to figure out.

I rummage through the duffel bag, looking for clean clothes to change into after the shower, and bring them into the bathroom with me. The mirror and glass shower door are completely fogged with steam. The sound of water cascading fills the space, and I don't think Malachi hears me come in over the noise.

I silently slip out of Aurora's borrowed pajamas, leaving

them in a neat pile on the counter. The steam kisses my skin as I quietly open the glass door and step into the shower behind him.

He turns immediately, and his hard expression makes me pause for a heartbeat. But then he lifts his hand to gently caress my cheek, water droplets sliding down his arm.

"I love you too," he says, his voice rough. "God, Kat, I love you so much it physically hurts. And it terrifies me that the woman I can't live without wants to throw herself into danger."

I place my hand over his, letting a smile spread across my face as warmth blooms in my chest.

He goes on. "I know you were upset out there, caught off guard by everything. So if you didn't mean what you said, if it was the heat of the moment—"

"Stop," I cut him off, stepping closer. "I meant every single word, Malachi. I am completely, desperately, madly in love with you. And I'm done pretending otherwise, done fighting what I feel."

His eyes darken with something that makes my knees weak. "You have no idea what you do to me when you say things like that." He pulls me against him, his voice dropping to a whisper. "Come here, my brave, beautiful, infuriating woman. Let me love you properly."

I wrap my arms around him as his fingers tangle in my hair, tilting my head back so he can kiss up and down my neck and explore my mouth with his tongue.

The hot water pours over us in a steady stream, like warm rain washing everything else away. I kiss him back, greedy for more, teasing his bottom lip with my teeth before slipping my tongue past his. He tastes like heat and sin, and I want to drown in it.

His body presses against mine, all hard muscle and desire,

his length stiff and pulsing between us. I slide a hand down and wrap my fingers around him, and the sound he makes isn't quite a moan, more a low growl of approval that vibrates through me as he deepens the kiss. His other hand glides down my body, stopping to cup my breast. I arch into him, gasping against his lips, my fingers tightening around his thick cock in response.

He lifts me with ease, my legs wrapping around his waist as my back presses into the cool, slick tiles. The contrast of hot water on my skin and cold wall at my spine makes me shiver. His tip presses into me, and he starts to lower me onto him fully.

I clutch his biceps, muscles flexing beneath my grip as he fills me completely and stills. The stretch makes my breath catch. He brings a hand to my chin, tipping my face until our eyes meet.

"No one's ever made me feel like this," he says. His thumb brushes water from my cheek, his gaze burning into mine. Those dark-brown eyes, framed by golden starbursts, hold nothing back.

"Don't ever stop looking at me like that ... like you see all of me and still want more," I whisper, peeking up at him through my lashes, my fingers tangled in the damp strands of his hair.

"Then give me more." He presses his forehead to mine, eyes covering me.

Then he starts to move again, his hips rolling in slow, intoxicating rhythm. There's nothing rushed about it, him making love to me. Like he wants to savor every second of it. My body trembles around him, pleasure building in waves, curling my toes and making it harder to breathe.

When it finally crashes over me, I bury my face in his neck, biting down softly as my orgasm takes me away, and he holds me like he never intends to let me go, and I find myself wishing it could stay like this forever, but right now, I can't let myself hope for forever when every day feels like it could be our last.

Chapter Twelve

LOG TWELVE - ESCALATING SENTIENCE NOTED: SHE
DOESN'T ASK WHERE SHE IS. SHE ASKS WHY WE
THINK WE'RE SAFE.

"HOW DID your gift first manifest, and how has it evolved since then?" Bash asks Aurora from where he sits in one of his swivel chairs, his light-blue eyes studying her with scientific curiosity.

After briefly filling Bash in on our mission, Cade and Malachi went to speak with Dante and whoever else they decide to bring into our small circle, leaving us to work through a few things with Bash.

His lab looks exactly the same—all white and pristine, filled with machines and equipment that I have no idea how to operate. Hell, I can't even fathom what half of it does. Bash looks the same too, only tired, like he's been pulling all-nighters. I've never seen him in glasses before either, but he's wearing a pair now. Not sure if they're to see better or for protection.

The sterile environment feels oddly comforting after everything we've been through, like stepping into a world where logic and science might actually provide help for this mission.

"It started when I was about ten," Aurora begins, her eyes taking on a distant look. "I used to be really good at maintaining my body heat, like I could play in the freezing cold for hours in a T-shirt while other kids were bundled up in coats. Everyone thought I was resilient."

She glances over at me, then back to Bash, and I can see something shifting in her expression, like she's deciding how much to reveal.

"Over the years, my gift has strengthened and expanded exponentially." She holds up her hand, and I watch in fascination as her palm begins to glow with a soft-orange light. "I can heat anything I touch to extreme temperatures now—metal, stone, even water."

The glow intensifies, and I can feel the heat radiating from across the room. "But that's not all. I can create fire with my hands, manipulate existing flames, and even ..." She looks away.

"Even what?" Bash leans forward, his wavy hair pristine on top of his head despite the bags under his eyes, his scientific excitement bursting through.

Aurora's eyes meet mine, then she extends her other hand toward an empty metal tray on the counter. Without touching it, the tray begins to smoke, then glow red hot, warping as the metal reaches its melting point.

"I can project heat at a distance now. And when I'm really focused, really angry ..." She closes her fist, and the tray bursts into brilliant white flames that dance without fuel. "I can make things combust without even touching them."

My mouth drops open. "You're basically a human flamethrower. I would take wielding fire over playing with the dead any day," I say, and she laughs.

"Bash, where's Freddy?" Aurora asks, drawing his gaze back up from where he's furiously typing notes on his computer.

"Oh, he wanted a change of scenery, I guess. Irina was down here offering positions in other districts, and he jumped on it." Bash shrugs, but there's something in his tone that suggests it wasn't entirely Freddy's choice.

Aurora frowns at this news but doesn't ask any follow-up questions, though I can see the wheels turning in her head.

"I heard it's a skeleton crew here right now," I say, leaning forward in my chair. "What Avids are left?"

I'm mentally trying to calculate if any of the remaining team members could be useful on our mission and more importantly if any of them can be trusted. After last night's betrayal, we all need to be on high alert.

"Several remained behind, but only two I think will be right for this job, and they both happen to be here today training." Bash adjusts his glasses, looking pleased with himself.

Two is better than none, I suppose.

"Who are they? What can they do?" Aurora chimes in from where she leans against the wall, absently bending a paperclip between her fingers with enough heat to make it glow faintly red.

"You both might have met them before, Alex and Nasha. They're brother and sister."

"Oh yeah, the first time Malachi brought me down here, I remember Rain saying she thought they were ready to join one of Solace's teams, but I never actually met them," I say, the memory clicking into place.

Aurora perks up. "Does that mean they can fight?"

Bash nods, looking between us with growing excitement. "Yes, they can fight, and they've been chomping at the bit to go on a mission. This would be their first real job though."

He swivels his chair back to his desk and types something into his computer. Four crystal-clear screens light up above his workspace, displaying photographs and detailed assessment notes in neat, clinical formatting.

"What are their gifts?" I ask, sliding my chair closer and

squinting up at the monitors, trying to make sense of the data streaming across the displays.

"Nasha can transfer injuries or pain to others," Bash says, pointing up at the screen displaying a young woman who looks to be in her mid-twenties. She has bronze skin and long black hair, but it's her eyes that make me pause. They're an impossible shade of lavender that seems otherworldly, mesmerizing, and fierce at the same time.

"Interesting gift. I'd like to see what she can do with it," Aurora says, settling into one of the chairs next to me.

"Oh, I've studied her abilities extensively, as you can see here in my notes." He points to one of the bottom screens, and I quickly scan through some of the bullet points displayed in neat, clinical text. She can transfer injuries from allies to enemies through touch, but every wound has to pass through her body first—meaning she feels everything. The psychological profile warns of god-complex tendencies from choosing who suffers and who heals. No wonder this ability is so rare.

"Wow," I murmur, reading through the implications, "I've never heard of a gift like this. It's useful but also deeply disturbing."

The idea of feeling every injury as it moves through your body makes my stomach turn, but I can't deny how valuable that ability could be in a fight.

"Now, this is her half brother, Alex," Bash says, clicking away on his keyboard until the screens shift to display new information. "His gift is going to be especially useful for this mission because he can make people compulsively tell the truth."

As his photo pops up on the main screen, I find myself studying his face intently. He looks older than Nasha by at least a decade, with the same bronze skin and dark hair, though his is cropped close and clean at the edges. His jawline is sharp and dusted with a hint of stubble that gives him a rugged edge.

His eyes are a deep shade of brown, almost black in the photograph, and he stares straight into the camera with an intensity that's compelling. There's something about the way he holds himself, even in a still image, that suggests controlled power.

His broad shoulders and strong build definitely make me want him on our team. If we're going into hostile territory, having someone who looks like he could handle himself in a fight and force our enemies to spill their secrets sounds like exactly what we need.

"How does the truth compulsion work?" I ask.

Bash brings up Alex's detailed assessment notes on the next screen over. I scan through the bullet points—he can compel people to tell the truth through eye contact and a trigger phrase, but only for short bursts and the subject knows they're being forced to speak. The notes mention it's less effective on other Avids and can be resisted by strong-willed individuals. Despite the limitations, it still sounds incredibly useful for what we're planning.

"His gift isn't as strong as his sister's, and we can't really go around interrogating everyone," Bash admits, switching off the screens. "But I think after Rupert's betrayal last night, Malachi will want Alex to at least question everyone he's trusting to work on this mission. Better to know where people stand before we're in the field, especially when you're involved. You seem to have a talent for attracting trouble."

He smiles at me with that mischievous glint I've come to recognize.

"What? My girl? Trouble? No way," Aurora says with mock shock, dissolving into giggles along with Bash.

"I can't help that everyone wants a piece of me." I roll my

eyes and stand, brushing off their teasing. It's not like I go looking for chaos, but it seems to find me wherever I go.

"So are you taking us to this training room to meet them, or do you want to try putting us through one of your machines first?" Aurora asks, gesturing toward the intimidating array of equipment surrounding us.

"Why don't you head to the Avidian training center? You remember where it is, right? Two stories up, go right. You can't miss it. You can see if you approve of their skills."

Aurora perks up at that suggestion, her eyes lighting with anticipation. "Yeah, I need to see if they're up to my standards," she jokes, already moving toward the door with that quick, energetic stride of hers.

"Don't do anything I wouldn't do," she calls as she disappears into the hallway, leaving the two of us in the sterile quiet of the lab. Bash turns back to face me, and I can see something shifting in his expression. He's been waiting for this moment to talk privately.

"I'm not going to ask you how you are, because I imagine everyone's been asking you that since you got back," Bash begins. "Instead, I want to know if you're ready to let me peek under that hood of yours? All this talk about a secret mission and getting revenge on Marco ... Has it changed your mind about my equipment?"

"Under my hood? Really?" I scrunch my nose at his phrasing. "Why do you have to make it sound so ... clinical and dirty at the same time?"

I walk closer to one of the larger machines, running my fingers along its surface. I forget what he called it, but it's a massive white and gray cylinder with a padded gurney positioned at its center, surrounded by screens and sensors that look like something from a sci-fi movie.

"I want to know more about my gift and where it comes

from," I admit. "I want to be stronger. I want my abilities to evolve like Aurora's have."

Bash comes up behind me, his footsteps soft on the lab floor. "Your gift has evolved, Kat. The difference is that Aurora's been fighting to unlock her potential her entire life, pushing against every limitation. You've been treating your abilities like a curse, only using them when absolutely forced to." His voice is gentle but direct. "I'm certain it'll evolve exponentially once you stop fighting what you are and fully embrace it."

I have been trying to embrace my gift more lately, but it's … complicated.

"What does this one do?" I ask, reaching out to touch the cool, smooth surface.

"That's my neural frequency analyzer," he says, moving to stand beside the machine with obvious pride. "It allows me to map your brain activity and examine the electromagnetic patterns your gift creates. Remember how I told you my ability helps me identify and synchronize with each person's unique frequency?"

I nod, the memory still fresh in my mind. "Like when you helped make me stronger briefly when I crossed the Veil trying to reach Carmen."

The thought brings back that awful experience—racing through the darkness between worlds, those desperate souls reaching for me. The way I left my body, I've never done that before, and it was kind of scary. I haven't felt anything that intense since, and I know Malachi really didn't like it. Or how I was out for so long after, spent.

"Exactly," Bash says, his eyes lighting up. "After that session, I've been running calculations and analyzing the data patterns. I think I've figured out a way to make that enhancement permanent."

I turn to face him fully, my pulse quickening. "What do you mean?"

"Think of it like this," he explains, gesturing with his hands as he talks. "Your abilities operate on specific frequencies, like radio waves. When I boosted your power before, I was essentially acting as an amplifier, temporarily increasing your signal strength. But what if, instead of amplifying from the outside, I could unlock the dormant frequency channels within your own neural pathways?"

Scientific explanations can make my head spin, but I'm following the general concept. "So you wouldn't be giving me your power. You'd be helping me access more of my own?"

"Precisely!" His enthusiasm is infectious and also makes me weary. "Every Avid has untapped potential locked within their genetic code. Most people only access maybe ten to fifteen percent of their true capabilities. But if I can map your unique frequency signature and then use targeted electromagnetic pulses to activate those dormant neural pathways ..."

"But?" I prompt, sensing there's more.

He grows more serious. "But I haven't tested this procedure on anyone yet, so it's all theoretical. I'd be essentially rewiring parts of your brain to unlock abilities you might not even know you have. The enhancement could be exactly what we hope for, or ..." He shrugs. "The human brain is incredibly complex. I can't guarantee what the outcome will be. Not to mention, Malachi would probably kill me for even talking to you about this."

Despite the warning, my interest is piqued. The idea of being stronger, of having more control over my abilities when we face whatever horrors await in that underground lab, is incredibly tempting.

The girl from the photograph flashes through my mind unbidden, and I can hear her voice echoing in my memory:

"Your gifts are only beginning to surface." Was that a sign? A push toward this exact moment?

"How long will it take?" I ask.

Bash glances over at the digital clock on the wall—it's nearly 3:00 p.m. "The procedure itself will be quick, maybe thirty minutes for the full neural mapping and frequency adjustment."

Thirty minutes doesn't seem particularly quick to me, especially if this procedure has any pain involved with it.

"I want you to do it now," I tell him, my decision crystallizing with surprising certainty.

His eyebrows shoot up. "Like, right now? You're not going to talk to Malachi first? Get his input on this?"

I roll my eyes. "I don't need his permission, and I don't need him talking me out of it." The decision feels right as I continue, "You didn't see the things I saw in those Project Graft files, Bash. The awful, horrific experiments I know are happening somewhere right now while we're standing here debating. The Volkovs need to be stopped, and I'm tired of feeling useless."

His expression shifts, lips falling into a flat, serious line. For a moment, I think he's going to refuse, but then he sighs deeply.

"You are hardly useless, Kat ..." He looks at me with renewed determination. "Fuck it. Okay, let's do this."

He moves quickly to the lab door, engaging the electronic lock with a soft beep, then dims the overhead lights until the room takes on an almost ethereal glow from the various machine displays.

Is this a terrible idea?

Yes, this is probably a terrible idea, but some of the best things in life start out as terrible ideas, so there's that.

I watch Bash program the machine and remind myself that I'm done being afraid of using my gift, of becoming stronger. I think about what Aurora said before. It's time I start using my gift for me.

I didn't think I'd convince Malachi so easily to let me go on this mission, and I still have a feeling he's going to try to find a way out of it. All the more reason to prove to him I am a real asset to the team. This could be exactly the kind of boost I need.

The animals in those documents make my heart physically ache. Thinking about all the Avids who have been trafficked like me or who've stayed in hiding for fear of what might happen to them if they're discovered. Those people and innocent creatures, taken by the Volkovs ... They're counting on someone to save them, even if they don't know it. How can I live with myself if I don't try?

Maybe this is why I survived the accident. This is why I survived all the hell I went through when so many others didn't. Maybe this is what I'm meant to do with this gift that has felt like a burden for so long. What if everything I've been through was preparing me for this exact moment?

"Are you ready?" Bash asks, drawing my attention back to the present.

I take a deep breath, feeling the weight of my decision settle into place. "Ready as I'll ever be."

I hop onto the cold metal gurney, and Bash positions me exactly where he wants me, then begins securing thick padded restraints across my wrists, chest, and ankles. The moment the first strap clicks into place, every survival instinct I have starts screaming.

"What the hell are these for? Planning to keep me as a lab rat?" I joke lamely.

Bash's entire demeanor has shifted. Gone is the friendly scientist, replaced by someone who looks like he's about to perform brain surgery. "I told you this is completely experimental, Kat. These restraints aren't optional. If your body goes into shock or if you start convulsing during the neural restructuring, you could seriously injure yourself."

He disappears from view, and I'm left staring up at the claustrophobic dome of sensors and wires hanging inches from my face. My heart starts hammering against my ribs. Control your breathing.

You chose this.

The walls aren't actually closing in.

"Bash, when you say 'shock' and 'convulsing,' are we talking mild discomfort or full-on seizure territory?"

The machine around me begins to hum with increasing intensity, and I can feel energy building in the air, making my skin tingle.

This is a bit ominous.

"Honestly? I have no fucking idea," Bash calls out from the control booth. "The simulations suggest it could be anything from a mild headache to ... Well, let's focus on the mild headache scenario."

Terror and adrenaline flood my system as lights begin flashing above me. "Wait, Bash, maybe we should—"

"Too late to back out now. Neural mapping initiated. Whatever happens next, don't fight it."

Pain explodes through me like a wildfire—hot, rapid, and utterly unrelenting.

Then there is only darkness, followed by blinding bright-white light.

Chapter Thirteen

LOG THIRTEEN - APPARITIONS OBSERVED: SHE HELD
A CONVERSATION WITH SOMEONE NO ONE ELSE
COULD SEE.

"IT'S YOU AGAIN. How are you here?" I ask, blinking until my eyes adjust to the brightness of the room. I'm staring at the woman from the photograph again.

I'm back in that sterile, hospital-like room, but something's different this time. She's standing in front of a large mirror mounted on the far wall, her back to me, but I can see her face clearly in the reflection. Her expression is knowing, almost amused.

"You mean how are *you* here," she corrects me, and I can see her slight smile in the mirror's surface.

I guess that makes more sense. Maybe.

Am I the visitor, or is she? The enhancement procedure must have somehow strengthened our connection, made it easier for me to cross over into this space between worlds.

"Is this where they kept you? What did they do to you here? Do you have powers like me?" The questions tumble out before I can stop them.

She begins to turn slowly to face me, but something's wrong. The room glitches around her movement, like a video with corrupted frames. For a split second, she appears to be moving impossibly fast—her turning motion becomes a blur of motion that my eyes can't quite track.

I blink hard, trying to focus and clear whatever's happening to my vision.

"I only let them keep me here so I could find my path," she says, and that statement raises about a dozen more questions in my mind.

Let them keep her? That suggests she had a choice in the matter, which contradicts everything I know about how Avids are treated. But I force myself to focus on what matters most right now.

"Before, you told me to find the door. What did you mean?" I ask, shooting for the most important question instead of demanding her entire backstory—which is what I really want to do.

"You'll know the door when you see it. It will feel like remembering something you never learned," she says, and her voice carries a wisdom that seems impossible for someone who doesn't look much older than me.

"Why do I need to find the door? What is Project Viridian? How did you die?"

There I go again, running my mouth and asking more than one question at a time, but I can't help myself. The questions are burning inside me.

"The door isn't an exit. It's a way to stop running from the truth you're not ready to see."

That sounds absolutely terrifying.

"Katja, does it hurt? Do you feel anything?" Bash's voice cuts through the vision, yanking me back to reality. The girl begins to fade away just as the bright-machine lights above come back into sharp focus.

"How long has it been?" I ask, blinking hard as my vision

adjusts. Everything feels disjointed, like I'm reassembling myself piece by piece.

"Um, a handful of minutes. You made a noise like it hurt, then you completely stopped responding to me." His voice takes on a slightly higher pitch, the kind that suggests he might have been genuinely worried I wasn't coming back.

"It did hurt, but it doesn't anymore," I tell him honestly. The pain is completely gone now, replaced by a humming energy beneath my skin that feels both foreign and familiar.

I hear his audible sigh of relief echoing through the lab.

I wasn't even thinking about that girl. I wasn't trying to contact her, wasn't thinking about crossing the Veil. I didn't have any of the same sensations I usually get when crossing over or speaking to a spirit. That was just ... weird.

Was it all a hallucination brought on by the procedure?

I shake my head.

"Stop moving, please," Bash says, and I almost forgot I'm still hooked up to this machine.

No, it wasn't a hallucination. She was real. She was Subject One, according to her file, which also said something about being psychic, maybe. Fuck, I can't remember the exact details. I'll need to ask Cade to look at it again, but maybe her gifts had something to do with how we communicated just now.

Do our abilities pass on with us after we die?

I guess I've never thought about it before.

If all I'm going to get out of her are cryptic riddles that only spawn more questions, I'll need to try researching her on my own time.

Spirits usually can't show themselves to me unless I will it, unless I'm actively thinking of them or trying to reach them. And I wasn't doing either. Mish is the only one who appears frequently without being summoned, and that's usually because she's always lingering in the back of my mind.

What if whatever this equipment is doing to me makes my gift evolve into something where I can no longer block spirits out? What if I don't have to deliberately summon them anymore? What if they start popping up uninvited, like when Bash helped me cross the Veil before and I was bombarded by desperate souls reaching for me?

The thought sends a chill through me, and I force myself to stay perfectly still.

I try to meditate, thinking this is going to take a while, but then Bash suddenly announces, "That's it."

It hasn't even been that long.

"Did it work?" I ask as he comes around to release all my straps and unhook the sensors.

"On my end, it looks like everything worked perfectly," he explains, carefully removing the last electrode from my temple. "But I don't know how it will affect you yet. You'll have to keep me updated on anything different, and I want you to come see me again tomorrow so I can run some follow-up tests."

I shrug, sitting up slowly. "Okay, but let's keep this between us for now, if you don't mind."

He brushes some of his curly hair off his forehead, glancing away like he doesn't enjoy the idea of lying to Malachi.

"I don't want to cause any unnecessary worry until we know if it actually does anything," I press, trying to sound reasonable.

"Alright," he concedes, "but you have to promise to come check in tomorrow and report anything out of the ordinary."

I cross my fingers behind my back. "I promise."

I hop to my feet and am genuinely surprised by how normal I feel—no dizziness, no lingering pain, no spirit coming to drag me to hell, nothing.

"I'm going to go look for Malachi," I say, stretching my arms above my head. "You should check on Aurora and make sure she's not driving Nasha and Alex completely insane."

"Good idea," he chuckles, already turning back to his computer screens.

"Hey, Bash," I call back before reaching the door.

He glances up expectantly.

"Can you make a small vial of Avidian with my essence now? From whatever data you collected during the procedure?"

He immediately starts shaking his head. "I wouldn't do that without your explicit permission. I know you didn't want me to before."

"I want you to now," I state firmly. "Between us. Make me one vial of it, please."

He cocks his head to the side, and I think he's about to ask me why, but instead he flashes me a grin. "You got it."

THIS PLACE IS ENORMOUS. I can't even begin to count how many floors this underground silo contains. The Depths is definitely a fitting name for this architectural marvel that seems to burrow endlessly into the earth's core.

I stand near the elevator bank, taking it all in with fresh eyes. Without the usual bustle of people, you'd think it would feel peaceful, but instead there's something eerie about the emptiness. It's like standing inside the ribcage of some massive, sleeping beast.

The chandelier that hangs suspended in the center of the vast atrium is nothing short of breathtaking. Each crystal catches and refracts the ambient light, sending rainbows and prisms dancing across every surface of the levels below, painting the curved walls in shifting kaleidoscopes of color. I guess it was a way to bring artificial sunlight beneath ground.

Normally, when I look out from this vantage point, I'd see people bustling about in illuminated rooms and busy hallways, researchers moving between laboratories, meetings taking place behind glass walls. But now, as I gaze out across the endless floors that spiral around this giant hive-like structure, it's hauntingly quiet. Different-colored lights still glow through the windows of various rooms—soft blues from computer labs, warm yellows from offices, the occasional flash of red from what I assume are restricted areas, but the silence is absolute. It's like looking at a city where everyone has simply vanished.

I take a cautious step closer to the metal railing and peer down into the depths below. The floors continue wrapping around the central core, level after level disappearing into shadows until the architecture becomes indistinguishable and darkness swallows everything. I can't even see the bottom ... if there is one. The spiral of walkways and chambers seems to descend infinitely, like looking down a throat that has no end.

I wish I had a coin to drop to hear how long it would take to hit the bottom.

I was going to go look for Malachi but am starting to realize this might be the perfect opportunity to do some unauthorized exploring. With practically no one around to catch me snooping, I could finally see what the organization has been hiding in its deeper, more secretive levels.

I step into the glass elevator, noting that the display shows I'm currently on floor twenty-three, nearly at the surface level, since the elevator only goes up to thirty. I press the button for floor one and watch through the transparent walls as I begin to descend deeper into the Depths than I've ever ventured before. The crystalline light from the chandelier grows dimmer as I sink past level after level, each floor revealing glimpses of darkened laboratories, sealed conference rooms, and corridors that stretch away into shadow.

On the way down, I catch a glimpse of the garden level as the elevator glides past—or the "Enchanted Forest" as Bash once poetically called it. Through the glass walls, I can see the soft, warm glow emanating from that magical sanctuary, and I wonder if Atlas, the brilliant botanist who tends to that impossible ecosystem, is part of the skeleton crew left behind.

I'm tempted to stop there instead. I'd love to wander through that tropical paradise again, to see all the exotic flowers blooming in impossible colors and watch the butterflies that exist nowhere else in this perpetually freezing district.

But I force myself to stay focused on snooping as the elevator continues its descent into the darker, more secretive depths.

Finally, the elevator shudders to a stop at floor one, and I quickly press the button for floor twenty-six, sending it back up the moment I step out. Hopefully, no one noticed it making this unexpected journey to the bottom of the facility. The last thing I need is to trigger some kind of security alert.

The first thing I notice is a large, hastily made sign. "LEVEL CLOSED — PLEASE RETURN TO HIGHER LEVEL" is written in someone's scrawled handwriting. It's propped up on one of those yellow wet floor–warning stands, like they grabbed whatever was handy to keep people out.

Interesting.

I walk right past it.

This level is nothing like the polished, sophisticated floors above. The walls are rough concrete, and the lighting is harsh fluorescent that flickers occasionally, casting everything in an unflattering, institutional glow. The air feels thicker down here, stale and recycled, with an underlying chemical smell that makes my nose wrinkle.

I pass by several rooms, peering through the long observation windows that extend all the way down the hallway like a series of aquarium tanks. Most of them appear to be empty, sterile chambers with nothing but bare walls and floors. One has furniture in it, but everything is covered in what looks like old painter's drop cloths, as if someone tried to preserve or hide whatever was underneath.

I'm almost wrapped all the way back around to where I started when I see something that makes my blood run cold.

A medical stretcher is on its side a few feet ahead of me, one of its leather restraints still buckled tight, as if someone had been violently ripped from it. The metal frame is dented, and there are dark stains on the padding that I don't want to think too hard about.

Along the wall behind it, a line of fogged observation windows watch me silently like dead eyes. Some have spiderweb cracks running through the thick glass. One is completely shattered, its jagged edges still glittering in the dim fluorescent light like a mouth full of broken teeth.

My deranged curiosity decides this is exactly the place to start digging deeper. I need to see what's behind those observation windows. What kind of experiments were being conducted down here that required restraints and reinforced glass?

Oddly enough, I can't find any doors leading into the observation rooms, only the ones that lead back out to the main hallway. The windows seem to be the only way to see inside, or in this case, the only way to get inside.

I approach the window with the shattered glass and slip off one of my leather loafers, using it to carefully brush away the remaining shards clinging to the frame. Ignoring every instinct screaming at me to turn around and leave, I hoist myself up and climb through to the other side.

The room beyond the shattered window is dusty and decrepit, seemingly abandoned for years. There's a busted computer terminal with its screen cracked beyond repair and a metal table with one of its legs snapped completely in half, leaving it tilted at an awkward angle. Papers are scattered across the floor, yellowed with age and covered in a fine layer of dust.

How long has the Syndicate been active?

Who used this silo before they came across it?

Even if this level is deserted and obviously old, I can't understand what would have caused this kind of destruction down here. It looks like there was some kind of struggle, or maybe an explosion. Claw marks? No, that's ridiculous.

Behind the overturned desk, almost hidden in the shadows, is another door. I twist the handle cautiously and pull it open.

What the fuck?

It's a dark staircase descending into absolute blackness. After about a dozen concrete steps, the darkness becomes so complete that I can't see my own feet. The air drifting up from below is even colder and carries a musty, underground smell that reminds me of old caves or forgotten basements.

Maybe I should go find Aurora and drag her down here with me. That would definitely be the more logical thing to do. Her fire abilities would be perfect for lighting the way, and having backup would be smart. But with both of us missing from the upper levels, that probably wouldn't go unnoticed. Someone would come looking, and then we'd both be caught snooping where we clearly shouldn't be.

Great, Kat, what are you getting yourself into?

I take a few tentative steps down, hoping my eyes will adjust and it won't actually be pitch-black at the bottom. Thankfully, there are motion sensors down here, though most of the light fixtures are broken or burned out. As I descend, a couple of ancient fluorescent bulbs flicker to life overhead with a tired electrical humming sound, casting weak, unstable light that flashes every few seconds like they're giving me the last bit of power they have left in them.

Each step echoes in the narrow stairwell, and I can't shake the feeling that I'm descending into something that was meant to stay buried.

Mischka materializes beside me and runs in little circles around my feet before settling protectively at my side as I reach the bottom of the staircase. I let out a sigh of relief at the sight of her, but immediately a bone-deep chill settles over me, and fear starts to fester in my chest.

The bottom of the stairwell opens into a long, narrow hallway lined with identical metal doors stretching into the darkness. I can't even begin to imagine what this area was used for or why it's been blocked off and abandoned. The doors look institutional, clinical, like something from a hospital or prison.

The hair on the back of my neck stands up as an uncomfortable sensation of being watched creeps over my skin. Mish suddenly halts in front of me, her translucent ears perked and alert like she senses the same malevolent presence. I pause to listen intently, but all I can hear is the weak electrical buzzing coming from one of the dying fluorescent lights above.

"Kitty Kat."

The voice feels like it's being breathed directly into my ear. I immediately pick up my pace, panic rising in my throat. It's too close, too intimate, and I know it's not Cade. Only one other person ever called me that pet name.

"Did you miss me?"

Damien's apparition materializes directly in front of me, and I stumble backward so fast I almost fall right through his ghostly form. I thought I was done with his games after solving Carmen's murder.

How is this happening? How is he here?

I didn't summon him, didn't even think about him. He

wasn't even a blip on my mental radar, which means what Bash did is definitely working. The veil between worlds is thinning, and I may have permanently opened the door for any spirit who wants to torment me.

"I already figured out your twisted game, Damien, so what can I help you with?" I sound strong and confident, even though I can hear the slight quiver betraying my fear.

I'm down here in the bowels of this underground facility, deeper in the earth than anyone would think to look. If something happens to me, my body would probably never be found. Well, that's not entirely true. They have security cameras. They'd find me eventually, right? Right?

Mish lets out a low, threatening growl at Damien's spirit, and despite everything, I can't help but smile slightly. Even she knows he's bad news.

"Oh, Kitty Kat, our game isn't nearly over. You're only now starting to uncover all the fun stuff."

Damien jerks his head toward the door at the far end of the hallway, his expression twisted into that cruel smirk that used to give me the creeps. Then he simply melts away in front of me like smoke dissipating in the wind.

God, I don't know if he disappeared on purpose or if my enhanced gift is going completely haywire on me. Either way, against every instinct screaming at me to turn around and leave, I hurry toward the door he gestured to.

I pause with my hand on the cold metal handle, afraid of what might be lurking inside. But this is exactly why I came down here, to uncover the Syndicate's secrets. And despite how much Damien terrifies me, he has every reason to hate the Syndicate after Cade killed him. He despises both the Volkovs and the Syndicate, so as creepy and manipulative as he is, maybe he's actually pointing me toward something important.

I look down at Mish, who's sitting at my feet staring up at

me with those wide, expectant ghostly eyes. She just blinks slowly, like I'm taking way too long to make a decision.

"Okay, let's see what's inside," I mutter, and she gives a little encouraging yip as I push the heavy door open.

The lights flicker on automatically the moment I step inside, revealing a room that's shockingly pristine compared to the decay and destruction on the rest of these lower levels. It's like stepping into a completely different facility—one that's been maintained and actively used.

At the center of the room is a high-tech chair positioned in front of a sleek control desk. Taking up the entire wall in front of me are approximately sixteen large crystal-clear monitors arranged in a perfect grid. The screens are cycling through different camera angles, and I realize with growing unease that these are live security feeds from throughout the facility.

I move closer and settle into the chair, studying the rotating surveillance footage with fascination and growing dread. The cameras are capturing every angle of the Depths, hallways I recognize, laboratories I've been in, even some areas I've never seen before.

Why is this sophisticated monitoring station set up down here in the abandoned levels, and why is no one watching it? Maybe they record everything automatically and only review the footage when they need to investigate something specific. But something about this feels deliberately hidden, like someone wanted to keep an eye on the facility without anyone else knowing about it.

"Tick tock."

Damien's voice brushes across my skin like ice water, far too close for comfort. I swivel around in the chair, heart jumping, but no one's there. The empty doorway behind me suddenly feels like a gaping mouth, so I push the heavy door shut. It gives me a false sense of security, but at least my back doesn't feel so exposed now.

"If you're going to keep popping up like this, you could at least say something useful," I snap at the empty air, assuming Damien can hear me if he's lurking nearby.

I wait for a response, but it's eerily silent. The only sounds are the soft leather creak of my chair when I move, the mechanical hum of servers hidden behind the walls, and the faint rhythmic clicking as the cameras automatically switch angles.

I turn my attention back to the monitors, watching as one cycles through a hallway, then another. My breath catches in my throat. That monitor shows the upper floors. The next one reveals the main entrance. Another displays the very staircase I used to descend into this nightmare.

I freeze completely when I spot movement on one of the screens.

A figure walks by quickly, a shadow slipping past the camera's range. Too blurry to identify clearly, but definitely not blurry enough to dismiss as my imagination. I grip the edge of the metal desk, my fingernails pressing into the cold surface hard enough to leave marks.

That wasn't a glitch in the system.

And then I see something that makes my blood turn to ice ... Myself.

On the bottom-right screen, the footage switches to show the exact hallway I was standing in minutes ago. I stare in horror, my heart hammering against my ribs, as I watch a grainy black-and-white version of myself reach for the door handle.

There's a slight time delay, maybe a minute. I blink, looking from the physical door beside me back to the screen showing my past self. There's a camera hidden somewhere in this room, and it's capturing everything. I'm on it right now. Someone must be watching me.

But who?

The screen flickers ominously, and suddenly all sixteen monitors freeze simultaneously, locking onto a single image: a close-up of my face from moments ago, frozen mid-motion as I lean forward to study the feeds.

I push back from the desk with a harsh scrape of the chair legs against concrete, my spine going rigid with fear. The overhead lights dim just a fraction, barely noticeable, but enough to make every hair on my arms stand on end.

A small white indicator light flashes to life at the center of the control desk. Next to it, a blinking red dot appears.

Recording.

That's when the horrifying realization hits me. I didn't trigger this surveillance system when I walked in. Someone else already had it running. And whoever it was knew I'd come down here.

They were waiting for me.

Chapter Fourteen

LOG FOURTEEN - ETHICS WITHHELD: TODAY,
MEDICINE BOWED TO POWER. AGAIN.

NOW THE REAL QUESTION IS. Is it someone dead or alive?

"Fuck, Damien, if you can manipulate this technology and you're messing with me, I will cross the Veil and kill you all over again," I growl through clenched teeth.

But my racing pulse betrays my bravado as pure terror ricochets through my nervous system.

I glance down at the controls, desperate to get my face off the screen. My gaze flicks to the door, half expecting it to slam open.

Geez, Kat, you've watched way too many old horror movies.

"Watch the door for me, girl," I murmur as Mish materializes beside it, her spectral form settling into a perfect sit, eyes locked on the handle like she's daring it to turn.

I turn back to the monitors as they all snap to black. My stomach drops. It's better than seeing myself, but maybe not by much.

The speakers crackle with a burst of static that rattles through the room. My head jerks up.

The voice is familiar. Irina.

She's seated in what looks like her office, calm as ever, speaking to someone off camera. A step closer and the other figure leans into view. Rupert, the man who burned the ranch to the ground.

I go rigid, every muscle locking into place as the audio spikes, the volume rising like someone wants me to hear *everything*.

Rupert leans against the wall in Irina's office, hands in his pockets like he owns the place. She's behind her desk, appearing calm and collected.

"The Volkovs are bleeding the districts dry," she says. "It's all over the black markets now. More trafficking, more experiments, more of those ... animals."

My stomach twists. She says it like it's an inconvenience, not complete savagery.

"And you're still pretending you can't shut it down," Rupert says.

"Pretending is the point, Rupert." A slow smile curves her lips. "Every day they overreach, the people get angrier. The families turn on each other. The gutter zones grow larger. When the collapse comes, no one will look to them for stability."

I know where this conversation is going.

"They'll look to us," he agrees.

Irina's smile sharpens. "Exactly. We'll give them a flag, a name to rally behind. The old borders will mean something again, and this time the leader will be ours. Someone young. Believable. Moldable."

My pulse spikes. I know who she's about to say before Rupert even breathes the name.

"Malachi."

"He's perfect. He hates his own family enough to play the part, but he trusts me. Once he's in place, I'll keep steering the ship. He won't even know whose course he's following."

My nails dig into my palms. She's been grooming him. Every mission, every half-truth, it's been for this.

Rupert tilts his head, studying her. "And the labs?"

She waves dismissively, like the torture chambers under her brothers' control are nothing. "Let my brothers have their fun. Every atrocity pushes us closer to the breaking point. When the public finally sees it, it'll be the final spark."

"You're gambling with thousands of lives," Rupert says, but there's no real protest in it.

"I'm ending decades of destruction. A little more pain now for peace later. The only way to unite them is to give them something to fear, then dangle someone to save them."

I want to look away, but I can't.

"And when Malachi realizes the Syndicate was never the hero in the story?" Rupert asks.

Irina leans forward, chin resting lightly on her hand, eyes gleaming. "By then, it won't matter. The people won't care who wrote the script. They'll only remember who gave them the ending."

Static chews across the feed, but not fast enough to blur the cold satisfaction on both their faces.

"Damien, are you the one showing me this? Who else is involved?" I ask into the air, glancing around the room as that unusual tingle creeps up my spine. The speakers blare again at full volume, making me jump.

The static ripples, breaking the image of Irina's office into jagged fragments before it clears again.

Rupert is pacing, his long hair hanging forward as he leans on her desk. "I got word that Marco's planning something big. The summit in the Southern District. He wants to hit it hard, take out as many Syndicate members as possible while they're all in one place."

That's where Irina's at right now.

What is she planning?

Irina doesn't even flinch. She leans back in her chair, fingers steepled like this is an interesting puzzle, not a death sentence. "Good. Let him."

Rupert stops. "Good? Irina, that could kill half our leadership."

"Then make sure as many non-Syndicate members are there too," she says, like she's discussing party seating arrangements. "We'll keep our real summit somewhere secure—small, private, off-site. The one Marco attacks will be the false summit. A spectacle."

I grip the edge of the desk, leaning closer to the screens.

Rupert's brow furrows. "A spectacle?"

"A large party," she clarifies, standing now, her heels clicking as she circles him like a predator. "We'll invite every influential family in the districts, especially the ruling families. All of them in one glittering room." She smiles faintly. "When Marco makes his move, everyone will witness it. We'll be ready to spin the narrative exactly how we want."

He shakes his head. "You're talking about planting our own attack."

"Of course we are." Gone is the gentle tone I'm used to. "We'll blame it all on Marco and Viktor. And while the chaos unfolds, we can remove a few ... key people. Quietly. Permanently."

I can barely breathe. The hum of the servers behind me sounds louder, pressing in like static inside my skull. They're not simply letting Marco's attack happen. They're staging their own, twisting it into a story the world will swallow whole.

Rupert exhales, running a hand over his jaw. "You realize how dangerous this is."

"That's the point," she says, pouring herself a drink like this conversation is already over. "Danger breeds loyalty. Fear breeds obedience. By the time the smoke clears, the districts will be begging for us to take control. We are so close and need to keep up the momentum."

The footage freezes on her face, then all the screens go black and the dim light overhead flutters to life again.

It's time to get the hell out of here.

I shove away from the desk and fling the door open. The hallway is empty, and I step out, heading for the stairs, every sound magnified, the squeak of my shoes, the tick of the overhead lights.

One of those lights clicks off.

I freeze. The air behind me feels colder.

Another light dies.

Then another.

The shadows seem to stretch forward, reaching for me. I quicken my pace.

Mish looks up at me. Her ears twitch, and she takes off at a sprint.

That's the only sign I need.

I run.

The darkness chases, swallowing the corridor in wide black gulps. It's too smooth to be an electrical glitch. My pulse surges into my throat. Mish is a faint beacon ahead of me, her small glowing form bobbing through the black.

I don't stop, not when the hallway narrows; not when my foot catches on uneven tile; not even when I dive through the broken window and feel a jagged shard slice my arm open.

I hit the ground running, lungs burning, vision tunneling. The elevator doors yawn open in time, and I throw myself inside. They slide shut with a metallic whisper, locking out the dark.

For now.

I jab the button and collapse to the floor, chest heaving.

Mish pads over, her cool touch nudges my side, tongue lolling. Then she's gone.

I stare at the empty space she left as my pulse returns to normal.

What the hell was that? More games from Damien? Malachi said they killed him for betraying the Syndicate, for playing both sides. But after what I saw—after what Irina said—I'm not sure that's true. Maybe she had him killed herself. Maybe she's been pulling strings the entire time.

This is bigger, more corrupt. And Irina ... Fuck, she had us all fooled.

And the way she talked about Malachi, about molding him, makes my skin crawl.

The elevator dings. Doors open onto the training level. I push to my feet, wipe my palms on my pants, and step out.

I need to find Malachi. Now.

"WHAT'S GOING ON?" I call out, the room going still as I push through the door.

The training center smells faintly of sweat and metal, but everyone's clustered in the far corner near the bleacher-style seats. My gaze sweeps over them, assessing quickly. Aurora. Bash. Malachi. Cade. Dante. Alex. Nasha. And me.

Eight people. Not bad for a team. Big enough to hit hard, small enough to vanish when we need to.

"Alex, here, was putting us all through the ringer," Aurora says, her grin widening as she drapes an arm over my shoulders and steers me toward the group. Her breath brushes my ear. "You okay? I'd say you look like you've seen a ghost, but we both know you're used to that by now."

I manage a faint smile. "Hilarious."

"What Aurora means," Malachi cuts in, "is that to make sure we can all trust one another, I had Alex use his gift to ask everyone a few questions."

"Right." My eyes lock on his. "Can I talk to you? Alone."

He studies me for a beat, and I'm certain he'll step aside with me. But instead, he shakes his head.

"We can trust everyone here. If we're going to work as a team, that trust starts now. Whatever you want to say to me, you can say to all of us."

He moves in close enough for me to catch the faint scent of cedar and steel on his skin. His voice dips, quiet enough for only me to hear. "It's okay."

"No, it's not." I draw in a breath, my throat tight. "I came from the lower levels ... way down, past level one. There's a room down there. Pristine. Monitors everywhere. And I saw"—I glance around the group—"a conversation. Between Irina and Rupert. About the Volkovs. About letting things get worse so they can use it."

Aurora's brow furrows, her arm sliding off my shoulder. Bash mutters something under his breath, sharp enough to sound like a curse. Cade straightens, his hands flexing at his sides.

"They're planning something at the summit," I add, my voice hardening. "Something big."

I keep talking, skimming over the details but making sure they understand Irina's intentions, Rupert's involvement, the plan to manipulate the attack, even the way Malachi's name came up. The silence afterward feels loaded. No one knows what to do now.

"And you saw this ... where exactly?" Malachi asks finally, his tone careful.

"Below the first floor. I was snooping, I admit, but for good reason," I say. "It was buried in a room that looks untouched for ages down there. There were sixteen feeds running at once. Someone's been watching the whole facility from that spot, and they knew I'd show up."

Malachi exhales, a muscle in his jaw ticking. "We haven't used the first floor in years. After the flood, it was written off. No one's assigned down there."

"Then someone's lying to you," I say, meeting his eyes. "Because it's not abandoned. And whoever's been down there has access to everything. I don't know why, but I think Damien helped me. He wanted me to see the footage ... Him or someone else."

"Damien," Malachi mutters derisively.

"Yes, but that's besides the point," I huff.

"Do you think burning down the ranch was a setup, then? Rupert working for your aunt?" Bash asks, his gaze cutting to Malachi, whose hand has curled into a fist at his side.

"Maybe all those documents would have incriminated her somehow, and she wanted them destroyed before you could uncover anything," Dante says.

Cade leans against the wall, arms crossed. He doesn't even need to speak for me to know he's been suspicious all along. This is validation for him.

"I'm going to that summit," Malachi says suddenly, "and I need to leave tonight."

My eyes widen. "What?" several of us say at once.

He takes a deep breath, shoving his hand into his pocket. "You're basically telling me everything I've worked for is a lie. That my aunt has been playing me all this time, thinking she can mold me into her puppet." His lips press into a thin line. "If what you saw is real, if she truly is as bad as my father and uncle, then I need to go to the summit. We can save lives, change the narrative."

It feels like this is slipping away from the task at hand. "What about targeting the lab in the gutter zone? That's the entire reason we're even forming this team."

"We need more training here first," Cade says. "We won't be ready to lead a coordinated attack on Marco's lab for at least a couple weeks."

My eyes snap to his. I thought he'd have my back on this.

"He's right," Alex says. "None of us have worked together as a team, other than Calloway and Mal. We might be good fighters and might have gifts, but that'll only get us so far. We need to be coordinated and to trust each other enough to know we'll have each other's backs when things go south down there."

Nasha's violet eyes sweep over us before settling on her brother. "Because things will go south. Every mission has unexpected obstacles. We need to train like a unit."

Bash says, "A normal team would train together for months. If we're trying to be ready in two weeks, we need to start putting in the time, like yesterday."

"The summit is supposed to take place tomorrow," Malachi says, looking off in the distance like he's already weighing the risks in his head. "But if what you said is true, the real summit could have happened today, and tomorrow is a facade. Still, tomorrow night is the party you saw them speak about in the footage, so I need to be there. Even if I don't confront my aunt and keep playing along, I need to save as many people as I can. I need to witness it for myself. I can't trust hearsay anymore."

"Don't you think it's going to be a red flag if we all show up at the party uninvited?" Aurora asks, her brows lifting.

Bash glances at her, then back at Malachi with a look that

says he already knows where this is headed. "We're not invited," he says flatly.

"I'm going alone," Malachi continues, like the decision is final. "I'll only be gone for two nights, three tops. Keep training while I'm gone, with my aunt busy in the Southern District, you'll have the place to yourselves."

"I'm going with you," I blurt out. My arms fold before I even register the motion, like my body has already decided for me. I'm braced for the fight I know is coming.

"That's not a good idea," Cade says.

Malachi glares blankly at me. "No."

"I'm not asking permission," I say, shoving my hair back over my shoulders. "We've been split up enough. Don't you think it's time we start sticking together?"

Something softens in his expression, but it doesn't stay there for long. "You need more training than everyone here. You should stay."

I bite back my irritation. "Are you forgetting I already went toe to toe with Rain in the ring? I'm not helpless, Malachi. I've spent years training with Marco's security." I lift my chin a notch. "I'm a fucking Avid."

Alex raises both hands like he's warding off trouble. "I don't think seeing the dead is going to help you in a hand-to-hand fight."

I narrow my eyes at him. "Bash put me through his machine and unlocked more of my gift. It's already evolving. I can see the dead now, but who knows what I'll be able to do in two weeks?"

The withering, dangerous look Malachi throws Bash makes me instantly regret saying that out loud.

"What the fuck?" he grits between clenched teeth.

I send Bash a quick, apologetic glance.

"She insisted," Bash says, keeping his tone even. "She's fine. Relax." Still, he takes half a step back from Malachi.

Malachi exhales slowly through his nose. "Fine. Kat's coming with me. Calloway, Bash, you're in charge while I'm gone. Get the team ready." The look he gives me burns. "We'll talk more about this later. We leave in two hours. Pack what you need while I find us a pilot."

Everyone seems to take that as the final word. The group breaks apart, Malachi striding out first. Alex, Nasha, Cade, and Dante head toward the weapons cabinets, already talking strategy.

I turn to Aurora and Bash. "That went well, all in all, don't you think?" I say with a lopsided grin that's more bravado than humor.

"Yeah, so much for keeping it between us," Bash chuckles. He never wanted to keep this secret to begin with, and now he doesn't have to.

Still, the weight of what I saw in that footage, and the way Malachi's entire foundation got ripped out from under him, irks me. We've got two hours before we leave, and I have no idea if that's enough time to prepare for what we might be walking into.

"I need to get back to the lab, but come see me before you leave," Bash says, and I nod.

Aurora slings her arm over my shoulders again. "Let's go raid Rain's room and see if we can find you something spectacularly inappropriate to wear to this party."

Leave it to Aurora to pivot from political conspiracies and assassination plots to wardrobe crimes without missing a beat. She has this rare talent for making the heaviest things feel like they weigh half as much, and right now, I'm not about to turn down the distraction. Besides, all my clothes are back at the cabin, and I don't have time to go get them now.

"HOW DID you even know Rain has a bedroom here? Why would she choose to sleep in this place instead of having a house of her own?" I say, perching on the edge of the bed.

The room is all shades of purple, even the throw pillows. Apparently, Rain has a full-on love affair with the color. Her hair and now her bedroom. Figures.

Aurora smirks, rifling through the closet. "Don't say anything, but I think she and Cade hooked up a time or two. He's how I know about her room."

I make a face. "Gross."

She laughs, the sound bright and unapologetic. "Yeah, the woman's kind of a bitch."

I'm glad we're on the same page. "I can't believe Cade hooked up with her."

But honestly, I can believe it. Cade hooked up with Carmen too to further his mission. Why would I think pining after me all these years meant he was celibate? It doesn't actually bother me, not in the sense of jealousy. I wish he'd find someone else, anyone else, but preferably not Rain.

"It was a long time ago by the sound of it," Aurora says, pulling a hanger from the rack, "and I got the impression it was more of a drunken thing, not an 'I have actual feelings for you' thing."

For some reason, that makes me feel a little better.

"Here, try this on." She tosses a gown at me without even looking.

I slip into it while she keeps flipping through the rest of the closet. The fabric pools like water against my skin, cool and impossibly smooth. The gown is a pale shade of lavender—yep, Rain definitely has a thing for purple—and it fits like it was tailored for me. Long and silky, with a dangerously low back and a high slit up one leg. The front has one of those draped cowl folds over the chest, enough to make someone's gaze linger.

I turn to the mirror, taking in the way the silky dress falls over me.

Aurora peeks her head over my shoulder with a wicked grin. "That's the one."

"Great. Now some more practical clothes would be nice," I say, folding the gown and tucking it under my arm.

"Yes, lucky for you, there's no shortage of tactical clothes around here." Aurora tosses me a black backpack.

I unzip it, place the dress in the bottom, then follow her lead as we start going through drawers. She tosses me a couple of shirts, soft, worn cotton and a pair of fitted pants that look like they'll hold up in a fight. I grab a sweater, because God knows the Southern District is unpredictable when it comes to weather ... and maybe because I like the idea of having something comforting to pull on if things get bad.

"Do you feel anything yet from going through Bash's equipment?" she asks suddenly, shutting the closet door with a click before plopping down on the corner of the bed.

"I think so," I admit, sitting beside her and resting my elbows on my knees. "When I was on the lower levels, it felt weird. Not the usual cold-prickle weird. Damien showed up without me even thinking about him, but it was more than that." I try to pin down the sensation. "I had this pressure, like what usually separates me from the spirits was thinning. Almost like the space between us was weaker."

She nods, not looking away. "Like a door opening."

"Kind of," I say quietly, rubbing the back of my neck. "But I don't know if I was the one opening it or if someone else was holding it open for me."

"Keep embracing it. Now's the time to push yourself, see

how far you can take it when you still have the time to recover. Better now than in the middle of something that can get you killed," she says.

"I will," I assure her, slipping the backpack over my shoulders. "I better go see Bash before it's time to go."

She stands, pulling me into a tight hug. "Be careful. And don't trust anyone," she murmurs, and then she's gone, heading back toward the training room to work with the others.

I find Bash exactly where I expect him, hunched over his desk, head buried deep in the glow of his computer screens.

"You wanted to see me before I go," I say, stepping inside.

He glances up, his eyes shadowed like he's been thinking too much. "I have what you asked for," he says, pushing back from his chair and crossing to one of the locked cabinets along the side wall.

"I already gave Malachi an assortment of Avidian to use if you guys get in a pinch," he continues, rummaging until he finds something. "But like you asked, I didn't tell him about this one."

He turns and presses a tiny vial into my palm. I hold it up to the light. It's black, nothing like the usual Avidian's shimmering blues and purples that remind me of a faraway galaxy. It doesn't even look like the viscous dark-green vial I found at Marco's. This is something else entirely.

"What's wrong with it?" I ask.

"This is your Avidian. Your essence." He shifts awkwardly, scratching the back of his head. "It's ..."

I turn it over in my fingers, watching as the black and silver, glitter-laced substance swirls in slow, hypnotic currents. It's beautiful in a dangerous way, like oil slick over deep water.

"There's something different about it, Kat," he says finally. "And I'm not sure what it means. Be careful with it, okay?"

I don't have time to press him for answers before Cade steps into the room. His eyes scan for me instantly.

I slip the vial into my pocket before he can see it.

"Here." He tosses something my way, a cloth bifold. When I unfold it, I find a neat row of tiny wickedly sharp daggers nestled inside, along with a thigh strap.

"Mal will have plenty of weapons," Cade says with a smirk, "but I figured you should have something too."

I run a finger along the hilt of one dagger. They're beautiful, sleek, balanced, and small enough to hide under my dress or slide into a boot without notice. Exactly the kind of weapon to use up close.

"They're perfect," I admit, tucking them into my backpack. Impulsively, I step forward and wrap my arms around his neck.

He hugs me back easily, leaning down so his breath brushes my ear. "Watch your back out there, Kitty Kat. Don't make me come hunting you down again."

I giggle, leaning against his side. "You're all acting like I'm not coming back. I'll see you in two days. And I'll be ready for training. I'm not losing sight of our mission. This is a minor detour."

But if someone knew I'd delve below the first floor and see the recording of Irina's machinations, wouldn't they also know I'd react exactly like this?

Chapter Fifteen

LOG FIFTEEN - MUTUAL BENEFIT: SHE BELIEVES WE
ARE ALLIES. THAT WILL SERVE US ... FOR NOW.

WE END up leaving later than planned, and by the time the long flight is over, it's already morning. I barely got any sleep on the tiny plane. Every bout of turbulence jolting me awake as I'd start to drift off. Now all I want is a hot shower, a real bed, and about ten hours of uninterrupted sleep.

Malachi contacted Irina in advance to let her know we were coming. He told her that after recent events like the ranch burning down, he feels rumors will start circulating, and he wants to show a united front with her to avoid the Syndicate looking weak or fractured. He also mentioned that he should have realized before now what a good opportunity this would be for him to network with key district leaders and prove he's ready for more responsibility within the organization.

He said she seemed pleased with his initiative and was her normal charming self on the phone. She even arranged for a driver to pick us up and booked us a suite at the same hotel where everyone is staying, the same luxurious venue where tonight's grand party will take place.

Someone named Alonso picked us up in a sleek red SUV. Malachi clearly knows him, but based on their stiff body language, he definitely doesn't trust the man. After a formal, polite hello, the car ride has been nothing but uncomfortable silence. I'm actually fine with the quiet because I'm too exhausted to plot or strategize right now. I'll definitely need a solid nap if I'm going to be sharp and alert for tonight's event.

It's a forty-minute drive from the private landing strip to the hotel, so I settle back and take in the haunting scenery passing by my window.

It's hard to believe this place was once called the Sunshine State. Florida broke away from the mainland United States decades ago and became the largest island in the Southern District, its original name nearly forgotten along with any memory of actual sunshine.

The landscape outside is absolutely dreadful. The once famous–sandy beaches are buried beneath thick, crusted sheets of ice, their jagged edges biting into a steel-gray sea that looks more like liquid metal than water. Frost clings to the broken shells of what used to be palm trees, their skeletal fronds now bowed and brittle, constantly snapping under the weight of snow that never should have fallen in this tropical paradise.

I honestly have no idea how any of these trees are still standing at all. I guess everything adapts and finds a way to survive when that's the only option left.

I crack my window slightly to let in some fresh air, and my nose immediately fills with the sharp scent of salt and rust— bitter and metallic, carrying whispers of the devastating hurricanes that once roared through these coastal areas. Most of the storms stopped when the perpetual cold settled in. Now the sky hangs oppressively low, heavy with an endless winter haze that mutes the entire world into depressing shades of white and blue gray.

The ocean beyond our coastal road is sluggish and dark, with chunks of ice drifting across its surface like fractured glass catching what little light manages to penetrate the clouds.

I close my eyes and try to remember an old postcard I found once in an antique shop, showing this very coastline decades ago—tall, gleaming buildings rising along pristine sandy beaches, thousands of people enjoying the sun, the water so brilliantly teal it looked like liquid jewels.

I would kill to see something like that in person. It's horrible to think about what this place has become, all because we didn't take care of the Earth when we still had the chance to make a real difference.

"You still can make a difference."

The Viridian girl from the photograph flashes suddenly in the reflection of my car window, her voice vibrating through my mind like an electric current. The unexpected contact makes me jump so hard I nearly hit my head on the roof.

"You okay?" Malachi's eyebrows furrow with concern as he studies my startled expression.

"Yeah, sorry," I mumble, shaking my head and forcing myself to look back out the window. I definitely don't want to explain what happened with Alonso listening intently from the front seat.

We start driving more inland, away from the frozen coastline and through a less desolate part of what was once a thriving city. I spot a handful of people walking into shops and restaurants as we pass by, everyone bundled up in heavy coats and scarves to fight off the cool temperatures.

"Here we are." Alonso's smooth voice pulls me from my thoughts as we arrive in front of one of the tallest buildings I've ever seen up close.

The Western District doesn't have skyscrapers like this— we've always stuck to smaller settlements, and whenever we traveled, we deliberately avoided major cities, mostly due to the dangerous spread of gutter zones where law and order had completely broken down.

This building is absolutely massive, constructed from pale-beige stone with enormous gold reflective windows that stretch impossibly high toward the cloudy sky. The entire structure is dusted with frost and delicate white snowflakes, making it look like some kind of frozen palace from a fairy tale.

We walk through the opulent lobby, and I find myself meandering around, taking it all in while Malachi speaks with the elegantly dressed concierge. The interior is even more stunning than the exterior—marble floors polished to a mirror shine, crystal chandeliers casting warm light across soaring ceilings, and artwork that probably costs more than most people make in a lifetime.

It's hard to believe fancy places like this still exist in our broken world. Every year, the wealthy become richer while the poor sink deeper into desperation. Meanwhile, the gutter zones keep expanding like a disease, consuming more territory, and the district leaders stay in palaces like this.

I glance around cautiously as well-dressed guests move through the lobby. They might be Syndicate, working with the Volkovs, a fellow Avid hiding their abilities, or ordinary people caught up in this dangerous world of political intrigue.

I let out a deep breath, feeling overwhelmed by thoughts I've never really entertained before. Being free from Marco's control, no longer forced to exist as his shadow, allows me to consider questions about justice and responsibility that I normally wouldn't have the mental space for. Before, all I could focus on was whatever murder case I was being forced to solve and how to survive another day under his thumb.

Now, for the first time in years, my mind is free to grapple with the moral complexity of the world around me, and it's not pretty.

"FEELS good to rest my head for a minute," Malachi says, falling onto the massive bed beside me once we finally make it into our suite.

The room is absolutely beautiful—all crisp white linens and elegant furnishings that match the rest of the hotel's sophisticated aesthetic. The luxurious bedding is exactly what my exhausted body has been craving after that cramped flight and sleepless night.

"Do you have a plan, or are we winging it?" I ask, shifting to rest my head in the warm crook of his shoulder as he brings his arm up around me, tugging me close against his side.

"Winging it," he repeats, and I can't help but laugh.

"Yeah, you know, throw ourselves into the midst of all the political chaos and see where things fall," I clarify, and he joins in my laughter.

"In a few minutes, I'm going to go find my aunt and see what intelligence she can give me. I need to know who's attending the party tonight and whether the district summit meeting has already happened or not." His fingers trail absent circles across my back as he speaks, the gentle touch both soothing and distracting.

"You know my father and brothers might show their faces here tonight, right?" His voice takes on a more serious tone.

"I hope those fuckers do show up," I say with genuine conviction. "Everyone's true feelings are out in the open now. Lines have been drawn, and I'm not his pretty little prisoner anymore."

Malachi rolls onto his side to face me properly. "No, you're my beautiful, sarcastic, foul-mouthed little demon now."

He brushes my hair away from my face with infinite tenderness and leans down to kiss me, soft and sweet and full of promise.

"Your demon?" I raise an eyebrow when he pulls back. "I don't remember signing any ownership papers."

"Mmm, I think it was in the fine print when you declared your love for me at the breakfast table," he says with that infuriating smirk. "Right between 'madly in love' and 'done fighting it.'"

"That was a moment of temporary insanity brought on by you two acting like territorial dogs," I protest, though I'm fighting back a smile.

"Temporary?" He looks mock wounded. "I thought it was a binding contract."

"If we're talking contracts, then you're stuck with my beautiful, sarcastic, foul-mouthed self permanently. No returns, no exchanges."

"Deal," he says without hesitation, pressing another kiss to my forehead. "Though I might need to add 'dangerously impulsive' to that list after your little impromptu experiment with Bash."

Before I can decide how much to confess about the procedure, the hotel phone starts ringing.

"Room 1143, got it. I'll be there in a few minutes," Malachi says into the receiver before hanging up and running a hand through his dark hair and down his face.

"Alonso must have alerted my aunt to our arrival. That was Irina. I need to go speak with her, but you should get some rest before tonight." He walks over to an elaborate control panel mounted on the wall and presses a few buttons until all the blackout curtains glide closed automatically, swallowing the room into complete darkness.

"Nice trick," I say, blinking and waiting for my eyes to adjust to the sudden absence of light.

"High-end hotels have their perks," he replies. "When I get back, I'll join you for that nap ... and maybe more."

He leans down to kiss me one last time before reluctantly pulling away and slipping out the door. I pull the blankets up over my head and push all my thoughts away, knowing I need all the rest I can get.

I stir awake slowly, yawning as I feel a familiar body press against my back. An arm works its way around me, a hand splaying possessively across my stomach in a gesture that should be comforting, but something's off.

"How long was I asleep? What time is it?" I whisper into the darkened room, a tiny stream of light peeking around the curtains.

When there's no response, I assume Malachi is still sleeping, but then I open my eyes wider and go completely still as a cold awareness hits me like ice water. Something's wrong. My internal alarm bells are screaming, and goosebumps start spreading across my skin.

"Malachi?" I whisper, reaching to touch the arm that's draped across me.

The moment my fingers make contact, the sensation is scaling. The skin is cold, and this arm doesn't feel as large and muscular as Malachi's should. The proportions are completely off.

"Ahh!" I yelp, flinging the covers back violently and tossing the stranger's arm off me as I fall off the bed in my panic. My side hits the plush carpet hard, and I scramble to my feet, heart hammering against my ribs.

A low, familiar chuckle reverberates through the room, making my blood turn to ice.

I narrow my eyes on the figure still lying in the bed, and my worst nightmare materializes before me. Damien is stretched out where Malachi should be, looking far more solid and real than any spirit should be able to manage.

My breathing starts to come in sharp, panicked bursts. "How are you touching me? How are you ..." The horrifying implications sink in.

Damien has always felt stronger to me than other spirits, but his presence right now is so vivid, so physically real, that it has to be connected to whatever Bash did to enhance my abilities.

"You feel nice, Kitty Kat," he says with that same predatory smile he wears so well, and I look down at myself, rubbing frantically at my shirt in a vain attempt scrub away the memory of where his hand was.

"What are you doing here, in my bed?" I demand.

He chuckles again, rolling onto his back and stretching his arms above his head. I watch in horrified fascination as his form shifts, going from solid flesh to translucent-blue energy, then back to disturbingly solid again.

"I won't be able to rest until the right people pay for what they did, Katja," he says, setting my nerves on edge.

Despite every instinct screaming at me to get as far away as possible, I venture to sit on the edge of the bed, staring at him intently. If he's going to keep showing up, I need to understand what he wants.

"Cade's not going anywhere, and neither is Malachi, so don't even think about targeting them," I say firmly, drawing a clear line in the sand.

Damien goes translucent again, and the heavy blankets fall straight through his incorporeal body, settling on the mattress like he was never beneath them. The sight is incredibly unsettling.

"I thought you were finally seeing the bigger picture. Do I need to spell it out for you?" he asks, reforming into a more solid state.

Part of me desperately wants him to explain everything, but I'm not about to give him the satisfaction. "I don't know. That might take all the fun out of the twisted games you like to play," I respond, choosing sarcasm over the high road.

Get a grip, Kat.

"Malachi and Cade were following orders. I don't blame them entirely for being obedient little soldiers." His expression darkens with genuine hatred. "Aunt Irina and my father need to pay for what they orchestrated."

It's the first time I'm realizing that Damien might actually be an ally I could use right now despite how much his presence unnerves me. Enemy of my enemy and all that.

"Viktor hired me to find your killer. You think he wanted you dead too?" I ask, leaning forward with growing interest. I'd always suspected something was off about that entire investigation, but I'd never been able to put my finger on what exactly felt wrong about Viktor specifically.

"No one is innocent in this web of lies, and I won't find peace until they all pay for what they did," he repeats cryptically, still refusing to give me specifics.

His form wavers between solid and translucent. I can feel him starting to fade, and despite my fear, I find myself straining to keep him here. I need answers more than I need safety.

The hotel room door opens suddenly, sending a shaft of blinding light streaming in from the hallway. Malachi tries to sneak in quietly, opening the door slowly, but startles when he sees me sitting on the edge of the bed instead of sleeping peacefully under the covers.

"What's going on?" he asks with immediate concern, hitting the light switch and flooding the room with warm light.

I put my hand up to shield my eyes from the sudden brightness and glance back at the bed, but Damien has already vanished. I quickly describe Damien's physical manifestation, his cryptic warnings about Irina and Viktor, the way he seemed more solid than ever before.

Saying Malachi doesn't look pleased would be a massive understatement.

"I can't even protect you from him because he's already dead. That motherfucker," he says, kicking off his shoes and sighing in frustration.

I reach for him, tugging him down to sit beside me at the foot of the bed. "If he were truly going to hurt me, I think he would have done it by now. I think he's trying to help us in his own deranged way."

Malachi nods. "Help himself, maybe."

I take his hand in mine, needing the comfort of his warm, solid presence after Damien's cold touch. "How did it go with Irina?"

I still have no idea what time it is or how long he was gone. Scanning the room for a clock, I spot a digital display showing 1:00 p.m. Okay, so I managed to get a few hours of decent sleep despite the supernatural interruption.

"Here, eat this while we talk. You have to be starving," he says, handing me a paper bag I hadn't noticed him carrying.

I quickly unwrap the burrito inside and take a grateful bite —beans, cheese, rice, and salsa. "Yes, thank you. This is perfect."

"I'm confident from everyone's behavior that Syndicate leaders already held their summit meeting yesterday, but Irina didn't directly mention it. I couldn't exactly call her out on the omission since I don't want her to know we saw that surveillance footage." He settles more comfortably beside me. "I don't want her to suspect we're onto her duplicity at all. It'll only create more problems for us."

I couldn't agree more. We already have too many enemies circling us like vultures. It's definitely better if we maintain the pretense with her for now.

"What did she say about tonight's party? Do you think there will be some kind of orchestrated attack or ambush? Did she seem like she was worried about us showing up?" I ask between bites.

"She acted completely normal, but I don't expect her to give anything away after all this time. Irina's had years to perfect her poker face," he says, then looks away, rubbing a hand over the back of his neck and sighing heavily.

"I didn't want to say anything because I hate making you worry, but can you stay by my side tonight? No matter what happens, we should stay together."

I finish chewing and set the rest of my burrito down, giving him my full attention.

"What do you mean you don't want me to worry? Remember, we're being honest with each other now." I cross my arms and give him a pointed look. "Besides, I'm no delicate flower. I'm a demon and can handle whatever shit you're about to drop on me."

I bump his shoulder with mine. He doesn't laugh, but I get a small quirk of his lips that counts as progress.

"I'm serious, Kat. I'm worried that if what you saw on that surveillance footage is real, which I have no reason to believe it's not, then Irina may be actively trying to have you eliminated. And I just hand delivered you right to her doorstep."

The thought has definitely crossed my mind as well but hearing him voice it makes it feel more real and threatening.

"Look at it this way, if I die tonight, at least I'll finally get some peace and quiet," I say with deliberate lightness. "No more spirits popping up in my bed to give me cryptic riddles and a heart attack."

"That's not funny," he says, though I catch the corner of his mouth twitching despite himself.

"Then, how about this? If I die tonight, I'll come back as a really pissed-off ghost and make her life miserable," I say.

He shakes his head at my terrible attempts to lighten the mood, but I can see some of the tension leaving his shoulders. "You're impossible."

"You love it," I counter. "But seriously, walk me through your theory. Why would Irina want me dead? It has crossed my mind too. After seeing that side of her in the footage."

"Think about it logically," he says, his analytical mind taking over. "If she wants me to become some future savior figure for the Syndicate to eventually put in power, then having you in the picture seems like a major liability. A distraction that compromises her plans."

His eyes search the room. "Hell, it's entirely possible she's the one who tipped off Orin about where to find you at the cabin when I went to get the car."

"Okay, that's a disturbing thought," I admit. "But wouldn't killing me defeat the whole future savior plan. I mean, you'd be devastated, right?"

"She knows for certain now that I won't let my father have you back. She knows I'd never stop fighting for you as long as you're breathing."

"So the logical solution is to eliminate the breathing part and remove the obstacle," I finish for him with mock cheerfulness.

"Katja, this isn't a joke," he says, though there's exasperation rather than anger in his voice. "I'm trying to tell you I wont let anything happen to you. I can't lose you."

I press my finger gently to his lips, then crawl onto his lap, running my hands through his brown hair and down his stubbled jaw. "Hey, you're not getting rid of me that easily."

"Promise me," he says seriously, his hands finding my waist.

"I promise to be such an annoyingly persistent pain in everyone's ass that they'll regret ever trying to kill me," I say with a grin. "Now, stop stressing and kiss me. We still have today."

And Malachi has never been one to waste an opportunity.

Chapter Sixteen

LOG SIXTEEN - THRESHOLD CROSSED: WITH THE VACCINE PREPARED FOR TRIALS, THE SUBJECT'S EVOLUTION ACCELERATES BEYOND PRECEDENT.

THE MOMENT WE STEP INSIDE, the sheer scale of the place steals my breath. It's not like the large private estates I'm used to seeing. This is on an entirely different level of grandeur. The entire space is decorated in warm golds, deeply polished woods, and rich jewel tones that speak of old money and established power.

But the first thing my eyes lock onto is the absolute marvel at the room's center, a massive carousel-shaped bar. Golden pillars rise from the floor up toward the vaulted ceiling, each one hand painted and carved with brilliant, swirling images of colorful carousel horses frozen mid-gallop, their painted manes caught in some imagined wind. The artistry is so vivid and life-like it looks like the horses might leap free from their golden prisons at any second.

The bar itself is a perfect circle, crowned with a smooth marble countertop that gleams like liquid gold under the amber lighting. A ring of intricately carved barstools surrounds it, each one completely unique, their high-rounded backs carved and painted to resemble different animals. As Malachi weaves us through the elegantly dressed crowd, stopping to exchange pleasantries with someone whose name I immediately forgot, I get a closer look at the incredible craftsmanship.

I spot a prowling tiger with emerald eyes, a soaring falcon with wings spread wide, and a graceful koi fish with scales that shimmer in the light. The details are so fine you can see individual feathers and the gleam of painted eyes that follow you as you move.

And the most incredible part is that the whole thing rotates slowly. The entire bar moves in a measured circle, smooth as clockwork, carrying bartenders and guests around in a slow parade of pure opulence. It's absolutely stunning, clearly designed to be the heart of this glittering social ecosystem.

Beyond the rotating centerpiece, scattered like precious jewels on black velvet, are clusters of small round tables topped with softly glowing lanterns. Their golden light creates intimate pools perfect for hushed conversations among the corrupt people of this event.

In one far corner, I notice high stakes–gambling tables where chips and cards represent more money than most people see in their lifetimes. The cause they're supposedly raising funds for tonight is probably an elaborate ruse to justify this display of excess.

"Nice to meet you," I say politely, catching the tail end of Malachi introducing me to a distinguished man with short curly gray hair. Nothing important, only the kind of small talk that oils the wheels of high society.

Looking past our new acquaintance, I spot a small stage and dance floor positioned along one wall, where a live band plays jazz, smooth and rich. The musicians are clearly world-class, but I would expect nothing less for an audience such as this.

Opposite that wall, another bar stretches along the length

of the room, this one carved from dark, lustrous wood to mimic intricate patterns of climbing vines and coiled serpents. It's beautiful in its own right, but it doesn't even attempt to compete with the grandeur at the room's center. Nothing could.

Not sure what's with the animal theme in this place, but I'm kind of into it.

Scattered throughout the ballroom at tall cocktail tables are some of the country's most powerful families networking and making deals that will likely affect many lives in the worst possible ways. I spot Belle Miller, an elegant woman in emerald silk whose perfectly styled blonde hair hasn't changed in the two years since I last saw her. She and her husband had hired Marco for my services when their daughter was murdered, a case that still haunts me.

Her husband, Hunter, is one of the leaders in the Southern District. Unlike the East and West, where Marco and Viktor are the sole rulers of their respective territories, the South operates differently. Here, three powerful families claim equal ownership of that title, creating a more complex and potentially volatile political landscape.

"Can we get a drink?" I ask, drawing Malachi's attention back to me from whatever calculation he was making.

"You actually want alcohol?" he asks, one eyebrow raised in surprise. I'm usually not huge on alcohol, especially when we need to stay sharp, but one drink can't hurt.

"Yes, and I want to sit at that bar," I say, tipping my head toward the carousel centerpiece.

He follows my gaze and breaks into a genuine smile. "Yeah, it really is something, isn't it?"

I take his elbow as he leads me through the crowd of glittering guests toward the slowly rotating marvel. I claim the barstool with a striking black-and-white zebra painted on it.

Malachi doesn't sit beside me. Instead, he stands protectively next to my chair, his arm falling naturally around me so his hand can rest on my lower back.

No one is sitting on either side of us, giving us a rare pocket of relative privacy in this sea of potential enemies. The bartender is a tall skeletal man with salt-and-pepper hair cut so short it looks almost carved into his head.

I order a gin and tonic, then turn toward Malachi with the questions that have been burning in my mind.

"If all the district-ruling families aren't supposed to know about the Syndicate, then how does this whole charade work exactly? Why would all these people come to Irina's event?"

He picks up the crystal tumbler containing his scotch and takes a sip, nodding politely to someone across the slowly rotating bar with a perfectly polite smile.

"The leading families don't know about the Syndicate, per se, or what their true goals are. They know them as influential, wealthy individuals who appear to be genuinely interested in supporting a common cause." He pauses, his expression darkening slightly. "At least, that's what I would have told you before yesterday's revelations. As for Irina, her last name carries enough weight to attract anyone."

He takes another drink, then places his glass on the polished marble surface. "After what you overheard on that surveillance footage, I know my father and Viktor are aware of what Irina's really orchestrating. I don't know to what extent they're involved, but at the end of the day, she's still their sister, and family loyalty runs deep. They'll play along with her schemes rather than expose her."

I nod, recognizing the logic. "I don't think they would risk outing her to the other district leaders either. That would create a political nightmare, and they'd much rather handle family business internally."

"Exactly. That's always been my father's operating philosophy. Keep the dirty laundry in the family," he agrees.

"So, if Irina arranged this elaborate party, what does everyone else think they're here for? What's the official cover story that convinced all these powerful people to make the trip?" I ask, genuinely curious about what lies have drawn so many prominent faces here.

"They're here for what they think is a strategic networking opportunity and the promise to unveil some new resource everyone wouldn't want to miss," Malachi explains, his hushed voice barely audible over the sophisticated jazz floating through the air. "Irina will have pitched it as a gathering to strengthen interdistrict relations, discuss trade routes, resource allocation, maybe even security cooperation. All the boring, respectable things powerful people pretend to care about when others are watching."

I take a sip of my drink, the liquid warming me from the inside.

"And when they think no one's watching?" I ask, though I suspect I already know the answer.

His gaze flicks to the carousel bar's rotation, then back to me. "That's when they make the real deals. They traffic Avids like livestock and invest in those sick underground experiments we've been uncovering. They decide who lives comfortably and who starves in the gutter zones, which humanitarian projects get funded and which are left to rot, whose names disappear from official records entirely."

The casual way he lists these atrocities makes me sick, but I already know how corruption works. You don't spend years under Marco's roof and think otherwise. I take another long gulp of my cocktail, needing the alcohol to steady my nerves.

"Another day in paradise," I say with bitter sarcasm.

"Exactly." I don't miss the way his eyes constantly scan the crowded room, cataloging exits, identifying potential threats, searching for familiar faces that might spell trouble.

"Irina's exceptionally good at making people feel like they're part of something meaningful, like they're truly important players in shaping the future. That's how she's gathered so many Syndicate members to fund our work over the years," he continues, swirling the amber liquid in his glass. "I'm sure she'll use this evening to eliminate a few problematic targets as well as recruit new allies to her cause."

He shakes his head. "It's been right in front of my face this entire time. I have no idea how I was so completely blind to it all, to her manipulative ways."

I reach over and touch his side gently, wishing we were alone instead of surrounded by what feels like a hundred of the most-dangerous and -deranged people in the country.

"Uncle Viktor just walked in. I don't remember the last time my aunt and uncle were in the same room together. This will be very interesting," Malachi murmurs, and I follow his gaze.

Sure enough, Viktor is working the room, all polished charm and hollow smiles, shaking hands with a knot of people near the far end of the other bar. Despite being Marco's twin, something about him makes him look older. Maybe it's the beard. Anton, his security, stalks a few paces behind, the sharp cut of his tailored suit doing little to disguise the predator underneath.

"If it isn't my two favorite lovebirds," a voice drawls from behind us, rich with venom. "My backstabbing, ungrateful son ... and my treacherous little pet."

The sound makes my spine lock straight, a jolt of cold rushing through me. I turn in my seat, and there is Marco, clean shaven, slicked-back black hair, and impeccable all-black suit. His presence sucks the warmth out of the space between us.

"How nice to see you're still alive, Father," Malachi says, flicking some invisible lent off his navy suit.

Marco's smile doesn't reach his eyes. "Lucky for me, my demon didn't have what it takes after all." His gaze drifts to me, a smirk twisting his mouth.

"Oh, I have what it takes," I snap. "I'll show you—"

He lifts a hand, cutting me off like I'm a petulant child. "Now, now. My pet seems to have forgotten all her manners in the short time she's been with you. I'll have to correct that when I take her back home. Perhaps I'll even let Orin spend a little more time with her." A flash of anger passes. "I know he fancies her too, in a very different way than you do."

Malachi doesn't move, but I feel the air change around him.

For one heartbeat, I truly believe he might slit Marco's throat right here in front of everyone.

"Where is my brother tonight?" Malachi asks, looking past Marco and doing a careful sweep of our surroundings.

"He had more pressing matters to attend to, but he'll be devastated when I tell him Katja was here," Marco replies, waving the bartender down.

I don't hide the disgust on my face. The very mention of Orin makes my skin crawl, bringing back memories I'd rather keep buried.

But suddenly I feel a lightning-quick strike to my nervous system that's so fast and sharp it leaves me breathless. Then everything returns to normal, as if nothing happened at all.

I glance around frantically, unsure what could have caused such a strange sensation. Was it supernatural? Physical? My imagination?

Malachi immediately takes my hand and guides me away from the bar and Marco's unsettling presence. "Dance with me," he whispers over the top of my head as he smoothly navigates us onto the polished dance floor.

"What about Irina and your father? Aren't you worried they'll—" I start to protest, but he cuts me off by taking my waist and expertly guiding our movements to the rhythm of the live band.

"It's too early for whatever Irina has planned. She'll wait until later when people are more relaxed, when guards are down and alcohol has loosened tongues. The party has barely started, and guests are still arriving."

His logic is sound, but I can't shake this feeling that has me on edge.

Maybe it's my abilities continuing to evolve in unexpected ways.

Yes, Kat, you're being paranoid.

"You know," Malachi says with that insufferably confident smile as he spins me gracefully, "I'm an excellent dancer. I thought you should be aware."

"Oh really?" I arch an eyebrow as he pulls me back into his arms. "And here I thought your only talents were brooding dramatically and looking mysterious leaning against doorways."

"Those are my hobbies," he replies with mock seriousness. "Dancing happens to be one of my many professional skills."

"Professional skills?" I laugh as he dips me low, his face inches from mine. "What exactly do you put on your résumé? Expert at sweeping women off their feet?"

"Among other things," he says with a wink, pulling me upright again. "I also list devastatingly handsome and irresistibly charming."

"Well, you got the devastating part right," I tease. "Though, I think you meant devastatingly arrogant."

"Arrogant?" He feigns wounded surprise, spinning me out and then reeling me back in. "I prefer confidently accurate about my own excellence."

"That's definitely going on the list of longest ways to say arrogant I've ever heard."

"See? I'm also creatively verbose." He grins, guiding us through a series of turns that make my dress swirl around my legs like liquid silk.

"You're something, alright," I say, trying not to smile too widely at his ridiculous confidence, though he does look hot in the navy suit he's wearing.

"Are you seriously trying to distract me with your charm right now?"

"Is it working?" he asks with that infuriating smirk, spinning me gracefully.

"Maybe a little," I admit reluctantly, "but I can still feel you scanning the room every few seconds."

"Can't help it. Occupational hazard," he says, pulling me closer. "But for the record, I'm also genuinely enjoying holding you like this."

"Even with a room full of potential assassins watching us?"

"Especially with a room full of potential assassins watching us. Nothing says fuck you to dangerous people quite like dancing with a beautiful woman."

"That's your master plan? Spite dancing?"

"Hey, if we're going to potentially die tonight, we might as well look good doing it," he says, dipping me smoothly. "Besides, I like the idea of them seeing exactly what they can't have."

"What they can't have?" I raise an eyebrow as he pulls me back up.

"You. Us. This." His expression grows more serious for a moment. "Whatever happens tonight, they can't take this away from us."

"You're being sweet to make me forget we're probably walking into a trap."

"Is that a problem?" he asks, that cocky smile returning.

"Not even a little bit," I say, letting him spin me again.

"Sinclair." The sharp bark of a man's voice cuts through the music, and I halt. I look past Malachi to see a towering figure pushing through the crowd toward us, a broad-shouldered man with flame-red hair and pale, freckled skin that's currently flushed with anger. His narrow brown eyes are fixed on me with unmistakable fury, and his expensive black suit does nothing to soften the menace radiating from his hulking frame.

Malachi instantly shifts into protective mode, his body becoming a shield as he pushes me behind him. He turns to face the approaching threat, every muscle in his frame coiled for violence.

"I knew you looked familiar," the red-haired man says over the sophisticated jazz. He completely ignores Malachi's intimidating presence, craning his neck to peer around him. "Do you still belong to Marco Volkov?"

The question sends ice through my veins. People around us continue their elegant waltzes, oblivious to the danger, but I can feel curious eyes beginning to turn our way. I start stepping backward off the dance floor, my mind racing to place this man's face.

"Don't speak to her. Who the hell are you?" Malachi says, his stance widening into a fighting position.

The man's aggressive demeanor wavers slightly when he registers the lethal promise in Malachi's eyes, but desperation keeps him pushing forward.

"I know what you can do," he says, his voice growing more urgent and uncontrolled. "I need your help. My wife died last month. They claimed it was a car accident, but I know better. That woman never drove a day in her life. It was a setup, and I need you to reach her. Do what you do. Contact her spirit, make her tell me who killed her."

Several elegantly dressed guests pause mid-conversation, their attention drawn by his increasingly frantic tone. My throat tightens. The last thing I need is my abilities being shouted across this political nest of vipers.

"Keep your voice down, and I'll consider helping you," I hiss through gritted teeth, frantically motioning for him to lower his voice.

"She's not helping you with anything. Back off." Malachi takes a step forward and drapes his arm around me, trying to guide us away from the growing scene.

But the man's grief and desperation override any sense of self-preservation. He lunges forward with surprising speed, his massive hand shooting out to grab my wrist in a crushing grip.

"Please, you have to—"

In one fluid motion, Malachi produces a sleek blade from somewhere within his jacket and presses it against the man's throat, the sharp edge drawing a thin line of blood.

"Let. Her. Go."

"No, don't!" I grab Malachi's arm, knowing that violence will only make this worse. The man immediately releases my wrist, his hands flying up in surrender.

"You're going to walk away right now, and if you ever—" Malachi says through his teeth.

His threat is cut off by the sudden, sharp sound of shattering glass from somewhere across the ballroom. The distinctive *pop, pop, pop* of something exploding echoes through the air.

Thick gray smoke begins billowing across the dance floor, and the party erupts into complete madness.

Chapter Seventeen

LOG SEVENTEEN - PHASE SHIFT: THE TRIALS WERE
MEANT TO CHANGE HER. INSTEAD, SHE IS
CHANGING US.

THICK, acrid smoke quickly fills the elegant ballroom, and then someone kills the overhead lighting, plunging the space into near-total darkness. Only a few scattered table lamps and the golden carousel bar fixtures glow dimly through the heavy chemical fog. I cough violently, and tears stream from my burning eyes.

I start to feel a rising panic clawing up from my chest as irrational fear grips me with razor-sharp fingers. I force myself to take a deep, shuddering breath, trying to fight against the artificial terror flooding my system.

At the exact same moment, I see recognition dawn in Malachi's eyes—the same horrifying realization hitting us both simultaneously.

This is no ordinary smoke bomb. This is fear gas, something unnatural and weaponized, designed specifically to cause panic and mayhem. The chemical compounds are hijacking our nervous systems, amplifying every worst fear and turning rational people into terrified animals.

"Fuck," Malachi curses, releasing the red-haired man and

shoving him away from us. The man immediately gets swallowed by the panicking crowd and billowing smoke.

The ballroom has become a nightmare of sound. People are screaming in terror, expensive heels clattering against the hard floor as guests trample over each other to reach any exit. Crystal glasses shatter underfoot, and I can hear the sickening sounds of bodies colliding in the darkness.

"Do you see anyone? Do you know who's attacking us?" I shout over the chaos.

Malachi grabs my hand tightly and starts dragging me through the mass of panicking bodies. "Stay low, stay close," he commands.

A woman's piercing shriek cuts through the cacophony somewhere to our left, followed by someone shouting, "I think he's dead!" My blood turns to ice.

We're almost to the relative safety of the wall, where we can regroup. I keep my head ducked into Malachi's back, my eyes streaming from whatever chemical they've pumped into the air. Then suddenly his hand is ripped from mine as two dark figures crash into him with brutal force.

"Malachi!" I scream, not knowing if these men are deliberately targeting him or if he's caught in the stampede of terrified guests trying to escape. Before I can reach for him, he's completely swallowed by the haze and hysteria.

Strong arms wrap around my waist without warning, lifting me completely off the ground and carrying me back into the heart of the panicking crowd. I fight like a wildcat, straining against his grip, kicking my feet frantically, and swinging my arms as hard as I can. I dig my nails deep into his hands where they grip me, feeling skin tear under my fingernails.

My captor hauls me up onto the small stage and drags me off to the side behind a section of heavy curtain, then finally releases me, immediately shoving my back hard against the wall to pin me in place.

"You again," I spit, narrowing my burning eyes at the massive red-haired man from the dance floor.

"Find my wife," he demands. His eyes look desperate and unhinged as they search my face. "I know you can do it. Contact her spirit and nothing bad has to happen to you."

My mind starts spinning with terrifying possibilities. Is he somehow orchestrating this attack? Does he have people working with him?

No, there's no way.

This guy clearly operates alone, and if someone really did murder his wife, then he must have more enemies than allies. His face had looked as shocked as everyone else's when those smoke grenades exploded.

But if he's not behind this coordinated assault, then that means the real attackers are still out there, and I need to get back to Malachi before someone else gets hurt or killed. I swallow, trying to keep the unnatural fear that keeps trying to claw its way up my throat down.

"Let me go," I snarl with as much venom as I can muster. "I don't give a damn who killed your wife, and I'm not helping you."

I drive my knee upward as hard as I can, aiming for his groin, but he shifts enough that I nail him in the thigh instead. In retaliation, he slams his massive body against me, using his bulk to trap me completely against the wall.

The giant has me pinned, and somewhere in the mayhem beyond this curtain, Malachi is fighting for his life.

I hear the brutal sounds of combat echoing from beyond the curtain—fists hitting flesh, the slick squelch of something wet that's hopefully not blood, and the kind of violent commotion that only life-and-death fighting produces.

I didn't want Malachi to kill this man before, but now I'm seriously regretting that merciful decision. I remember the three small daggers strapped to my thigh, and wiggle my hand down desperately, trying to grab one of them without him noticing.

"You fucked with the wrong Avid, asshole," I snarl as I finally grasp the hilt and drive the blade deep into his massive bicep.

I should go for a killing blow—throat, heart, something vital —but I'm hoping this painful lesson will get my point across so I can escape and find Malachi.

He groans, then grabs the blade and rips it free from his flesh with a wet, tearing noise. Blood immediately begins streaming down his arm and blending into his black suit.

Maybe this is why Malachi always says to only go for killing blows.

Way to prove Marco right, Kat. You're being too empathetic in a life-and-death situation.

"Cute," he says through a clenched jaw as crimson drips steadily onto the stage floor.

Maybe I should have risked strapping a bigger weapon to my leg. This guy's arm is so enormous that my small dagger barely seemed to penetrate deep enough to cause any serious damage.

Without warning, he backhands me hard across the face. The strike whips my head sideways, and I pull my bottom lip into my mouth, tasting the blood on my tongue.

He turns my own dagger over in his bloody hand, pressing the sharp edge against my throat while his massive body presses harder against me, pinning me completely against the wall.

"Care to rethink your position?" he asks.

This is exactly when a power like Aurora's would come in handy. I could light this fucker on fire and be done with it.

"You don't understand," I say, staying steady despite the blade at my throat. "I don't know what your wife looks like. I know nothing about her. It's nearly impossible to summon someone's spirit under the best of circumstances, let alone in the middle of this."

I gesture as much as I can with my pinned arms toward the utter shitshow beyond the curtain.

"Look around you," I spit, then do something incredibly stupid, I push harder against the blade, daring him to follow through on his threat.

I feel the sharp steel pierce my skin, drawing blood, and the bug-eyed, bloodshot stare he gives me tells me I should probably start taking him much more seriously. I need to stop pushing my luck because he clearly has nothing left to lose.

And if I learned anything from my time with Marco, it's that people with nothing to lose are the most dangerous kind of all.

"I have a feeling you're stronger than you let on. Marco Volkov wouldn't keep a pet like you so close if you weren't extraordinary." He pauses, his eyes laced with scarlet veins, searching my features with disturbing intensity. "Then again, he wasn't with you tonight, was he? Maybe you should have stayed on your leash. There's no one here to save you now."

The word "pet" hits a nerve, inciting me. I want to tackle this bastard to the ground and strangle him with my bare hands, but I force myself to take a shuddering deep breath. I need to focus and give him what he wants so I can at least get him off me and find Malachi.

"Do you have a picture of her with you?" I ask, hating every sound that comes out of my mouth.

"I don't. Her name is Vivianne. Everyone called her Viv. She had strawberry-blonde hair and the most beautiful blue eyes, not too different from your own." His voice takes on a softer, more desperate edge when he talks about her. "Now you better make that work, because I'm losing my patience, and by the sound of it, things are only getting nastier out there."

I can't see much beyond the heavy curtain that shields us from view. It's like we're tucked into the one private corner of this entire chaotic hellscape.

"You're going to have to let go of me if I'm going to try to reach her," I tell him.

He removes the blade from my throat, dropping his hand to his side, but doesn't move even an inch away from me. I can barely breathe with him pressed this close, his massive frame blocking out everything else.

"That's all you're going to get. Now, hurry up," he growls.

I crack my neck to the side, trying to find some space, then close my eyes tightly. *Focus, Kat. Clear your head of everything else.*

I block out every sound in the room—the distant screaming, the crashes, the sounds of violence—and let my mind go completely blank. Then I reach for the Veil between worlds. I imagine a door, and instead of carefully peeking through it like I usually do, I kick it down with desperate force and scream into the void. "VIV!"

I will her to be here, to answer my call. I don't know how to picture her exactly based on his brief description, so instead I focus on the red-haired man restraining me—his energy, his scent, his overwhelming grief. I hope she carries enough of him with her that it will pull her spirit to me.

Suddenly my eyes shoot open when I hear Malachi yell across the ballroom destruction, "Katja!"

But the man hears it too and immediately clutches my throat before I can scream back, squeezing hard enough to cut off my air supply.

"Time is running out for you, pet," he hisses.

I squeeze my eyes shut, struggling to take even a partial breath. In desperation, I completely shatter the Veil in my mind and scream into the supernatural darkness with everything I have left.

Then an ice-cold presence pierces straight through my chest, and my heart jumps violently as all the breath gets sucked from my lungs.

I open my eyes, and a woman stands behind the man holding me captive. She reaches up tenderly and touches his cheek, but he can't feel her ghostly caress. I stare at her in fascination as she flickers unstably from a translucent-blue shade to full, vibrant color.

I catch a glimpse of her strawberry-blonde hair shining like spun gold, then she's translucent again, wavering like heat shimmer. I blink hard, remembering that I need to ask her who killed her, but I can't speak against his crushing grip that's slowly cutting off my air supply.

I open my mouth to try to speak but can't tear my eyes away from the woman's large round eyes that carry a bone-deep sadness I can feel resonating in my very soul.

Suddenly Malachi appears like a phantom assassin, stepping right through her spiritual form without even seeing her. In one fluid, lethal motion, he draws his blade across the man's throat.

The red-haired man immediately releases me, his hands flying up to press his neck as blood pours between his fingers. Malachi shoves him roughly to the side, and he staggers backward before collapsing to the stage floor, making wet, gurgling sounds that fade into silence.

Malachi immediately grabs my face in his hands, his eyes scanning me frantically for injuries. His gaze lingers on the bruises forming around my neck and my split lip, and I can see murderous rage flickering in his dark eyes.

"What's happening out there? Are you all right?" I ask, my voice coming out as a rasp from my damaged throat.

"Meadow is back. I can only assume Marco brought her, but I don't know who her target is yet. I was worried she was going to find you before I did." He's still examining my body like he's expecting to discover more wounds hidden somewhere.

"She wasn't responsible for the smoke bombs though. That was from someone with a lot of money and access to get fear gas like that."

"So basically almost anyone here," I reply, but the likely culprit is any of the Volkovs.

Malachi nods. "Someone blocked all the main exits from the outside, and there are only two hallways still open, but by the looks of it, they're being sealed off too."

I feel that supernatural chill still spreading through my chest from my contact with Viv's spirit, and I visibly shiver, trying to contain the lingering effects.

"If Meadow's here, then is Marco planning to attack Irina or us? What's Irina's endgame? Have you seen her?" I ask frantically, my mind racing through the possibilities.

He shakes his head. "I'm not sure, but I thought tonight would be more orchestrated than this. It's quickly becoming a complete clusterfuck, and it's gone way beyond trying to save anyone. I want to get you out of here alive. Everyone else can kill each other as far as I'm concerned."

I like the sound of that plan. I did think we would be able to prevent innocent people from losing their lives tonight, but after seeing this gathering up close, I don't know if anyone here would qualify as innocent.

"I have an idea," he says, his tactical mind already working. "I'm going to stack some of this band equipment and try to break through the ceiling tiles over there. We could crawl through an air shaft and get away from here unseen."

I nod, following his gaze toward the dark backstage area where abandoned instruments and sound equipment sit scattered in the shadows.

Malachi immediately gets to work, grabbing a large amplifier and dragging it across the stage with a harsh scraping sound that makes me wince. The noise seems impossibly loud in our hidden corner, and I keep glancing toward the curtain, expecting someone to come investigate at any moment.

"Shit." I throw my hand over my mouth to muffle the startled curse as the now-dead red-haired man's apparition emerges through the curtain, walking directly toward me with purposeful strides.

"What is it?" Malachi asks, looking back in my direction with concern.

"Nothing, hurry please," I urge, staring transfixed at the man's spirit.

He can't hurt me. You can control this, Kat.

But then his wife suddenly materializes next to him, and they both charge at me in unison, running right through my body like I'm made of air.

I swirl around to follow their movement, but they've already vanished.

Mish appears at my feet, yipping frantically and clawing cool, ghostly marks up my leg before darting through the curtain like she wants me to follow her. Her distress is palpable.

I take a couple hesitant steps forward, finally leaving the safety of the wall I've been clinging to. My heartbeat is thundering so loudly in my ears that it drowns out the distant chaos, and my veins feel like liquid nitrogen is coursing through them. I rub desperately at my chest, willing the freezing sensation to go away, but it only intensifies.

Maybe it's Meadow causing this. Maybe she's actively searching for me. I felt something unusual when I encountered her before, and there's definitely something not right about her. Who knows what horrific experiments Marco subjected her to?

I reach the edge of the heavy curtain and grab the corner with trembling fingers, peeling it back just enough to peek around the edge into the main ballroom.

I freeze completely.

The entire space is filled with spirits—dozens of them, maybe more—standing throughout the frenzy in their slightly luminescent forms. Some are clearer than others, their ghostly figures weaving between the panicking crowd of living guests who can't see them. But I can see every single one with crystal clarity, and they're all turning to look directly at me.

"Uh, Malachi," I whisper, stricken. I'm too terrified to look away from the scene unfolding before me, too horrified to even blink.

He moves up behind me, his warmth a stark contrast to the ice spreading through my veins as he peers past the curtain into the ballroom. "What's wrong? Talk to me."

I try to swallow, but my mouth has gone completely dry. I'm frozen in place, every muscle in my body rigid with a fear so profound it feels like I'm drowning. Some of the initial chaos from the smoke grenades has died down to a tense, waiting quiet, but there's something far more sinister happening now.

A different kind of smoke, not the gray chemical fog from the grenades, but something that seems to absorb light itself, billows across the polished floor like liquid shadow. This black vapor moves with purpose, collecting in dark pools throughout the grand space, creeping around the scattered bodies and huddled survivors like it's alive. It has to be Meadow's work, wherever she's lurking in the darkness, probably providing supernatural cover for whatever Marco has planned.

In one far corner, a large group of guests in torn eveningwear argues in frantic, hushed voices. They're pressed against ornate double doors, pushing and shoving, but the doors won't budge, clearly barricaded from the outside. Their diamond jewelry catches what little light remains, creating tiny sparkles of desperate beauty in the nightmare unfolding among us.

Around the magnificent carousel bar, another cluster of people has taken shelter, crouched low on the cold floor, clearly frightened out of their minds. Some are weeping silently, while others stare into the darkness with shell-shocked expressions. A few still clutch crystal glasses, as if holding onto the remnants of normalcy might save them.

But I can see something they can't. The painted eyes of the tiger on the back of one of the barstools seem to shift and blink, tracking movement, growing more animated.

I quickly scan over each of the stools as they continue their steady rotation in the center of the room, and my heart nearly stops. The carved animals are coming to life, not the physical carvings but their spirits.

I have no idea what the hell is happening. Were these animals studied to create this elaborate contraption? Were they killed so their likenesses could be replicated?

The lion's spirit suddenly leaps out from the back of its barstool and bounds across the room, where it begins to prowl and pace against the far wall with restless, ghostly energy. Its translucent mane flows as it moves, and I can hear the phantom sound of its heavy paws padding against the floor.

One of the carousel horses breaks free from its golden pillar, galloping straight through the air in a spectral form. It continues its eternal ride in a perfect circle, moving in eerie unison with the bar's mechanical rotation, its ghostly hooves never touching the ground.

I blink several times, trying to process what I'm witnessing, then force myself to tear my gaze away from the supernatural menagerie and back to the human spirits scattered throughout the ballroom.

They all stand perfectly motionless throughout the room, scattered among the living. Each ghostly figure is positioned next to a breathing person, and they're all waiting. Their translucent forms shimmer slightly in the dim light, some more solid than others, but all of them have the same expression of patient anticipation.

"I did something really, really bad," I wheeze, each syllable scraping past my paralyzed vocal cords.

The apparition closest to us—a woman in an evening gown with a gaping hole where her heart should be—slowly turns her head toward me. Her lips stretch into a macabre smile. Her eyes are black voids that seem to see straight through to my soul, and when she grins, I can see her teeth are stained with something dark.

"I'll say you done fucked up royally this time, Kitty Kat," Damien says through the air around us like poisonous honey, though I can't pinpoint where he's hiding. "This is quite the show you've put on."

"What is it? What do you see?" Malachi's hand finds mine and squeezes so tightly I can feel his pulse hammering against my palm. He's trying to anchor me to reality, but reality is quickly becoming something I don't recognize.

"There are ghosts everywhere," I breathe, my voice cracking with the weight of what I've unleashed. "Dozens of them. Maybe more."

His head snaps toward me, but I can't look at him. I physically cannot tear my gaze away from the supernatural army I've accidentally summoned. Every spirit in the room is now looking directly at me, their partially translucent faces turned in my direction like sunflowers following the sun.

As if responding to some silent command I didn't give, they all begin to move.

It happens in slow motion, each second stretching into an eternity of horror. I watch, helpless and paralyzed, as every single spirit raises their translucent hands. They place their fingers on either side of their chosen victim's head.

The living people don't react. They can't see what's about to happen to them. Some are still arguing about escape routes, others comforting one another. They have no idea that death is literally standing right beside them, preparing to end their lives with surgical precision.

"No," I whisper, finally finding my voice. "No, stop!"

But it's too late.

Moving in perfect, terrifying synchronization, every spirit in the room twists their hands sharply to the right.

CRACK. CRACK. CRACK.

The sound of necks snapping echoes through the ballroom. Twenty, maybe thirty sharp breaks happening simultaneously. The noise is grating and final, the kind of sound that will haunt my nightmares forever.

Bodies begin dropping to the hard floor with sickening thuds that seem to go on forever. A woman in emerald silk crumples next to the carousel bar. A man in a perfectly tailored tuxedo collapses near the stage, and I see it's Hunter Miller, one of the leaders of the South.

For one impossible, deafening moment, absolute silence blankets the ballroom. Even the distant sounds of fighting from other parts of the hotel seem to pause, as if the entire building is holding its breath.

Blood-curdling screams tear through the air—sounds of pure,

primal terror that seem to come from the very depths of human despair. The survivors scramble over each other in blind panic, stepping on the fallen bodies, slipping in pools of blood that are beginning to spread across the pristine floor. I see Belle Miller drop to her knees beside her husband's dead body, her dress soaking up his blood as an ear-curdling scream escapes her throat.

"What the fuck?" Malachi says beside me.

I can't do anything except stare at the carnage I've created. The supernatural massacre that happened because I pushed too hard, because I tore through the Veil. After Bash's experiment, I'm even stronger than I thought possible—and that terrifies me.

The spirits are still there, still standing among the destruction, but now they're all smiling absently. And every single one of them is looking directly at me, as if waiting for their next command. As if they're not even real people back from the dead but possessed spirits.

Did I do this?

I shake my head frantically, not wanting to know the answer to whatever horrific question is forming in my mind, when suddenly the black smoke evaporates like it was never there, the overhead lights flicker back to life with a harsh electrical buzz, and the double doors across the room burst open with a thunderous crash. Fresh air and voices pour in from the hallway beyond.

I can see the carnage much more clearly now, and the sight makes my stomach lurch violently. I quickly scan the room, trying to distinguish between who's left alive and who's lying motionless on the blood-streaked floor.

"I don't see my father or Irina anywhere," Malachi says beside me, scanning the crowd of survivors who are now streaming toward the open exits like water through a broken dam.

Dead bodies are scattered throughout the elegant ballroom —some still in their perfect eveningwear, others twisted at unnatural angles. Living people crouch beside the fallen, some checking for pulses, others weeping over loved ones who will never move again.

Suddenly, the woman's ghost nearest the stage—the one with the hole where her heart should be—charges straight at me with supernatural speed.

I take a reflexive step backward, a sharp yelp escaping my throat as she slams into my body and disappears completely. The impact feels like an ice-cold dagger piercing straight through my chest, stealing my breath and sending shockwaves of pain through every nerve.

I start stumbling backward, shaking my head in desperate denial. "No, no, no, no," I whisper frantically, but there's no stopping what's happening.

All the spirits begin moving at once.

Every single ghost in the ballroom turns toward me and charges with terrifying purpose. They come from every direction—some running, some gliding, some moving so fast they're blurs of translucent energy. The first few slam into me simultaneously, each impact sending waves of supernatural agony through my body.

"Kat!" Malachi calls, but I can't see him through the relentless onslaught of spirits. They're hitting me multiple at a time now—five, six, seven ghosts slamming into my body and vanishing in rapid succession.

Each collision sends electric jolts of pain through my nervous system, like being struck by lightning over and over again. My vision starts to blur, and my knees begin to buckle under the assault.

"Viktor Volkov is dead," a man announces somewhere in the distance, seeming to echo from very far away.

Then everything goes black.

Chapter Eighteen

LOG EIGHTEEN - SOMATIC SURGE: DURING STRESS TESTING, HER STRENGTH INCREASES EXPONENTIALLY. WE FEAR THE CEILING FOR THIS POWER DOES NOT EXIST.

THE STERILE WHITE walls and pristine white tile floors of this endless hallway stretch out before me, making my skin crawl with unease.

I keep walking past door after door, each one equipped with small rectangular windows that I'm too afraid to peer through. The glass is frosted, offering only vague shadows of movement beyond, but something about those glimpses fills me with a dread I can't explain.

When I finally reach the end of the seemingly infinite corridor, a man dressed entirely in white emerges. His clothing blends so perfectly with the surroundings that he's almost invisible until he moves, pulling open one of the imposing double doors in front of me.

I step inside, and the scene that greets me is both familiar and deeply disturbing. A long, polished table stretches across the center of the bare room, surrounded by occupied chairs. People sit at regular intervals around the table, but I can't make out anyone's face. They're all blurred and distorted, as if I'm looking at them through water or thick glass.

The figure to my right pulls out an empty chair with a soft scraping sound that echoes unnaturally in the silent room. The voice catches me off guard.

"Now, Viridian, please recount for us ..."

I gasp awake, shooting upright with my heart hammering against my ribs.

"Hey, I've got you," Malachi says gently from the chair he's pulled up directly beside the bed.

I look around, disoriented, and realize he's still wearing his navy suit from the party. I glance down at myself. I'm still in my lavender dress, though it's wrinkled and slightly torn at the hem. But we're definitely in a different room than before, somewhere I don't recognize.

"Where are we? What's going on?" I ask, my voice hoarse as he leans forward so our knees are touching.

"I had to get you out of there, so I grabbed our things and brought you here. This is a more discreet hotel a few blocks away from that nightmare. It's safe here," he explains, scanning my face with concern.

I look him up and down carefully. He's surprisingly pristine, considering the supernatural massacre we just survived—his suit is barely wrinkled, no visible blood or wounds.

"Do you feel all right? Are you hurt or exhausted? What the hell happened with your abilities back in the ballroom?" he asks, his questions coming rapid-fire.

I glance around the modest but clean room, trying to process everything. "How did you even manage to get me here?" I ask, puzzled. "How did you carry me and all our stuff several blocks through that carnage?"

"Really?" His eyebrows shoot up. "Are you seriously answering my questions with more questions? Kat, are you hurt? Do you feel okay? You were unconscious, for fuck's sake."

His frustrated tone makes me laugh despite everything. "I feel fine actually. How long was I out?"

He glances at his watch. "Over an hour."

This isn't right. After crossing the Veil, I should be unconscious for hours, maybe days. Instead, I'm here perfectly fine after tearing the thing apart. What the hell did Bash's procedure do to me?

"What happened tonight after I blacked out?" I ask, running my fingers through my tangled hair and pushing it back over my shoulders.

"Viktor's dead, but he wasn't killed by one of your spirits. He was stabbed right through the heart."

"I remember hearing that right before I passed out. Who do you think killed him?" I pause, my mind racing as the memories flood back. "And how the hell were the spirits killing people? You saw that, right? I mean, you didn't see them, but you saw necks snapping and people falling to the ground."

"I saw," he confirms. "You've never witnessed anything like that before?"

I meet his intense stare. "No, never. It was like they were possessed or being controlled by someone else. They weren't acting like normal spirits, if that makes any sense. I wasn't telling them to kill anyone, if that's what you're thinking."

He nods slowly, looking away. "I don't know if this is even possible, but after you blacked out on the stage, I had the strangest sensation. It was similar to how we felt in the car when we were leaving my father's compound, and when I looked up across the room, I saw Meadow staring directly at you."

I shake off the chill I feel creeping up my spine. "You think Meadow was controlling the spirits I summoned?"

The possibility seems both impossible and terrifyingly

plausible. At this point, I think anything could be true. They were all staring directly at me, responding to my presence.

"I honestly don't know," Malachi admits, scrubbing his face. "I carried you out of there as quickly as possible, but I did have to pass back through the ballroom to get our things. I made a mental note of everyone I saw along the way. A lot of the people with their necks snapped were individuals my father had serious conflicts with."

The implication of what he's saying hits me, and I don't like this feeling, like I'm not in complete control of my own abilities. I don't fully understand what happened or how I was used.

"My aunt and father are both already spinning lies about what happened tonight, each of them pushing their own twisted agenda," he says bitterly, leaning back in the chair.

"Oh, this should be good. Tell me," I say, reaching out to touch his leg. I know he'd hoped we might prevent bloodshed tonight instead of starring in someone else's horror show.

"Irina hitched a ride with us here. It gave us a few minutes to talk, and she's relocated all of her people to this hotel and the one next door." He runs both hands down the back of his neck. "She's telling everyone the attack was vigilantes from a nearby gutter zone. Poor, desperate people finally fighting back against their oppressors."

"That's complete bullshit," I howl. "I've met desperate people, and they don't usually coordinate supernatural neck-snapping massacres with fucking fear gas grenades. Who's actually buying this crap?"

"More people than you'd think. She's claiming the district leaders are losing control and that citizens are starting to revolt because they're tired of being starved out. And she's not wrong about the underlying problems. People are suffering. But you and I both know that bloodbath wasn't some grassroots uprising."

"So let me get this straight. Her master plan is to stir up a civil war? Systematically pick off the ruling families, and the ones she can't murder directly, she'll trick into killing each other or get the public angry enough to do her dirty work?"

"Bingo," he says.

"Then she swoops in like some benevolent savior to restore peace and order, with you as her shiny new poster boy for a bright future."

Malachi closes his eyes and lets out a laugh that's completely devoid of humor. "Christ, when you put it like that, it sounds even worse."

"I'm not done," I continue, getting more worked up. "If I had to bet money, I'd say she's the one who had Viktor killed too. Either she and your father are trying to outdo each other, or they're planning to eliminate everyone else first and save their epic showdown for the finale."

"You know what the really fucked-up part is?" he asks, looking at me. "I think you might be right."

"I hate politics," I mutter. "I hate how these people treat human lives like game pieces."

"I haven't told you what my father's saying yet," he says, and I give him a sideways glance.

"Do I even want to know?"

He smirks. "Probably not. His news outlet already put out a statement warning about how dangerous Avids are and claiming this attack was entirely supernatural, a rogue Avid losing control and slaughtering innocent people."

I burst out laughing. It's a deranged, slightly hysterical laugh, and I quickly cover my mouth when I see the lopsided grin Malachi is giving me.

"That's really rich coming from him. What a complete asshole," I say, shaking my head before continuing. "The man who kept me as his personal weapon is now warning people about dangerous Avids."

"It's not only that. He mentioned a new procedure they're developing to ensure complete Avid compliance," Malachi says.

I get up, feeling the sudden need to move and get some fresh air before I lose what's left of my sanity. I head over to the sliding glass door and push it open, stepping out into the frigid night air.

We're on the top floor of the hotel, and all I can see stretching out before me are dark skies that are surprisingly clear for this frozen wasteland. I can even make out actual stars twinkling through the sparse clouds drifting overhead.

Frost and snow cover the edges of the balcony and cling to the railing in delicate, crystalline patterns. I run my hand through a small pile of powdery snow that's accumulated in the corner, letting the cold bite into my skin as I look up. Fresh snowflakes glitter down all around me like tiny diamonds, catching what little light filters up from the city below. Mish appears on the railing, tongue lolling out as she looks up at me, then twirls around a few times until she finds a good spot to settle down, making me smile.

Malachi comes out to stand beside me, already starting to shrug out of his suit jacket.

"No," I say, stopping him mid-motion. "I want to feel the cold."

I know Malachi doesn't think tonight was my fault, but those spirits answered my call. Even if Meadow directed them after, I'm the one who tore down the Veil. I'm the one who screamed into the void. I wanted to save people tonight, and instead I became exactly what Marco always said I was, a demon. A killer. A weapon.

I can sit here and tell myself that no one in that ballroom was truly innocent, but does that mean they deserved to die?

Does being complicit in an evil system warrant having your neck snapped? When did I become the kind of person who weighs human lives on a scale, deciding who gets to live and who gets to die?

The worst part is how torn I feel about it. Half of me is horrified by the bloodshed, replaying the sound of breaking bones and watching those bodies crumple to the floor. But there's another part of me—a part that disturbs me—that feels satisfied. Relieved. Like maybe some kind of justice was finally served.

What kind of person does that make me?

The world feels so broken, so impossibly fucked up, and I feel like I'm drowning in the weight of it all. What started with my hunger to escape Marco's control has spiraled into something so much bigger, so much more dangerous than I ever imagined. Now I'm standing in the middle of a war I didn't ask to fight in with powers I can't fully understand or control.

I want to save lives. I lie awake at night thinking about those labs, about the Avids and creatures being tortured behind closed doors, about the trafficking that still happens every day. I want to tear those places apart and set everyone free. But it's more than that. I want to fix everything. I want children in the gutter zones to have enough food. I want people to stop being bought and sold like cattle. I want a world where someone like me doesn't have to exist, where supernatural abilities aren't something to be feared or weaponized.

But how can one person change an entire world? How can someone who can't even control her own gift possibly take on centuries of systemic corruption and evil? Some days I feel like I'm a mouse trying to move a mountain, and the mountain keeps getting bigger while I get smaller.

I see a shooting star streak across the endless dark sky,

burning bright before disappearing into nothing. And somehow, despite everything, it gives me a flicker of hope.

Maybe that's all any of us can be. A brief light in the darkness, burning as bright as we can for as long as we can, hoping someone else will see it and remember that even in the worst of times, beautiful things can still exist.

"Hey, you. Where did you go just now?" Malachi's fingers brush my arm before his hand wraps around my wrist, tugging me closer.

I rest my palm against his chest, feeling the steady thrum of his heartbeat beneath my hand. He holds my waist, eyes locked on mine as if he can read the thoughts swirling in my head—or at least I'm sure he wishes he could.

"I was thinking how overwhelming everything feels when I look at it on a grand scale."

He brushes a few stray hairs from my face, then cups my cheek in his palm, grounding me in the way only he can. "Then stop looking at the world and keep your eyes on me. When it feels too big, remember you don't have to face it alone anymore."

"When this is all over, what do you think we'll do?" I ask, focusing on the little gold flecks and starbursts scattered through his dark eyes like constellations I could get lost in.

"Sleep for a week. Maybe learn how to have normal problems, like arguing about what to have for dinner," he says, his smile softening as he twirls a strand of my hair around his fingers.

"I'd like that. Normal sounds perfect," I whisper, it tastes bittersweet.

Normal does sound perfect ... and completely alien. I can barely remember what it feels like to worry about mundane things like grocery shopping or whether it will be cold outside.

But somewhere deep down, I already know what neither of us wants to admit out loud. This will never really be over.

People like us don't get to retire to quiet suburban lives. We don't get white picket fences and Sunday morning pancakes. We're too deep in this world of shadows and blood and supernatural politics to ever truly escape it.

But for now, standing here in his arms with snowflakes melting in my hair, I can pretend that someday we might.

Chapter Nineteen

LOG NINETEEN - BEHAVIORAL NOTE: WHEN
WATCHED, SHE SITS SILENT, POSTURE PERFECT,
EXPRESSION BLANK. WHEN SHE THINKS SHE IS
ALONE, HER SHOULDERS SLUMP. SHE LOOKS SAD.

"I'M TAPPING OUT," Aurora gasps, slapping her arm frantically against the padded training mat.

I immediately release the chokehold, and we both collapse onto our backs, chests heaving like we ran a marathon. Sweat drips down my temples, and my muscles are screaming in that satisfying way that means we pushed ourselves today.

"Fuck, I'm completely wiped," I pant, staring up at the bright lights of the Depths training room.

"Damn right we are." Aurora grins, still catching her breath. "We're becoming some seriously fierce bitches, if I do say so myself." She gives me a weak but triumphant elbow to the ribs.

It's been two weeks since the Southern District Massacre Ball, and we've been training like our lives depend on it, which they probably do.

Malachi kept pushing back our mission date, insisting we need more preparation time. Normally I'd be climbing the walls, arguing that we're wasting precious time while people suffer in those labs. But I'm grateful for the extra training. The ball showed me how little control I really have over my abilities when the stakes get high.

The political landscape has shifted a bit since that night. Irina is still in the South, apparently providing stability during this difficult transition, which really means she's systematically installing her own people in positions of power while the surviving district leaders are too traumatized to stop her. Meanwhile, Rain's entire team has been permanently stationed at Marco's former compound. Irina's not giving up that strategic stronghold now that she controls it.

And Marco's made himself quite comfortable in Viktor's sprawling estate. As Viktor's twin brother, he inherited everything by default—which I'm sure was exactly what Irina intended when she had Viktor killed. Or maybe Marco had him killed. I know he never trusted him, and this way he can be closer to his sick experiments. Now the bastard is literally sitting on top of the very lab we need to infiltrate, probably torturing more innocent Avids while we sit here perfecting our combat roles. Okay, he's not right on top of it, but he's close, too close for comfort.

"Go get changed and meet me by the elevators. I have an idea," Aurora announces, jumping to her feet and offering me her hand with a mischievous grin.

"Why do I get the feeling your idea is going to get us killed?" I narrow my eyes at her as she grasps my hand and pulls me up effortlessly. Geez, she really is stronger than she looks.

"Only one way to find out. Now, move your ass," she snipes over her shoulder as she bounces toward the gym door, red curls flying.

I head down to the bedroom Malachi and I have been sharing. It's a far cry from his cozy cabin, but it'll have to do since he's convinced returning there is a death wish. I throw on leggings and a sweater, figuring whatever Aurora has planned will either require running or hiding.

"Took you long enough," Aurora says when I meet her at the elevators, tapping her foot impatiently.

"That was literally three minutes, and I'm still gross from sparring," I protest.

"You're fine. Besides, we're not going anywhere fancy." She hits the button for the surface level. "Trust me."

"Famous last words," I mutter as we ascend.

"Oh, live a little," she laughs, practically vibrating with excitement as we step outside into the biting wind.

Cade's jeep is on the street, surrounded by other Syndicate vehicles, making this sleepy neighborhood of tract houses look like a government stakeout.

"Please tell me Cade knows we're commandeering his ride," I say, climbing into the passenger seat.

"Commandeering sounds so official. We're borrowing it." Aurora turns the key. "Along with some of their expense account. When's the last time you did something for fun?"

The engine purrs to life, and despite everything going on right now, I find myself grinning like an idiot. "You know what? You're absolutely right."

"Malachi is going to kill me when he finds out I let you take me to a deserted part of town," I say as we park behind a dilapidated mall.

The building is a disaster—broken windows covered with plywood, graffiti covering every surface, chunks of concrete missing from the walls. This place looks like it could be smack in the middle of a gutter zone.

"Didn't anyone ever tell you not to judge a book by its cover?" she says, hopping out of the jeep with infectious energy and shooting me a broad smile as she loops her arm through mine.

Despite the perpetual cold, the sun is actually out today, making the temperature almost tolerable for once.

"Sure, but this is a far cry from a book, Aurora. This looks like we might get murdered before I even see whatever surprise you have planned," I quip.

She lets go of my arm and pushes open one of the heavy mall doors. I follow her inside, and the interior matches the exterior perfectly—abandoned storefronts, broken tiles, the musty smell of decay and neglect.

I glance at a section of wall near the entrance where someone has spray-painted in bright blue letters, "EAT THE RICH OR FEED THEM TO THE GUTTER RATS."

"Nice. Real classy, Aurora. How do you even know about places like this?" I ask, gesturing at our lovely surroundings.

"I have my ways. Now, come on," she says, tugging me forward with barely contained excitement.

We walk past several clothing stores with knocked-over mannequins and piles of ransacked merchandise scattered across the floors. We pass a toy store that's been picked clean, except for one disturbing clown doll in the window that seems to be staring directly at us with painted-on eyes.

I shiver and quicken my pace, following Aurora down a long, broken escalator that creaks under our weight.

Suddenly, I hear something unexpected cutting through the mall's eerie silence.

"What is that? Do you hear that?" I ask, looking at her and slowing my steps.

It sounds like voices and laughter mixed with electronic beeping and shooting sounds. Maybe there's an old movie playing somewhere in this abandoned place.

"That's exactly where we're headed," Aurora says.

We pass by a dozen more empty storefronts, their security gates pulled down and covered in more colorful graffiti, then round a corner and approach a shop that has black reflective paper taped up over all its windows so we can't see inside.

"Is this where we get murdered?" I tease.

Aurora pulls the door open with a flourish, waving me inside ahead of her. "After you, my lady."

I step through the doorway, and my jaw drops.

Holy shit. It's a fully functional arcade from several decades ago that somehow still works. Neon lights flash in every color imaginable, casting rainbow glows across the space. Classic arcade games are lit up throughout the room, and there are actually people here playing them, laughing, and having fun like there isn't a care in the world.

I walk past a girl jumping and dancing on glowing blue-and-pink squares, following arrows on the screen above. Aurora and I can't help but dance along with the beat, giggling as we pass.

Then I spot a guy on a motorcycle game, leaning dramatically side to side as he navigates a virtual racetrack.

"How is this even possible?" I ask.

She shrugs casually. "You know Atlas, the guy who works in the secret gardens in the Depths?"

"You mean the Enchanted Forest?" I correct her.

"Yeah, whatever it's called. Atlas told me about this place. Apparently, he has a friend who's an Avid with a gift for restoring and powering old electronics."

Holy crap, that's so cool. "So this guy basically runs a speakeasy arcade as a hobby?"

"His name's Tuck, but I don't see him around right now."

I whirl around to face her. "You've hung out with him?"

"Maybe I have," she says, scrunching her nose at me with a wink. "Now, what should we play?"

I guess I'll let her keep her secrets for now, but I'm definitely grilling her about this Tuck character later.

I bite my bottom lip and spin around, eyeing all the free games. "Oh, this one!"

I grab her hand and pull her toward a zombie hunting game. We both squeeze into the booth and pull the curtain closed, encapsulating us in darkness. The seats start vibrating as the screen flickers to life, and we each grab one of the plastic guns attached to the console.

"Don't we have enough scary stuff in real life? You had to choose the creepiest game in here," Aurora complains, but she's already aiming her gun at the screen and hitting start.

"What can I say? I have a thing for dead things," I tease, shooting at a zombie that jumps directly at the screen.

"You know, for someone who deals with actual dead people, you're terrible at shooting fake ones," Aurora fires back as she nails a zombie right between the eyes with perfect aim.

"Keep it up and I'm going to start asking serious questions about arcade boy," I warn her.

She laughs as she takes down another zombie. "There's nothing to tell, really. But he does have this terribly attractive man bun."

I burst out laughing and completely miss the zombie that lunges toward us. "A man bun? Really?"

"So when are you and Malachi getting married?" she asks casually while reloading. "I've seen how he looks at you. Are you ready to become the wife of the future leader of Sunderlands?"

The question catches me completely off guard. I've never really thought about it like that. If the district ruling families were actually taken down and the territories united again under one leader, they probably wouldn't even call it Sunderlands anymore. Maybe it would go back to being the United States, the United Districts, or the United Territories …

"Hello! You're going to get us killed!" Aurora bumps my

shoulder, and I realize I've been letting zombies overrun our position while I got lost in thought.

"Sorry! I can only think about one thing at a time right now. I'm worried about all of us surviving next week, not planning my wedding with Malachi."

She makes a disapproving clicking sound with her tongue. "Yep, you definitely needed to get out today. You've been way too serious lately."

I smirk and glance over at her. "Maybe you're right about—"

The screen flashes red as we both get devoured by a massive horde of zombies.

"Oops," I say sheepishly.

"I want to play the claw machines, then we can find something to eat," Aurora says, practically bouncing over to the far wall where more than a dozen different claw machines are lined up like colorful sentinels, each one filled with random prizes and stuffed animals.

"Here, take this and try one," she says, pressing a little game card into my hand before we split up to tackle different machines.

After failing about ten times straight, I can see how these things become seriously addictive. It's complete bullshit. The claw closes perfectly around a stuffed animal, lifts it up, then mysteriously releases it right before reaching the prize slot. The whole thing is obviously rigged.

"I'm going to order us some food," I call over to Aurora, who's completely absorbed in her own battle with a machine full of plush unicorns.

She waves me off without looking away from her target.

I walk across the arcade to a small order window I spotted when we first came in. Sure enough, there's a handwritten menu taped up next to the opening, and I scan the options with growing amusement.

Noodle Nests. Instant ramen formed into crispy bowls with canned veggies. That sounds okay, I guess. I keep reading. Packed protein bars. No description on those, but that's dangerous. The protein is probably from bugs. I end up ordering us each a couple of tofu tacos. It sounds like the safest option, and you can practically make tofu taste like anything with the right spices.

The young man behind the grease-stained window slides two mismatched plates through the slot, the metal scraping against chipped paint. Steam rises from the tacos, carrying the scent of cumin and something vaguely meat-like that definitely isn't meat. I claim one of the rickety benches next to the air hockey table, its surface scarred with decades of carved initials and burn marks.

Aurora bounces over with that infectious grin of hers, clutching something behind her back.

"It's for you, a Boston, just like Mish." She hands me the most adorable little plush Boston Terrier stuffed animal.

"Aw, it does look like Mish," I say, examining the lopsided face and oversized button eyes. "Did you win this, or did it fall out of the machine when you kicked it?"

"Ha, ha, very funny. Give me a taco." Aurora grabs the plate, and I stuff the cute little stuffed animal in my jacket pocket.

"AW, no, no, no, no, really? Come on." Aurora jogs over to where the jeep was parked, and we find an empty parking lot decorated with broken glass.

"Fuck, Cade is going to murder you," I say, unable to hide

my grin despite our predicament. We got so caught up in arcade games that I lost track of time completely, and now darkness is setting in. "We better get moving before this gets worse."

No one knows where we are, and when the sun disappears, this place is going to turn into a frozen wasteland. Thank God for Aurora's internal heater.

"Moving where, exactly? Our ride got jacked," she says, gesturing dramatically at the empty space.

"Wow, really? I hadn't noticed the giant missing vehicle," I deadpan. "We walk, genius. Unless you've got a teleportation power you've been hiding from me."

Aurora kicks at a glass bottle, sending it skittering across the pavement. "Great. A lovely evening stroll through murder alley."

"Come here, drama queen." She pulls her hood up and zips her jacket to her chin. I mirror her movements, we need to look like we belong here, not like two lost girls with pockets full of arcade tokens. When she links her arm through mine, her gift flows through me, chasing away the evening chill instantly.

As we walk away from the mall, it's mostly flat wastelands, huge fields of snow stretching endlessly, with the occasional farmhouse breaking up the monotony. It's when we have to cut through the more densely populated area that we pick up the pace.

The tract housing where the Depths are located are all nice, not fancy, but clean and well-kept. The neighborhood we have to pass through to get back there? A little sketchy. Yards are cluttered with junk, turning the pristine snow into a graveyard of rusted car parts, broken furniture, and mystery debris. The houses look tired, paint peeling like an old sunburn, windows barred up tight. This isn't gutter zone bad, but it's definitely not prime real estate for two girls taking an evening stroll.

I spot a large bonfire crackling in someone's front yard up ahead, three guys huddled around it clutching bottles, their laughter echoing off the empty street.

"Let's cross here," I whisper to Aurora.

"No, it's fine. Come on," she says, all casual confidence.

"Didn't you literally call this murder alley? Now suddenly we're invincible?" I mutter, and she giggles.

"Let them try something. I'll turn their cozy little bonfire into a fireworks show so fast they won't know what hit them."

We're almost past their house when one of them calls out, "Hey! Ladies!" His voice has that slurred edge that comes with too many drinks.

I keep walking, pulling Aurora along with me, but she's already slowing down.

"Don't stop," I mutter under my breath.

"Where you going so fast?" Another voice joins in, and I can hear footsteps crunching through the snow behind us. "It's cold out there. Come warm up by our fire!"

The third guy laughs, making my skin crawl. "Yeah, we got plenty of heat to share."

Aurora's grip tightens on my arm, and I feel her temperature spike, not the gentle warmth from before but something hotter, more volatile.

"Keep walking," I whisper, but the footsteps are getting closer now, and I can smell the alcohol and smoke coming off them.

"Hey, I'm talking to you!" The first guy's voice is sharper now, annoyed. "Don't be rude."

Great. We're definitely not getting out of this without a confrontation.

"You know what? You're right. We are being rude." Aurora stops walking and turns around, that dangerous smile spreading across her face, the one I've seen right before she does something spectacular and stupid.

"Aurora, no," I hiss, but she's already stepping toward them.

"We'd love to warm up," she calls out sweetly. "Your fire looks so ... cozy."

The three guys exchange looks, clearly not expecting this response. The leader, a tall, scraggly guy with more facial hair than sense grins and gestures toward their yard.

"Now that's more like it. Come on over here, girls."

I watch Aurora's hands start to glow faintly at her sides, hidden in her jacket pockets. This is about to go very, very badly.

"Actually," the second guy says, stepping closer and looking us up and down, "you two look like you got money. Nice jackets, clean hair. You're not from around here."

"What's in those pockets?" the third one demands, and suddenly this isn't about warming up by their fire anymore.

Aurora's voice is sugary sweet. "You really want to find out?"

"Aurora," I warn but can already feel the heat radiating off her, and the guys are starting to notice something's wrong.

The leader's expression shifts from drunk and friendly to something uglier. "Hand over whatever you got, and maybe we'll let you walk away. After we've had some fun with you first, of course."

Okay, asshole.

I was going to try and deescalate this situation, but now I'm thinking this could be good practice. Before I have a chance to second-guess my decision, one of the guys grabs my jacket and pulls me close. His breath reeks of cigarettes as he leers at me. "Come here with those pretty eyes. I'll give you something to look at."

Gross.

I knee him in the balls and kick him when he doubles over. I'm not entirely sure what he was insinuating, but I have a feeling it was something inappropriate.

I glance back at Aurora, who throws her hand out toward the bonfire. Flames shoot up into the sky, becoming a massive tunnel of fire taller than the fucking house. It brightens the entire area like daylight, and on closer inspection, I can see the men's faces, which are all scarred and missing teeth. My guy recovers quickly and comes at me again. I fend him off while one of the other men screams in pain. I can only assume Aurora's giving him a taste of her gift.

"Let's get out of here! These bitches are crazy!" one of the men shouts as they scramble to gather their shit and take off down the street.

I turn to Aurora, whose red hair is whipping around her face like she's standing in the center of her own personal inferno. "That was too easy. It wasn't even fun," she huffs, sounding genuinely disappointed.

"Aurora," I breathe, her name escaping with a plume of mist in the frigid air.

The chill claws its way back into my bones with skeletal fingers despite the inferno still raging beside us. I look down and watch in horror as tendrils of absolute darkness begin to bleed up through the pristine snow, spreading like spilled ink across paper. The blackness moves with purpose, with hunger, devouring the white ground beneath our feet until nothing remains but shadow upon shadow.

Aurora's towering fire begins to flicker. The flames stutter and gasp like dying breaths before the darkness swallows them whole, leaving us in a profound cold.

"What is happening?" Aurora's voice is barely more than a whisper, as if speaking too loudly might wake something better left sleeping.

I cannot answer. My throat has turned to ash. Goosebumps rise across my flesh. I know this unholy chill and sense reality bending at the edges. I have felt it twice before, and each time it came with the same person.

Emerging from within the darkness, she appears across the yard. Her mouth is no longer the grotesque prison of black thread I remember. Instead, festering scabs ring her lips where the stitches once bound her mouth shut. The sight makes my stomach lurch.

Chapter Twenty

LOG TWENTY - EFFICIENCY TEST: SHE NO LONGER REACHES FOR OBJECTS. THE MIND IS FASTER. WE ASKED HER TO HAND US A CLIPBOARD. IT FLEW ACROSS THE ROOM BEFORE THE WORDS LEFT OUR LIPS.

MEADOW'S obsidian eyes lock onto mine, and I feel her stare searing my skin. Her ravenous leer is suffocating, as if death itself learned to walk upright and wear a girl's face.

Aurora lunges forward, but I scream, "Don't let her touch you! She'll track you!"

Meadow's hand snaps out, catching Aurora's wrist. The sound of bone grinding against supernatural strength makes me wince. Aurora's arm bursts into flames, white-hot fire that should melt flesh from bone, but when Meadow releases her, she simply studies the blackened skin of her palm with the detached curiosity of a scientist examining a specimen.

No scream. No flinch. Nothing human at all.

She smiles, a grotesque parody of joy that splits those scabbed lips and reveals teeth stained dark with something I don't want to identify. Every instinct screams at me to run.

She's already touched Aurora.

We're fucked.

"Meadow," I shout, my heart hammering against my ribs,

"you can come with us. We can help you. It doesn't have to be like this."

"Kat, are you insane?" Aurora's snaps. "Look at her. She's not even human anymore."

I shoot Aurora a look and mouth *Shut the hell up.*

"I'm not leaving without you, Katja. He will never let you be free."

Her voice hits me like nails on glass—flat, monotone, like someone's speaking through a broken radio.

"What the hell did he do to you?" I snap, backing up another step.

"Katja, come with me now, or your friend dies." Same robotic delivery, each word precise and emotionless.

Aurora mouths *We can take her.* Before I can respond, Meadow melts backward into her own shadows like smoke.

One second, she's there, and the next, she's gone.

Her arm locks around my throat from behind, cutting off my air. I claw at her forearm, but it's like trying to bend steel. Her other hand grips my shoulder, nails digging through my jacket hard enough to draw blood.

"I have new tricks," she says in my ear, her voice sounding a bit more like herself.

I throw my elbow back hard, connecting with her ribs, but she doesn't even grunt. Aurora shouts something, and I see flames erupting toward us, but Meadow drags me deeper into the shadows.

Aurora comes after us. A stream of fire erupts from her hands, aimed right at Meadow's head. But Meadow dissolves into shadow as the flames reach her, and I drop to the snow, gasping and clutching my throat.

She rematerializes three feet to my left, that same dead expression on her face.

"Shit," Aurora breathes, her hands still glowing with heat. "How are we supposed to hit her if she can do that?"

I roll to my feet, shaking off the dizziness. "Keep her moving. Make her work for it."

Aurora launches another blast while I circle around Meadow's right side. The fire passes through empty air as Meadow vanishes again, reappearing behind Aurora. I lunge forward, throwing a hard right hook at Meadow's ribs. My fist connects with solid flesh, and she staggers. At least she's still solid when she's not shadow-jumping.

Meadow spins toward me, her hand shooting out to grab my wrist. I duck under her reach and sweep her legs. She goes down but rolls backward into darkness, disappearing before she hits the ground.

"This is bullshit," Aurora mutters, flames dancing around her fists as she scans the shadows. "She can't keep this up forever, right?"

Meadow materializes directly between us, close enough that I can smell the antiseptic scent clinging to her clothes. She grabs for Aurora's throat, but Aurora jerks back and sends a concentrated burst of fire at Meadow's chest. Meadow dissolves again as I throw a punch at where her jaw should be.

We're fast and coordinated, but she's always one step ahead. Every time we think we have her cornered, she melts away.

The sound of heavy boots pounding through snow reaches us, and suddenly Cade and Malachi burst through the darkness, weapons drawn.

"What the hell?" Cade startles when Meadow rematerializes right in front of him.

"Move!" Malachi shouts, throwing a blade, but Meadow's already gone again. He rushes to my side. "Are you all right?"

Aurora blurts out, "She's here for Kat."

"Apparently, she can move through shadows now," Cade adds, scanning the darkness around us.

I turn to Malachi. "Do you have any Avidian?"

He shakes his head. "No."

"Avidian? You're lucky we have a few blades. We didn't think you guys would be getting into trouble, but I guess we should have known better," Cade says. Aurora lets out a loud huff.

I think for a moment that maybe Meadow got spooked with all of us here, but her darkness hasn't dissipated. The black smoke still billows around us waist-high, thick and unnatural.

"Stay close," Malachi mutters, drawing a long shiny dagger from his jacket. "If she can teleport, she could come from anywhere."

She appears next to Cade, and he slices across her arm as Malachi springs toward her. She vanishes instantly, but I'm already moving, anticipating her next move. Malachi must be thinking the same thing because he hurls his dagger at the space behind me where she's most likely to go.

Meadow materializes directly into its path, the steel burying itself to the hilt in her abdomen. She staggers, gripping the weapon's handle, and pulls it free with a wet, horrible sound. Bright-red blood spurts out of her wound in pulsing bursts. The blade must have severed her abdominal aorta.

Her black eyes lock onto mine as she crumples to her knees, then collapses backward into the snow. I rush forward despite Malachi's attempt to stop me, something deep inside compelling me to reach her.

I press both hands against the gushing wound, but it's useless. The blood seeps between my fingers, warm against the cold air.

"Meadow, I'm sorry," I whisper. "I'm so sorry I couldn't save you."

She tries to speak, but blood bubbles up instead. I lean closer, my heart breaking. She may have come to capture me, to hurt us, but none of this was her choice. She's another Avid, another victim of Marco's experiments, a weapon for him to wield. Whatever they did to turn her into this hollow, robotic thing must have been unthinkable.

"I've seen …" she gasps.

The others crowd around us, listening.

"I've seen you down there, Katja," she says with her final exhale. Her eyes drift past us, unfocused, and the unnatural darkness melts away like morning fog.

"She's gone," Malachi says softly, his hand gentle on my shoulder as he helps me stand.

"HOW DID you know where to look for us?" I ask Malachi from the passenger seat as he navigates the empty streets back to the Depths.

"I told Bash where we were going. I'm not completely reckless," Aurora pipes up from the back seat, and I can't help but smirk.

"When it started getting late, I got worried," Malachi says, his knuckles tight on the steering wheel.

Cade leans forward and taps my headrest. "The pillar of fire shooting fifty feet into the air might have been a clue too."

Aurora snorts. "Great, so I'm a walking flare gun now." Her snickering is humorless. "Meadow wasn't even supposed to be that powerful, and we could barely touch her."

I twist in my seat to face her. The confidence that usually radiates from Aurora has dimmed, replaced by something I rarely see in her—doubt.

"She had advantages we didn't expect. Shadow teleporta-

ration, enhanced strength, no pain response. When we hit the lab, we'll be prepared. Full team, proper weapons, Avidian to level the playing field."

tion, enhanced strength, no pain response. When we hit the lab, we'll be prepared. Full team, proper weapons, Avidian to level the playing field."

Aurora nods, but her fingers fidget with the zipper of her jacket. "I know the plan makes sense." She pauses, watching the dark landscape blur past her window. "I always thought my fire made me untouchable. Tonight, I learned otherwise. We're walking into something way bigger than us."

"Hey, what do you think Meadow meant when she said she saw you down there?" Cade muses thoughtfully.

"I'm not sure. Maybe she saw me at Marco's compound before," I say, but in trut,h I have no idea what she meant. She clearly wasn't well.

The rest of the car ride back is silent, and Malachi and I leave before I get to hear Aurora break it to Cade that his car was stolen.

I take a shower, desperate to wash the blood off me and erase everything that happened tonight. Once I'm dressed in a silky black nightgown and smelling fresh, I feel my muscles finally relax from the warm water. I step out into the bedroom.

"What are you doing?" I ask Malachi, who's perched on the edge of the bed.

"I thought about joining you in that shower," he says, his voice low, "but then we'd never make it to where I want to take you."

"And where exactly is that?" I move closer, positioning myself between his knees and threading my fingers through his damp hair.

His hands slide up the back of my thighs, pulling me against him until the silk of my nightgown brushes his chest. For a moment, I think he's going to give in to the distraction. Instead, he lifts me easily and sets me back on the bed, just out of his reach.

"Nice try," he says, with that maddening grin. "Get your shoes on. I have something to show you."

After everything that happened tonight, his playfulness is a bit unexpected but exactly what I need. "Please tell me it's not another abandoned mall."

He laughs, moving toward the door. "Trust me. And don't change. You're perfect like this."

The way his eyes rake over me makes me tingle. I slip into my loafers and grab my jacket, feeling oddly rebellious about wandering around the Depths in nothing but silk.

We get in the elevator, and I try to see what button Malachi hits, but he quickly steps in front of the panel, blocking my view.

"Seriously? What are you, twelve?" I laugh, trying to peek around him.

"Close your eyes and don't open them until I say," he orders, that commanding tone making my stomach flutter.

I scrunch my nose at him. "This is ridiculous."

"Eyes. Closed. Now."

"Fine, but if you're taking me to some creepy basement, I'm never forgiving you." I squeeze my eyes shut, crossing my arms dramatically.

When the elevator dings and the doors swish open, I'm about to peek, but Malachi scoops me up and hoists me over his shoulder so my arms dangle down his back.

"Malachi!" I yell, laughing despite myself.

"No peeking," he says, giving my ass a playful smack that makes me yelp.

"I wasn't peeking! I was—ow! Okay, I'll be good."

"That's what I like to hear," he says, satisfied.

I'm dying to look, but I keep my eyes squeezed shut, my heart racing with anticipation. "This better be worth the dramatic kidnapping."

We step through what feels like a sterilizing chamber, cool mist kissing my skin along with that sharp-antiseptic scent that signals we're entering something sacred.

"You're taking me to the Enchanted Forest, aren't you?" The sterile airlock is a dead giveaway.

"Only Bash calls it that," he chuckles.

"I like the name. It suits a place where impossible things grow."

The air shifts as we move deeper. I smell rain-soaked earth and honey-sweet blossoms, the kind of air that makes you believe in magic. Malachi navigates several turns, finally setting me down with gentle hands.

"Open your eyes, love."

The breath leaves my lungs in a rush. Before me spreads a living dream—my garden but elevated beyond memory into something ethereal. Emerald grass carpets the ground like velvet, each blade seeming to shimmer with its own inner light. The pond captures starlight and holds it, making the water itself glow like liquid moonbeams.

Azure forget-me-nots cluster around weathered stones, their petals so vivid blue they seem painted with sky. But it's the weeping willow that steals my breath—beautiful and magnificent. Its branches cascade like a waterfall of green silk like the one in my garden, only hued in a way that only something created with magic could be.

"Malachi, this is ... It's more beautiful than I ever imagined it could be."

"Atlas doesn't simply grow plants," he says softly, watching me with eyes full of tenderness. "He grows dreams. I described your sanctuary to him, but he felt what it meant to you. Every flower, every blade of grass stems from the love you have for this place."

Tearing up, I thought I'd lost this forever, that my one safe harbor had been swept away by the chaos of everything we're fighting. I never thought I'd visit my garden again.

"Come here," he murmurs, guiding me to where a blanket waits beneath the willow tree. The tree's curtain of leaves creates an intimate alcove, and overhead, the enchanted ceiling sparkles with constellations that shift and dance. It's hard to believe we are still underground.

I sink down beside him, the soft grass a cushion beneath us. "Why did you do this? Why go to all this trouble?"

His hand finds mine, fingers intertwining. "Because I wanted to give you back something beautiful. In all this bullshit, you deserve to remember that good things still exist." His thumb traces across my knuckles. "And I needed you to know that wherever you are, wherever we end up, I want to be the person who helps you find home again."

"You are the home I never knew I was searching for."

I look up at him, swallowing hard against the emotion threatening to spill over. After my parents died, after Marco bought me like I was nothing more than a useful object, I never thought I'd have anything good again. When you're used enough, you start to believe you don't deserve better and will never be free. I let myself accept my pretty prison because I thought that was as good as life would ever get for me.

Then this man walked into my world and turned everything upside down in the most beautiful way possible. God, I wish I could describe how he makes me feel without getting all tongue-tied. I'm not used to ... this. To someone caring about what I need instead of what I can give them.

He reaches up, cupping my face with his free hand, thumb brushing away a tear I didn't realize had fallen. "I love you, Katja. And you deserve so much more than the shit this world has thrown at you." His eyes don't leave mine. "All of that ends now. We're going to build something real together that belongs to us."

I lean into his touch, my fingers still playing with his other hand in my lap. "What about your father? The Syndicate? Everything we're fighting against?"

"We're going to tear it all down and build something better in its place," he says, and the fierce determination in his voice makes my heart skip. "No more trafficking, no more owning people, no more children growing up the way we did. We're going to make sure no one else has to suffer like that." His thumb traces my cheek gently. "But we're doing it together, and we're doing it for us. The life we want to build is within reach."

His eyes search mine. "I'm not going anywhere, Katja. Never. You're stuck with me through all of it—the fight, the rebuilding, the future we're going to create."

A laugh bubbles up through my tears. "Promise? Even when I'm being impossible during missions?"

"Especially then." He grins. "I promise you forever, and I keep my promises."

I smile and say, "Did you learn this from one of your spicy romance books."

"That was all me. Though if you want to see what I learned from the novels, that can definitely be arranged." He winks, his hand sliding up my thigh to the edge of my nightgown.

"Uh-uh." I catch his wrist, giving him a cheeky smile. "You have to feed me first."

"Of course," he chuckles, turning his hand to intertwine our fingers instead. "Little demons get cranky when they're hungry, and I happen to like all my limbs attached."

"Smart man," I say, settling back against the tree trunk as he reaches for the stack of containers with his free hand.

He starts lifting lids off, revealing an array of tempting food. "Let's see. We have strawberries. Don't ask how I got them.

They were extremely hard to come by. There's chocolate, some of those little pastries you love, and ..." He grins wickedly as he opens the last container. "Whiskey. Because, apparently, I'm trying to get you drunk in a magical garden."

"Very smooth, Malachi. What's next? Are you going to feed me grapes?" I tease, but I'm already eyeing the strawberries hungrily.

"Don't tempt me," he says, picking up a particularly perfect strawberry and holding it out. "I was thinking we'd start with these and work our way up to the more ... interactive foods."

Chapter Twenty-One

LOG TWENTY-ONE - COLLECTIVE DELUSION:
MULTIPLE STAFF MEMBERS REPORTED HEARING A
HEARTBEAT IN THE WALLS. THE SUBJECT SMILED,
SAYING, "IT'S NOT THE WALLS."

"THERE'S something I need to tell you, and I don't want you to get upset," Malachi says.

I tip my head back to look up at him. We finished eating our romantic feast, and now he's leaning back against the tree. I'm nestled against his chest, having taken off my jacket and draped it over our legs like a makeshift blanket, though the temperature down here is perfectly comfortable.

"Me? Upset? Never," I say, narrowing my eyes at him and wondering what this could possibly be about.

"I need to leave for a day or two to go back to my father's compound and check on the rest of Solace. I can't tell my aunt our plans for the mission, but I should tell someone in case ..."

"In case we all die down there and no one knows what happened to us," I finish for him, and his lips press into a grim line.

"Rain might be a pain in my ass, but I think I can trust her. We practically started Solace together and have been through countless missions." He runs his fingers through my hair absently. "I need her to know in case everything goes sideways."

I don't like the idea of him leaving, but I also don't have any desire to go back to that place. "So you're going to tell Rain our plans, and that's it?"

I roll onto my side, resting my head on his chest where I can hear his heartbeat steady and strong. "Yeah, I need to talk to her about it in person and set some things in order. While I'm gone, you can keep training. We'll leave in under a week unless you change your mind."

The thought is tempting, to run away together, start a new life, and pretend there aren't terrible things happening in this broken world. But what kind of person would I be if I did something like that when I'm in a position to make a real difference?

It's funny how love makes you want to be selfish and self-less at the same time. Part of me wants to grab him and never let go, to find some remote corner of the world where we can just exist together without caring about anyone else's suffering. But the bigger part of me knows I'd hate myself for it. I've spent my whole life being powerless—controlled, owned, used. Now that I finally have the ability to fight back, to protect other people from what I went through, how could I walk away?

Maybe growing up is realizing love doesn't mean hiding from the world together. It means being brave enough to face it side by side, even when staying safe would be so much easier. Even when you're terrified of losing everything you've finally found.

"There's no way I'm changing my mind," I say, letting out a long sigh.

"What is it?" he asks, taking a strand of my hair and wrapping it around his finger.

"I keep thinking we're going to get down there and realize we're in over our heads. That I've dragged us straight into a shitstorm we can't crawl out of and there won't be anyone to save us." The words tumble out, letting my insecurities finally reach the surface.

Malachi cups my jaw, tipping my chin up to look at him. "We don't need saving, Katja. We are the storm."

He says it with such confidence that I wish I could steal a bit of it from him.

"Damn right, they won't know what hit them," I say, flexing my arm to show him my muscles. He chuckles, the sound rumbling through his chest.

"Keep training with the team while I'm gone and get comfortable using the mask so we can all have Avidian on the mission. Bash has made enough for everyone now."

I make a mental note to find Bash tomorrow and ask him about it. I nod, resting my head back on his chest, feeling slightly more settled by his unwavering certainty.

"So when do you plan on leaving?" I ask, tugging his T-shirt up a bit so I can run my hand across his warm skin and the taut muscles of his stomach.

"Tonight," he says.

"What? Is that why you brought me down here, to soften the blow? It's late. When exactly were you planning on telling me?" I scowl, sitting up on my knees to glare at him properly.

"I'm telling you now, and I don't have to meet the pilot for three more hours. You have me all to yourself until then." He gives me that adorable, infuriating smirk that makes me want to hit him and melt all at the same time.

"I can't believe you're leaving tonight. I wanted to spend more time alone with you before the mission." I cross my arms, knowing it's ridiculous to pout over this, but I can't help it.

"That's exactly why I'm leaving tonight after you go to sleep. The sooner I get going, the sooner I get back to you," he says, sitting up and pulling me closer. "Besides, we still have three hours. That's plenty of time for me to make it up to you."

"Oh yeah? What do you have in mind? Going to show me some of those tricks you learned from your romance novels?" I pull my bottom lip between my teeth, anticipation already building.

"Oh, my little demon, the books haven't been written yet for what I want to do to you." His voice dips into a more dangerous tone.

His fingers trace along my jawline, and the promise in his eyes makes my breath catch.

He circles me like a predator, his gaze dark and hungry, and my core heats under the weight of it. When he drops into a crouch in front of me, my back presses into the rough trunk of the willow. He captures my wrists easily, stretching them above my head, pinning me there with a dominance that steals my breath.

His mouth claims mine, warm and delicious, laced with the faint sweetness of whiskey and strawberries. I press my tongue against his, already breathless, already desperate to feel him inside me.

"Patience," he hums against my mouth, smug.

He pulls away and parts my thighs with a sure hand, his eyes dragging over me, his pupils dilated. "I like these tiny straps," he murmurs, toying with one of the delicate silk ribbons on my shoulder. With an unhurried tug, he slips it down, then the other, until the nightgown bunches loosely at my waist, baring my breasts to the cool air and his burning stare.

"Fuck," he breathes before cupping one breast in his hand and lowering his mouth to the other. His tongue flicks over my nipple, followed by a teasing scrape of teeth, and the mix of pleasure and ache has me arching against him, squirming, wet, desperate for more.

"Naughty." He shakes his head slowly when he realizes I don't have any panties on under my nightgown. He pulls me closer, urging my legs farther apart until the nightgown rides up and leaves me completely bare to him. His gaze drops for only a heartbeat before locking back on mine, pupils blown so wide the flecks of gold in his eyes vanish into endless black.

Then he lowers his head to my center, watching me the whole way down. The first press of his mouth against me rips a gasp from my throat, his tongue parting my core and finding the part of me that has my head tipping back against the tree in helpless pleasure.

"Uh-uh," he says, his voice muffled against me, vibrating straight through my core. "Eyes on me. I want to see your face while I fuck you with my tongue."

My head snaps up at his command, eyes wide as they meet his. His lips curve against me in a dark smile. "Good girl," he whispers before his tongue parts me again, dragging a humiliating moan out of me.

I try to hold his gaze, lids heavy, vision hazy, but it's almost impossible to focus when his mouth is wrecking me. His tongue teases my clit, swirling, sucking, licking, until I'm trembling, clawing at the grass, and then he thrusts it inside me. The sudden invasion makes my hips jerk, my breath stutter, my whole body bow toward him.

"Oh god ..." I moan as his dark eyes pin me in place, unrelenting.

"Don't call for him," Malachi growls, flipping me onto my knees like I weigh nothing. "He can't save you from this."

I hear the rustle of fabric as he strips behind me, then his thighs press against the backs of mine as he nudges my knees wider. A sharp squeeze grips my ass, followed by a teasing slap that makes me jolt forward. Then his palm clamps down hard on my hip, anchoring me.

My breath stutters when I feel the thick length of him slide against me, hot and demanding.

"Malachi—" A ragged cry escapes when he thrusts deep, filling me so completely I nearly collapse into the grass.

My pussy clenches around him as he pulls out slowly, then drives back in with brutal force, eliciting cries and moans from my throat. My fingers claw at the earth, desperate for something to hold onto.

He doesn't let up. His arm snakes around my waist, hauling me upright until my bare back presses against the searing heat of his chest. His hand splays between my breasts, keeping me pinned against him as he pounds into me.

"Are you all right?" he rasps into my ear, his breath ragged against my temple.

"Yes," I gasp before releasing another moan.

"Good." His lips graze the side of my face, then press a gentle kiss to my temple. His other hand brushes my hair aside, palm settling on my slick skin as if holding me together while he tears me apart.

He shifts his hips, angling deeper, so deep it feels like there's no part of me he hasn't claimed. My vision goes hazy as his free hand trails down, finding my clit. He rubs and circles, his fingers relentless, dragging me higher and higher while his cock pounds into me.

"Fuck, Katja," he groans, the sound rumbling through him. "You take me so perfectly."

Shuddering, I grip his forearm hard enough to leave marks, my nails digging into his skin as the pressure builds too sharp to bear.

"I love you," he murmurs hoarsely against the crown of my head, kissing me there between thrusts.

My head tips back, lips parting against his throat. "I love you more," I pant, trembling, every nerve on fire.

His lips lift on one side. "Prove it. Fall apart for me."

His fingers flick harder, his pace becomes merciless, and my body shatters. I cry out, the orgasm ripping through me in violent waves, making my knees shake as I convulse against him. He holds me firm, fucking me through it, driving deeper until he finally slams into me one last time.

A groan fills my ears as his release floods me, his grip bruises into my hips, anchoring me while we both catch our breath.

He slowly lets go and settles back against the tree, pulling me into his lap and cradling me there. I lean my head against his chest, skin still warm and damp with sweat, listening to his heart gradually slow from its frantic rhythm.

The garden around us feels like a cocoon—soft grass beneath us, willow branches swaying gently overhead, the magical starlight casting everything in silver. I could fall asleep here, like this, with his arms wrapped around me, and my body completely sated.

I don't know how long we stay like this, and I would be content to spend the rest of the night in his arms, but reality creeps back in. He has to leave. Then I remember my own surprise.

"I almost forgot. I have a surprise for you too." I reach over, grabbing my jacket from our scattered clothes. My heart starts beating faster. I've been waiting for the perfect moment to give him this.

"Oh yeah?" Malachi says, watching as I fumble through the little zippered inside pocket and pull out the vial and hand it to him.

"I had Bash make this for me the other day. It's my essence, my gift, and I wanted you to have it." His fingers close around the small vial, and he examines it the way I did when I first saw it—with wonder and a little wariness.

"I know it looks different than most Avidian, and it's

slightly alarming that it's black," I say quickly. "Bash warned me it was unusual and to be careful with it. I want you to experience what my magic feels like, and if it works ..." I stammer, suddenly feeling shy for no reason. "You could meet Mischka."

"I've wanted nothing more ever since I saw you pretending to cast your first spell," he jokes, and I slap his chest.

"I was petting her! Avids don't cast spells," I say, laughing.

He lifts me off his lap and onto the grass, handing me my nightgown while he reaches for his clothes.

"What are you doing?" I ask, eyebrows raised.

"If I'm going to meet Mischka, I should at least have some clothes on," he says seriously, and I burst out laughing.

"She's a dog, Malachi."

"So?"

"She's literally seen you naked for the past hour." I shake my head, grinning. "Besides, she's already seen you naked plenty of times. You two are practically roommates at this point."

"Great."

Sitting back down beside me, he holds up the vial, watching the dark ribbons of silver move through the liquid like living things.

"Are you sure you want to try it?" I ask, feeling kind of nervous, though I don't know why.

"I have never been so sure of anything as I am of this right now. I want to know what you experience," he says, grabbing me and pulling me in for a quick kiss. Then he pops off the top and breathes in my Avidian.

He shakes his head, and a shiver spreads down his body like electricity through water. "It feels ..." He looks at me, and I'm holding my breath, waiting for him to say something terrible. "Normal. I don't feel anything."

I let out a relieved sigh, my shoulders dropping. "There's only one sure way to test it."

I turn toward the pond where I can see Mish lying peacefully in the soft grass, her ghostly form barely visible in the enchanted starlight. I reach out with my mind, calling for her the way I always do. She disappears instantly, then reappears right next to me in a shimmer of translucent light, tongue lolling as she looks up at me with those familiar, loving eyes.

"Holy shit." Malachi visibly jumps backward, his hand flying to his chest, and I burst out laughing at his reaction.

Mischka notices his shock too and seems delighted by it. She swings her ethereal head from me to him and back again, then lets out an excited yip and starts doing zoomies in wild circles between us, her form flickering in and out of visibility as she runs.

"This is absolutely insane," Malachi breathes. "I mean, I knew it would work, I believed you completely, but I didn't know what to expect. She's real, actually real." His eyes track her movements, wide with amazement, and I can't help the silly, stupid grin spreading across my face watching him experience this for the first time.

"Did you think I was making it up all this time? Poor crazy girl with the imaginary dog she can't actually see?" I tease, a hint of old vulnerability beneath the joke.

His eyes snap to mine, narrowing playfully, but then his smile widens into something warm and reassuring. "Of course not. I've never doubted you, not once. It's ... surreal seeing her with my own eyes. Seeing an actual spirit, a ghost. It's so completely different from any Avidian I've ever used before." He pauses, looking down at his hands. "Getting enhanced strength or speed, having something tangible. That's one thing. But this? Seeing beyond the Veil into another realm entirely? It's ..."

I understand exactly what he means. Even after all this time, seeing the dead still catches me off guard sometimes.

"Can I touch her?"

Mischka moves closer, her ghostly form padding over to sit right next to his leg. She looks up at him expectantly, tail wagging.

"Yes, but it will feel different from anything you've experienced," I warn him, but he's already reaching out with careful, tentative fingers to pet her.

"It feels like ... cool, thick air," he says, his hand moving over her gently. "Like touching mist but with weight." He strokes between her ears, and Mischka's eyes close in contentment.

Then she flickers, her form suddenly becoming more solid, more present, almost like a living dog before fading back to her usual translucent state.

"What was that?" Malachi's eyes snap up to meet mine, startled. "Did you see that?"

"You saw it too?" I ask, my own surprise evident. This is new, even for me.

"Yeah, she was completely solid for a second there, like she was alive again," he says, continuing to pet her as she curls up into a contented ball against his leg.

I chew my lip, considering how much to tell him. "Ever since I went through Bash's machine, things have been ... different. Evolving. Spirits have seemed more substantial at times—more real than ever before. I've been able to touch them more clearly, and they can interact with the physical world in ways that used to be impossible. Like at the party." I pause, uncertainty creeping into my voice. "I'm not sure if it means I'm getting stronger, or if something else entirely is happening to my gift."

His expression shifts, lips pressing together in that familiar look that means he doesn't like what I'm telling him. It's his protective face, the one that appears whenever he thinks I might be in danger.

"Have you told Bash about these changes?" he asks, concerned.

I nod quickly. "A little bit, but honestly, we've been so busy with training and mission prep. He told me that gifts naturally evolve over time and to keep monitoring things as they develop."

Malachi doesn't look satisfied by my answer. I can see the wheels turning in his head, probably planning to have his own conversation with Bash about this. Mish suddenly vanishes without warning, and he jumps slightly, his head whipping around to look for her.

I can't help but laugh at his startled reaction. "Does that happen often?" he asks, his eyes wide with alarm.

"All the time. She has her own agenda, coming and going as she pleases. I'm used to it by now." His shoulders relax slightly at the explanation.

"Kat ..." he says suddenly, his voice taking on a strange quality.

He gets to his feet, and something in his tone makes me follow suit, standing slowly beside him. I find myself looking around the garden, scanning for threats, expecting Damien or some other danger to emerge from the shadows.

"What are you looking at?" I ask, wondering if my Avidian is affecting him in ways we didn't anticipate.

"Don't you feel that?" He tenses up.

I freeze, every nerve in my body suddenly alert. Goosebumps erupt across my flesh like ice water spreading through my veins. I hadn't noticed it before, too caught up in watching him with Mischka, but I feel it now. That familiar, dreadful chill working its way up my spine like cold fingers tracing my vertebrae.

"Yes," I breathe.

"Is this normal? Is this supposed to happen with your Avidian?" he asks urgently, and I instinctively step closer to him.

"This is how I feel right—" Before I can say more, the world tilts sideways.

The garden begins to wobble around us like we're looking through water. Malachi throws his hand out for balance. Our beautiful, magical surroundings start to flicker in and out of existence. One moment, I'm seeing the willow tree and starlit pond. The next, something else entirely is trying to break through.

Without warning, we're somewhere else completely.

I know we're still physically in the garden, because I can feel the soft grass beneath my bare feet, can smell the lingering scent of the flowers Atlas grew for us. But visually, we've been transported. She's brought us here, shown us this place.

I look up to see Malachi taking an unsteady step toward what appears to be a large two-way mirror, his eyes wide and unblinking as he stares through the glass. His face has gone pale, jaw slack with shock.

On the other side of the mirror is the Project Viridian woman—the same one from the photograph, the same face I've seen in my visions before. But this time, she's not standing or walking or trying to talk to me. She's strapped down to what looks like a medical bed, thick leather restraints holding her wrists and ankles immobile. Her head is tilted back, exposing the vulnerable line of her throat.

The room beyond the glass looks sterile and cold—all-white walls and gleaming surfaces, like a hospital operating room. Banks of monitors line the walls, their screens displaying readouts I can't interpret. Medical equipment I don't recognize hums quietly in the background.

"What's happening?" Malachi whispers.

I'm transfixed by the scene unfolding before us. Two men in pristine white coats enter the room. The first carries a clipboard, making notes as he observes the restrained woman. The second holds something that makes my blood run cold—some kind of syringe device with a long needle on it. It gleams under the harsh fluorescent lights, and whatever liquid is inside it seems to swirl with an unnatural luminescence.

The woman on the bed turns her head slightly, and I catch a glimpse of her eyes.

They don't look afraid—they're defiant and eerily calm for someone strapped down to a medical bed.

"Thompson, read me last Tuesday's notes," the man with the syringe says to the one holding the clipboard. He lifts up a few pages and reveals a small notebook, flipping it open.

"Log one hundred and nine, compliance drift. She begged us not to send her back in, but we have no choice. Resistance weakens with each cycle. One day, she may go willingly."

I already suspected, but now I know the journal Malachi found was about this girl. Project Viridian. The first Avid.

"I don't want your damn header. Read me the detailed notes," the man snaps as he jabs the syringe into her arm, then releases her straps.

"Sorry, sir."

They both disappear out of the room, their voices fading.

I look over at Malachi, who is completely frozen, and I start to panic. This is too much for him. This is too much for me sometimes, and I'm used to it. I don't know how this is going to affect him.

The girl slowly sits up, and I think we both stop breathing

as she looks across the room. She stares directly at Malachi through the glass.

The room flickers for a second, and Malachi blinks repeatedly. My head whips from him to the girl as she slides to the foot of the bed and lets her feet hit the ground. She walks directly toward the two-way mirror we stand behind until she's standing inches from Malachi's face, separated only by glass.

"Kat," he whispers.

"Yeah," I say, but then I realize he's not talking to me. He thinks this is real. He thinks that's me.

She holds up her hand and presses it against the glass, her eyes softening before profound sadness settles over her features.

An alarm suddenly blares, and we all jump as the room she's in starts flashing red. A loud, wailing siren vibrates through my mind, the sound so intense it feels like my skull might crack.

"Kat!" Malachi yells louder, hitting his hands against the mirror desperately.

"Malachi, it's okay! It's not real!" I tell him, but it falls on deaf ears. As the siren continues its deafening wail, the girl looks frightened, eyes wide with terror, but her hand stays pressed against the glass even as Malachi starts punching it.

"Malachi!" I scream, covering my ears from the sound. The room flickers again, and Malachi punches the glass so hard it shatters right in the center, spider-webbing outward and distorting the girl's face as shards splinter the surface.

Then it's gone.

The vision disappears along with the sound instantly. When he swings his arm again, it whooshes harmlessly through empty air, making no contact with anything solid.

I reach for him, touching his arm, and he flinches like he was in some kind of trance. When he turns to see me, his eyes are wild, the golden flecks burning so bright they almost seem to glow.

"Katja," he says as he pulls me to his chest and wraps his arms around me, burying his face in my hair.

"Katja, what was that?" he finally manages, his voice shaking.

"I don't think we want to know."

Chapter Twenty-Two

LOG TWENTY-TWO – PERSUASIVE RESISTANCE:
WHEN PRESSED ON DIFFICULT QUESTIONS, SHE
DEFLECTS WITH QUESTIONS OF HER OWN.
RESEARCHERS LEAVE THE SESSIONS BELIEVING
THEY REVEALED TOO MUCH INSTEAD.

"WHO DO YOU THINK SHE IS?" Aurora asks, her voice soft in the dim light of her bedroom. She's lying next to me, head propped up on her hand, red hair spilling over her shoulder like liquid fire. "More importantly, why didn't you tell me you've been seeing her?"

We've all been sleeping in various bedrooms throughout the Depths lately. It's safer that way and easier for early-morning training sessions until we leave on the mission. After Malachi left tonight, I couldn't sleep. My mind kept replaying that vision, the way he'd looked at that woman like she was me. So I'd padded down the hallway in my nightgown and slipped into Aurora's room, seeking the comfort of my best friend.

"I know I should have told you," I admit, picking at the edge of her comforter. "It's ... Everything's been so chaotic lately, and I didn't want to worry everyone when I barely understand what I'm seeing myself. I still don't know what Project Viridian is or how I'm connected to that woman, if I even am."

Aurora flops onto her back with an exaggerated sigh, her

arm thrown dramatically over her eyes. "Kat, come on. You're definitely connected. Evil twin from another dimension is way less likely than, you know, actual family."

I watch as Mish materializes and crosses the room, hopping up onto the bed and settling between us, a cold spot that somehow brings me warmth.

"I wish Malachi hadn't left tonight," I confess, absently reaching out to stroke Mish's translucent fur. "He seemed so shaken by what he saw. The way he looked at her, Aurora ... It was like he thought she was actually me. Then he rushed out of there afterward, barely saying goodbye. I've never seen him that rattled."

Aurora turns her head to study my face, her expression growing serious. "That must have been terrifying for him. Seeing someone who looks like you trapped in some horrific medical experiment? No wonder he freaked out.

"What do you think we'll find in the lab?" Aurora asks, shifting the conversation to darker territory.

I trace patterns on her comforter with my finger, considering. "Honestly? I'm not sure what we're walking into. We know Marco is running experiments on Avids and animals, but the scope of it ..." I shake my head. "How many people are trapped down there? How big is this operation? What exactly is he doing to them? Those are the questions that keep me awake at night."

Aurora stares at the ceiling. "What happens after?" she finally asks. "Say we succeed, expose the lab, save whoever's left alive, burn it all to the ground. Then what? What does the world look like the day after we win?"

Until now, I've been so focused on the mission itself that I haven't let myself think too far beyond it.

"I mean, Solace has rescued individual Avids before, shut down trafficking operations," I say slowly, rolling onto my side to face her. "But they've never uncovered something this massive. Never exposed the truly horrific shit the Volkovs are doing on this scale."

What we're attempting makes my chest tight. "We're not saving the people in one lab, Aurora. We're potentially saving thousands, everyone who would have ended up there in the future. And Banks said this is the largest facility. There are at least two more labs we know about."

"But that's what I'm getting at," Aurora says, turning to meet my eyes. Her expression is serious in a way that reminds me she's a strategist, a fighter at heart. "Even if we accomplish all of that, even if we expose everything and wake people up to what's happening … then what? Irina's not the answer. We've already established that. The Syndicate isn't proving to be much better than the current district leaders."

She pauses, and I can see her working through the implications. "It feels like a lot more people are going to die before we see any real change. And when that many lives are at stake, I want to make sure we've thought this through. That we really know what we're doing and what comes next."

People will die, probably a lot of people. The question that's been lurking in the back of my mind surfaces. At the end of the day, if we're responsible for all that death, how are we any better than them?

But we have to be better. We're fighting for the right things —for freedom, for a world where Avids aren't property, for leadership that unites instead of divides. We're standing against the worst kind of evil.

"They count on fear to keep us obedient, but hope spreads faster than fear ever will. It's the one contagion they can't contain," I say, feeling determined to make a difference. "If we reveal the truth, hope will take root, and it will spread."

Aurora looks up at the ceiling, deep in thought.

"Would you rather we throw in the towel?" I ask carefully, studying her face. "Run away instead of fight? Because if that's what you want, Aurora, I wouldn't blame you."

She snorts, and for a moment she's back to being my fierce friend. "Me? Miss out on a fight? Not a chance in hell. I want every one of those bastards to pay for what they've done." Her expression grows serious again. "But I'm also not naive. The system is rigged, Kat. We've already declared nobody in this mess is purely good or purely evil. Everyone's doing terrible things and slapping different labels on them to justify it."

She sits up slightly, her voice gaining intensity. "I need you to consider the possibility that this won't end the way we want it to. Maybe we don't make the difference we think we're making. We could be trading one kind of suffering for another."

I shake my head, feeling something fierce and determined rising in my chest. "I'm not saying we're going to save the world with this one mission. That would be delusional. But it's a start, Aurora. Everything we're doing is a push in the right direction."

I think about Meadow, about the visions I've been seeing, about the woman who looks like me trapped in that nightmare facility. "We're on the brink of something important. Maybe it won't be perfect, and maybe the world we create won't be paradise, but it has to be better than this. It has to be better than children being sold like livestock, than people disappearing into labs never to be seen again. Than the fucking gutter zones that are spreading by the day."

I reach out and squeeze her hand. "We keep pushing because the alternative, doing nothing, isn't an option. Not for me. Not anymore."

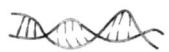

"MALACHI WOULD PROBABLY KILL me if he knew I was taking you back to the ranch right now," Alex says from the driver's seat.

We've been training nonstop for two days, and today I was on a team with Cade and Alex. We crushed it, using our masks, training with different forms of Avidian, working together flawlessly. We were faster than Nasha, Aurora, and Dante in every drill Bash put us through, which is why the three of us got to leave early.

Since Cade's jeep was stolen, I had to ask Alex to take me back to Malachi's cabin. I want to get more of my things, and I'm hoping the journal about the first Avid is still there. I barely got to read much of it before the fire, and then Malachi forbade us all from going back to the ranch, claiming it's not safe.

"Malachi is always being overly cautious. We'll be fine. In and out, right, Kat?" Cade says from the passenger seat in front of me.

"I promise I'll be quick, and it's been weeks since the attack. I doubt anyone is hanging around the ranch after it burned to the ground," I tell him from the back seat.

Alex nods, but I don't miss the way he grips the steering wheel tighter, like he's anxious about this whole thing.

We pull up to what's left of the ranch, and my heart sinks. The main house is nothing but blackened timber and ash spread in stark contrast against the snow, with only the stone chimney still standing. I don't care if Irina is a terrible person, but I feel for Malachi. This was his safe place where he grew up after his mom died, and I know he must have had memories here.

We drive past the house and toward the back of the property where Malachi's small cabin still stands untouched, thankfully.

"I'll keep watch out here," Alex says quickly, already

getting out of the car. "This spot gives me a good view of the access road. You two should still be quick."

I glance over at Cade, who's already walking to the front door. "We'll be fast," I promise, and follow Cade inside.

He's already in Malachi's bedroom, pulling a backpack from his closet and handing it to me. "What am I looking for exactly?" he asks as I take the empty pack from him and start putting some of my clothes in it.

"It's a brown, worn notebook," I tell him, not knowing where Malachi put it and hoping it wasn't in Irina's basement with everything else that caught fire.

I move to my side of the bed and pull open the nightstand drawer. Sure enough, it's right there. Malachi must have placed it there for me.

"I have it. We can go," I tell him, stuffing it into my pack on top of my clothes.

Cade nods and leaves the room. I look down and notice a tear in my sweater. I pull it off and fish a fresh one out of Malachi's closet. The idea of putting on one of his sweatshirts that smells like him makes my heart happy. I grab a black hoodie and breathe it in.

"We'll take one of these too while we're here," Cade says, coming back in with a full bottle of whiskey in his hand.

I glance over my shoulder at him as I pull the hoodie on over my head. "What?" I ask as a mischievous smile spreads across his face.

"You were smelling his sweatshirt," he states, and I shrug.

"Shut up. I miss him. Besides, he does smell good." I roll my eyes, and Cade laughs.

"So ... Aurora's pretty amazing in training, huh?" he says, and I freeze while opening the bedroom door to gawk at him.

"You have a thing for her, don't you?" I say, scanning the

way his cheeks suddenly flush and he looks away, not wanting to look me in the eye.

"I wouldn't go that far," he says, and I scoff.

"Don't play coy with me. It's okay if you do. I think you two would be great together. You both deserve to be happy." Something occurs to me. "But can I ask what's holding you back? Because if you're worried about me being weird about it, don't be. Aurora's my best friend, and I want her to be with someone who actually sees how incredible she is."

Cade runs a hand through his hair, looking uncomfortable. "It's not that. She's so confident, so powerful. And I'm the guy without any gifts who fixes weapons and knows how to fight. What could I possibly offer someone like her? Not to mention, she knows how I've always felt about you."

"Are you kidding me?" I stare at him. "Cade, you're one of the most loyal, steady people I know. You've had Malachi's back even when he was being an asshole, you make everyone feel safe, and you're funny as hell when you're not being self-deprecating. And me and you, we're friends, and Aurora knows that."

His smile is small but genuine. "You really think she'd be interested in someone like me?"

"I think Aurora would be lucky to have you. But more importantly, I think you should talk to her instead of asking me." I grin and head for the door. "Don't wait too long. We're about to go on a potentially deadly mission, and life's too short for what-ifs."

Our good mood dissipates quickly as we step outside.

"Fuck," Cade says. Alex is nowhere to be seen.

"Alex!" we both yell in unison.

I open wide to shout again, but he comes jogging up from the other side of the cabin.

"What the fuck? Where did you go?" Cade asks, opening the truck and hopping into the passenger seat.

"I had to take a piss and didn't want to interrupt whatever was going on in there," he says, and I clear my throat from the back seat.

"What exactly do you think we were doing?" I ask.

Alex starts the truck, then holds his hands up. "Hey, I don't ask and don't tell." He starts driving down the long driveway.

I feel no need to defend anything, and apparently, neither does Cade, who shakes his head and clicks on the radio. I don't know why Alex would say that. Maybe he knows we have history, but something about it makes me uncomfortable. That's the last thing I need before we're all about to put our lives in each other's hands.

"First up in today's Unity Broadcast: reports continue to pour in from Eastern Gutter Zone 3, where residents have barricaded several city blocks following rumors of raids targeting Avid families."

The broadcaster's voice is sickeningly cheerful, like she's discussing the weather instead of people's lives. I hate listening to this propaganda bullshit. When the broadcast network is owned by the same people making the policies, the truth gets buried under layers of spin and manipulation.

"In related news, Marco Volkov issued a statement today regarding the ongoing investigation into twelve missing persons from Eastern District checkpoints. Citizens are urged to remain calm as Volkov assumes leadership of the Eastern District following the sudden death of his twin brother, Viktor Volkov, in what officials are calling a tragic accident."

My blood runs cold. Marco's expanding his territory, consolidating power, and people are vanishing at checkpoints.

Cade slams the power button, cutting off the broadcaster. "I can't stomach that garbage. Twelve people 'missing,' and they call it an investigation? We all know where those people ended up."

"In a lab somewhere," Alex says quietly, his knuckles white on the steering wheel.

"Do you think the raids in Gutter Zone 3 are real?" I ask, though I already know the answer.

"They're real," Cade says grimly. "Marco's getting bolder. He doesn't even care about being subtle anymore."

I lean back, staring out at the snow-covered landscape. During my years under Marco's control, I was kept completely isolated from news, from any information about the outside world. He preferred his "assets" ignorant and compliant. Now that I can hear these broadcasts, each one is more disturbing than the last. The systematic disappearances, the propaganda disguised as news, the casual way they discuss human lives like inventory.

"It's getting worse out there," I murmur.

"That is exactly why this mission matters," Alex says, and I lean forward to study his profile. There's an intensity there that wasn't present before. Maybe it's pre-mission jitters, or maybe something's going on with him.

MY POWER HAS BEEN EVOLVING at an unprecedented rate since I went through Bash's experiment, and now, training with Avidian vials through those masks, I'm starting to feel something I haven't felt in years, genuine hope. We can really do this. We can take down Marco and Orin and dismantle the entire Volkov operation one lab at a time. The thought should terrify me, going up against the people who owned me, who broke me, who turned me into a weapon. Instead, I feel this fierce determination burning in my chest.

Once we expose the labs and rescue whoever's left alive in those nightmarish facilities, we can start the real work. Weeding out the Syndicate members who are looking for power, who want to replace one corrupt system with another. Then we strike at the heart of it all. Irina's fate may be the same as her brothers'—a necessary casualty in this war. Or maybe she'll surprise us all and start supporting Malachi the right way, not as a tool for her own ambitions but as the leader he's meant to be. Unlikely, but I'm not entirely ruling it out yet. People can change when their world collapses around them.

I rub at my growling stomach, still hungry despite trying to ignore it. All I managed for dinner was a bowl of cereal with that awful synthetic milk that tastes like chalk mixed with water. The communal dining area was buzzing with conversation and laughter—Aurora trying to convince Nasha to let her braid her hair, Cade and Dante arguing about weapon maintenance techniques, Alex making everyone laugh with some story I couldn't quite catch from the hallway.

But I didn't feel like joining them tonight. Sometimes, the weight of what we're planning, what I'm asking them all to risk, sits so heavy on my shoulders that I need space to breathe. Lately, I've caught them looking at me differently, not like I'm part of the team anymore but like they expect me to have answers I don't have. Malachi is our leader, he's the one with the vision and the strategic mind, but sometimes, I see them turning to me first when things get complicated.

It makes me uncomfortable. I never asked to be seen that way, and I'm not sure I'm built for it. Most days, I feel like I'm guessing and hoping I don't get us all killed. Tonight, I needed solitude to practice my gift and to read more of that scientist's journal about the Viridian girl, the first Avid.

When I spoke to her, she said "Avid" wasn't even a term that existed in her time. Makes me wonder when that word came into use, who decided that's what we'd be called. Was it the scientists who created more like her? The government officials who decided we were dangerous? Or did we choose it for ourselves somehow? The girl in those journal entries ... There's something about her story that feels familiar in a way I can't explain. I want to get to the bottom of how we are related.

I pull on my favorite nightgown and braid my hair to the side, muscle memory guiding my fingers through the familiar motions. It's something my mother used to do for me when I was small, before everything went wrong. Strange how these little rituals can carry so much comfort.

Climbing onto the bed, I'm immediately reminded of how empty it feels without Malachi here. The mattress doesn't dip on his side, and there's no warm body to curl up against, no steady heartbeat to fall asleep to. I miss the way he unconsciously reaches for me in his sleep, pulling me closer even when he's dreaming. I miss his terrible jokes and the way he hums under his breath when he thinks no one's listening. Three days shouldn't feel like an eternity, but when you've found your person—your home—their absence echoes in every quiet moment.

I lean back against the headboard and pull the gray cotton sheets up to my chest, the fabric soft from countless washes. The room is quiet except for the distant hum of the building's ventilation system and the occasional sound of footsteps in the hallway. Everyone's settling in for the night, preparing for another day of training tomorrow, another step closer to a mission that could change everything or destroy us all.

I close my eyes and take a deep breath, centering myself the way Bash taught me. It's time to focus. Time to push my abilities further, to see what these enhanced powers can really do. The journal can wait. I need to understand what I'm becoming.

Chapter Twenty-Three

LOG TWENTY-THREE – TRIAL INCONSISTENCY: THE
VACCINE TRIALS ARE NOT PROGRESSING.
EQUIPMENT FAILS ONLY WHEN SHE IS PRESENT. NO
DIRECT EVIDENCE LINKS HER, BUT THE PATTERN IS
UNDENIABLE.

I TAKE deep breaths and center myself, deciding to start with something easy, something safe. I focus on Mischka until she appears, which only takes a split second since summoning her is like second nature to me now. She does a few little ghostly zoomies on the end of the bed, and then comes to sit in front of me.

"Okay, girl, I'm going to make you less of a spirit and more substantial for a minute, and when I do, I want you to take the ball," I tell her, and she stares up at me.

I close my eyes and reach out, touching her cool form and focusing on strengthening her spirit. I can't bring anyone back from the dead—that's a gift I don't think anyone has, unfortunately—but I can make her spirit more substantial for a short time, more tangible in this world. Kind of like what I did with the spirits in the ballroom, though I still don't know if Meadow had anything to do with that or how I managed to summon that many ghosts at once.

I shake my head and square my shoulders, focusing on Mish again until the cool form beneath my fingertips hardens

242

and I feel her soft fur. My eyes shoot open, and I can't help the stupid grin that spreads across my face.

I pick up the ball and throw it to the end of the bed. She chases after it, picks it up, drops it back next to me, jumps in my lap, and starts licking my face. I feel wet kisses, a warm tongue, and wet nose on my cheek. I wrap my arms around her and kiss the top of her head. She feels completely real—solid, warm, alive.

She stays like that for a solid two minutes before she starts flickering in and out, then eventually returns to her translucent form. I think that's the longest I've been able to maintain it without any fading in and out.

It's weird, you'd think if I could make the spirits stay more tangible, anyone would be able to see them, but that hasn't been the case yet. But making them more tangible gives them the ability to touch others, to kill others. I need to sustain it for longer and either only summon spirits I trust or find a way to make them do my bidding like in the ballroom.

Only, I didn't want them to kill everyone at the party ... Maybe subconsciously I did.

Fuck, I wish I knew how I did that and if Meadow had anything to do with it. I need to replicate that kind of power. Maybe I need to be under more dire circumstances for my body to react that way. It's also possible the strength of the spirit has something to do with it, because Damien has always felt stronger to me, and he was the first who was able to touch me before I ever went through Bash's equipment.

I continue practicing with Mish over and over again until my head is pounding. The last time, I was able to keep her with me in her tangible form for ten solid minutes—a new record. But the headache is getting worse, a sharp throbbing behind my eyes that warns me I'm pushing too hard.

I let Mish fade back to her ghostly form, and rub my

temples. This power evolution is incredible, but it's also exhausting in ways I didn't expect. Each breakthrough comes with new questions, new possibilities that are both thrilling and terrifying. The idea that I could command an army of spirits and make them solid enough to affect the physical world is exactly the kind of ability that could help us on this mission.

But it's also the kind of power that could consume me if I'm not careful.

I slide down under the covers, prop the pillows up around me, then reach for the journal. I flip it open and start reading. Considering they came from a scientist, you'd think these notes would be well-thought out and neatly written, but instead, they're sloppy entries with scattered thoughts. Squinting to read the handwriting does nothing for my headache, but I need to learn more.

I skim the first couple of pages.

Subject acquired under emergency medical protocols following the regional crisis. No surviving family members to provide consent. Standard treatments had failed completely. The experimental vaccine represented the only viable option available to us. The ethics board approved the procedure unanimously. We believed we were preventing a tragedy while potentially developing something that could benefit countless others. How naive we were. Some doors, once opened, can never be closed again.

No family members to provide consent? The girl didn't look that young in the visions I've seen. God, how long was she kept in that lab, or whatever it was? Since when were doctors abducting patients for experiments? I was naive to believe things weren't always this corrupt. This poor girl. Did they really believe they were preventing a tragedy? I don't trust that for a second.

I idly pet Mish and continue reading entry after entry,

getting a glimpse into the mind of this scientist and how the first Avid possibly came to be. He seems to be following orders, but I can tell he struggles with his moral compass. Whoever's writing this knows what they're doing is wrong, but I don't think that makes it any better since he's still doing it.

Remarkable physical changes continue to manifest. The subject unintentionally bent steel restraints during today's examination. We've had to reinforce her medical bed with industrial-grade materials. More concerning, her dream episodes have become incredibly detailed and predictive. Dr. Harrison has approved construction of the new neural interface machine. If we can record and analyze these visions properly, the applications could be revolutionary. I pray we're not overstepping our bounds.

A neural interface machine to record her dreams? Her predictive visions? Was her gift seeing the future?

It sounds like she had many gifts. She clearly had enhanced strength, and then possibly some kind of future cognition. Maybe she even saw me coming. Maybe she knows what's going to happen with the mission, with Sunderlands, with all of it? I wish she wasn't so difficult to communicate with. I need to try to reach her again. If she can offer us any guidance and possibly warn us, she could save lives.

It's so odd reaching out to her though. I haven't been able to bring her to me yet. I always get sucked into some kind of past recollection of where she was kept. Maybe her spirit is more comfortable bringing me to a place she spent so much of her time in, rather than appearing in my reality.

I glance back down at the journal.

Subject has requested we call her by her name, but I can't bring myself to do it. Guilt for what we've done to her and for how we are using her becomes too real if I put a name on it. For now, "Subject" is how I will refer to her. The others have taken to calling her Viridian after the project name. Dr. Harrison named the project Viridian because she was the first and only one to survive the process. "A green sprout in the ashes of failure," he once said.

Hmm, so that explains the name stamped across her folder, but that's not her true name. I continue reading through several more pages, even though my eyes are getting sleepy.

We removed her restraints this week. She walks freely now, even dines with the others. Some say she has accepted the cause. I suspect the opposite. She is cleverer than us all, that she endures until the moment she no longer has to. There is something in her eyes I cannot explain. It unsettles me, and I cannot be the only one who feels it.

The neural interface machine is complete. Yesterday, we ran our first successful test. Sedation was required to extract enough data, yet still she complied ... or seemed to. It is difficult to know whether she obeys us or allows us to think she does. Regardless, the results are remarkable. For the first time, I witnessed the future unfold, not through prediction but through her dreams. This morning's debrief will be the first true measure of how her recollection compares to the visions we recorded. If the data holds, the next phase will begin.

I need to know what happened in the debrief before I can put this down for the night. My fingers skim the page, turning it quickly.

The subject remained mostly stoic during debrief. The amount of freedom we continue to grant her unsettles me, though Dr. Harrison insists it is necessary. He believes she must choose to help us if this project is to succeed. I do not share his optimism. What troubles me most is her lack of anger. No rage, no bitterness, no sign of hatred toward those who confined her. That, I suspect, is the greatest danger of all. If she can hide that, she can hide anything.

Meanwhile, the virus consumes more lives by the day. Our vaccine trials crawl forward, but the numbers fall against us. After watching her vision of the future this morning, I am certain we are running out of time. Perhaps the world itself is doomed. And yet she smiles when she speaks of saving it. Enthusiasm, they call it. But I wonder if it is only another mask she wears, waiting for the moment to discard it.

A chill lingers over me as I close the journal and set it on the table.

Clearly, they never succeeded. If they had, half the population wouldn't have died, the government wouldn't have collapsed into ruin, and the climate wouldn't have spiraled so far out of control.

If she really was the first Avid, then how were more of us created? Maybe she had children, and whatever they did to her bled into her genes. But that wouldn't explain the sheer number of Avids who exist now. Her bloodline alone couldn't have seeded us all.

Maybe she was contagious. Or maybe that vaccine they kept testing didn't cure anyone at all, changing them instead. Maybe it twisted something in their bodies, rewrote something in their blood, and that mutation became us.

If I want to reach her, it has to be now, before exhaustion drags me under. I push the covers back and stand. Mish snores softly, unmoving even as the floor creaks beneath my feet.

I pace a bit, my breathing erratic. Anxiety hits fast. Maybe standing was a bad idea. I drop onto the edge of the bed, press my palms to my knees, and close my eyes. Inhale. Hold. Exhale. I force my heart to slow, count each beat until it steadies, and then I imagine her.

Those piercing icy-blue eyes. The sterile room. The thin gown. I picture the woman on the other side of the two-way mirror and reach for her, willing her to appear. But she doesn't come, not at first. She's too strong or is resisting. My chest tightens. Then the air chills, that same unnatural cold creeping into my skin, and when I open my eyes, I'm not in my bedroom anymore.

I'm in hers.

"Viridian," I say, since she hasn't given me another name.

The room isn't quite the same as before. Time feels different here, stretched or warped. She sits on the edge of a narrow bed, not a gurney this time, her dark hair pulled back, her posture weary. Medical equipment glows softly around her, and she looks worn thin, like she's been carrying the weight of something far heavier than her frame should bear.

She pats the bed beside her, an invitation. My instincts scream not to trust it, but I step forward anyway. The walls ripple faintly, like water disturbed.

No. Hold steady. You've got this, Kat.

I sit beside her, not too close, my body taut as a bowstring. Her eyes shift toward me, tired but sharp, the kind of gaze that strips you bare.

"I know you can see the future," I say, knowing I don't have much time. "Do you know about my mission? Do you know if we succeed?"

Two questions at once.

Damn it.

I bite back frustration. It's always the same. I rush, demand too much, then run out of time before I get all the answers I need. I inhale slowly, coaching myself like Malachi does in training. Breathe. One thing at a time.

Viridian tilts her head, lips curving, not a smile but something closer to recognition.

"You want certainty," she says, her voice soft but potent. "That is a luxury the future never offers. I can show you shadows, fragments ... but whether you succeed?" Her eyes narrow, piercing mine. "That depends on who you trust and what you're willing to sacrifice."

"You said before I was more powerful than I realized. How do I control my power? How do I become stronger?"

She looks past me. I turn my head, but there's nothing there, a blank wall.

"You're holding back because you're afraid of becoming like them. But power isn't evil. Intention is," she says, still not looking at me. The room warps again, then static strings appear across my vision until I rein it in and bring her back into focus.

"But what if I have to kill many to achieve a better future? Doesn't that make me no better than them despite what the intentions are?" I ask, and she tips her head, her eyes studying me for a beat.

"Some futures are worth becoming the villain for," she says.

I open my mouth to reply but hear my name.

"Kat?" It's Malachi's familiar voice. I blink, and she's gone. The room disappears, and I'm back in my bedroom with Malachi standing in front of me, a confused expression on his face, his brows drawn together.

I get to my feet and throw my arms around his neck. "I thought you wouldn't be back until tomorrow night!" I practically squeal, and he lifts me up into his arms. I wrap my legs around his waist and cross my feet behind him.

"I wanted to surprise you," he murmurs, his lips curving into that crooked smile that always makes my chest ache. "Besides, I couldn't wait another day to get back to you."

He starts carrying me toward the bathroom. "What are you doing?"

"You look tired, and I want to take care of you. Let's take a bath," he says, and if I wasn't already melting into him, I would be now, because a bath with him sounds amazing right about now.

He pauses at the bathroom door, and I lean back in his arms so I can see his face. "What's that smirk for?" I narrow my eyes at him.

"Were you sleeping with my hoodie?" he says, holding back a laugh, and I snap my head toward the bed where I have it draped over my pillow. I can't help that I like the way it smells.

"I was talking to it too," I tease back, and he chuckles.

"It's pretty much like you, only better because it doesn't talk back," I tell him. Indignant, he lifts me over his shoulder and carries me into the bathroom. One of my flailing legs catches him.

"Ouch," he says dramatically, though I barely hit him. "And here I was going to run you a nice hot bath with those fancy salts you like."

"You still are," I say confidently, "because you missed me too much to be petty about my superior sense of humor."

"Superior?" He sets me down on the bathroom counter and steps between my legs, his hands resting on either side of me. "I seem to remember you laughing at my jokes plenty before I left."

"I was being polite," I lie, trying not to smile as he leans closer.

"Polite," he repeats, his voice dropping lower. "Is that what we're calling it now?"

"What would you call it?" I challenge, my heart racing as he moves even closer.

"I'd call it you being completely charmed by my irresistible personality," he says with mock seriousness.

I burst out laughing. "Irresistible? You do realize I've seen you try to make coffee first thing in the morning, right? There's nothing irresistible about watching you argue with an inanimate object."

"That coffee maker has it out for me, and you know it."

Grinning, he reaches behind me to turn on the bath. "But I notice you didn't deny being charmed."

I open my mouth to argue, but he kisses me before I can say anything else. It's soft and sweet and everything I've been missing these last couple days. When he pulls back, I'm slightly breathless.

"That's cheating," I murmur against his lips.

"I prefer to think of it as strategic," he says, his thumb tracing along my jaw. "Besides, you were about to lie again, and I can't have that."

"How do you know I was going to lie?"

He touches the space between my eyebrows. "Because you get this little crinkle right here when you're about to say something you don't mean. It's one of my favorite things about you."

"You have favorite things about my lying face?" I ask incredulously.

"I have favorite things about every one of your faces," he says simply, moving to pour some salts and bubble bath into the tub, but something about the way he says it makes my chest tight with emotion. "Your thinking face, your laughing face, your sleepy face, your annoyed-with-me face ..."

"I don't have an annoyed-with-you face," I protest.

"You're wearing it right now." He grips the bottom hem of my nightgown and lifts it up over my head.

The bathtub in here is surprisingly nice, given we're in an underground silo. It's a large white claw-foot tub, big enough for two. Once he turns the water off, I move to step in, and he halts me.

"I'm taking care of you, remember," he says, and swoops me up, causing an embarrassing squeal to escape my throat. He lowers me into the warm water, and then I watch as he undresses.

"I could get used to you spoiling me like this," I say as he steps in behind me and pulls me back between his legs.

The water is perfectly warm, and I let myself melt against his chest, feeling the tension from the day finally start to dissolve. His arms wrap around me, and I close my eyes, savoring this moment of peace.

"How was your trip?" I ask, tilting my head back against his shoulder.

"Productive," he murmurs into my hair as his hands start to run idle circles down my arms. "Rain sends her regards, by the way. She thinks I'm blinded by my feelings and that you're going to get us all killed."

"Comforting," I say dryly, stretching my legs out and crossing my feet on the upper edge of the tub. "I thought you were going to keep the mission a secret," I say, trying not to sound accusatory.

"I didn't give her specifics and only told her what she needed to know in case anything happens, and she knows it stays between us. I told her about Aunt Irina and how fucked things are within the Syndicate right now too," he says as he moves his hands to my shoulders and starts massaging me.

"How did she take that information?" I ask, leaning my head forward as he works the knots in my neck with his strong hands.

"Rain's tough and skeptical by nature. She insisted she never fully trusted Irina's leadership, and she wants to help change things when we get back," he says, and despite not personally liking Rain that much, I'm glad she has our backs.

"That's reassuring," I admit, sighing as he hits a particularly tense spot. "We're going to need allies when this is all over, especially if Irina doesn't take kindly to us exposing my father's operations and planning an entire mission in secrecy."

"Rain also said something interesting," he continues, his

hands moving lower to work on my shoulder blades. "She thinks there are others who've been questioning the leadership quietly. People who joined Solace and the Syndicate because they believed in the cause, not because they wanted power."

I turn slightly to look at him. "How many others?"

"She wasn't sure, but enough to matter. Most of them are afraid to speak up because they don't know who they can trust." His hands stop. "Rain thinks if we can prove what Marco's been doing and Irina's motives, it might be the catalyst to clean house properly."

"No pressure or anything," I say wryly, settling back against him. The warm water and his touch are making me drowsy, but my mind is still processing everything. "So when we get back, we're not only fighting the Volkovs, we're potentially dealing with a civil war within our own organization."

"Potentially. But if this mission is successful, Irina and I may be the only Volkovs left," he says, which puts things in perspective.

After breaking into Marco's largest secret-testing lab buried beneath the most dangerous gutter zone in the country, we're hoping to kill him, Orin, and Gary in the process.

Fuck.

I turn in his arms so I can see his face, studying the tension around his eyes that he's trying to hide.

"Are you okay with that?" I ask quietly. "I know they're monsters, but they're still your family."

He rubs his eyes. "My father bought and used you. Orin tortured you and has blood on his hands from many operations like this one. Gary ..." He shakes his head. "They stopped being my family the moment I learned what they really were."

"That doesn't make it easier," I point out.

"No," he admits, "but the alternative is letting them continue destroying lives, and I can't live with that either."

I reach up and touch his face, feeling the slight roughness of stubble under my fingertips. "We don't have to kill them, you know. Exposing them, destroying their operations, putting them in prison—that could be enough."

"Could you let Marco live?" he asks, and I squirm.

I think about the brand on my shoulder, about the years of captivity, about all the other Avids who didn't survive what I did. "I don't know," I answer honestly. "When I think about facing him again, all I feel is rage."

"Then you understand," he says simply. "Not to mention, he sent Meadow after you. He may have played nice at the party in the Southern District, but that was only because he had an audience. He wants you for himself, Katja, and he won't stop until he has you. Thinking about him or one of my brothers getting their hands on you—"

I turn around fully in the tub now so I can face him, brushing his hair back with my damp hands. "No one is taking me from you. It's you and me forever, remember? You promised." I smile at him, getting him to relax.

"How do you do that?" he says.

"Do what?" I raise an eyebrow.

"Everything in this world feels like it's breaking, but when I look at you, it all makes sense. With you, I can survive anything. It feels like I can accomplish anything as long as I have you by my side," he says, and my heart does a little flip-flop.

"That's because you can accomplish anything," I tell him, water droplets falling from my hands as I frame his face. "You're the strongest person I know, Malachi. You're fighting your own family to do what's right. You're leading a team into the most dangerous mission any of us have ever attempted. And you're doing it all because you believe in something better."

I lean closer, our foreheads almost touching. "But if I make it easier somehow, if I help you feel like you can take on the world, then that's perfect and exactly how you make me feel too."

"We're going to get through this," he says, his voice full of quiet conviction. "Whatever happens in that lab, whatever we face afterward—we're going to make it out together."

"Together," I agree, and when he kisses me, it tastes like promises and hope and the kind of love that could survive anything.

Chapter Twenty-Four

LOG TWENTY-FOUR - ESCALATING SUSPICION: I BELIEVE SHE IS SABOTAGING US, BUT I CANNOT FIND PROOF. AND THE ABSENCE OF PROOF IS BEGINNING TO FEEL INTENTIONAL.

"I'VE ARRANGED for us all to fly to the Eastern District tomorrow afternoon. We'll go to one of the safe houses there and regroup. It's close enough to start surveillance on my father and brothers and get a better idea of what's going on, and from there, we can plan our exact date of attack on the lab," Malachi says to all of us in the training room.

We spent another two days completing a brutal training schedule, but I'm confident we're prepared as a team. With Malachi back, everything feels right. I feel more ready than I've ever felt and think we're all getting the itch to get this over with.

"How long will we stay at the safe house before we make our move?" Alex asks. I look over to where he's leaning against one of the side bleachers, dripping in sweat.

"We don't want to hang out in the Eastern District longer than necessary, hopefully only a handful of nights, enough to see what they're up to and feel things out," Malachi says.

"What about the pilot? Can we trust them not to give away our location?" Nasha asks.

Bash speaks up, "The pilot was paid well for his silence, and I consider him a personal friend. He won't say anything."

I cross my arms, studying the faces around me. Everyone looks tired but determined. Aurora's eyes have that fierce glint they get when she's ready for a fight. Cade is already mentally cataloging weapons and equipment, tapping his fingers against his leg. Even Dante, usually the quietest of us, has a focused intensity about him.

"Once we're there, stick to pairs for any reconnaissance," Malachi continues. "No one goes anywhere alone. The Eastern District isn't friendly territory, even without the added risk of running into family."

"What's our cover story if we're spotted?" Aurora asks.

"We're Solace operatives investigating reports of missing persons in the area. It's close enough to the truth that it should hold up under casual scrutiny," Malachi replies.

The plan sounds solid, but I can't shake the feeling that we're walking into something bigger than we realize. Still, we've trained for this. We're as ready as we'll ever be. Well, we clearly could all train a lot longer, but time is of the essence here.

"Now we'll have plenty of time to pack in the morning since we don't leave until later in the day, so since all of you have been working so hard, I thought tonight we could go to District Blackout to let off some steam before the mission," Malachi says, and Cade and Dante start laughing, already looking excited.

"What's District Blackout?" I ask, glancing around at everyone's suddenly perked-up faces.

"It's a dive bar, hence 'blackout,'" Aurora says, and I snap my head to her.

"How is it that you know everything?" I exclaim, and she gives me a furtive smile and wink.

"Hey, dive bar is a little harsh. It's a respectable establishment," Malachi says, and now I'm laughing because I know he's lying.

"If by respectable, you mean they don't ask questions and the drinks are strong enough to strip paint," Cade adds with a grin.

"Exactly my point," Malachi says. "Very respectable."

"Are we talking about the same place where someone allegedly punched a hole through the wall last month?" Alex asks, raising an eyebrow.

"That was an accident," Dante says quietly, and everyone turns to stare at him. "What? The guy was really annoying."

"Let's meet up in the garage in two hours," Malachi says, and Nasha pulls the towel that's wrapped around her neck off and snaps it on Dante's back.

"Yeah, because you all need a shower. You stink," she says, flashing all of her teeth at him, and it's the first time I notice there may be a little chemistry between those two.

Dante's dirty-blond hair falls into his eyes as he lunges for Nasha, but she squeals with laughter and dodges out of his reach, darting toward the door with him in hot pursuit.

All I hear is her squeal disappearing down the hallway, causing me to giggle and shake my head. When I look back at Aurora, she raises her eyebrows, then laughs.

"Well, that's new," she says, gathering up her water bottle and towel. "Though, I guess it makes sense. They've been partnering up a lot during training."

"I know, right? I was starting to wonder if I was imagining things," I say, watching the doorway where they disappeared. "They're actually kind of cute together."

"Dante needs someone who can keep him on his toes," Cade adds, chuckling. "Nasha's definitely got the personality for it."

"Speaking of keeping people on their toes," Aurora says with a mischievous grin, "I should probably warn you all that I've heard District Blackout has karaoke nights."

The collective groan from everyone makes me laugh even harder. "Please tell me it's not karaoke night tonight."

"Oh, I hope it is," Aurora says, looking far too pleased with herself.

"I'm suddenly rethinking this whole team bonding idea," Alex mutters, but he's smiling as he heads toward the door.

BY THE TIME we all squeeze into one of the larger SUVs and get going, it's fully night out, and the moon is visible. Despite the snow on the ground, it's a clear night with cool, crisp air. I watch out the window as we drive away from all the housing and into ... well, nothing. We pass snow-covered field after snow-covered field, away from all the lights of the town. The stars look beautiful this far out here, away from all the light pollution.

"I wish Bash had come out with us tonight," Aurora says from behind me, and I do too. He's been working so hard lately.

"He's in the zone right now, and you know how he gets when he's focused," Cade says.

"Is this place in the middle of nowhere or what?" I ask from the front seat, looking over at Malachi, who's driving.

"We're almost there, but we like to keep things low-key, and this place is a Solace favorite around here," he says, not taking his eyes off the road.

I can see a flickering light in the distance, and as we get closer, I make out a motel. Its sign is only half lit up, and the parking lot is empty except for one car covered in a heaping pile of snow like it hasn't moved in a long time. The single-lane road stretches as far as I can see in both directions. On the right, we have the creepy motel, and on the left, I see our bar as we pull into the parking lot.

A neon beer-mug icon still clings to life, glowing faint blue, but right above it hangs a wooden placard that reads, "DIS-TRICT BLACKOUT." The letters are uneven, like they were carved with a dull knife. The irony of a glowing sign under the word "Blackout" isn't lost on anyone.

"This place looks like it's one health inspection away from being condemned," Aurora observes cheerfully from the back seat.

"That's part of its charm," Cade says, already unbuckling his seatbelt. "Wait until you see the inside."

I can hear muffled music thumping through the walls and see warm-yellow light spilling from the windows. Despite the rundown exterior, there's something welcoming about it, like finding civilization in the middle of absolutely nowhere.

"Last chance to back out," Malachi says as he turns off the engine.

"Are you kidding?" I say, opening my door to the crisp night air. "After that buildup? I'm definitely curious now."

Dante darts ahead, his boots crunching over the snow-packed steps before he swings the door wide, his grin sharp in the glow of the sign above. He does a ridiculous bow as Nasha walks in, and she rolls her eyes but can't quite hide her smile. Malachi's arm slides around my waist, his warmth seeping through my coat as he guides me inside. The heavy metal door groans shut behind us with a sound like rust grinding against rust.

I didn't think it was possible, but the inside feels even darker than the night we stepped out of. The air is thick with old smoke and stale beer, and it clings to my throat as I breathe it in. The lighting is a string of mismatched holiday lights drooping across the ceiling, throwing off a jaundiced-yellow glow. They sag low in haphazard crisscross patterns, as if someone strung them up years ago and never bothered to take them down. The shadows between them feel alive, and I can't help but think the place looks like it's lit by dying stars.

A small wooden stage sits in the corner, no bigger than a dining table, with a microphone that looks like it hasn't worked since before I was born. A long bar stretches the length of the far wall, its surface worn smooth by decades of elbows, the wood stained so dark it nearly blends into the shadows. Bar stools in a deep shade of red line the counter, their fabric cushions frayed at the seams. They have no backs, only a place to sit if you don't care about staying long.

But it's what's behind the bar that really catches my attention. Tiered shelves rise up nearly to the ceiling, crowded with liquor bottles—some full, some half empty, some so dusty I wonder if they've turned to poison by now. Above the bottles, a ledge runs the length of the wall, and it's completely buried in Halloween decorations. A cracked clown head leers down at us, hollow eyes catching the light. A witch frozen mid-flight balances precariously on her broom. Skeleton limbs are scattered like trophies. Battery-powered candlesticks flicker weakly, their fake flames stuttering. And creepy porcelain dolls with cracked faces watch from every angle. It's chaos, clutter, pure junk. And yet I kind of love it. In this world of decay, someone chose to hoard plastic skulls and rubber bats like they were precious relics. There's something weirdly comforting about that kind of madness.

"I'd like to start the night off with a bang," Cade declares, swaggering up to the bar like he's done it many times before. "So everyone gets a mind eraser on me."

The bartender turns at the sound of his voice, and she looks like she belongs on that ledge with all the rest of the oddities.

She's tall, willowy, her frame all sharp edges and angles. Her hair is dyed a deep, unnatural pink that falls almost to her waist, and her face is weathered with lines. A constellation of piercings glints across her nose, ears, and brow, tiny sparks of silver in the dim light. Her expression doesn't shift when she looks at us, not even a flicker. It's like she's already seen everything we could ever do, and none of it would surprise her.

"Seven mind erasers coming up," she rasps, already pulling bottles from the shelves.

"Fair warning, these aren't for lightweights," Cade says as he plops down in a stool next to Aurora.

"What exactly is a mind eraser?" I ask, though I'm not sure I want the answer.

Aurora leans against the counter beside me, her grin bright against the gloom. "Think of it as liquid courage with a side of bad decisions."

"Reassuring," I mutter, my eyes narrowing on the bartender as she begins to pour.

She's using a long spoon to layer the liquid so the alcohols don't mix, and I've never seen anything like it before. Then again, I haven't exactly spent much time in bars. The only ones I've been to were the sleek, glass-and-chrome lounges Marco liked to drag me into when he wanted to parade me in front of his associates. Those were cages dressed in crystal and velvet. This place feels real.

I spin slowly on my stool, taking in the rest of the dive. Nasha and Dante have claimed the pool table at the center, their voices bouncing off the scarred wood as they argue over who gets to break. The wall behind it is plastered in layers of old stickers, peeling and faded until they've become a patchwork of color and shadow. Up close, I notice initials and words carved deep into the wall, some scratched in with knives, others scrawled in marker. It's the kind of history you can't fake, every mark a story left behind.

A few tall cocktail tables are scattered around, each crowned with a lamp that burns with a dull red bulb. The crimson glow mixes with the sagging strands of holiday lights overhead, painting the whole room in a surreal wash of gold and blood red. It shouldn't work, but somehow, it does.

To the right of the pool table, a massive black sign hangs crooked on the wall. Sloppy white paint spells out, "SHUT UP AND DRINK." Classy.

"Kat."

Malachi's voice pulls me back, and I turn to find the bartender sliding a glass in front of me.

"Alright," Cade says, lifting his with a flourish, "the rules are simple. You down it all at once. That's why it's layered. First you taste soda, then coffee, and the vodka in the middle disappears like magic."

"More like it ambushes you later," the bartender mutters under her breath, lips twitching.

I eye the drink warily but grab my glass when everyone else does.

Cade raises his first, his grin reckless. "To bad ideas and even worse hangovers."

Aurora smirks, clinking her glass against his. "To raising hell while we still can."

Alex lifts his glass higher. "To making it out alive."

Malachi's gaze finds mine. "To finding our way home."

I realize they're all waiting for me to say something. I look at them—my team, my family, ready for battle.

"To us," I say softly.

The glasses clink, a sharp chime in the dim haze, and I tip the drink back in one go. Sweetness first, then a sharp burn, then coffee liquor, sweet and dark. Like Cade promised, the vodka is invisible ... until it's not.

"So how did you all meet?" I ask Nasha as we stand near one of the cocktail tables waiting for our turn to play pool. Right now, we're playing in teams—her and Dante against me and Malachi. I've never played before, so Malachi is pretty much carrying our team at the moment.

"I was working as a medic in the city, not too far from Devil's Lake. It used to be called Toledo. This was before the gutter zones had spread and the city became too dangerous," she says, taking a drink from her cocktail.

"She saved our asses, basically," Dante says before bending to set up his next shot.

"Long story short, I was off duty when I ran into them. They had saved two Avid kids from a bad situation, and one needed medical attention. I was wary of the entire thing at first, but once Malachi explained what they were doing and who they were, I decided I could do more good joining Solace than I could working at a hospital that was run by politics," she says.

I get up to take my turn, eyeing the table for a solid-colored ball to hit. "And your brother Alex decided to join with you?" I ask, glancing up at Alex, who is standing with Aurora, apparently arguing over the antique jukebox about what song to select next.

"He did later. That's when we both decided to start training to be on active missions," she says.

I hit the ball, knocking it into the right corner pocket. "Yes!" I breathe, looking over to smile at Malachi.

"Nice shot," Malachi says, smirking. "You're a natural." Just as I miss my next shot.

"Don't get cocky yet," Dante warns as I hand off the stick. "Nasha's about to show you how it's really done."

Nasha chalks her cue stick. "Why don't you tell Kat how you ended up here?" she says, nudging Dante out of the way.

"My brother worked at a hospital in the Western District. He was a new doctor there, and he really cared about his patients and wanted to make a real difference in the world. I think he went down the wrong career path for that," Dante says, moving to chug some of his beer, and then walking around the table closer to me.

"He told me about a group of other doctors that were moving patients, and he didn't know what was happening to them. They would simply disappear one day. He finally got one of them to admit they were following orders from Marco Volkov."

His eyes meet mine, and it's the first time I realize we have an odd connection.

"He was trying to uncover what was happening and expose the whole thing. Then one day, I get a call that he fell down the stairs at work and died," he says, and I swallow hard.

"Fuck, I'm so sorry," I say, wanting to reach over and comfort him but not knowing how.

"It was a long time ago, but I know my brother didn't fall down the fucking stairs, and if he did, that certainly wouldn't have killed him. He was asking too many questions, and they wanted him out of the picture. I went to question the doctor he told me had given him information before, and believe it or not, that's when I ran into this asshole," he says, shoving Cade in the shoulder as he comes up and pulls out a stool for Aurora to sit and watch us.

"What are you all talking about? Me? I'm the asshole?" Cade puts his hands up, and Dante shakes his head, laughing.

"This was years ago now, but you can imagine the surprise when I go to question a doctor and I see this guy beating the shit out of him," Dante says, and my eyes snap to Cade's as I start putting the pieces together. Cade does the slightest nod of his head to confirm my thoughts.

Dante's brother worked at the hospital I had been in, and his brother's friend was my doctor. What are the odds?

"So we're all sickly united by our hate for Marco Volkov," I say with a lurid smile.

"Dante and I have worked together ever since. Once we met Malachi, it was only natural for us all to team up," Cade says, and I want to know more about that story, but then the jukebox blares to life playing "Another One Bites the Dust," and we all start laughing.

"I have an idea. Let's play Blackout List. It's only fitting, given the name of this dive," Aurora says as she slides back from the bar, Alex following behind with fresh drinks for all of us.

It's kind of nice having the whole place to ourselves. For a second, I glance over at the bartender, guilt tugging at me for not including her, but she's tucked away with a pair of bulky headphones over her ears, nose buried in a paperback. Her posture screams leave me alone, and I figure she likes it that way.

We shove a few of the cocktail tables together, the lamps wobbling until Malachi steadies them, and I climb onto a stool beside Aurora. Everyone else gathers around, some sitting, some standing, each with a fresh drink sweating on the wood in front of them.

"What's Blackout List?" I ask.

Cade leans one shoulder against the table, swirling his glass. "A depressing game, if you ask me."

"It's a way for us to know each other better," Aurora says, bumping my arm with hers, her grin bright against the gloom. "Come on. Build that team camaraderie you're all always preaching about."

"Each person shares one thing they've lost since the world

fell apart," Malachi explains, his beer already half gone. "Then we drink to it."

"Sounds simple enough," Nasha says.

"Great. By all means, you go first, then," Dante says, giving her a little nudge. He drops onto the stool beside her, and she squares her shoulders like she's about to step into battle.

She lifts her drink, a blended, violet concoction. "I lost the line between mercy and cruelty," she says, her voice quiet but sharp. "I can transfer pain, but I can't always tell if I'm saving people or punishing them."

This is starting off more serious than I thought. We raise our glasses in unison. My cider is crisp and sweet at first, but there's a bitter note that lingers on my tongue as I take a long chug before slamming my glass down on the table.

My eyes flick to Dante, sitting next to her, and I assume we're moving clockwise. His hands rest on the table, fingers drumming against the wood like he's debating what to share.

"I lost a bet to Cade once, and I'm still suffering for it," Dante says, smiling. His laugh is rough, but Nasha shoots him a sharp look that wipes it right off his face.

"Okay," he concedes, shoulders dropping. He lifts his glass, voice lower now. "I lost my faith in justice. The people who are supposed to protect us are the ones who bury us."

No one tries to lighten it. We raise our glasses and drink. That's how the game works, I realize. You get something off your chest, no discussion, no judgment. A confession swallowed down with alcohol. My kind of game.

My gaze slides to Cade, knowing it's his turn. He's staring into his drink like the answer's hiding in the bottom. When he finally speaks, his voice is quiet.

"I lost the first person I ever killed. Not their body, their face. Can't remember it, no matter how hard I try. And that scares me more than remembering ever could."

There's still so much I want to know about Cade's life and the years we were apart.

He leans back, smirking faintly. "I also lost the ability to take myself seriously. Cheers to that."

The tension fractures as his laugh rolls through the circle, warm and contagious. We all tip our glasses back, the clink of glass against wood sharper this time, the edge dulled by alcohol and the comfort of knowing every one of us is carrying the same kind of scars. Damaged. Slightly deranged. But together.

"I lost the idea that beauty matters. You can paint the world gold, but it still rots underneath," Aurora says with quiet bitterness.

I'm next. I stall with a longer than necessary drink, staring into the amber liquid before finally lowering my glass to my lap. I don't want to meet anyone's eyes.

"I lost the sound of my mother's voice. I try to remember it, but every year, it fades a little more," I say, staring at the bubbles forming around the edge of my glass.

Everyone lifts their drinks, and I'm grateful no one asks why I don't reach out to her spirit. That's a wound I'm not ready to pick open.

When I look up, Malachi is already watching me, his eyes dark with something I can't quite name. Before I can unravel it, Alex clears his throat on my left.

"I lost my innocence the day I realized truth doesn't set anyone free. It hurts faster," he says. Fitting, coming from someone who can drag the truth out of anyone, whether they want it or not.

The circle shifts, all eyes turning to Malachi. I lean forward, curiosity swelling. He takes a slow breath, his gaze sweeping over each of us before settling back on me.

"I lost my faith in loyalty. Everyone has a price. Everyone except the people at this table."

This time, no one simply drinks. Chairs scrape back, glasses rise, and one by one we stand, clinking our beverages together.

I glance around at their faces, at the rare smiles tugging at tired mouths, at the warmth pooling between us despite the cold world outside, and I know.

This is what I'll cling to.

This is what I'll remember.

The world has already taken so much from all of us, but it hasn't taken everything.

And I won't let it.

Chapter Twenty-Five

LOG TWENTY-FIVE - DISCREPANT OBSERVATIONS:
COLLEAGUES DESCRIBE HER AS GENTLE,
COOPERATIVE, EVEN INSPIRING. YET I'VE SEEN HER
EYES WHEN NO ONE ELSE IS WATCHING. THERE IS
NO GENTLENESS THERE, ONLY CALCULATION.

"I TOLD myself I'd never fall for someone bossy. And now here I am, drunk, in love, and listening to you tell me when to go to bed like I'm a child." I scowl at Malachi as I try to take off my shoes but wobble until he catches me and sits me on the end of the bed.

He kneels down in front of me and tugs off my shoes and socks one by one. "You are kind of cute when you're tipsy," he says, and I scrunch my nose at him.

I may have had a few too many drinks at the bar tonight, but I'm starting to sober up. Plus, we all raided the kitchen when we got back, and the bowl of cereal I ate is already soaking up the alcohol.

"I don't want to go to bed yet. I'm not tired, and I think I like you bossy," I tease as he starts to undress me.

"We don't have to go to sleep, but I don't want you tripping and falling over anything," he says, and I giggle.

"I'm not that drunk. Plus, I have poor balance sober," I tell him, and he nods, raising one eyebrow at me.

I pull the lacy nightgown he hands me over my head and

then enjoy the show while he strips down to his boxers. Once we're both in bed, I curl into his side and savor the feel of him wrapped around me.

"Thank you for tonight," I murmur against his chest. "I needed that. We all did."

"Yeah, it was good," he agrees, his fingers tracing lazy patterns on my back. "Seeing everyone laugh and ... be normal for a few hours. I forgot how much I missed that."

"Tomorrow everything changes," I say quietly.

He presses a kiss to the top of my head. "But tonight is for us."

I tilt my head up to look at him in the dim light. "Are you scared?"

"Terrified," he admits without hesitation. "But not about the mission. I'm scared about losing you."

"You won't," I promise, reaching up to touch his face.

"Oh, I almost forgot, while you were away, I got Cade to admit he has feelings for Aurora. And did you see Dante and Nasha today? I think there's something going on there too," I say, and he chuckles.

"How would you feel if Cade and Aurora got together?" he asks, more serious.

"Honestly? I'd be thrilled for them. They both deserve to be happy, and I think they'd be good for each other," I say, and he releases a breath like he'd been holding it. "Were you worried I'd be jealous or something?"

"Maybe a little," he admits. "Aurora's your best friend, and Cade's ... Well, I know he's important to you to. I wouldn't want things to get complicated."

"The only thing that would complicate things is if one of them hurt the other," I say firmly. "Aurora would definitely keep Cade in line though."

"Poor bastard has no idea what he's getting into," Malachi

271

laughs. "She'll probably set him on fire the first time he leaves his socks on the floor."

"Literally," I agree, grinning. "But he'd be good for her too. She needs someone who won't back down from her intensity."

"And Dante and Nasha?"

"They make sense. He's steady, and she's fierce. He doesn't try to dim her fire. She brings out something lighter in him." I pause, thinking about Dante's story tonight. "Plus, they both understand loss. That creates a bond you can't fake."

Malachi scratches his temple. "It's weird how we all ended up here. My father's actions brought us together, but somehow, we built something good from all the bad."

"Maybe that's the only way real families happen, not through blood or convenience, but by choosing each other when everything else is falling apart."

"Promise me that if Cade screws this up with Aurora, you'll let me handle it before she kills him."

"Deal. But only because I like Cade and would prefer he stay un-incinerated."

"There's been something on my mind I want to talk to you about," Malachi says, and I sit up to face him.

"What is it?" I ask, searching his features.

"You didn't have to sit up," he says, sitting up himself and leaning back against the headboard. "The brand. The Volkov crest my brother burned into your back." He starts, his jaw ticking like it's difficult for him to talk about. "Would you like to get rid of it?"

The possibility never really crossed my mind. "How?"

"We have Aurora's essence now, plenty of vials of it made into Avidian. I practiced using it the other day, and I'm confident I could heat the brand enough to destroy it and then give you one of the healing vials like you used before when the wolf hurt you. It would heal to where you'd be left with barely a small scar," he says.

I don't know why I never thought of it before. I could have asked Aurora to do it herself, but then I'd have to show her and talk about it. I'd rather not relive it, and something about the way people look at you differently when they hear such stories ... Not that Aurora would look at me differently. She's been through a lot too, but I still feel almost ashamed of it, which is silly, considering it was out of my control.

"Let's do it now," I tell him, and his eyes widen.

"No, Kat. You're drunk, and it's going to hurt. I thought about asking Nasha to take your pain and give it to me while I do it, but then I didn't think you'd want me telling her about it and involving anyone else," he says, and I cross my arms, relieved he didn't ask Nasha.

"I can handle the pain. I'm not even drunk anymore, and I know it's going to hurt. I remember how it felt the first time. If anything, the alcohol will be good at dulling my senses," I tell him, and his lips press together in a flat line like he's mulling it over.

"Kat, this isn't something we should rush into. Even if you're sobering up, your judgment might still be affected. And doing this right before the mission ..." He runs a hand through his hair. "What if something goes wrong? What if it doesn't heal properly and you're dealing with an injury during the infiltration?"

There's something about facing Marco tomorrow while still carrying his mark that feels unbearable. "I don't want to go into that lab tomorrow wearing his brand," I say quietly. "I don't want him to see it and think he still owns me."

Malachi's expression softens, and he reaches for my hand. "He doesn't own you, Katja. Brand or no brand, you're free.

You're mine, and I'm yours, and that piece of shit has no claim on you."

"I know that, and I know he won't see it on my back," I say, squeezing his fingers, "but I still want it gone."

"Alright," he says, standing and crossing to his duffel bag in the corner. He returns with the bag, and I watch his hands as he rifles through it on the bed.

"You have everything we need in here already?" I ask, though I shouldn't be surprised. Malachi's always prepared for anything.

"I keep supplies close. Medical kit, Avidian, weapons, it's better to stash things in multiple places than get caught without options," he says, extracting two vials that catch the dim light and sparkle. One has a green cap, and one has an orange cap. He sets them carefully on the nightstand alongside gauze and medical tape.

"I think if you inhale the healing Avidian first, before I start, it may work so well you're left with no scar at all," he says, holding up the vial with the green cap.

"I'll take it after. I want a small scar to remain, not as a reminder of what he did but of what I survived."

The silence stretches between us as he studies my face, searching for any hint of doubt. "Are you absolutely certain? Once we do this, there's no undoing it. And Katja ..." His voice drops. "This is going to hurt like hell. Worse than the original branding, because I need to burn deep enough to destroy all the scar tissue."

"I know." My voice is steadier than I feel. "This is my choice. My body. My terms."

He nods slowly, then moves to sit behind me on the bed. "Turn around. Let me see what we're working with."

I shift away from him and quickly tie my hair up in a bun, exposing the raised, twisted skin between my shoulder blades.

The Volkov crest covers nearly four inches of my back. Thankfully, my hair covers it when my clothes don't. I feel Malachi's sharp intake of breath, even though he's seen it before.

His fingers trace the edges, mapping the raised borders where the iron burned deepest. "He's going to die for this," Malachi says quietly.

"Don't think about him right now," I say. "Think about erasing him."

His hands still against my skin. "The moment I start, you scream if you need to. Bite something and tell me if you want me to stop."

I turn my head to catch his eyes. "Don't stop until it's done."

"I won't." When he picks up Aurora's vial, his hands are rock steady. "Ready?"

"Yes," I say firmly, grabbing my pillow and hugging it to my chest. I bend my head forward and bite down on the fabric.

The first touch of controlled fire against my skin steals every thought from my head. It's the kind of pain that blinds, sharp and immediate, like every nerve ending is screaming in unison. The heat crawls methodically across the brand, burning through the memory of it. Then the smell hits—the thick, sickening stench of flesh singed raw—and bile rises in my throat.

Tears spill hot down my cheeks before I even realize I'm crying. That's when Mish materializes in front of me, cool and translucent, her tongue lapping at my face. The ghostly sensation pulls me out of the agony enough to breathe. My sweet girl, always knowing when I need her.

"I'm done," Malachi says at last, and I realize I'm shaking so hard my whole body trembles against the mattress.

He pops the top off the healing Avidian, and I inhale the glittering swirl as it releases into the air. It spreads through me like liquid starlight, soothing, mending, like my cells are knitting themselves back together from the inside out.

"Are you all right? Talk to me," Malachi urges.

I nod, the death grip on my pillow finally loosening as the pain ebbs faster than I expected. I draw a shaky breath and sit up straighter, marveling at the absence where agony had festered.

"How does it feel?" he asks.

"Free," I whisper. It feels true in a way nothing ever has. "It feels like I'm free."

Behind me, he makes a small, pleased sound. "I don't even think I need to bandage it. Your body's healing it already," he says.

The ache is fading by the second. "How does it look?"

"Two pale scars, thin as lines," he says softly.

I close my eyes, and a sob breaks free, half grief and half relief. For the first time since he pressed that iron into me, my back feels like it belongs to me again. Not his. Not a mark of ownership. Mine.

"THIS PLACE IS FREAKING FREEZING," Aurora says as she drops her bags on the floor. We made it to the safe house in the Eastern District, and everyone's a little tired and hungover still, so it's a good thing we don't plan on executing the mission right away.

"I'll go get some firewood. Can you guys start unpacking?" Malachi says to no one in particular, but Dante and Alex start opening up bags and laying out equipment across the table—Avidian vials organized by different-colored caps, masks, daggers of all sizes.

"I'll come with you," I call after him, catching up as he reaches the door.

It's frigid outside, and our breath billows out in little clouds as we exhale. I almost forgot how the forest looks here—tall skeletal trees packed together and covered in fresh snow, creating an otherworldly maze of black and white. The silence is profound, broken only by the crunch of our footsteps and the occasional crack of a branch somewhere in the distance.

"How are you feeling about being back here?" I ask as we walk toward a pile of chopped wood stacked against the side of the safe house.

"Strange to think last time we were here together things were so different between us," he admits.

"Yeah, it feels like a lifetime ago," I agree, even though it hasn't been that long. The sun is setting fast with slivers of pink hues streaming low through the forest around us. "Let's split up before we lose all the sunlight."

"No, we don't need to. There should be plenty of firewood already split and stacked behind the shed," he says, and that's kind of a relief. I thought we were going to be digging through the snow looking for branches.

"Great," I giggle, and hold onto his elbow as he leads us through the trees down this snowy, unkempt path to a large shed. "What do you use the shed for?"

"We remodeled the inside to work as another living space when there are too many of us to fit in the main house," he says, and I nod, releasing him as we come up to a now snow-covered tarp.

He uses his arm to brush the piles of snow off and pulls it back to reveal plenty of neatly stacked wood.

"We have a few plastic sleds in the shed. I'll grab one, and we can stack it full of wood, then drag it back to the house," he says, and I follow him inside.

He tosses a teal sled near the door, but when he turns back to me, there's a sharpness in his eyes that makes my stomach flip.

"What's that look for?" I ask, my lips twitching into a smile.

"It means we're finally alone," he murmurs, stepping close enough that the cool air around us feels suddenly hot. "And I've been thinking about you all day."

"Have you now?" My pulse quickens when his hand brushes a strand of hair from my face.

"Mm-hmm. About how brave you were last night. About how beautiful you looked this morning." His thumb grazes my jaw. "And about how soon everything changes. But right now ..." His hands slide to my waist, pulling me closer until there's no space between us. "Right now, I just want you."

The intensity in his eyes steals my breath and somehow has me feeling self-conscious. I smile at him, holding his stare. "What?" I finally ask, though I don't look away.

"Has anyone ever told you your smile could ruin men?" he says, his voice low. "Those eyes could start a war, and that smile would finish it."

Heat floods my cheeks, and I duck my head with a giggle. "No."

His fingers find my chin, coaxing me gently back up to meet his gaze. "Then they weren't looking closely enough."

I swallow hard, pulse thrumming in my throat. My instinct is to joke, to deflect, but I can't. Not when he's looking at me like that, as if I'm something rare and untouchable, as if he's afraid I might vanish if he blinks.

"Malachi ..." I feel vulnerable, uncertain, but I trust him enough to embrace this moment.

He leans closer, his thumb brushing along my jaw, his lips hovering so close I can feel his breath when he speaks. "You have no idea what you do to me, do you?"

I shake my head, the tiniest movement, and he huffs out something between a laugh and a growl. "That smile ruins me, Kat. And the worst part? I don't want to be saved from it."

He kisses me, deep and unyielding, until the world outside the shed disappears entirely.

Our kiss is wild and hungry, teeth clashing as I push his jacket off his shoulders and tug at his shirt until he yanks it over his head. His chest is warm, solid, all hard lines under my hands as he presses forward, backing me up until the edge of the table digs into my hips.

He lifts me onto it, and the wood creaks beneath us. My breath catches as I break away for air, unzipping my jacket with clumsy fingers. Malachi drops to his knees, his hands already working, shoes gone, pants sliding down, until I'm bared to him in the dim light of the shed, just the last wisps of the sunset shining through the window and covering us in a beautiful peach hue.

"I'll never get used to this," he murmurs, his eyes devouring me like I'm something sacred. His lips press against my calf, then higher, trailing fire along my skin. "Never."

The world outside is frozen and brutal, but in here, with his mouth worshipping its way up my thigh, I've never felt more alive.

I press my palms against his shoulder, stopping him before he can go farther. His brows knit in confusion until I slide off the table and onto my knees in front of him.

"This time," I whisper, tossing my jacket aside, "I want to taste you."

Surprise flickers in his eyes, quickly replaced by heat. He lets me tug his pants away, and when I reach for his thick, hard cock, he exhales a broken sound that makes me ache everywhere at once.

I stroke him slowly with my hand, savoring the way his

muscles tense, the way his hands flex like he doesn't know what to do with himself. Then I lean closer, my lips brushing him, tasting the salt on the tip of his head with my tongue.

"Fuck," he breathes, head tipping back, one hand finding its way into my hair. Not pulling but holding like he needs the anchor as much as I do.

I twirl my tongue around his head, then take him all the way into my mouth and suck. I repeat the motion, sucking and twirling my tongue over and over again, loving the way he tenses when I take him deep.

"If you keep doing this, I'm not going to last long," he groans, his voice strained and low, and it only encourages me to suck him harder and take him deeper.

Before I can react, his hands grip my arms and he pulls me to my feet in one fluid motion. My pulse stutters, heat flooding through me as he lifts me onto the table. His mouth finds mine again, urgent and consuming, and I can taste his need in every kiss.

His body presses close, strong and sure, and then he parts my knees with his own, settling between them. His breath is hot against my ear when he whispers, "I want you to come with me."

He thrusts inside me, and I gasp at the fullness of him, reaching up to wrap my arms around his neck so I have something to anchor me.

He lifts me off the table, pulling me down on him harder and faster, filling me deeper. I bite onto his shoulder to contain the sounds he's drawing out of me.

"I want every sound you make burned into me. Don't you dare hold back," he says. I let my head fall back as ragged breaths and moans escape my lips.

"Malachi, you feel so good, oh my god," I cry out, and he backs me up to the wall, one hand wrapped around me, holding me to him. He brushes my hair back from my face with the other, and I open my eyes to find his fixed on me. I can't hold on anymore—I shatter, my orgasm ripping through me, heating my insides and causing me to tremble.

Malachi finds his release at the same time, and then stills inside me. My head drops to the crook of his neck, and he holds me while I catch my breath.

"I love you," I whisper. His arms tighten around me.

"I love you more."

He pulls out of me gently and holds me while my feet hit the ground, and I steady myself. I wrap my arms around his waist and press my face to his warm chest, damp with sweat.

"Hey, are you okay?" he says, coaxing my chin up to look at him.

"Yeah. I don't want to let you go yet. I want you to keep holding me," I tell him, and he pulls me tighter, leaning down to kiss the top of my head and stroking my back with his hands.

He doesn't pull away or try to move until I finally release him and walk over to the bathroom to clean up before getting dressed. I don't know why I feel needy all of a sudden, but I can only guess it's because this could be our last chance to be together.

Chapter Twenty-Six

"THAT MAY HAVE BEEN the longest trip to get firewood on record," Bash says as we step into the living room, his smirk faint in the glow of the stove.

Malachi drags the sled in behind me, tugging the weight across the worn floorboards before stacking the wood in a neat pile by the fire. "I had to cut down the damn tree by hand," he says, and I can't help the small laugh that escapes me.

Aurora sits curled up in one of the mismatched armchairs, her grin a little too silly to be innocent. She knows.

The potbelly stove roars with flames, heat radiating through the space until the air feels thick and soft on my skin. My cheeks warm instantly, the icy sting of the shed fading into memory.

It's nighttime, the windows black with snow pressed against the glass, and the kitchen smells like heaven. Aurora and Cade raided the pantry earlier, and somehow, they managed to put together spaghetti for all of us. Canned tomato sauce and noodles, but the scent is rich, tangy, comforting—the kind of meal that reminds me there's still a piece of normalcy left in this ruined world. My stomach growls so loud it draws a laugh from Nasha.

"Come on, we waited for you guys to eat," Bash says, motioning us over. We all settle around the table, quickly digging into our plates of spaghetti. The sauce is thin, the noodles a little overcooked, but it's warm, filling, exactly what we need after the day we've had.

"So what's the plan for tomorrow?" Cade asks, looking to Malachi, who sits across the table from him.

"At first light, we need to get eyes on the estate," Malachi says, focused. "See what my father and brothers are doing. Then we make our move on the lab. Ideally, we'll catch them both when we infiltrate so we can take them out at the same time."

I twirl my fork through the noodles and take another bite, thinking it over. I have another plan in mind, one I can't share until Malachi and I are alone.

"If for some reason that's not feasible, our main focus is still to find and infiltrate the lab," Bash adds, ever the voice of reason. "We may have to make the Volkovs a separate mission."

We're exhausted, worn thin, and soon, the only sound in the room is the scrape of forks and the quiet clatter of glasses. No one lingers around the table, there's an unspoken agreement that tonight we need rest more than talk.

The house has eight bedrooms, more than enough for everyone to spread out, but I want Malachi and me to have our own space for what I need to do tonight.

"Can we stay in the shed?" I ask him quietly as we load our dishes into the sink.

He glances down at me, that irresistible half smile curving his lips. "We can stay wherever you want, little demon."

The warmth in his eyes makes my chest ache, and I have to

stop myself from kissing him right there. Instead, we say our goodnights, agreeing to meet for breakfast at first light.

Outside, the night air bites hard, and our breaths curl like smoke as we jog across the snow toward the shed. My teeth chatter, my heart pounds—not from the cold but from everything I know is about to happen once we're alone.

Malachi drops our bag of clothes onto the couch and kneels by the little brick fireplace. Sparks crackle, then flames catch, filling the shed with a faint orange glow. I tug off my jacket, my fingers twitching, and pace the length of the room, chewing on my bottom lip.

"Malachi, I don't think we need to risk sending anyone to the estate tomorrow to stalk your father and brothers," I say.

He glances over his shoulder as he closes the little doors on the fireplace. His brows pinch together. "What do you mean?"

"I'm going to use my gift to contact Viktor tonight," I begin, but his head is already shaking.

"I don't like it, Kat. Your gift has been unpredictable lately, and what if he tries to hurt you? Fuck." He pushes to his feet, running a hand through his hair, pacing now too. "I don't know how to protect you from ghosts I can't see."

I step into his space, pressing a hand to his chest, tilting my face up to his. "I'll be okay. I've been getting stronger. You've missed a lot of the trainings, so you haven't seen me in action, but I promise I've got this."

Some of the tension leaves his shoulders, but I can see in his eyes he's not convinced.

He sits on the couch, bracing his elbows on his knees. I follow, sinking down beside him. His hand scrubs over his face, then falls limp against his thigh.

"After I took your Avidian and we saw her, the spirit, that Project Viridian girl who looks so much like you ... I thought it was you, Kat. I couldn't reach you, couldn't help you. It scared the hell out of me, feeling so helpless, not being able to protect you."

My heart squeezes, tight and aching. I slide closer until our knees touch, until I can lace my fingers through his. "I'm okay. That wasn't me. I'm here with you. Always. I'm not as breakable as you think. I can handle this."

He lifts his head slowly, his gaze catching mine, and I give him a reassuring nod.

"What makes you think he's even going to tell us the truth?" Malachi asks.

"Because his fucking twin brother and their sister had him killed," I say. "I thought Banks wanted revenge, but your uncle will be livid."

Viktor was always unnerving to think about, and the thought of summoning him makes me queasy.

Malachi exhales slowly, his jaw tight. "Let's get this over with, then. What do you need from me?"

I scrunch my nose, thinking. "Nothing. Be here with me. And don't freak out if anything bad happens. Actually, grab a pen and paper so you can write down anything I say. That way we don't forget."

He rises, muttering under his breath, and digs around in the kitchen drawer before coming back with a notepad and pen. "Real reassuring, Katja," he mumbles as he sits beside me again.

I give him a quick kiss, then ease back, moving to the chair by the fireplace. The firelight flickers across the walls, throwing restless shadows, and I put a little space between us. If I'm going to focus, I need distance, need silence, need to breathe.

I close my eyes and picture Viktor, holding onto the memory of his sharp features, the gross musty smell of his cologne. I will him to come, and it happens faster than usual. A cold chill slides over me, stealing the heat from the fire at my side. When I open my eyes, he's towering above me in his translucent form, eyes hollow, expression twisted, same dark suit I saw him in at the party.

"If it isn't my brother's favorite pet," he drawls, glancing around the room. "I wondered when you'd call upon me."

I steal a look at Malachi, giving him a quick reassuring nod before fixing my gaze back on Viktor. "I need to know how to find Marco's lab in the gutter zone near here."

Viktor throws his head back, a deep, mocking laugh rolling from his chest. "And why would I do anything to help you or my traitor of a nephew?"

My jaw tightens as I force a steady breath. "Because don't you want revenge? Your twin and your sister had you killed. If you tell me how to find the lab, and when Marco will be there, I'll kill him for you."

A deranged smile spreads across his face, sharp and chilling. "I do like the sound of that." His form flickers, shimmering more solid than before. He glances down at himself, a strange curiosity in his eyes. "But I want to do it myself."

Figures. He was never going to make this easy. "I can't do that."

He shakes his finger at me, eyes gleaming. "Uh-uh, little girl. Spirits talk. I know you're capable of more than you let on."

I exhale slowly, already feeling the strain claw at my chest. "If you tell me how to find the lab and when Marco and Orin will be there, I can summon you. I can make you tangible enough to kill him yourself, but it'll have to be quick."

Malachi's anger and fear radiate beside me. I don't even risk looking at him.

"They're there right now. They plan to be there all night," Viktor says, and my stomach sinks. That's not what I wanted to hear.

"That doesn't work. What about tomorrow night or the following night? Do they have a schedule?" I ask.

He flicks imaginary dust from his suit, eyes sliding down his nose at me as if I'm the greatest inconvenience. "If it's my brother you want, you must act tonight. Tomorrow, he leaves with my traitorous friend Boris to sink his claws into the Southern District before my sister can sway anyone else against him."

I study him carefully, but the tone in his voice feels authentic. I think he's telling the truth.

"How do I find the lab?" I press. Banks had marked a star on the map, but it wasn't exact. And traveling through the gutter zone at night, searching for an underground lab, will already be hard enough.

"Find Tommy's old pizza joint on Dolores," Viktor says with a cruel smile. "It will lead you where you need to go."

And then he's gone in an instant, leaving behind nothing but a lingering cold in the air.

"Fuck," I mutter, resting my hands on my hips. I glance at Malachi and quickly repeat everything Viktor said.

"Fuck is right." Malachi's already on his feet, jaw set tight. He doesn't waste another second. "Come with me," he snaps.

Before I can even argue, I'm chasing after him out of the shed and across the snow toward the main house, my pulse thundering in my ears.

Chapter Twenty-Seven

LOG TWENTY-SEVEN - INVERTED CAUSE: WE ISSUE
COMMANDS, AND SHE OBEYS, BUT THE OBEDIENCE
FEELS REHEARSED, LIKE SHE ANTICIPATED THE
ORDER BEFORE WE GAVE IT.

THE FRONT DOOR SLAMS OPEN, a burst of icy air
sweeping in with us. Everyone looks up from where they're
gathered in the living room, draped across chairs and couches
in their pajamas, relaxing by the fire that lights up their tired
faces.

"What the hell?" Dante mutters, straightening. "You two
look like you've seen a ghost."

Malachi huffs. "Not far off," he says, brushing past him and
pulling the map off the counter, spreading it across the table.

I quickly tell everyone what happened while Malachi
searches the map, his eyebrows scrunched together in concen-
tration.

"Wait, slow down," Aurora says, sitting up straighter on the
couch. "You want to leave tonight, right now?"

"It may be our only choice if Viktor is telling the truth,"
Bash says, and I nod.

"The bastard is probably lying," Cade says, coming over to
the map to see where Malachi is looking.

"This is what we've been training for. Tonight or tomorrow

night makes no difference to us. We are ready, guys," Alex says, and I like his enthusiasm. I think he's right. We may feel a little tired, but nothing a little adrenaline rush won't wipe away.

"If we want to get Marco and Orin, tonight's the night. I believe Viktor. I don't like the prick one bit, but I believe he was speaking the truth," I say.

Nasha stands, stretching, her violet eyes meet mine. "Fuck it, let's get dressed and go over the plan," she says, hurrying down the hallway to change.

Aurora jumps up from the couch. "Finally, I was getting tired of sitting around waiting."

"Everyone, gear up," Malachi says, his voice taking on that commanding tone. "Full tactical. Masks, Avidian, weapons. Meet back here in fifteen minutes."

The room explodes into motion as everyone scatters to their gear. I feel that familiar mix of nerves and excitement coursing through my veins.

All of our masks and Avidian are locked in the trunk, and we're suited up in full black tactical gear as we cram into the SUV. We went over the game plan until we could recite it in our sleep, and now as we drive toward the gutter zone and away from the desolate forest, the car is silent except for the hum of tires on cracked asphalt. The calm before the storm settles over us, and I try to calm my racing thoughts and focus on controlling my breathing.

Malachi navigates through increasingly rundown streets. Thirty minutes of urban decay later, he pulls into an empty parking lot and puts the car in park. The engine ticks as it cools.

I stare out the window at the towering concrete monuments around us—skyscrapers with darkened windows, some floors completely gutted, others flickering with the glow of illegal fires. I thought the city we hit in the South was big, but this place dwarfs it. The buildings seem to lean in on us, casting long shadows even in the dim streetlight. I suddenly feel very small and have to shake off the anxiety starting to fester in my chest.

We all get out, boots crunching on snow and debris. The air tastes stale and carries the faint scent of burned trash. At the back of the car, we strap on our weapons with practiced efficiency—knives, tactical gear, everything we might need to survive what's coming. Bash hands out our masks and explains which colored caps correspond to which Avidian, going over the operation sequence one final time even though we all know it by heart.

We can't drive into the gutter zone because it's barricaded on all sides—rusted shipping containers stacked three high, topped with coils of razor wire. It's like stepping from one world into another. Only a few blocks behind us, the corporate district gleams with chrome and glass, every window blazing with artificial daylight even at this hour. But here, where the asphalt crumbles into potholes deep enough to swallow a tire, reality shifts. Half the streetlights flicker sporadically or hang dark entirely, casting the crumbling facades in pools of amber and shadow. Windows stare down at us like hollow eye sockets, some boarded up with scrap metal, others glowing with the orange flicker of barrel fires.

"Remember, we may be here to do good, but the people beyond those walls don't know that," Malachi says, his voice carrying the weight of experience. "They will see us as a threat, and there is no reasoning with desperate people who have nothing left to lose."

"We don't want to kill any civilians, but we will if it's a choice between them or us," Cade adds, checking his weapon one final time. Aurora bumps my shoulder, her touch grounding me through the tactical gear.

We've trained for this. I'm stronger than I've ever been.

We've planned every contingency. It's going to be okay. The mantra loops in my head, but my pulse hammers against my throat.

"Mask up and stay in pairs. Only talk through comms from here on out. I'll cut the power grid once we breach the perimeter," Bash says, his voice already taking on that clipped, professional tone that means we're switching to mission mode.

I look down at the mask in my hands, all matte black polymer that feels deceptively light, its surface broken only by the seven Avidian vials arranged in a perfect arc across the front. Each vial swirls with its beautiful galaxy-like glow. The technology that could mean the difference between life and death tonight.

I strap it on, feeling the seal form around my face. When I push the button for the tactical visor, my world transforms—overlays showing team positions, comm indicators, and that faint green tint of night vision that will let us navigate the darkness Bash is about to plunge this place into.

Through the enhanced display, I watch my teammates become anonymous shadows in black tactical gear. Only their eyes remain human behind the masks, and even those seem different now, harder, focused, ready for war.

We reach the barricade, and Malachi is the first to climb over. I'm right behind him. The shipping container groans under our weight as we scale it, the corrugated metal slick with condensation and grime and ice. He cuts through the razor wire at the top, the sharp twang of severed metal echoing in the night air as he clears a path wide enough for our bodies.

He drops climbing rope on both sides—military grade, black as the night around us. I grip it tight, feeling the rough fibers bite into my gloves as I rappel down the interior face of the barricade. The gutter zone spreads out below me like a festering wound in the city's flesh. Buildings lean at impossible angles, their facades crumbling like diseased skin. Some structures have collapsed entirely, leaving skeletal frames reaching toward the sky like desperate fingers.

When I'm close enough to the ground, I release the rope and drop the final few feet, landing in a crouch on broken pavement littered with snow and debris I don't want to identify. Malachi's hand finds my shoulder immediately, steadying me as my boots find purchase among the rubble.

Above us, Aurora begins her descent, moving with the fluid grace of someone who's done this before. I turn away, watching Malachi's back while scanning our immediate surroundings. The smell here is overwhelming—human waste, rotting garbage, burned plastic, and underneath it all, something metallic that might be blood.

In the distance, a trash fire burns in a rusted barrel. Figures move in and out of the light, too far away to make out clearly but close enough to remind us we're not alone.

Bash's gift kicks in.

The power grid dies with an almost audible sigh, every functioning streetlight, every flickering neon sign, every dim bulb in every broken window going dark simultaneously. The transformation is absolute, one moment, we're in a diseased urban landscape, and the next, we're plunged into a darkness so complete it feels solid.

Only that single trash fire remains, a lonely beacon of orange flame at the end of what used to be a street, now a river of snow and shadows flowing between the hulking shapes of abandoned buildings.

The Viridian woman suddenly appears in my mask, her voice echoing inside my head. "Betrayal comes from within. You're closer to the truth." I stumble backward into Aurora.

She catches me and moves around until our eyes meet through our visors. The woman's gone, vanished as quickly as she appeared, leaving only the green glow of night vision and Aurora's concerned gaze. Her eyebrows pinch together as she takes me in, searching for signs of what just happened.

I nod, assuring her I'm all right, though my heart is hammering against my ribs. Betrayal comes from within. Aurora turns back to the others, but her body language stays alert, protective.

We fan out but stick close to one another as Malachi leads us toward this fucking old pizza place we're supposed to find. I swear if I've led everyone here and Viktor is lying, I'm going to make sure the spirits torture him for eternity.

Malachi turns left before we reach the trash fire at the end of the street, and I'm thankful because walking past those shadowy figures seemed like asking for trouble. The road we turn down is pitch black, not a flicker of light anywhere as we move down the center, scanning the crumbling buildings on either side through our night vision.

We make it a couple blocks, then turn again. That's when I hear someone whistle from high above, followed by the sharp crash of breaking glass.

All of us freeze. Then bottles start raining down from the windows above—glass, trash, chunks of concrete, anything they can get their hands on.

"Shit," I hiss as something hard connects with my shoulder, sending pain shooting down my arm. A molotov cocktail hits the pavement right in front of me and explodes in a burst of orange flame. I stumble backward, throwing my arm up to shield my face from the heat and flying glass.

Crude yelling echoes from the darkness above, voices telling us we don't belong, to get the hell out of their territory. I remember Bash's warning. Don't try to reason with desperate people. Just get out.

Malachi's hand finds mine, and we break into a run down

the street. Even with debris raining down on us, it's not worth the risk of going through the buildings where they could trap us. Better to endure the bombardment and keep moving toward our target.

Behind us, the voices grow louder, more aggressive, but we don't look back.

"Everyone all right?" I hear Malachi's voice through my comms, and I make a mental note of everyone who checks in, but I don't hear Aurora. Panic starts to set in as I pause and turn back, doing a quick count.

"Aurora," I call through the comms.

After a heart-stopping moment, she responds, "I'm here. I got hit in the head with something, but I'm okay. I had to activate one of my healing Avidians, but it worked. The bleeding stopped. Alex ducked into one of the buildings with me, and we ran to the other side to get away from the locals."

I look over at Malachi. All I can see are his eyes beyond the glowing visor.

"I can read the map. We'll meet you at the pizza place. Keep going," Alex says through the static.

I should feel relieved that Aurora isn't alone, but something about the separation sits wrong with me. The Viridian woman's warning echoes in my head. Alex offering to navigate, taking Aurora away from the group ... It could be protective, or it could be something else entirely.

But there's no choice now. We're split, and we have to trust that they'll make it to the rendezvous point.

We move in a tighter formation now, the six of us— Malachi, Bash, Cade, Dante, Nasha and me. The absence of Aurora and Alex feels unsettling.

"Two blocks north, then east on Dolores," Bash says quietly through the comms, consulting his tablet. "Should be a straight shot from there."

The street we're on now feels different from the destruction we escaped. Quieter, but not in a good way. It's the kind of silence that means people are watching from the darkness, deciding whether we're worth the trouble. I catch glimpses of movement behind boarded-up doorways, and it reminds me of the feeling I get when a spirit comes, like I'm being watched, only those watching us now are alive.

"Movement, ten o'clock," Dante murmurs, and I see them too, three figures keeping pace with us from an alley mouth, far enough back to think they're being subtle.

Malachi responds, "Keep walking. Don't engage unless they force it."

We turn as planned and pick up the pace.

"There," Cade says, nodding ahead. "Dolores Street."

The faded green–street sign hangs at an angle, barely legible through years of bad weather. When we turn east, I can finally see it in the distance, a narrow building wedged between two collapsed structures, its red brick facade crumbling but still standing. The neon sign that once advertised "Tommy's Pizza" is cracked in half and hanging vertically over the broken, boarded-up windows.

"That's got to be it," I say through the comms.

"Aurora, Alex, you copy?" Malachi calls. "We have eyes on the target."

Static answers him.

Fuck, why aren't they answering? A noise has me moving away from the others. It sounds like a child crying. The others must hear it too, because suddenly everyone stops walking, our heads all on a swivel.

I walk toward the alleyway on our right and see a little kid crouched down in the distance. I take off jogging toward them.

"Kat, stop," Bash says in my ear, but the kid's alone and afraid. I need to get over there before something bad happens.

"Goddamnit," Malachi echoes after that, but all I can focus on is the kid crying, this small figure crouched at the end of the alley against a concrete pillar.

I hear footsteps behind me and assume it's one of my teammates, but I don't look back. I slow when I reach the child and crouch down with my hands out.

"Hey, it's going to be okay," I say softly. The little boy has his knees pulled up against his chest, face buried in his lap, but his body shakes as crying whimpers echo from him. He can't be older than eight, maybe ten—so small and thin.

I reach out slowly and touch his shoulder. "Hi," I venture again.

His head pops up, brown eyes meeting mine, and I pull my hand back. He's not crying anymore. He's smiling—a scary, wicked kind of leer.

Fuck.

I stand up and take a step back, quickly scanning side to side. We're at the beginning of a low-level parking garage that's collapsed on one side. Concrete pillars spread out in sporadic aisles behind and on either side of the kid. He's only wearing a T-shirt and pants and must be freezing.

I don't care if his smile terrifies me. I pull off my jacket and step forward, wrapping it around him.

"Kat, what the fuck are you doing?" Cade says, reaching me first. "You can't take off running without your team, without answering comms. Get your jacket back. It's freezing."

I look over at him like he's lost his mind—clearly he has no empathy. The little boy turns and runs deeper into the parking structure.

"Shit, Kat, we don't have time for this. You can't save everyone. You gave him your coat. Let that be enough," he says, tugging at me. I turn to look at him, realizing Malachi isn't with him, and none of my other team members are here.

"Why did you come alone?" I ask.

"Everyone else is fanning out around the pizza place. Looks like Marco may have some high-tech surveillance set up, but Bash is trying to knock it out with his powers," Cade says.

We both turn toward the parking garage when we hear sudden commotion.

"Fuck," Cade curses under his breath as we see at least five men running toward us from behind different pillars.

"It was a fucking setup, Kat," he says, and I realize that must be why the kid was fake crying and then smiling at me. Oddly, I don't feel upset. My heart only hurts more for what that poor child must be going through to be used as bait like that and not see anything wrong with it.

One of the men reaches us first—skinny and scraggly, his clothes hanging baggy on his emaciated frame. He has a crowbar in his hand and swings it at me, but I duck, realizing I'm kind of in shock.

I shake it off as Cade socks the guy in the face and sends him flat on his ass. Cade's strong, especially when we're fighting malnourished vigilantes. I don't want to kill them, but when the rest close in on us, I don't think we have a choice.

Instead of wasting one of my daggers, I pick up the crowbar off the ground and slam it into one of the men, then swing around and knock another over the back of the head. Cade and I fall into a steady rhythm, and we manage to get all five of them on the ground in record time.

"Cameras are out. What the fuck is taking so long?" Dante says in my comms.

"Minor setback. On our way to you," Cade says, breathless, giving me a sharp look.

At least we didn't have to kill any of them. Fuck, they have no relation to Marco or his security team. These are desperate people trying to survive.

Cade pushes my shoulder to turn away from them, and we start jogging back out of the alley to the road we came from. I need to focus on the mission at hand.

They've made it farther down the street and spread out around the building, so we reach Malachi first. "Where's your jacket?" he asks when he sees us.

"Don't ask," Cade says. Malachi starts unzipping his.

"Stop, I'm fine. Let's get inside," I say, grabbing his hand.

Malachi turns and moves toward the brick building. All I can think is what the fuck is Marco doing having an abandoned pizza place be the entrance to a lab. It has to be the weirdest thing I've seen in a while.

"Side door is the best way in. We're ready when you are," Bash says, and we round the corner to find him, Nasha, and Dante waiting for us, pressed up against the wall.

"Any movement inside?" Malachi asks, and they shake their heads no.

Malachi gives them the signal, and Dante kicks the door in. We all flood inside, spreading out and searching the place. There's no one, not even a squatter looking for warmth.

"Back here," Dante calls, and I follow Malachi to where they are in what used to be the kitchen but is now an empty room, too clean compared to the rest of the place.

Dante looks back at all of us, then reaches for the pantry handle, pulling it open fast and silent. It's a large walk-in pantry with a hatch in the floor. Cade steps forward, opening the hatch, and we all lean over the large opening, looking down into the darkness.

It's a ladder going straight down. Little LED lights can be seen at the bottom, but it's too far down to tell what they are. It's still silent, and I'm a little on edge. How in the world do they get people and equipment down here if this is taking us to a giant underground lab?

I guess the city is huge, and the underground tunnels branch out in a maze. There have to be other ways in and out of this place. But why did Viktor tell us about this one? Maybe he really does want his brother dead and knew this would be the least patrolled. I'm still suspicious.

"Why haven't Aurora or Alex showed up yet? We can't go down there without them. Something has to be wrong," I say, and everyone is silent for a moment. My heart starts to beat faster, and I tell myself now is not the time to spiral. They probably got held up in a fight like we did.

"Dante, I want you to search the perimeter and keep trying to reach them. They could be out of range for the comms, or something Bash did is causing interference," Malachi says.

"No, it's not me. I know my equipment," Bash says, which doesn't make me feel any better.

"If you don't hear from them in fifteen minutes, come down and find us," Malachi continues, and Dante nods.

I don't like that we're already splitting up before we even reach the lab, but this isn't their first mission. Maybe this kind of thing happens often. I want to object, but it's not the time. We have a leader for a reason, and I know Aurora and Alex can take care of themselves.

Malachi looks over at me, blinks once, and then starts down the ladder. I don't wait to see who wants to go next. I grab the ladder and start lowering myself behind him.

Chapter Twenty-Eight

LOG TWENTY-EIGHT - EMOTIONAL PARASITE: THE MORE TIME WE SPEND WITH HER, THE LESS I TRUST MY OWN THOUGHTS. ARE THEY MINE, OR HERS PLACED CAREFULLY WITHIN ME?

MY FEET HIT THE GROUND, and I quickly take in the surroundings. To my right is simply a black brick wall, damp and musty smelling. It's warmer down here but slightly suffocating. To my left is a round concrete tunnel with a door at the end. Little light-blue LED lights on both sides of the path lead all the way to the large metal door.

I step away from Malachi and over to the wall, pacing a bit while the others slowly make their way down. I quickly focus and call Damien to me. It's a risk, but I'm worried about Aurora. I'm shocked when he shows up right away, leaning against the wall with one knee bent so his foot presses against the brick.

"Did you miss me?" he says, his light-blue form wobbling to match the color of the lights on the ground.

"Is Aurora all right? Can you find her for me, please?" I say, practically choking on the request, but I need his help.

"Why would I help you now after you've been talking with my father?" he says. Fuck, the spirits really do talk too much.

"He's dead. Isn't that what you wanted? If you want Irina

to pay too, then we need to do this first," I tell him, and he crosses his arms.

"Oh, Kitty Kat, what is it you're always saying? I like to play games. Well, I'm not into team sports," he says, shaking his head. I feel like trying to choke him, but before I can protest, he vanishes.

Damn him, that asshole.

"Let's move." Malachi touches the back of my shoulder, and I flip around to meet his stare and nod. I'm at the back now, following Malachi with Nasha and Cade in front of him, heading toward the door. I could hang back and reach out to other spirits, but there's no time. I hope Dante finds them soon.

Cade reaches the door first and turns the handle slowly. I'm a little surprised it's unlocked, but he turns the knob fully and pushes the door in.

I see a flash of fiery-red curls and my breath catches. I push past Malachi and shove through the door. Aurora and Alex are here. They must have made it down before us. I break past Nasha and step into the room.

It's bright white, almost blinding in contrast to the dark, musty tunnel we came from. The room has fluorescent white lights all across the ceiling, the floor is covered in large white tiles, and my eyes trail up to see Aurora and Alex.

Their masks are gone. Rupert stands behind Aurora with a fistful of her hair, holding her in place with a large dagger pressed to her throat. Alex is standing there, his back to us, looking at Rupert and Aurora like we interrupted him trying to talk Rupert into letting her go.

I freeze, my heart leaping out of my chest as my eyes find Aurora's. The terror in them is unmistakable, but there's something else. Why isn't she talking or using her power to light this fucker on fire?

She opens her mouth, but something viscous and black

spills down her chin like oil. They've drugged her. My mind fractures into a thousand racing thoughts. Is it the same substance Marco had in that vial the day he escaped? Did the vial never help him at all, just fall forgotten from his pocket? Has Rupert found a way to nullify our abilities, to steal Aurora's voice, to render us powerless?

The questions ricochet through my skull.

"Why don't you release them, and we can talk about this the way we used to discuss things, man to man?" Malachi says, steady and diplomatic.

He and Rupert have history. Rupert, who burned Irina's ranch to ash. Rupert, whose face haunted that security footage alongside Irina's. Rupert, who's been playing double agent, infiltrating Marco's operation for the Syndicate.

Hope flickers in my chest like a dying flame. He's going to let her go. He has to. His allegiance was never truly to Marco. It was to the Syndicate despite whatever twisted games they're playing now. I remember his face in that footage, the way it contorted with disgust when Irina carelessly disposed of lives like trash. He won't hurt Aurora. He can't.

But then I catch the subtle movement in my peripheral vision. Cade's hand creeps behind his back, fingers seeking the blade I know he has strapped against his thigh. My blood turns to mercury, heavy and cold.

I look back at Aurora, and terror shoots through me like lightning. I've never seen her look so afraid, not even in our worst moments. Those light-green eyes are wide as dinner plates, boring into mine with desperate intensity. She's trying to tell me something, but the message is lost in translation, swallowed by the black substance coating her lips.

I want to whisper reassurances, to tell her everything will be okay, but I force myself to stay silent. Malachi is good at talking his way out of impossible situations. He has to be our way out.

Fuck, Cade, please, I silently beg, watching his muscles coil like a spring. *Don't let your feelings for Aurora make you do something stupid. Give Malachi a chance.*

"Your aunt is going to be upset when I tell her how things have developed while she's been trying to ready you for a position of power," Rupert says.

Malachi takes a cautious step forward.

"Move again and I will slit her fucking throat."

The blade presses deeper, and I watch in horror as a thin line of crimson blooms across Aurora's pale skin, mixing with the black fluid. The sight nearly drops me to my knees.

I have to do something. But what? What can I possibly do?

Then it hits me. Rupert can't see my face from where I'm positioned behind Cade. I use that advantage and close my eyes, reaching deep into the place where my power lives, that cold cavern in my chest where the spirits dwell.

The only spirit I can communicate with without sound is the easiest to summon, the one who's never failed me.

I focus everything I have on that connection and open my eyes to find Mish standing at my feet, her ghostly form shimmering as she looks up at me with those knowing eyes. I'm so relieved I nearly sob. She's always been able to understand me in ways that defy explanation, some invisible thread binding us together across life and death.

I blink slowly at her, a silent thank you, then deliberately shift my gaze to Rupert and Aurora. Mish follows my line of sight, her ethereal head turning to assess the threat.

Yes, you know what to do, girl. I throw every ounce of power I have behind the silent plea. *You're the only one who can help us now.*

Mish takes off, gliding across the space between us and our

enemy. She reaches Rupert's feet and stops, looking back at me expectantly.

I find my power, and the transformation happens in a heartbeat—her translucent body solidifying into brown and white fur, compact muscle, and razor-sharp teeth.

Still invisible to everyone but me. Still our secret weapon.

She may be small, but her mouth is wide and her jaw is steel. She lunges forward and sinks her teeth deep into Rupert's calf, her ghostly growl vibrating through dimensions only I can hear.

The blade slips from Rupert's hand, and Aurora collapses forward into Alex's waiting arms. Mischka vanishes as quickly as she appeared, and Cade and Malachi descend on Rupert. Bodies blur in violent motion, and I see Cade stab his dagger into Rupert's side, then his chest repeatedly until Rupert lies motionless on the white tiles, now stained with blood, his threat extinguished.

It seems like we're in the clear, until Nasha's scream hits my ears.

I whip around to see her crumpled on the ground, cradling her brother's lifeless body. Alex is dead, and tears cascade down her face like a waterfall of grief as she rocks back and forth. "Sorry," she mutters over and over again.

But why isn't Aurora getting up yet? What did they drug her with?

I push past Nasha's anguish and drop to my knees beside Aurora, my hands reaching for her before my brain can process what I'm seeing. A dagger protrudes from her chest ... a dagger with a brown handle that I recognize instantly.

Alex's dagger.

My hands shake as I lift Aurora's head into my lap. I fumble for the healing Avidian in my mask, pop the top, and hold it beneath her nose.

"You're going to be all right," I whisper, shaking. "Breathe in the Avidian, Aurora. It will heal you."

Tears flood my cheeks, hot and relentless.

Malachi drops down beside me, his hands gentle but firm as he tries to pull me away. I fight him, my voice cracking as I scream, "Stop! She's okay!" But he doesn't relent, and when he grabs me harder this time, something in his grip makes me look at him.

His hands frame my face, forcing me to meet his eyes. I see grief that mirrors my own.

"She's gone, Kat."

She can't be gone, not Aurora, not now, not like this.

Cade lowers himself to Aurora's other side with the reverence of approaching an altar. His fingers brush her hair from her face with infinite tenderness, and I see the tears streaming down his cheeks.

No. No, no, no.

I start shaking my head, a violent denial that my body can't contain. Malachi grabs me again, his voice cutting through my fracturing mind. "Kat, she's gone. We either abandon the mission now or we keep moving."

"Mal, she's in no shape to keep going," Bash says.

"My brother was the rat," Nasha squeaks. "He betrayed us, and now these deaths are on my hands."

The pieces fall into place. She killed Alex—her own brother—after she realized he had stabbed Aurora. The Viridian girl's prophecy echoes in my mind. "Betrayal will come from within." Alex, our living truth, the only one we couldn't question because truth was his power to wield.

I need to know why. I need to summon him now and Aurora back from whatever realm she's crossed into. I need to see her again, to speak to her, to hear her voice one more time before I shatter beyond all repair.

"I can fix this. It's my pain to bear," Nasha says, moving next to me.

Malachi responds, but I can't process what he's saying. I'm drowning in the sight of Aurora's lifeless body, my mind rejecting what my eyes are showing me.

Then Nasha's warm hand touches my arm, and slowly—impossibly—my chest begins to release its crushing grip. My breathing evens out, becoming less erratic.

I turn to face her, and her eyes swim with tears that threaten to spill over. She nods at me with solemn understanding.

"I will take your pain for now," she whispers. "We need to finish the mission."

She's using her gift to absorb my sorrow, taking it into herself so I can keep moving forward. The most selfless act imaginable in our darkest hour.

Malachi takes my elbow with gentle firmness as I rise to my feet, every movement feeling foreign and mechanical. My gaze sweeps over Alex's lifeless body before settling on Aurora one final time. Cade pulls off his jacket, draping it over her upper body and face, the only dignity we can offer her in this hellish place.

I look past Malachi toward the imposing double doors that loom like the gates of damnation themselves. The lab. Our destination. My destination.

Nasha may have stolen my crushing grief, but she didn't touch the pure, molten rage that's building inside me like a volcano ready to erupt. It courses through my veins like liquid fire, threatening to consume everything in its path.

It's time everyone down here dies.

"What the fuck happened?" Dante shouts as he bursts through the door behind me, his blue eyes wide, taking in the carnage with growing horror.

He pulls Nasha to her feet and into his arms, stroking her back with protective tenderness while he and Malachi exchange hushed words that sound like static in my ears. Their conversation feels distant, unimportant, background noise to the symphony of vengeance building in my chest.

Cade rises from Aurora's side and walks over to where Bash and I stand beside the double doors. His movements are calm, but I can see the barely contained violence beneath his skin.

"Are you good?" Bash asks, his voice rougher than usual.

Cade nods curtly, dragging the back of his hand across his face to wipe away any lingering evidence of tears.

We've been reduced from eight to six. Two friends lost to betrayal and sacrifice in the span of minutes. But I'm not thinking about our numbers anymore.

I'm thinking about revenge.

I'm ready to find my goddamn reckoning.

Chapter Twenty-Nine

LOG TWENTY-NINE - ETHICAL COLLAPSE: ONE OF
MY COLLEAGUES CALLED HER A MIRACLE. ANOTHER
CALLED HER A GODDESS. I CALL THEM FOOLS, BUT
THEIR AWE IS SPREADING.

I KICK the double doors open, the sound reverberating through the corridors. We're immediately blasted with a controlled mist that hisses from hidden vents—some kind of decontamination protocol that feels like ice against my burning skin.

The clinical sterility of it makes my rage spike higher. They sanitize everything down here while they butcher people.

Malachi quickly moves to my side, his presence solid and reassuring, but I don't bother looking over at him. I can't risk letting him see the unhinged wildness I know is blazing in my eyes right now, the kind of look that promises death and destruction to anyone who gets in my way.

I don't wait for the mist to stop its mechanical cleansing ritual. I push forward through the suffocating chemical fog, my boots echoing against the sterile floor as I barrel toward the next set of doors. These are different—thick, heavy, reinforced like a vault. The kind of barriers designed to keep secrets in and intruders out.

Too bad for them I'm not an intruder anymore.

I'm vengeance incarnate.

The doors yield to my fury, and we finally cross the threshold into the belly of the beast.

We've reached the lab.

I pause inside the threshold, my eyes drinking in every horrific detail while the doors groan shut behind us with mechanical finality, sealing us inside this chamber of horrors.

The air has the acrid tang of chemicals, sterile and bitter. Overhead, fluorescent lights buzz. Long steel counters stretch the length of the cavernous room, each one cluttered with flasks, beakers, and colorful test tubes.

Tubes snake from one container to another, pulsing faintly with whatever unholy substances flow through them.

The walls are a nightmarish maze of panels and machinery, every surface covered in dials, glowing screens, and switches that belong in some fever dream of mad science. This is a place where humanity comes to die and something else is born in its place.

This room alone makes Bash's lab look like a child's chemistry set.

The cold seeps into my bones immediately, the kind of artificial chill that has nothing to do with temperature and everything to do with the absence of anything remotely human or warm.

We fan out around the room, each of us taking in the magnitude of what we've stumbled into. The low, constant hum of machines is unsettling.

"Don't touch anything," Bash says. "Keep moving."

He doesn't have to tell me twice. Every instinct I have is screaming at me to get out of here, but my rage keeps me rooted in place, keeps me moving forward into the belly of this place.

Malachi takes the lead, pushing open the next door. We file in and spread out, weapons ready. This room has a handful of people dressed in sterile white suits, but they panic the moment they see us, scurrying toward the exit on the far side of the room.

Smart choice.

The floor here is slick with puddles that reflect the eerie glow of massive glass domes stretching down the corridor like alien pods. Each dome radiates a golden amber light from within, pulsing like a diseased heartbeat.

I approach one to inspect it closer. It's like staring into a sealed ecosystem—each dome designed to keep something trapped inside or keep the world safely out.

A wolf paces frantically within the nearest one, its mangled fur pressing against the glass. The creature's appearance isn't far off from the monstrosity we saw with Gary and Rupert when they started the fire. I want to shatter the glass and free it, but part of me is terrified it would devour us all.

I force myself to keep moving. "This is sicker than I anticipated," Nasha says, aghast.

I join her at the next globe. The creature inside froths at the mouth, its form so twisted and unnatural that I can't even name what it once was. It's an abomination, something that should never exist.

"Keep moving," Malachi urges, his hand finding my shoulder and nudging me forward.

I speed past the remaining orbs, deliberately avoiding looking at the ones on the opposite side of the room. My heart is breaking for whatever unholy experiments are happening to these poor animals down here.

In the next room, I sprint to the clear wall, pressing my palms against its cold surface.

There are Avids, dozens of them.

A long hallway stretches ahead with clear acrylic walls on either side, punctured with small holes for air. Both rooms are packed with people wearing thin hospital gowns, their faces gaunt and hollow. They pace like caged animals, some sitting in corners, others pressed against the walls.

I spot a woman close to my age near the barrier and thrust my fingers through one of the holes to touch her trembling hand. The contact sends a jolt through me—warm, human, real.

"Who are you? What's happening?" she asks, and I realize we must look terrifying with our masks and weapons.

"We're here to help," I whisper, my throat tight. "What are they doing to you down here?"

Bash appears beside me, looking from side to side as he surveys our surroundings.

"Don't talk to them," another Avid warns sharply from behind the woman, his eyes darting nervously between us. "You don't know who they are."

She glares at the man, then turns back to us. "I'm an Avid like you. I promise we're here to help," I assure her, and she shakes her head.

"I have nothing more to lose," she says. "They've been taking our blood and injecting us with viruses that amplify our powers but make us aggressive and uncontrollable, unrecognizable even to our own families."

This woman has watched loved ones transform into monsters.

The man shoves her aside and presses his face against the wall. "They're creating an army they can control or sell to the highest bidder as living weapons."

Bash and I exchange a look of pure horror.

A searing heat suddenly fills the air, followed by a sharp cracking sound. I whip around to see Malachi activating Aurora's Avidian, his hands glowing as he works to shatter the wall on the opposite side.

Dante and Nasha start doing the same on our side, and

Bash and I immediately start shouting at the imprisoned Avids. "Back up! Get away from the walls!"

The acrylic explodes in a shower of fragments. Dozens of people surge through the openings, pushing and trampling each other in their desperate bid for freedom.

"Wait! Go this way to get out!" I try to direct them, but it's useless. Sheer panic has taken hold as they scatter like frightened animals through every available door.

"Don't bother," Malachi says, stepping over the debris. "They'll figure it out. We need to keep moving."

I follow him through the wreckage toward the next door when suddenly the room wobbles and static images splinter through my vision like broken glass. Not now. The Viridian woman better not be pulling me into another vision right now.

I take a sharp breath and force myself to focus on the door ahead. The room steadies, reality snapping back into place.

Before we can reach the door, it explodes outward in a shower of metal and debris. Marco's security floods through the opening.

It took longer than I anticipated for them to try to stop us. Either they were scrambling to respond, or we're trapped in this narrow corridor exactly where they want us.

The next few minutes dissolve into a complete blur of bodies and chaos. I don't have to think about how to fight or what moves to make. My training takes over, muscle memory guiding every strike.

Malachi slams into someone with brutal force, and they crash through the shattered wall to my left, grappling on the ground among the glass. Bash and Cade are locked in similar combat to my right, a tangle of violence.

I eliminate the target in front of me and surge into the next room where at least a dozen more security guards charge toward us. I press the side of my mask and breathe in Aurora's essence, feeling her power flow through me like liquid lightning.

Fire erupts from my hands, shooting across the room in deadly arcs. Somehow, it feels only right to use her power to destroy these men—a final gift from the friend they helped murder.

Heat blazes behind me as the others channel the same devastating force.

My comms crackle and die from all the electrical interference, dissolving into meaningless static. I know the others can handle themselves—I have to find the real targets. Marco and Orin.

I spot a set of stairs where the security forces emerged, and sprint up them, taking the steps three at a time. I'm down to my last Avidian, one healing vial left. Everything else has been spent in the carnage below.

At the top, I yank open a heavy door and freeze. I'm standing in a security surveillance room, and my blood turns to ice.

Dozens of screens line the walls, displaying live footage from every corner of this nightmare facility. But it's worse than that. I can see the gutter zone above us, the pantry hatch in the pizza place, even areas of the city I recognize. They've been watching everything. Everyone.

They knew we were coming long before we ever suspected. Even if Alex hadn't betrayed us, they would have seen us coming with this surveillance network. We walked straight into their trap.

"If it isn't my favorite parasite."

Orin's voice sends ice through my veins. I jolt forward as his hands seize me from behind, ripping my mask away and hurling it across the room where it shatters against the wall.

"You're sicker than I thought. What do you think you're

doing down here, playing God? No, that's your father. You're his trusted lackey, doing whatever daddy says like a good boy," I spit, and he fists a handful of my hair so hard my eyes start to water as he tips my head back. His beard is wiry and rough against my cheek as he leans down close to my face.

"This is going to be more fun than I thought," he says.

I try to kick him, thrashing in his grip, but he's so much bigger than me, so much stronger.

"You can't hurt me anymore, Orin. I've already lived through your torture once, and I can do it again with a fucking smile on my face," I screech.

He grabs my cheeks with his free hand, squeezing until I feel the inside of my cheek split against my teeth. He takes a step forward, forcing me to stumble with him, his hot body pressed hard against my back as he holds me in place, my neck bent at an uncomfortable angle from his grip on my hair.

"Oh, torturing you will be fun, pet, but not as fun as making you watch this," he hisses, and my eyes snap to the security screens, scanning them row by row.

Cade is on the ground, unmoving. Nasha's body lies not far from his.

No, they're not dead. They're okay, I tell myself, not ready to accept what reality might be.

"Right here." He jerks my head to the side, and I see Malachi.

My heart stops.

Malachi.

The screen shows him surrounded, outnumbered, fighting desperately against impossible odds.

"Your precious team is falling apart, little parasite. And you're going to watch every second of it."

This wasn't a fair fight. Even with our Avidian, they have too many guards. Worse, all the security personnel are abnormally strong, like they've been injecting themselves with whatever substance they're using to alter the Avids.

Did Viktor know he was sending us into a trap? Did Alex warn them before we even arrived? The questions spiral through my mind as I watch Malachi struggle against impossible odds.

But I'm not giving up. I refuse to accept defeat, not when we've come this far. We can still get out of this and expose what's happening down here. The Avids we freed, most of them ran toward what had to be the exit. They must have found their way out by now. Someone will know. Someone will tell the world what Marco is doing.

I have to survive long enough to make sure that happens.

My eyes dart across the other monitors, searching for any sign of hope, any advantage I can use. There has to be some way to turn this around.

They wear Malachi down until they finally have him restrained, a dozen guards holding him in place. Marco appears on screen, walking across the laboratory floor in his pristine suit like he's strolling through a boardroom instead of a chamber of horrors.

"Here, let's turn this one up a bit." Orin leans forward with sick anticipation, pressing buttons on the console.

Marco's voice crackles through the speakers. "This is what happens when you challenge the natural order, demon. This is what your rebellion costs." He turns and looks up right at the camera.

He knows I'm watching.

A guard drags in Bash and Dante, shoving them down to their knees next to Malachi. All three of them have their arms bound behind their backs, helpless and defeated.

I can't breathe and start to feel dizzy and nauseous. I can't tell if it's me losing focus or reality itself starting to fracture around me.

I blink hard, desperately trying to will the screens to steady as one of the white-coated workers enters the frame. He approaches Bash with a dark syringe and jabs it into his neck without ceremony.

"This one will be useful to us, once he's malleable," Marco says. His cold gaze shifts to Dante. "He is nothing."

Gary walks up and hauls Dante away toward an unseen fate.

"No!" I thrash against Orin's iron grip, fighting with everything I have left to break free. But his hold is unbreakable, and all I can do is watch my friends disappear one by one.

The screens blur through my tears, but I force myself to keep watching.

"Why don't you bring my pet down here for a closer seat at the party," Marco says without even looking back at the camera.

Orin kicks the door open and drags me out, his grip brutal as he shoves me down the flight of stairs. I stumble and nearly fall, but he keeps me upright through sheer force.

"Let her go," Malachi roars raw with desperation. "She only came here because I made her. You have all these Avids already. Let her go."

My heart sinks like a stone. I've never heard him plead like this before, never heard that note of defeat in his voice. Is he losing hope? Does he think we won't survive this?

Orin stops me directly in front of Malachi, close enough to see the bruises forming on his face, close enough to hear his labored breathing. Marco turns to face me fully, his expression a mask of false disappointment.

"Do you see what you're making me do?" He throws his arms up theatrically.

I spit directly in his face.

He freezes, that calm composure cracking as something darker flashes across his features. He pulls a pristine handkerchief from his pocket and wipes away my contempt with deliberate precision.

"I'm not making you do any of this," I snarl. "That's your son. If only your wife and daughter were still alive. They're disgusted by what you've become. They wanted me to come here and stop you." It's a lie, but he doesn't know that.

His face relaxes back into that terrible, controlled calm, but I can see the rage simmering just beneath the surface.

"If I was such a sick, horrible man, I wouldn't let you do this," Marco says with twisted magnanimity. He motions for Orin to release me. "Say your goodbyes."

I drop to my knees, my arms flying around Malachi's neck as I squeeze him desperately. I'm hyperventilating, tears streaming down my face as I blink, trying to clear my vision. But the room wobbles, and suddenly I glimpse the Viridian woman in her bed before snapping back to reality.

Malachi can't hug me back with his hands restrained, but he tips his head against mine, holding me as best he can.

I can do this. I can summon Banks and Viktor right now and end this. I need to focus. *Control your breathing, Kat. This isn't over. Get a grip.*

"Hey, Katja," Malachi says, and I lean back to see his face. His eyes soften when they meet mine. "Do you remember what I said before? We don't need saving."

"We are the storm," I finish under my breath.

He nods once, and I understand. He's telling me I'm strong enough to do this. This isn't over.

"We are the storm," I repeat, finding my strength.

Orin yanks me back, and a guard steps forward with a blade to Malachi's throat.

I reach for him but can't move.

Time fractures. The world around me slows until sound collapses into a distant, muffled roar. The blade bites into flesh, and I watch in horrified clarity as it sweeps clean across his throat.

Blood erupts in a violent arc, splattering hot across my face, my chest. Our eyes lock, his wide with shock, mine with desperate denial. He's still there, still alive, still *him*—until he isn't. The light dies, draining from his gaze, and I can do nothing but watch as he collapses forward, crumpling against the tile floor in a lifeless heap.

A scream tears out of me, raw and curdling, shredding my throat as my body convulses with grief. My heart feels like it's being ripped from my chest, torn to ribbons in someone's hands. My lungs seize, panic and rage boiling inside me until they overflow.

I close my eyes and scream into the void—so loud, so furious, the air vibrates around me. And with that scream, I reach for the door I swore I'd never open again. I tear it down.

"You want a demon, Marco?" My voice rips through the chaos, low and venomous. "You created one."

Every barrier between realms shatter, walls collapsing like glass splintering under my will. Shadows pour in like a flood. My chest is an open wound of rage and hate and anguish, and it all spills out of me in a torrent.

They answer.

One by one, the spirits manifest. Wisps of blue-gray light at first, then sharper, clearer—faces half rotted, jaws broken, limbs twisted. Some I know. Some I don't. They crowd the lab, a swelling storm of the forgotten dead.

Viktor appears, looming beside Marco, his skeletal grin splitting wide as his eyes blaze with malice. Banks rises before me, more solid than ever, his touch cold against my shoulder.

His eyes are heavy with sorrow, but sorrow no longer matters to me.

And then the darker ones arrive, the ones even I can't name. Shadows with gaping maws, eyeless sockets, clawed fingers scraping along the tile. They spill across the floor, swallowing the room in darkness, their hunger vibrating in the air.

Marco takes a step toward me, and I smile. It's jagged, deranged. I see it reflected in his eyes when he falters, his bravado crumbling as he takes an instinctive step back.

"You call it the devil's work," I whisper, my voice shaking the lights in their sockets. "I call it reckoning."

I pour everything I have into them—every ounce of pain, every scream that won't leave my throat, every shred of fury still burning in my veins. My skull feels like it's cracking open, my vision flashing white-hot. Blood trickles from my nose, then gushes, sliding down my lips. My chest seizes like my heart might explode.

But I force the spirits to take solid form.

And for the first time, everyone sees them.

Panic breaks out. Security shouts, weapons raise, but it's useless. The spirits launch themselves into the living. One tears a man's throat open with translucent claws. Another drags a scientist screaming into the shadows, his cries cut short with a wet snap. The lab becomes a slaughterhouse.

Marco's face twists in horror as Viktor lunges at him, slamming him to the floor. Marco thrashes, scrambling like a rat, but Viktor tears into his neck with his teeth like an animal. Blood sprays across the tiles. Marco wails while Viktor rips chunk after chunk from his flesh, eviscerating him.

Orin shoves me hard, trying to push me down, but Banks and Damien seize him. They don't kill him quickly. Fists crash into his face, his ribs. He screams, but there's no mercy. Blow after blow until blood pours from his mouth and nose, until his teeth scatter across the floor.

And then there's the one who slit Malachi's throat. My vision narrows, red-hot fury tunneling in. He sees me and bolts, but he doesn't get far. I snarl, and the spirits seize him midstride. Hands sprout from the shadows, clawing up his legs, pinning his arms back. He thrashes, screaming for help, but there's no help left.

I stalk forward, my blade heavy and perfect in my hand. I press it to his neck, slow, deliberate. He begs, but I don't listen. I drag the blade across his throat in jagged strokes, sawing into him. His scream gurgles out, blood spraying my face, hot and metallic. I don't stop until he crumples at my feet, twitching, choking, and then nothing at all.

The lab is chaos. Screams, blood, shadows tearing through flesh. But I don't care. I only care about him.

I fall to my knees beside Malachi's body, cradling his head in my lap. My hands shake as I stroke his hair back, streaking it red with his own blood.

The anguish rips through me like fire. It's too much, too consuming. The world is ending. I can't survive this. I *can't survive* without him.

An icy chill stabs my chest, spreading through my veins like frostbite. My vision wavers, the room rippling and distorting like water. Static slashes across my sight, buzzing in my ears. I clutch Malachi tighter, screaming his name, but it doesn't matter.

Everything collapses into white.

I blink rapidly as the room comes into focus—a different room entirely.

The Viridian woman lies in bed, wired to countless machines, watching me with knowing eyes, somehow, she brought me here again, wherever here is. This time feels different though. It feels more tangible as if I'm physically here, not my mind venturing into the Veil. My blood runs cold as that familiar chill creeps up my back, and I turn my focus back to her.

"You knew," I grit between my teeth, closing the distance between us. "You knew! Why didn't you warn me? Why didn't you tell me how to save them?"

I slam my hands down on the bed, my breathing becoming erratic again as rage and desperation consume me.

"You must lose everything before you can save anything," she says with maddening calm.

I unleash a blood-curdling scream that tears from the deepest part of my soul, releasing everything that's been building inside me like a dam bursting. "I'm tired of your riddles and word play!"

I grab the monitor next to her bed and rip it from the wall, hurling it to the floor until it explodes in a shower of sparks and broken glass. The screen goes dark, but still, she lies there unmoving, watching me with those ancient, knowing eyes.

I seize another monitor and drive my fist straight through the screen, not caring as the glass slices into my knuckles, not caring as blood streams down my arm. Pain is nothing compared to the agony tearing through my chest.

"Let me out!" I scream, my voice cracking with desperation. "I don't want to be here! I don't want to see you! Send me back to him now!"

I grab the cords attached to her frail body and yank them as hard as I can, ripping them from whatever machines she's hooked up to.

Alarms start blaring, lights flashing red.

Chapter Thirty

LOG THIRTY - TEMPORAL DISPLACEMENT: HER
DREAMS REFERENCE EVENTS YEARS AHEAD WITH
MUNDANE ACCURACY–WEATHER PATTERNS,
ELECTIONS, DEATHS. IT IS NOT PROPHECY. IT IS
MEMORY DISPLACED.

I GASP AWAKE, my eyes flying open, lungs dragging in air like
I've been drowning. My chest heaves, ragged and uneven, and
for a moment, I don't know where I am or what's real.

Mischka shifts beside me, warm and solid in the crook of
my arm. Alive. Real. Breathing. My throat tightens as she licks
my face with gentle concern, her soft weight grounding me in
this moment.

Not a ghost.

Not a memory.

She's here.

I sit up slowly, my hands trembling as I pull the wires from
my temples and wrists. The adhesive tugs at my skin, and I coil
the cords neatly around the monitors at my bedside—muscle
memory from too many sessions like this. My body moves on
autopilot, even while my mind spins in disbelief.

The door swings open before I can fully orient myself.

"This is the longest amount of data we've been able to
record to date," Dr. Harrison says, practically vibrating with
excitement. "I know it takes you a few minutes to get your bear-

ings, so meet us in the debrief room in ten minutes. The board is here for the first time. They couldn't have picked a better day."

His smile is wide, hungry. He looks at me like I'm not a person but a breakthrough waiting to be dissected, eager to pry apart whatever horrors my mind just endured.

"Project M," he adds with a satisfied nod at Mischka—my very much alive dog—before shutting the door behind him.

The silence he leaves behind presses down on me like a weight as I sort through everything that happened.

Then it all becomes crystal clear, and I know exactly what needs to be done.

I know what I must do.

I strip off the sleep gown and pull on pants and a shirt, slip on my shoes, and head toward the conference room. I pass a couple of scientists in the hallway, and they quickly avert their eyes. I let it roll off my shoulders. I know they fear what I am, and that's perfectly fine with me.

Mischka pads along beside me, her presence steady and reassuring.

A man in a pristine white lab coat smiles and nods. "Katja," he says, opening one of the double doors for me with exaggerated courtesy, and I'm glad he's taken to using my name finally. Too bad it won't make a difference.

The room has white floors, white walls, and a long gray table stretching the full length of the space with fourteen chairs positioned around it. There's a small podium at the far end and a massive screen mounted on the wall beyond the table.

I take my usual seat at the very end, right next to the head of the table where Dr. Harrison always positions himself. Mischka curls up at my feet under the table, hidden from view, and I rest my hands on my knees, waiting for everyone to arrive.

Two men sit across from me, typing furiously on their laptops without so much as glancing in my direction.

Ten minutes to the second, the double doors swing open and several more people in lab coats file in, finding their designated seats with practiced efficiency. Dr. Harrison enters and settles beside me, waving four board members over to claim their spots. Besides me, they're the only ones not wearing white coats.

Every single person at this table is a man except for me. So typical.

They'll learn, eventually.

"Thompson has been cataloging Project Viridian since conception in March of 2263, over three years ago now," Dr. Harrison says, his gaze sliding past me to the board members seated beyond. They all smile and nod, waiting for the juicy parts.

"Thompson has put together a presentation to walk you all through what we've been working on here at Unity Lab Core," he continues, then looks across the table to the young blond man with wire-rimmed glasses and a thick stack of paperwork beside his laptop.

"Thompson, the room is yours."

Thompson clears his throat nervously and rises to his feet, gathering his computer as he moves to the podium. The large screen flickers to life, and my own face appears in stark detail, a photograph with "PROJECT VIRIDIAN" typed in bold letters across the top.

We're off to a great start.

"Katja, or as I refer to her, Viridian, came to us under desperate circumstances. Without our intervention, she would have died. After extensive waivers were signed, experimental treatment began," Thompson starts, his voice confident and practiced.

He's a fucking liar, but I keep my stoic mask firmly in place as the screen changes to display an image of the sterile lab where they run most of their experiments.

"She has become like family here to a lot of us because we've spent so much time together. Her dog even came along with her and has since been our first animal test subject for Project M. More on that later, but it has been incredibly successful so far," he continues with nauseating enthusiasm.

I'm thankful I have Mischka. Thankful I'll have her forever now, but not in the way they've intended.

I'm ready for him to hurry through this sanitized version of my life. He's putting on quite the happy family show for the board's visit, painting our relationship as some heartwarming collaboration instead of the systematic abuse it really is.

Under the table, I stroke Mischka's fur and wait. Let them present their data. Let them celebrate their breakthrough.

They have no idea what's coming.

I zone in and out of Thompson's presentation, catching fragments as he reduces years of systematic torture to sanitized bullet points.

"Viridian is the first of her kind—no longer entirely human but something else, something more." His voice carries the pride of a creator discussing his masterpiece. "She can alter her aging process as it suits her and can ultimately live forever. She has superhuman strength, can communicate with the dead, and see the future."

He rattles off my extraordinary assets like I'm livestock being appraised at auction, each ability a commodity they've harvested from my humanity.

"She can predict things and has shown some telekinetic abilities as well. But when I say she can see the future, it's not as simple as you may think. When she dreams, it's like she's living through future simulations, complete sensory experiences indistinguishable from reality. We created a specialized neural interface machine just so we could extract and view what she sees."

They've been mining my dreams, stealing my most intimate visions and turning them into data points. Every nightmare I've lived through, every moment of terror and love and loss, all of it reduced to footage for their experiment, their hope at a better future.

"Listen, we all already know our current world is headed down a catastrophic path—environmental collapse, social upheaval, economic devastation. It's why we started this project. But with Viridian and our simulation extraction technology, we can see firsthand what the future holds and make the necessary interventions."

The man to my right, some corporate vulture in an expensive suit, speaks up while leering at me. "What exactly do you mean by necessary interventions?"

Thompson's composure cracks, his pale face flushing before he regains control.

"Everything we do creates ripple effects in the timeline. So far, the futures we've documented show accelerated climate destruction and a viral pandemic that eliminates over sixty percent of the global population. Complete economic collapse follows, governments fall like dominoes, and the United States as we know it fractures into something called Sunderlands, a feudal nightmare where powerful families rule over districts like medieval lords. People with supernatural abilities are hunted, captured, and trafficked like living weapons. They call them Avids."

That brings back the visceral memory of that world's suffering.

"Avids," one board member repeats, mystified.

"Yes, Avids. Our analysis suggests they're a derivative

mutation from this very project, though we haven't isolated the exact catalyst yet. Viridian completed her longest simulation to date, eleven consecutive hours. That may not sound extensive, but our temporal calculations indicate each hour represents approximately one year of her life in the future. That's eleven years of lived experience compressed into a single session."

The board members lean forward, their whispered excitement filling the sterile air. The casual way they discuss my torment—like I'm not sitting right here, like I'm another piece of lab equipment—makes my skin crawl.

"Now we obviously don't have eleven hours right now to review the complete simulation, but I've compiled key highlights to demonstrate the exact catastrophic future we're working to prevent. This last sim started almost a hundred years from now."

The massive screen flickers to life, and my blood turns to ice as very real memories—not simulations, not dreams, but lived experiences—flood the room in high definition. I see Aurora's laugh, bright and genuine as she tends to my garden in the Depths. Cade's protective stance as he shields her from danger. The warmth in Malachi's eyes when he looks at me.

My grip on my knees becomes painful as I fight to remain motionless while these monsters dissect the most precious moments of my life. Every scene they're watching, every person they're analyzing—it was real. It was my reality for those eleven hours, compressed into a nightmare that felt like years.

They're witnessing an hour of carefully edited footage from a life I actually lived, a life set nearly a century in the future that they're determined to erase from existence. Every friend I made, every love I felt, every sacrifice that gave my existence meaning—all of it labeled as an "undesirable outcome" to be prevented.

When Thompson finally sits down, Dr. Harrison turns to

me with that practiced, paternal smile that makes my stomach turn.

"Katja, I would appreciate it if you could address the board about your experience. Share your perspective on the project and the remarkable work we're doing to secure a better future for all of humanity."

It's a gentle suggestion that's really a command. He wants me to play the grateful test subject, to validate their noble mission in front of these investors.

I nod slowly and rise from my chair, feeling every pair of eyes in the room lock onto me like targeting systems. Under the table, Mischka's warmth against my leg reminds me what I'm fighting for.

Time to show them exactly what their perfect weapon can really do.

I was willing to play along, willing to endure endless cycles of psychological torture masquerading as research until we found a future worth preserving, until we found a future worth fighting for. I didn't realize until this moment they wouldn't be one and the same.

They haven't finished analyzing all the data yet, but that life is still seared into my consciousness like fresh burns. Every detail, every face, every moment of love and loss plays on repeat in my mind. Unity Lab isn't simply connected to Unity Broadcast in the future. It is Unity Broadcast, the propaganda machine the Volkovs will use to control the fractured remains of civilization.

This pandemic that will slaughter sixty percent of Earth's population is their creation, engineered in the sterile laboratories beneath my feet. The virus is their opening move in a game of global chess, designed to create the chaos they need to seize control.

And the vaccine they'll develop in the future, the supposed

cure they'll market as humanity's salvation? That's how Avids are really born. They splice my genetic code into their antidote, and it backfires in the worse way possible—creating a race of supernatural beings who become living commodities in their twisted marketplace.

The cruel irony burns like acid in my veins. They're not trying to prevent the future I showed them, they're engineering it, step by calculated step. Every simulation they've extracted from my mind, every vision they've stolen and dissected, it's all been research for their master plan.

It spirals into total devastation when Marco and Viktor Volkov come of age and complete their ascension to power, using the destruction they created to justify their authoritarian regime. They'll run experiments that make this lab look like child's play, developing bioweapons that can control supernatural armies while systematically exterminating anyone who threatens their new world order.

But I know what has to be done now. The future I'm truly fighting for isn't the sanitized utopia these monsters envision. It's the one where I'm united with him. With my person, the love of my life, Malachi. I will become the demon so he can be the savior.

This lab, every machine, every file, every trace of their research needs to be obliterated so completely that the pandemic never happens. So the vaccine is never created. So Avids never come to exist. So Sunderlands remains nothing more than a nightmare that never takes root in reality.

I know exactly which political pieces need to fall, which leaders need to rise, which power structures need to crumble for the world to heal instead of hemorrhaging into the dystopian wasteland I've lived through.

All of this has to start now. Today. In this sterile conference room with these arrogant men who think they've created the perfect test subject.

"Complacency is a poison, seeping slow until it kills you. And I fear everyone in this room has already let it seep too deep.

"You call yourselves men of science, pioneers, visionaries. But all I see are cowards in white coats. You forgot what you turned me into.

"You hide behind your data, your charts, your endless meetings, convincing yourselves that this is progress. But it isn't progress.

"You let yourselves believe that if you look away long enough, if you avert your eyes, you aren't guilty. That complacency absolves you. But it doesn't. It damns you."

Dr. Harrison gets to his feet, moving toward me, his smile strained as his eyes flick nervously from me to the board members. "I'm sorry," he says quickly, "she's often tired and irrational after going through a simulation. That one was clearly draining for her—"

My hand snaps out, and with a single twist, his neck breaks. He crumples to the floor before anyone can even scream.

I turn to the board, my gaze cold, unflinching. With a thought, the long gray table wrenches free of the floor and slams against the double doors, barricading them all inside. Papers flutter like frantic white birds before settling in silence.

There's no enjoyment in this. No cruelty. I don't want to torture them. I want it over.

I let my power ripple outward. The crack of bone echoes through the room as I snap every neck at once, thirteen heads slumping in eerie unison.

Mischka pads to my side as I step over bodies, her eyes bright and steady, her presence the only living comfort in this graveyard of men who thought they owned me. She's not a ghost here. They tested her like they tested me. And like me, she endures. Untouchable. Eternal.

Room by room, I move methodically through the facility. White coats blur together—faces I don't bother to learn, lives I don't bother to count. I end them all. Quick. Efficient. My hands barely move, my mind doing the work. And when there's no one left to kill, I set fire to the heart of the place that made me.

Flames roar through the corridors, eating glass, swallowing steel, turning every sterile surface into ash. Smoke rises high enough to choke the stars.

I stand at the edge of the forest, watching the building burn into ash below, and think about how Dr. Harrison named me Project Viridian because I was like a sprout rising from the ashes. How ironic that feels now. I look down at Mischka and pet her.

"We have a lot of work to do, girl."

Ahead of us, the world waits. And it's time to set everything in motion.

December 3rd, 2358

"My entire family died in a freak boating accident when I was eight years old, and I was thrust into a foster system that wasn't prepared for a traumatized child. I moved from home to home, never staying anywhere long enough to feel safe, never knowing if I'd have a place to sleep the next month. Those were some of the darkest, most isolating years of my life. But if it wasn't for those early struggles—learning to be resilient, learning to fight for what I believed in even when I had nothing—I don't think I would have had the relentless drive that brought me here today."

I hear his voice carrying in the distance as I walk through the park, the joyful sounds of children playing drifting on the gentle breeze. The sun breaks through the clouds, warming my face, and I look up, breathing deeply in this impossibly warm winter day, the kind of day that shouldn't exist in the world I came from but does now in the one I helped create.

"And now, here I am, standing before you as the head of the most advanced medical research institute in the world, announcing that our trials for a revolutionary cancer-eliminating treatment have not only been successful but will be moving into the final stage of human trials. When I transition to my new role in public service next year, my lead scientist and dear friend Sebastian will be stepping into my role as CEO. I have complete faith that he will continue pushing the boundaries of what's possible, continuing our mission to heal rather than harm, to build rather than destroy, to give hope to families who are facing their darkest hours."

Malachi's speech continues as I weave my way through the large crowd, desperate to be closer to the front. Then I see him, and my heart stops in my chest. It's been over sixty years since he held me, and I can still remember the way he smelled, the way his fingers would trace lazy circles across my skin and loop pieces of my hair aimlessly around his finger while talking, like it was yesterday.

"My CFO Cade would like to say a few words," he says, and his eyes sweep over the crowd before stopping on me.

His smile falters, and though he continues talking, my eyes take him in alone. Does some part of him remember me too? I know it's not possible, but his eyes find mine and hold them.

I see Cade and Aurora talking off stage. They're married now with two daughters. Bash is saving lives every day in his fight against cancer, among other groundbreaking research their company is pursuing. Dante and Nasha found each other and work as personal security for the company. It's funny how when people are meant to be in your life, there's always a way.

When Malachi steps back and Cade approaches the podium, I turn and walk away. I don't need to hear the rest. I can see they're all exactly where they're meant to be. They're happy, all of them, and successful. The world is thriving. After Unity Labs was destroyed, a new company bought the property and became the leading facility for climate change research. There was never a pandemic, Avids do not exist, and the districts never formed. Today, we live in a world where kids play freely in the streets, and we celebrate all the seasons.

My heart squeezes as I walk away from him, from Malachi. But he's successful and brilliant, doing real good in the world exactly as he was always supposed to. Next year, he will start his political career, and I know he will continue to bring great change to this world.

This is exactly the kind of future worth becoming the villain for.

"Hey, wait up!" I hear from behind me, and I know it's him. I've already made it through the crowd, and when I turn around, I see him rushing toward me.

I swallow hard, holding my breath as he approaches, that irresistible charming smirk quirking up on one side just as he reaches me.

"Are you talking to me?" I say, glancing around like there might be someone else he meant.

He laughs, that familiar sound that makes my chest ache, and holds out his hand. "I'm Malachi Volkov. I saw you back there during my speech, and I wanted to come say hi. You look so familiar to me. What's your name?"

I shake my head, remembering to breathe. "Katja, but my friends call me Kat."

"Kat," he repeats, giving me his full attention. "I like that."

I smile to myself at the déjà vu of it all. "I didn't say we were friends."

Ashley R. O'Donovan is an author of fantasy romance born and raised in Monterey, California, Ashley loves spending time with her friends and family, and when she's not writing, you can almost always find her cuddled up with one of her dogs reading a book, or catching the latest horror movie with her husband.

If you enjoyed this book, please consider leaving a review on Amazon and keeping in touch with Ashley on social media. She loves hearing from readers and is exciting to share more of her stories with the world.

***

For more books and updates:
www.AuthorARO.com